Other books in this collection:

WHEN LOVE SIZZLES

PEEL AWAY YOUR INHIBITIONS WITH THESE SEXY STORIES

The timeless love stories from
True Romance and True Love live on.

Edited by Barbara Weller,
Cynthia Cleveland and Nancy Cushing-Jones

A BROADLIT BOOK

BroadLit

October 2012

Published by

BroadLit ®
14011 Ventura Blvd.
Suite 206 E
Sherman Oaks, CA 91423

ISBN 978-0-9859596-4-7
Produced in the United States of America.

Visit us online at www.TruLOVEstories.com

*This collection is dedicated to all of you who are
looking for true love or have already found it.*

WHEN LOVE
SIZZLES

PEEL AWAY YOUR
INHIBITIONS WITH
THESE SEXY STORIES

Table Of Contents

INTRODUCTION

WHEN LOVE SIZZLES
Peel Away Your Inhibitions with These Sexy Stories

There's sex and then there's sizzling sex—and the difference between them is like the difference between vegetables and dessert. We may need the former, but the latter is infinitely more luscious.

You have to shed more than your clothes for this kind of romp. Mainly you have to shed your inhibitions, thus exposing your deepest sexual desires to your partner. It's an opportunity to explore a new aspect of your sexuality—and your personality. Consequently, when love sizzles, it can be both exhausting *and* energizing at the same time.

So how does sizzling sex happen? How does it, pardon the pun, come about?

Sometimes it means setting rules with your partner, like absolutely no talking during sex or insisting that the room is in total darkness. Sometimes it involves role-playing—complete with costumes or wigs —or acting as if you are strangers. (And sometimes you really are strangers!) For the more intrepid, it means venturing into forbidden territory—like spouse-swapping.

Sizzling sex might be the result of forethought. You might go out and buy your first pair of stiletto heels, or find just the right music for dirty dancing in front of your partner, or perhaps you have to ask a favor and get someone to take your kids for the night.

But then there is sizzling sex that is purely spontaneous—perhaps the result of a dare from a girlfriend or an impulsive response to a broken heart.

And as several of the stories here illustrate, you shouldn't underestimate the potent aphrodisiac nature of the weather! An extraordinarily hot and humid day can inspire you to match its temperature. The same with a wet and wild storm. Like record-breaking weather, sizzling sex is the result of going beyond the boundaries of your normal daily ranges.

Wherever it takes place, whomever it is with, you can count on sizzling sex to be a game-changer. It can revitalize a tired relationship or kick-start a new one. At the very least, it will unleash a side of yourself that has been yearning to be discovered.

LUST WITH THE PROPER STRANGER

Have you ever wanted to break free from being "a good girl" and have an uninhibited fling with a sexy stranger? Just find a handsome hunk and let your desires go wild? It had always been a secret fantasy of mine that I never could admit to anyone. . .until the day I decided to make it come true.

It was hot and humid that summer evening when I pulled my car into the Sweets & Treats parking lot. I dashed up the steps. If I hurried, I would have just enough time to pick up something for dessert and get to Luanne's barbecue party without being late.

A wave of cool air engulfed me as I yanked open the glass door. I paused for a second and inhaled. Strawberry, lemon, watermelon. . .the zesty aromas flooded over me as I gazed around the quaint baked goods shop. It was almost like stepping back in time.

The open oak beams told me that the bakery was at least a hundred years old, probably older. I've always loved antique buildings, and this place caught my eye. The high ceiling twinkled with multi-colored lights. Red, white, and blue balloons, flag paper cut-outs, and streamers decorated the display tables and high archways. My three-inch black heels echoed on the wide hardwood floors as I made my way to the rounded glass and oak counter.

I tucked my hair behind my ear and peered into the case filled with cupcakes, sugar cookies, pies, and muffins. Everything looked delicious. As I glanced around the country-style store, I realized that I was the only customer. *Where was everyone?* After checking my watch, I noticed the stenciled sign in the window. "Summer Hours: 9-6pm." The store closed at six o'clock, and it was already six-fifteen.

Can I help you?" a male voice asked.

I turned around. The man leaning against the kitchen doorway took my breath away. He wore black jeans and a green and white striped polo shirt. His sky-blue eyes locked onto mine, and he looked me over as he ran a hand through his wavy honey-colored hair.

"Can I get you something, Miss?"

I flashed him my best smile. "I'm Diane. I'm sorry to barge in like this, but the front door was open, and I didn't realize you were closed. If it's a bother, I can go."

"No. Not at all, Diane. My name's Josh." He grinned, showing off a set of dimples. "I've got some time. What would you like?" he asked with a wink.

I licked my lips and relaxed. The pleasing fragrances in the shop drained my need to hurry. I could be late, Luanne would understand. Besides, Josh was handsome and acting flirty, how could I leave now?

"I was driving past and I thought I'd stop in for a dessert. I never noticed this store before, but it's interesting," I replied.

"I opened up two months ago. This used to be an old ice cream parlor. I was a pastry chef in a restaurant, but I always wanted to own my own business. I can show you around, if you're not in a rush," he offered.

"That'd be great. I've got some time to kill." All the time in the world, I wanted to add. Luanne's party could wait. Every time Josh spoke, a tingling sensation ran up my spine. There was no doubt about it—Josh was hot, even hotter than last week's weather when the temperature soared to ninety-five degrees.

I decided to give in to my body's signals and see where this was leading. What harm could there be in flirting back, or even teasing a little? Josh was attractive, and I certainly wouldn't mind snuggling up next to him after a day at the beach.

I followed Josh through the shop decorated with sunflowers and ice cream cone-shaped lights. "I bought the place at foreclosure. It came within a week of being torn down. I couldn't let that happen. I'm too sentimental, and they don't make buildings like this anymore," he said as he steered me toward a black walnut cabinet.

It was obvious that Josh had put a lot of work into the place. A gift section was devoted to decorative candles, lime and lilac scented potpourri, exotic iced teas, and flavored coffees. He seemed proud of the store, and rightfully so. The place looked gorgeous.

"The store is beautiful. I love old buildings, and antiques are one of my hobbies," I said as I examined a display of daisy-themed party items. As I bent over, my black dress rode higher up the back of my thighs. It was short and sexy, and showed off every curve. Wearing it made me feel like a sexy seductress, and tonight that's just what I wanted to be.

I turned and caught Josh staring at my legs. Obviously the dress had done its job and captured his attention.

He looked at me and our gazes locked. Despite the cool air conditioning, the temperature in the room had just shot up ten degrees. A warm rush flooded over me, and I felt my heart race in my chest.

Josh bowed his head and looked away, but not before I saw the hint of a blush on his cheeks.

"So, you've seen the place. Tell me, Diane, what would you like?"

"Everything looks so tasty, I can't decide."

That was a lie. At that moment, I knew exactly what I wanted— him. I swept my auburn bangs away from my eyes. "I'm not keeping you from something, am I?"

"Absolutely not. Stay as long as you like. I don't mind."

His deep voice sent a scorching burst of heat through my body.

Normally, I wasn't the type to size up a complete stranger, but my instincts told me that Josh was different. My body didn't lie, and right now it was begging for his affection. But what should I do about it? My courage faltered for a second. Did I dare risk rejection and make the first move?

Josh stepped closer and I caught a whiff of his cologne. The masculine mix of citrus and musk made my heart pound faster, and my lower body flashed into a state of arousal. He was close enough to kiss me, yet I could sense he was holding back. . .

"Don't be shy, Diane. If you see something you like, just let me know." Josh's wide hand covered mine, and he gave it a gentle squeeze. "Now, what did you say you came in for?"

"Dessert." I found myself drawn into Josh's blue eyes. He would definitely make a delicious dessert—and there'd be no need to add any whipped cream. I stared at his well-defined jaw accented with a hint of scruff and imagined the rough feel of it brushing against the side of my neck, nuzzling my bare stomach, then traveling lower. . .

I quickly broke from the fantasy and cleared my throat. "I'm on my way to a party, and I'd like to bring something extraordinary."

"A party, huh?" Josh smirked. "Well then, come in the back. I think I have just what you're looking for."

I eagerly followed him into the kitchen through a set of swinging double doors. A row of pies sat cooling on wire racks.

"This is a new recipe, and I'd like an honest opinion," Josh said, as he cut into the nearest pie. He put a slice on a plate and broke off a piece with a fork. "You can be the first to taste it."

I couldn't help but smile as Josh fed me the pie. I closed my eyes, anticipating the familiar taste of apple or cherry. Instead, a zingy raspberry puree teased my tongue. My taste buds came alive, and I felt my pulse surge. "That's fantastic," I said, opening my eyes.

Just for Josh's benefit, I relished the lingering flavor and took my time, licking every drop of raspberry off my lips.

Josh swallowed hard. "Good! I'm glad you enjoyed it. Would you like some more?" he asked as he leaned closer to me. I felt an electric heat searing between us. *Did Josh have any idea what he was doing to me?*

"I'd love it," I replied.

I closed my eyes and waited. My body tingled with excitement as Josh's lips tenderly covered mine. His strong arms encircled my waist and he pulled me to his chest. I didn't waste time. I responded as my body commanded. I ran my hands along Josh's muscular back and down to his tight pants. He moaned as I squeezed his buttocks, and then pulled his hips toward mine. A welcome hardness jutted against my belly.

What seemed like hours later, Josh broke the sizzling embrace.

He gazed into my eyes and trailed his thumb across my lips. "I hope I wasn't being too forward, but I couldn't help myself. Trust me, I don't behave like this with all my customers." He flashed me a boyish grin. "I know it sounds strange, but something just clicked the second I saw you. It's like we've known each other before."

I stroked the front of his chest and curled my arms around his neck. "That's good to hear. I've never done anything like this either. But I'm looking forward to doing it again. "

I angled Josh's head down to mine and kissed him again. It was bold and uncharacteristic of me, but I couldn't help myself. Josh tasted so good that I just had to have a second helping. My heart thundered as he slid his hands under my dress. *Finally.* He was taking charge and acting on my wild fantasy.

"No panties. Good, I like that," he muttered.

As Josh's tongue teased mine, I raised my left leg and bent it around his hip. I bit back a cry as his fingertips brushed against me, teasing my already sensitive body. "Oh, yes. Don't stop," I whispered.

He stroked and teased me for what seemed like blissful eternity. When he nuzzled the side of my throat, the last of my self-control melted away. I ran my hands down his chest and stomach, then went lower, until I found what I was looking for. "My, what a big pastry you have," I said, rubbing the front of his pants.

Josh released me. "Why don't you have a taste? I think you'll like it."

My mouth watered at the thought of devouring him. It was something I didn't ordinarily do, but just for tonight, why not? This wanton encounter was something out of a naughty movie. *Who knew when I'd ever be so bold again?*

I unbuttoned Josh's pants and gave him a light squeeze. He gasped as I bent my head down. Within seconds, the kitchen was filled with the sounds of Josh's groans and sighs of pleasure as I sampled his tasty treat.

A few minutes later, he begged me to stop. "Please, I can't take anymore. . ."

"What's wrong?" I asked as I straightened up.

Josh coiled his arms around me and rocked his hips against mine. "All this teasing. I need to have you, now," he said, his deep voice sounding raspy.

I nodded. It was about time. I knew I could seduce Josh and that we'd both end up with a sweet release.

Josh led me out of the kitchen and into a small office. He closed the door and kissed me down to my soul. I leaned back on the desk and unzipped his jeans, eager to satisfy my craving.

"Hurry," I whispered, as he shoved my dress over my hips.

I wrapped my arms around his neck, clinging to him as he filled me. I went wild, moaning and grunting encouragement. Right now it didn't matter that we were in a public place and might get caught, I wanted him more than anything.

A few moments later, Josh shuddered and cried out. "Oh, God, Alice!"

He clutched me tight as I squealed and whimpered, writhing against him. Fireworks danced in front of my eyes as we climaxed in unison.

We held each other for several minutes before we separated. Josh let out a sigh of contentment as he readjusted his pants. "You should come here more often. I like being seduced by sexy customers who walk in off the street." He winked. "As long as they look like you."

I smoothed my rumpled dress and giggled. "Maybe we should make this our Friday night ritual. It was pretty hot."

Josh kissed me on the cheek. "Anytime you want to pick me up after work and rock my world, it's fine with me. So, what brought all this on?"

I smirked and tossed my hair over my shoulder. "I was reading one of those women's magazines you always make fun of, and I came across an article about secret fantasies." I felt my cheeks flush as I confessed. "They had a few suggestions for spicy encounters, so I decided, why not?" I shrugged. "I'm glad it worked."

"Oh, it worked, all right. The second I saw you in that short and slinky dress, I knew I was in for it. I knew I had no choice but to play along and be seduced," he joked. "I hope I didn't wreck your outfit.

You weren't planning on wearing that to Luanne's party, were you?"

"Are you kidding?" I laughed. "This dress is for seduction purposes only. My 'sweet, good-girl' sundress and sandals are in the car." I gave him a flirty look. "And if you liked this, wait till you see what I've got planned for next Friday."

"I can't wait," he said, running his hands up my thighs. "Why don't we stay a little longer and have second helpings?"

I playfully batted his hands away. "Don't worry, I've got something else in mind for when we get home later tonight. Let's get the desserts and get going. If we show up too late, your sister will be annoyed."

"Don't worry." Josh chuckled as we left his office. "If she complains, tell her you were sampling your husband's dessert and let her wonder."

That summer night was one of the hottest we'd had together in a long time. After ten years of marriage, Josh and I opened up a new chapter in our love life. Instead of the same old lovemaking, we've started exploring our hidden desires and secret fantasies, and things are certainly spiced up in the bedroom! THE END

SUNTANS FADE . . . TRUE LOVE LASTS FOREVER!

What Happens In Vegas . . . Sometimes Carries On Into The Sunset Of Your Wildest Dreams!

It was good to see Calliope again. She looked exactly like she did back in school, only now, her hair was lighter, her smile brighter, and she'd perfected a golden tan from living in the land of sun and surf. We were having a great time catching up on all the gossip, while taking in the magnificent view of the Pacific. The California climate was a pleasant change for me from the cooler temperatures back home, but I was missing Tony big time and I couldn't *wait* to see him again.

I wondered why I hadn't heard from him since the night before, so I decided to give him a call.

"I'm coming home tomorrow," I told him over the phone while sipping a delicious cocktail Calliope concocted.

"But I thought you were going to Vegas with Calliope." Tony's voice had an edge to it. "Why the sudden change of plans?"

"I miss you. Two weeks is a long time to be apart."

"I wanna see you, too, Krista, but it's crazy to miss out on a trip to Vegas. I know how much you love it there."

"But it's not the same without you."

"You're being silly. It's only a few more days. And do you realize how much it'll cost to change the ticket? I'm not made of gold, you know. Now, promise me you'll have a good time and stop this nonsense."

"I *am* having a good time," I admitted. "But I—"

"I don't want to hear it," he said. "Gotta go. Say hi to Calliope for me, and don't forget to put a little something on sixteen red for me."

"I won't forget," I promised. "I'll see you on Monday. You're picking me up, aren't you?"

"I'll be there."

"I love you."

"Love you, too, babe."

I hung up with a sinking feeling in the pit of my stomach and all kinds of questions swirling through my mind. I even thought about changing the ticket myself, despite Tony's objections.

"Well? How's your handsome fireman doing?" Calliope asked as she crossed the patio and handed me a fresh drink.

"Okay, I suppose," I said quietly. "He said to say hi to you."

If Calliope noticed that I was upset, she chose to ignore it. Instead, she talked about her new job, our trip to Vegas, and some guy she met at Las Brisas, an upscale Mexican restaurant that's the perfect spot for sunset viewing and *awesome* margaritas.

"Said he'd call me this week," she told me as we relaxed on her patio perched high above the ocean, soaking up the last bit of sunshine and the lazy charm of Southern California. "I won't hold my breath, though—with my luck, he's probably a bouncer in some strip club!"

I lifted my sunglasses and looked at her. "You're too much!" I said with a burst of laughter. Calliope always knows how to make me laugh even when I'm completely miserable.

A flock of seagulls flew low along the horizon as a pink-and-orange sunset filled the sky and I suddenly decided to take Tony's advice and enjoy my time with my friend, pushing aside my worries because, quite plainly—he didn't seem to be missing me at all.

With my gaze fixed on the ocean, I took a deep breath. "Staying here makes me realize things back home aren't as simple as I thought they were," I began.

"Trust me; life isn't as simple as it seems out here," Calliope said, rising out of her chair. "It's all a façade. People can be just as deceptive as they are back east; they're just dressed up in prettier packages, that's all. Hey—I'm getting hungry. What about you?"

"Maybe a little."

"A little?"

Calliope knows me all too well. "Okay; I'm *famished*. And these drinks have quite a kick to them—I'm beginning to see two of you!"

"Then let's go inside and I'll make you the best beef fajitas you've ever tasted!"

"When did *you* learn how to cook?" I asked, stepping through the doorway and padding barefoot across the cool, tile floor. Shoes aren't allowed past the doormat in Calliope's home.

"I've learned a *lot* of things since I moved out here."

"Like what?" I placed my empty glass in the sink and looked at her pointedly.

She grinned devilishly—elusively. "Like, well . . . minding my own business, for a change!"

"What's that supposed to mean?" I questioned, crossing my arms over my chest. "When have you *ever* minded your own business?"

"I promised myself I wouldn't go digging through the past," she said, opening her fridge and pulling out the sirloin strips that'd been marinating all day in a mixture of garlic and Calliope's "secret spices." "I don't want to spoil your visit."

"I appreciate that—but we're friends. You can say anything to me."

Calliope's eyes grew moist. "I want you to understand . . . I said those things because I love you and I didn't want to see you get hurt." She paused and leaned against the counter.

Suddenly I wished I hadn't opened the door to the past, because I knew what was coming and it was too painful for me to even contemplate.

"Watching you go through that," Calliope continued, "seeing you cry all the time—and over what? Someone who wasn't even worth it?" She shook her head vehemently. "I had to tell you how I felt about him—about how he treated you."

"I know, I know—but that was a long time ago," I said, my mind clouded by instant sadness as I remembered how crushed I was when I found Tony with his hand down the front of Tanya Joyner's pants. "We were just kids back then; things are different now."

"I'm glad everything's working out for you—and Tony," she said, opening a cabinet and reaching for a pan. "I'm sure he's changed."

"He has—he really has," I said quickly . . . as if I were trying to convince myself.

"It's good to be home," I said as Tony handed me a pink rose and patted my bottom.

"You look great, babe."

Tony: A six-foot-two hunk of man with dimples so deep and alluring that they gave me a flush of desire I could barely control whenever he smiled at me. Even back in high school, I never could resist that crooked smile of his.

I tickled his nose with the rose and he draped his arm around me as we took the escalator down to the baggage claim area. We picked up my luggage and when I settled into the car, a hint of something spicy touched my olfactory nerves. My heart twisted and a wave of nausea hit me as I realized it was perfume I smelled.

Opium, I thought. *A scent I never wear.*

I felt like I was going to be sick right there in the car while he raced onto the turnpike and headed for Hoboken.

"You're awfully quiet," he said after awhile, driving along the Hudson and running his hand over my arm. "Must be jetlagged."

"I am pretty tired." Avoiding his eyes, I glanced across the river at New York—and wasn't sure if I could keep from asking him whose goddamn perfume was stinking up the car.

"I hope you're not too tired for a little lovin'." He turned the corner and eased into the garage next to the creaky brownstone we lived in. "It's been too long since I had some and I'm ready to pop."

He grabbed my bag out of the trunk and we hiked up the two flights of stairs to our small, one-bedroom apartment. As soon as we were inside, he dropped my luggage on the hardwood floor and crushed me against him. His hands grabbed my butt and his tongue pushed its way through my lips.

"Tony, please—we just walked in the door, for Pete's sake!" I squirmed out of his arms and stepped over to the sink, where he had dirty dishes piled to the moon.

"What the hell's going on? I don't see my wife for two whole weeks and all of a sudden—she doesn't want me anymore?"

"It's not that I don't want you. It's—"

Tony rushed over to me, grabbing my arm with a sweaty hand. "It's what? You got a little side action going on?" He leaned back, staring at me. His eyes turned to black glass and he tightened his grip as I tried to pull away.

"Don't be insane, Tony—I'm tired, that's all."

He yanked me toward him and I felt then as if my arm had been pulled right out of its socket. Grinding his hips into mine, he whispered huskily, "You don't have to do a thing, baby. I'll do all the work." He slipped my blouse over my head; a devilish smile curved his lips as he unhooked my bra and gazed at my bare breasts. "Now, *that's* what I'm talking about. . . ."

I gave in.

There's no point in arguing with him when he's like that. When Tony wants sex, he gets it. And usually, I was just as turned on as he was.

But as he pushed me against the counter, his fingers pressing hard into my flesh and his mouth hungrily covering mine, I couldn't forget the scent of another woman in our car.

For the next few nights I told Tony I wasn't feeling well. As it was, just the mere thought of his hands on me made me want to scream. I'd wait until he was asleep before slipping into bed and, even then, with an ocean of space between us, I'd lie awake and wonder why he couldn't be satisfied with me alone. I only spoke to him when I had to. When he started to question what was going on, instead of confronting him with my suspicions, I decided to forget the whole thing.

Oh, but he was on his best behavior. Like a vampire, he knew he had me completely under his spell.

So I tried to convince myself that it was his mother's perfume. *Maybe Marie decided to try something new.* But deep down, I knew

I was only fooling myself. Tony's mother only wears Shalimar, the perfume Tony's father, Big Tony, usually buys her for Christmas or her birthday.

No matter what, though, I *still* wasn't ready to end my marriage. I loved Tony, despite the man I knew him to be.

Eventually, things returned to normal. And then one unbearably warm afternoon, I was out showing property, burning up in my suit while driving around Hudson County with a couple of first-time buyers looking for that "perfect starter home." I usually have the metabolism of a hummingbird, but that day all I wanted was to go home and collapse into bed with a cold washcloth on my forehead. As it was, I'd been with them for hours when my head started to pound.

It was the onset of a bad migraine, and as the day progressed it only grew worse and after awhile, I honestly wasn't sure if I'd make it. I rushed the couple through the last showing and *finally* dropped them off at my office.

"Can you take us out again tomorrow?" the young man asked as we stood in the blinding sunlight.

I nodded, causing my head to spin, so I quickly handed him my card. I couldn't go back into the office; the pain was excruciating and I knew it wouldn't be long before I started to black out. Cold sweat seeped through my clothes as I drove home.

I stuck my hand in my purse, searching for my pills. *I must've left them at home*, I thought, emptying my purse's contents onto the passenger seat.

I'm not even sure if I parked in the right parking space or not; I didn't care. All I could think about was finding relief from the pain screaming through my head. The humidity was on overdrive and the heat nearly pushed me back into the car as I opened the door and climbed out of my seat.

I practically *crawled* up the narrow staircase to the apartment, feeling as if I were moving through quicksand. Each step sent spears of pain through every cell in my body and I had to stop a couple of times just to catch my breath before I finally reached the door.

Inside, the air conditioner was on full blast and music was playing softly in the bedroom. I tossed my purse onto the counter and pulled out a clean glass from the dishwasher. I figured Tony must've called in sick because his shift usually starts at one.

Rather disappointed to realize that he was home, I poured myself a glass of water, peeled off my jacket, and reached for the vial of Darvocet I kept in the cabinet above the sink. It was empty and I realized I'd forgotten to pick up my prescription at CVS. I took a few aspirin, instead, hoping I'd be able to sleep the pain away. As it was, I knew I needed to rest, but because Tony was home, I figured he'd probably bug me for a mid-afternoon lovemaking session.

The music was still playing and I smelled incense burning as I padded down the hallway. "Hey, baby. I didn't think you'd be—"

I stopped in mid-sentence as I pushed open the bedroom door. My feet seemed glued to the floor and my mouth filled with a horrible acidic taste as I stared in stunned silence at Tony—on his back in our bed with his eyes closed and his hands on the very *ample* ass of a sexy blonde.

"What the hell—?" Tony yelled, opening his eyes in horror as the girl rolled off him and covered her big, bare breasts with my pillow.

Tony was silent then, waiting for me to make a move—to scream, to hit him—anything but stand there witnessing the terrible thing he did. In a matter of milliseconds my whole world was shattered, and my stomach lurched as I looked at him for what I knew—even then—was the last time.

It dawned on me then: *Our relationship was built on a mountain of lies. Nothing more.*

I could've killed them both with my bare hands. But instead, I walked out and never looked back.

I buried my pain in my work and became the top realtor in the tri-state area, but the dull ache in my heart was always there, reminding me of that awful day.

Calliope called almost every night and finally persuaded me to meet her in Vegas for a few days, hoping it would cheer me up. But when I arrived, ready to forget the past and party with my best friend, I discovered she had a completely different agenda in mind.

"This is Valentine," she said with a mischievous grin. "He's my attorney and I thought it'd be fun if he joined us!"

Valentine: Undeniably handsome, with a scorching smile and dark eyes that seemed to gaze right into my very soul. But I wasn't about to fall for *that* again. I shot Calliope a warning glance and planned on talking to her about this scheme of hers once we were alone. But at that moment, with Valentine standing just a few feet away, I'd been put on the spot and I had no choice but to join them for dinner.

"What do you think you're doing?" I asked Calliope once we were in the privacy of our suite at Mandalay Bay. "Why on *earth* would you bring your *attorney?*"

She shrugged haplessly, conveying the very picture of guileless innocence. "He's a real estate attorney and I thought because you're in the business, you two would have something in common."

"And just *what*, precisely, makes you think I want to spend my vacation with a total stranger?"

"Because it's time you get over Tony and have a little fun."

"Spare me the pep talk," I said, slipping a T-shirt over my head.

"You don't have to *marry* the guy. Just hang out with him and see what happens."

"*Hang out with him?* I don't even want to *talk* to him!" I snapped, storming off into the enormous bathroom and wondering, *What the hell is she thinking? She's about as subtle as a train wreck and I'm not about to get on board!*

The following day I was polite to Valentine, but I only spoke to him when necessary, hoping he'd take the hint and disappear.

He didn't. And I have to admit—his manners were impeccable, his conversation engaging, and his disarming grin had all the girls in Vegas going nuts.

After a quick dinner, we went our separate ways. Calliope headed straight for the slots, Valentine strode over to a crowded craps table, and I instinctively headed for the roulette wheels. That's when I suddenly heard Tony's voice—a phantom echo from the misery of my past—telling me to put money on sixteen red. Sixteen is *my* lucky number, but because I always win, he'd often ask me to play it for him.

With a lump the size of a golf ball in my throat, I changed directions and ended up watching a magic show in the lounge. When the show was over I stayed in my seat and ordered a drink; I noticed a Rubenesque, redheaded beauty sitting at the bar, blinging from head to toe. She was talking to a guy whose eyes were glued to her boobs.

Men! I thought with disgust. *They're all pigs.*

Sipping my drink and thinking about what to do next, I spotted Valentine striding in. Instantly, the curvaceous redhead spun around in her seat and fired a seductive smile right at him. I figured with her in the room, he wouldn't even notice me, but nevertheless he homed right in on me like a heat-seeking missile. Needless to say—the redhead looked shocked that he didn't even make eye contact with her.

"Mind if I join you?" He sat down next to me before I had a chance to answer.

"Look, Valentine—I'm sure you're a nice guy and all, but I'm not interested."

"Wow. You must really think you're all that!" he said with a laugh. "Calliope asked me to see if I could find you. She's worried about you."

"Then why didn't she come looking for me herself?"

"She's winning and doesn't want to break her lucky streak."

All of a sudden I felt silly; after all, the guy was just doing what Calliope asked of him and wasn't actually hitting on me. So we ended up sitting there for a while as I tapped my swizzle stick on the table, trying to come up with fascinating topics of conversation. At one point, I thought he was about to get up because I realized I was about as exciting as watching my nails dry, but instead, he waved over the cocktail waitress and asked me if I wanted another drink.

Once we had our drinks, we started to talk and I realized then that Valentine's a nice guy, after all—not to mention the fact that he was *also* trying to get over a broken heart. It turned out he was just as uneasy about this little getaway as I was.

"I just *knew* you two would hit it off!" Calliope said delightedly a while later when she joined us. "The next round's on me, guys; I won two hundred bucks! Can you *believe* it?"

Valentine looked at me, a smile spread across his face, and he waved his forefinger in a cautioning manner at Calliope. "We know what you're up to, sweetheart, and it's not working."

"What are you talking about?" She fluttered her eyelashes in feigned innocence.

"I'd sleep with one eye open tonight if I were you, Calli. Krista's on to you," he said, and I couldn't keep from laughing.

The rest of the trip was more fun than I imagined and Valentine, well—let's just say, we became . . . *friends*.

"He's a bit of a babe magnet, y'know," Calliope said as we watched him carry our bags to the car. They were dropping me off at the airport before heading home to California and, crazy as it sounds—I found myself wanting to go with them.

"Really? I hadn't noticed." But it was impossible *not* to notice. *Valentine's built to perfection, I thought with a lusty, hungry sigh, and his smoldering eyes never leave mine whenever he talks to me.*

At the airport Calliope and I hugged tearfully, promising to plan another "girlfriend trip" as soon as possible. *A trip without Valentine, I suppose,* I mused rather dismally. But when he gave me a soft kiss on my cheek—*wow*. . . . I don't know what happened. Suddenly, I forgot where I was.

"You're going to miss your flight, chica," he said, gazing at me through his thick fans of long, dark lashes.

I hurried to my departure gate and the whole trip home, Valentine and his sexy good looks possessed my every thought. I found myself thanking God that we lived three thousand miles apart, because that little kiss of his kept me warm for *days*.

It was fall and I was so busy at work that I rarely thought of Valentine—okay, I'll admit it—every once in a while the memory of that exquisite, albeit brief, kiss would worm its way into my brain and stop me in my tracks. As it was, if I closed my eyes, I could *still* feel the sizzle of his full, soft lips on my cheek.

Just before Halloween, Calliope surprised me and came to New York for a business trip, and I was so glad to have my friend in town, even if it was just for a few days. After a morning filled with meetings, she met me in Central Park and we walked a bit along the reservoir. The trees were aflame with their autumnal glory and families, couples, and tourists were all happily taking advantage of the sunny day and crisp air.

We ended up at The Loeb Boathouse, and over lunch, Calliope casually mentioned that Valentine had moved to San Francisco.

Not that I really care, I immediately told myself.

"You know, he asked about you, Krista," she said with a grin. "He thinks you're really cool—despite your hang-ups."

"What hang-ups?" I asked, looking over at the rowboats that dotted the lake.

"Your hang-ups with men. You know—the way you're always sparring with them as if they're all Tony and you hate their guts."

My eyes shot to hers. "Calliope, you *didn't* discuss my personal affairs with Valentine, did you?"

"No. But it's apparent that you have a Hummer-size chip on your shoulder when it comes to men. I think he was actually *relieved,* though; I mean—you didn't drool all over him like most women do. I think he likes that about you."

"He told me he split up with his girlfriend a few months ago."

"He told you about Marina? I'm surprised."

I shrugged. "He didn't give me all the details—he just told me that he isn't interested in dating anyone right now because he had a really bad experience."

" 'Really bad experience' doesn't even *begin* to explain what she did to him," Calliope said grimly, shaking her head. "She squeezed the *life* out of him."

"Anyway, it's none of my business; I don't even know why we're talking about him," I said, glancing at my watch. "Hey—we can make the two o'clock matinee if we leave now."

"Valentine's a good guy—and sexy as all get-out. It wouldn't hurt you to give him a call, you know. Just talk to—"

"Forget it," I said as the waiter appeared with our check.

She gave me his number, anyway.

After that, every night for the next two weeks, I thought about calling him, but never did. One night I actually started to dial his number, but fortunately I stopped myself before it was too late. Then one day, as I was working on a contract for a potential client, the receptionist buzzed me on the intercom.

"A Mr. Niarchos is here to see you."

"Who?" I couldn't remember meeting anyone by that name. "Do you know what he wants?" I asked, flipping through my appointment book, trying to jog my memory.

"He says it's a private matter."

"I'll come out," I said, getting up from my desk and walking out to the reception area. There stood Valentine, smiling that devastating smile.

"Hey. What's up?" he asked pleasantly.

"Valentine . . . w-what are you doing here?" He looked as hot as ever and the receptionist actually turned bright red when he shook her hand and thanked her.

"I have some business in the city and I thought I'd cross the river and see if you'd like to have dinner with me."

Immediately, I just about freaked and thought, *Oh, jeez—why didn't I wear something nicer to work? Do I even have makeup on?* I couldn't remember. It was a day that I planned on using to get through the mountain of paperwork on my desk and since I didn't have any appointments, I didn't dress up.

"Well?" Valentine's searching eyes sought mine.

My heart fluttered.

We went to a bistro perched along the Hudson. He was amazed by the awesome view of the Manhattan skyline and later, we strolled along the river, watching the ferry make its way to New York. It was nice, sharing the sights with someone who was experiencing them for the very first time, seeing as I suppose I often took them for granted.

We walked out to the pier and talked about our jobs, Vegas, Calliope—basically, everything but ourselves. A cool breeze came off the water and made me shudder; the light sweater I wore wasn't keeping me warm at all and I started to shiver. Valentine gave me his jacket, draping it over my shoulders as we headed back to my office.

"Krista," he said, suddenly stopping and turning to face me, "my business in the city—it's not work related. It has to do with . . . Marina."

My heart dropped as it dawned on me: *He came to see her, not me. I'm an afterthought, a courtesy call.*

"She took my son away, Krista. She's convinced him that I don't want him and she left and took him away without so much as a word to me." The anguish in his face was heart-wrenching and I instinctively put my hand on his arm. "I had a lead that they were in New York, but it turned out to be nothing—a dead end."

"I'm so sorry, Valentine—I—I had no idea."

"Sometimes . . . for a brief moment or two, I forget he's gone. . . . And then it slams into me all over again—the fact that I may never see him again—never play with him or hold him again. . . ." He looked at me, his eyes filled with tears. "I don't know why I'm telling you this. But you listen when I talk; that's a quality most people lack. . . . I felt a real friendship developing between us when we were in Vegas, Krista. I hope you did, too."

I wasn't really sure what I was feeling at that moment.

"You're an oasis in a crazy world, Krista. I was drawn to you from the moment I met you." He cupped my chin and pressed his lips against mine. "You like to gamble, don't you?"

I nodded as he drew me closer and my whole body melted.

"Then why don't you roll the dice and take a chance on us?"

I pulled away, not sure that I'd heard him correctly, but the look on his face was unmistakable: He wanted to take our friendship to the next level.

And I wasn't ready for that.

I didn't feel like going back to work, so Valentine walked me home, instead. My pace had quickened and he caught my elbow as we crossed the street.

"Did I scare you back there?" he asked suddenly.

I looked at him and could hardly believe it—he was blushing!

"I mean, I guess I came on a little strong back there."

"There's my place." I pointed to my building. "I love being so close to the office, especially in the wintertime."

"*And* . . . she deftly changes the subject," he said with a wry smile.

I couldn't bring myself to meet his gaze, so I fumbled for my key and invited him in and gave him the two-minute tour of my airy loft. As we stood in the living room, I told him about the plans I had for the place. I was clearly uncomfortable and I could sense his own frustration. After a few more minutes of me babbling away about my decorating ideas, he told me he had an early morning flight to catch and that he should take off.

We said good-bye at my doorstep. That time, he aimed a kiss right at my mouth. I must've been shell-shocked, because I let his tongue trace the outline of my lips and didn't stop him when he pulled me even closer. I wrapped my arms around his neck and I could feel the pounding of his heart as I opened my mouth and let him in. I don't know how much time passed, but we were definitely making out like a couple of kids on a first date.

And God help me—I *loved* it!

Okay—so maybe I felt a little more than "friendship" for him, but I was too confused then to admit that to Valentine . . . or to myself. When I finally pried myself out of his arms, he smiled, kissed my hand, and started down the stairs. By that point the sky had turned a fiery orange, and I just stood there and watched him walk down the street and out of my life.

He left for California the next day. I never gave him an answer and he didn't push it. In fact, he didn't call me until a week later and I *still* didn't know how to respond.

"I won't call you again," he said. "Not until you know what you want."

"Why can't we remain friends? Do we have to jump into a romance right away?"

"Do you honestly want to just be friends?" Valentine asked. "After the intimacy we've shared?"

I cleared my throat, but the words didn't come.

"Krista, I know this Tony guy really hurt you, and believe me—I understand more than most what heartbreak like that can do to a person. But I'm nothing like him, Krista. And unless you give me a chance, you'll never know for sure."

As it was, I already knew that he wasn't anything like Tony, but I couldn't bring myself to jump off that cliff again and into Valentine's waiting, open arms. I was too afraid to open up my heart—too afraid of the pain that I was sure would come.

"I'm ready to let go of the past, Krista. Are you?"

"How can you be ready?" I asked him plainly. "How can you forget the woman you once loved? The woman who took your child from you?"

"I'll never stop looking for my son, Krista. Never," he said, pain running like an icy stream through his voice, "but his mother's dead to me. Our relationship was over and done with long before she left me, anyway. I stayed for my son's sake, but I realize now that was a tragic mistake."

"You can't beat yourself up over something you had no control over."

"Maybe so. Still, it's the first time in my life that I feel helpless."

"I'm sure you're doing everything you can, Valentine."

There was a long pause and my heart went out to him; I knew there was nothing I could say to make it any better.

"My world stopped the day Marina took my son and left," he finally said, breaking the silence. "Happiness wasn't an option for me anymore, but when I met you, I . . . I felt alive for the very first time in *years*, Krista. You're the woman who fills my thoughts . . . my dreams. . . . I don't want to be alone anymore, Krista."

"Maybe feeling like you don't want to be alone has nothing to do with me."

"You're *impossible*, Krista!" he cried suddenly. Then, with a deep sigh of exasperation, he muttered, "I give up. Have a nice life."

Then he hung up on me.

I spent the holidays with my folks and tried to put a smile on my face and Valentine out of my mind. Every year they throw a huge

Christmas Eve party for the neighborhood and everybody brings their favorite dishes. That year Mom's friend, Sophia, brought her famous baked ziti, a big dish of eggplant parmigiana, and her son, Charles. Charles is a regular fixture at these holiday parties and I suppose he's always had a thing for me—for as long as I can remember, at least. He's funny, sweet, and attractive—everything a girl could hope for—and he's got a high-paying, high-profile government job and a lovely summer house in the Hamptons.

But it wasn't enough.

He isn't Valentine, I realized glumly, tucking into my festive paper plate piled high with baked ziti, London broil, green bean casserole, and Swedish meatballs.

Needless to say, I was lonelier than ever when New Year's Eve rolled around. I watched the ball drop, at home, by myself, with a big bag of greasy potato chips and a bottle of champagne for consolation. I spent the rest of the night observing droplets of condensation sliding down the stem of my champagne glass and landing on my lap. Obviously, I found myself wondering what Valentine was doing; I pictured him at a party, surrounded by skinny model types with gigantic, gravity-defying fake boobs and pouty, silicone-filled lips, and my insides flipped over a couple hundred times.

I blamed the queasiness on the champagne and went to bed, but still had his face seared in my brain. The room was spinning and I couldn't sleep, so I tried to focus my eyes on the cracks in my ceiling.

In the morning, sunlight flooded my loft, forcing me out of bed. My head felt like I had a tennis match going on inside of it. I drank a full bottle of water and made myself a trucker's breakfast—skipping the mimosas I planned on having.

And the whole time Valentine was still in every corner of my mind.

The sun's appearance was brief that day. Come noontime, it started to rain and as I sat in front of my bay window with a second bottle of water, staring at the view and remembering Valentine's reaction to the skyline, I realized that I *did* want to be with him, despite his problems—and despite my fears.

After all, I realized, *he could have any woman he wanted, and yet— he's chosen me to fill the hole in his heart.*

Calliope had told me it was a big step for him—letting me in. Marina cheated on him from day one; she was an aspiring actress, playing any bit part that came along and screwing whomever she had to to get those minor roles. It nearly destroyed Valentine when he found out and he thought he'd never give his heart to another.

But he tried—tried with me.

And I tossed his heart right out the window.

"You don't see it, do you?" Calliope said later in the day when she called to wish me a Happy New Year. "You and Valentine *belong* together. The way you light up when you talk about him . . . the intensity between you two is obvious to everyone *but* you, Krista!"

She's right, I realized. *Valentine's under my skin and no matter how hard I scratch, the itch for him will never go away.*

So I took a chance and booked a flight to California, not even sure if he'd still want me—not even sure if he'd already moved on and found a life with someone else.

A pleasant-looking woman sat next to me on the flight, chatting my ear off the whole way. I nodded every few minutes, just to be polite, but I honestly didn't even hear a single word she said because my thoughts were on Valentine and what I was going to say to him once I found him.

As it was, he'd sent me a Christmas card, so I had his address, but I had no idea as to whether or not he'd be home when I arrived. Upon landing, I rented a car at the airport and headed for the Bay Area. I'd never been to San Francisco before and I had to stop a couple of times for directions.

As the sun began to set, I started to lose my nerve. I'd come so far, though, and I wasn't about to give in to my fears. All I kept thinking about was the way Valentine looked at me, and that thought alone fueled my determination to keep on going.

My mouth was as dry as the air when I finally found the street he lived on—a steep side street—and I let out a big breath when I reached the top. I began to shake as I pulled into his driveway. I parked, and then I just sat there for a long time, rehearsing the words I planned to say and gathering my courage before going up to his door.

And then I saw him.

He turned the corner, his lean, muscular body sweaty and sexy as his jog slowed to a brisk walk. He stopped when he saw me there, sitting in my parked car, just staring at him, watching him, and a smile as big as the Golden Gate Bridge filled his sun-kissed face.

Molten heat surged through my veins as I hopped out of the car and, in my enthusiasm, I managed to trip over the curb and fell straight into his strapping arms. What a klutz!

He laughed, righting me and leading me along the walkway, covering my face with kisses. "I can't believe you're really here!" he kept saying over and over again as I tried to find my voice.

The front of his house was draped in bougainvillea and when we stepped inside, my whole body went numb. I realized then that I desperately needed some "liquid courage" before I could even begin to truly *contemplate* telling him that I wanted to take this "thing" we had—whatever it was, or wasn't—a step further. So I asked him if he had any beer in the house and he took two bottles of Corona from the fridge.

"What are you doing here?" he finally asked as we both took healthy swigs from our ice-cold beers.

"I . . . uh . . . wanted to see you," I said, taking another big gulp of beer. "I've been . . . thinking about you. A lot."

"So you flew all the way out here just to tell me that?" His eyes held mine and my knees began to buckle.

"Valentine, please. . . . This is hard enough for me as it is."

"Oh, don't get me wrong, Krista; I'm glad you came," he said, raking a hand through his thick, dark hair. He sighed and seemed to compose himself. "We'll talk later, okay? Right now, I need a long, hot shower."

The whole front of my shirt was damp from his sweat and my own nervous perspiration was trickling a steady path down my back. "So do I," I whispered impulsively, drowning in the intensity of his eyes and trembling at the mere thought of being naked with him . . . being in a shower with him . . . making love with him. . . .

We stood silently in his small, old-fashioned kitchen and quickly finished our Coronas. Then he led me down the hallway into the bathroom and we slipped out of our clothes. He turned on the shower and I stepped under the cool, refreshing stream of water, letting it run along my body as Valentine glided his soapy hands over my shoulders and back. I turned to kiss him and the soap fell from his hand; his lips were on fire as they blazed a trail along my neck and over my bare breasts.

"I want you, Krista," he whispered huskily, hungrily against my skin as he slowly made his way back to my lips.

He pressed me up against the shower wall as his mouth conquered mine. We made hot, passionate love in that shower—hot, wet, crazy, uninhibited love—and I felt . . . reborn. Then we did it again—but that time, in his bed, where Valentine took his time, kissing and licking and caressing every inch of my body until I begged him to take me again and again and again and again. . . .

Thank goodness—he had a whole box of condoms!

"I guess this means you're giving us a shot?" he said later—much, *much* later—as I snuggled against the warmth of him.

My fingers danced over his chest, tenderly stroking his dark, silky chest hair as I looked up at him. What I saw in his eyes made my heart sing; I knew then—with all of the certainty any woman can ever feel about a man: *This guy's for real.*

"You bet I'm giving us a shot," I said through happy, love-filled tears. "And the odds are the best I've ever had."

We tried the bicoastal thing for a while, but in the long run, it was too complicated—and *waay* too expensive. And after my last visit, I knew that Valentine was the only man for me, and I finally told him that I loved him. He was ecstatic; instantly, he asked me to move in with him, and even though I knew I'd miss my folks terribly, I called them and discussed the situation with them and they wholeheartedly encouraged me to go and explore my future with Valentine, giving me their blessings, genuinely happy because I finally met a man who'd do just about anything for me.

Two months later Valentine and I were sitting on the patio of a romantic, bayside restaurant and had just started eating. He kept clearing his throat and he had this silly grin on his face.

"Okay; 'fess up," I finally said as the tiki torches flickered in the breeze. "What's going on with you?"

Valentine put his fork down and his grin disappeared. "You have my heart," he said, taking my hand and slipping a diamond the size of Texas onto my married-lady finger. "Do I have yours?"

Tears rained on my food as I sat there with my mouth wide open.

"I know you're afraid, Krista . . . I am, too. But I'm willing to bet that we'll have a wonderful—"

I rose and went to him—sat in his lap and put my fingers to his lips. "I'm not afraid anymore, Valentine . . . not with you."

His smile reappeared and reached his eyes as he kissed my fingertips, tears like mine shimmering in his beautiful eyes.

"And just for the record—you had my heart the day you kissed my cheek in Vegas."

Valentine had a smug look in his eyes as he quickly paid the bill and we left without finishing our meals. We made it home in record time. Sweeping me up into his arms, he stumbled into the bedroom and the love we made that night was, well—incredibly . . . *amazing*. My tears vanished instantly, replaced by contented sighs of pure happiness and a passion I never knew before that night that anyone could feel.

We were married in the Graceland Chapel in Vegas; after all— that's where we met! We wrote our own vows and chose the theme song to that beautiful movie, *Somewhere In Time*, to play throughout the ceremony. It was all very simple, beautiful, and without a doubt the happiest day of my life. Valentine's sister flew down from Oregon and my folks flew out, too, to celebrate our joyous, blessed union. Calliope and her new boyfriend, a hotshot Hollywood producer who seems totally crazy about her, stood up for us as my maid of honor and Valentine's best man, respectively.

Honestly—Calliope cried more than I did, using up a whole box of tissues!

"The two of you getting married gives the rest of us some hope!" she whispered in my ear, hugging me after the ceremony. "You can thank me later, girlfriend!" she added with a giggle.

After the ceremony, we enjoyed a fabulous, five-course, celebratory wedding dinner at Emeril's in the MGM Grand. I almost fell out of my seat when the world-famous chef, himself, came over to congratulate us on our joyous occasion! He even sent over a special dessert and autographed our menu, which I had framed and now hangs on a wall in our kitchen.

I rarely have headaches these days. Even when I do, they're nothing like the blinding flashes of pain I used to get when I was married to Tony. I guess the West Coast suits me well.

And so does the man I married!

San Francisco is a unique and spectacular metropolis, but we're currently looking for a larger house outside the city. I've had my fling with big cities; now I want something with a huge backyard where I can plant a garden, with lots of shady trees and tons of kids in the neighborhood. I earned my California real estate license a few months ago and this week, I'm in the process of closing my first sale! It's a multimillion-dollar deal and I plan on putting my commission toward a down payment on our dream home.

Valentine recently opened his own law practice and he's still relentlessly searching for his son, Marcus. He'll never give up, and I'm helping him any way I can. We've hired a topnotch private investigator who's had some solid leads. God only knows what kind of damage Marina's done to Marcus, but when he's found—and I truly believe that it will happen—I want him to live with us . . . and his baby sister.

That's right . . . I'm six months pregnant!

Valentine can't wait to spoil his little girl the way he's been spoiling me. THE END

"$2 TURNS MY MAN INTO A SEX FIEND!"
One Wife's Secret

It all started with a blonde wig. I spotted it while I was browsing at the local thrift store with my best friend, Monica. It was pretty sexy looking—a shiny, platinum color—with shoulder-length, silky locks. It looked like something Cher would wear.

"Get a load of this!" I said, holding it up.

"Try it on!" Monica urged.

I laughed, and slipped the wig on over my own short, dark hair. When I turned to a nearby mirror, a stranger stared back at me. My skin seemed darker and my eyes looked huge and dark against all that pale hair. It felt . . . kind of sexy.

"Look at you!" Monica hooted. She reached out and flipped over the price tag dangling from the back. "It's only two bucks. You should buy it."

I took the wig off and considered it. "Why not?" I shrugged. "Davis will get a kick out of it. And I can use it at Halloween as a part of my costume."

Later that afternoon, when it was almost time for Davis to get home, I changed into a short, sleeveless sundress that I hadn't worn since a Caribbean vacation we'd taken three years before. Then, I slipped on the wig. I coated my lashes with dark mascara and added vamp-red lipstick. I grinned at my reflection in the mirror. I looked like I ought to be standing on a street corner, asking strange men if they were "going my way!"

Davis was going to *die* when he saw me!

When I heard his car pull up in the driveway, I positioned myself seductively, draped over the arm of the sofa. He came in, but he didn't notice me right away. He was too busy putting down his briefcase and sorting through the mail.

I cleared my throat.

Why hadn't I thought to have a camera ready? I would've given anything to capture the look on his face. In a split second, Davis's expression went from shock, to disbelief, to definite interest. "Hannah, is that you?" Grinning, he walked closer.

I laughed and stood. "Can you believe it?" I did a slow turn.

He continued to stare. "Did you dye your hair?"

"And grow it out six inches? Come on, Davis. It's a wig. I found it at the thrift store and bought it as a joke."

"You look great." He pulled me into his arms and gave me a big kiss. A definite step up from the usual "honey-I'm-home" peck on the cheek.

I smiled up at him. "Maybe I ought to play dress up more often."

"Maybe so." Davis smoothed his hand down my back. "I've always wanted to make love to a gorgeous blonde." There was a definite gleam in his eye—one that I hadn't seen in a long time.

"Is that so?" I stood on tiptoe and kissed him hard. "That could be arranged."

The next thing I knew, we'd gone from kissing in the living room to tearing each other's clothes off in the bedroom. I was thrilled. I couldn't even remember the last time Davis had been so eager to get me into bed. After twenty years of marriage, I guess our love life had gotten a little . . . routine. When you've been with someone that long, the excitement of the unknown is long gone. Not that there aren't *good* things about familiarity, but warm companionship isn't the same as red-hot lust. And lust was definitely heating up between us this afternoon.

When we were both naked, I started to take the wig off, but Davis put his hand over mine. "No. Leave it on. It's kind of fun."

I shrugged. "Sure. Why not?" It was kind of fun pretending to be a more exotic version of myself.

I kept the wig on in bed, in the shower afterward, through supper, and even when Davis dragged me into the bedroom a second time after the evening news. It was the most amazing night ever. If it took a cheap wig to get Davis *that* turned on, then I'd buy a whole closet full!

The next morning, Monica called to see how the evening had gone. "What did Davis think of the wig?" she asked.

"He went wild. I mean—absolutely *wild*." I smiled, remembering the night we'd shared. I was sore in places that hadn't been sore in years!

"What do you mean? Was he angry?"

I laughed. "Not exactly. I mean 'wild' as in totally turned on. He couldn't wait to get me into the bedroom. We haven't acted like that since we were newlyweds."

Monica laughed, too. "Maybe I should try a wig on Ted. In any case, it sounds like that two dollars was well spent."

"You know it. I can't wait to see if the dividends continue to pay off—if you know what I mean."

"Better watch it. The next thing you know, you'll be swinging from the chandelier."

That evening, I was in the kitchen fixing supper when Davis came home. Instead of puttering around in the living room the way he usually did, he headed straight for the kitchen. He stopped in the doorway. "Where's my sexy blonde?" he asked, grinning.

I laughed. "In the closet. You'll have to settle for a sexy brunette."

He kissed me—on the cheek. I had to admit that I was a bit disappointed. Was it only my alter ego that got the attention?

"Maybe after supper we can convince the blonde to come out and play," he said.

"Maybe." Or maybe not. His infatuation with that wig was beginning to annoy me. But after supper, I let him talk me into taking the wig out of the closet and putting it on. Immediately, my mild-mannered husband was once again transformed into a stud.

That's pretty much how things went for the next week. Davis would come home and persuade me to put the wig on, and then we'd go at it like bunnies. Even outside of the bedroom, Davis paid me more attention. One night, he even brought home flowers! But was it the wig he was courting, or was it me?

I complained to Monica. "I've never seen Davis like this," I said. "It's like he's having an affair, or something."

"So he's cheating on you with yourself?" She laughed.

"It isn't funny, Monica," I said. "How would you like it if the only time Ted wanted sex with you was when you were dressed up like someone else?"

"I guess that depends on how good the sex is."

The sex was good, but that wasn't the point. The point was that Davis was supposed to love *me*, not some floozy! I decided the best thing to do was to give him a taste of his own medicine. I went back to the thrift store and purchased a pair of cheap sunglasses, a phony moustache, and a beret. Then I went home, donned the wig, and waited.

Davis grinned as soon as he saw me. "Hello, you sexy thing," he growled and headed toward me, arms outstretched.

I held up my hand to stop him. "First, I have a few things I want *you* to wear for me." I handed him the sack with my purchases.

Clearly puzzled, he looked into the bag, then drew out the sunglasses. "Go on, Davis—put them on," I said. "And the rest of the stuff, too."

He shrugged. "Okay." On went the sunglasses, the moustache, and finally, the beret. I had to bite the insides of my cheek to keep from laughing. Oh, my! He looked ridiculous. But I pretended to be enthralled. "You look *so* handsome!" I raved.

He grinned. "You think so, Hannah?" He reached for me. "Come to me, doll!"

I would have burst out laughing if his lips hadn't covered mine. But my mirth was quickly forgotten in that searing kiss. And, with my eyes closed, I couldn't see his silly costume. I could only feel his lips and hands doing wonderful things to me.

Later, as we cuddled in bed, I reached up and removed the sunglasses. "I can't believe you're still wearing this getup," I said.

Davis hugged me close. "I'll have to admit, I felt silly, but you seemed to like it, and if this is what turns you on, then I'm all for it." He kissed the top of my head. "I just want to please you, baby."

A lump formed in my throat at the words. That was so sweet! "I love you," I told him, and kissed his cheek.

"I love you too, sweetie. More and more all the time."

The next night I told Davis that I'd changed my mind about the sunglasses, beret, and moustache. "I think I like the real you better," I said, hoping he'd get the hint.

He tossed his "disguise" onto the bathroom counter. "Whatever you say, sweetie." He bowed. "Your wish is my command." He plucked the wig off its stand on my dresser and settled it onto my head. "You know you turn me on in that thing, don't you?"

"Yes, but—" I didn't get a chance to finish my sentence. It's hard to speak when your husband is kissing you passionately.

But I wasn't going to let this go on any longer. As soon as I was able, I pushed him away and took off the wig. "I'm beginning to think you're not in love with me anymore—you're in love with this wig!"

Davis's eyes widened in shock. "Hannah, how can you say that? I've been in love with you for twenty years; I'm not about to stop now."

He pulled me close and kissed me. I relaxed a little. Maybe I was making too much of this. When he broke off the kiss, I smiled up at him. "Tonight, I'll leave the wig off."

Did I imagine his look of regret? "Okay, hon. Whatever you say."

But things weren't the same when we made love that night. Something was missing. Had that blond wig come between us again?

I didn't plan to say anything to anyone about my worries, but when I had lunch with Monica the next day, she asked me what was wrong.

"What makes you think anything's wrong?" I added sugar to my iced tea and stirred vigorously, my teaspoon ringing against the sides of the glass.

"*Hannah.*" Monica touched my wrist. I grew still, avoiding her eyes. "Honey, what is it?" she asked. "What's gotten you so upset?"

I shook my head and laid down my spoon. "It's that wig, Monica. I wish I'd never bought that thing!"

"What do you mean? I thought you said it drove Davis wild—that it made the two of you act like newlyweds again!"

"It did. But now. . . ." I choked back sudden tears. "Now he's not even interested unless I'm wearing the wig! He doesn't want me anymore; he just wants some fantasy woman!"

"Oh, honey!" Hannah patted my shoulder. "It can't be that bad. Davis loves you."

"He says he does. But . . . when we make love without that wig, it's not the same. It's like he's just going through the motions!" I cried.

"Maybe he's just tired." Monica smiled. "After all, you two have been going at it pretty hot and heavy for an old married couple."

I swatted at her. "We're not old."

She laughed. "Okay. But maybe you need to find some way to remind Davis that it's not about the wig—it's about the two of you, together."

I sighed. "Maybe I should throw the wig away and tell him I gave it to someone who needed it more than I did."

"That's one idea. You could give it to me."

"I could, Monica. But then you might end up with the same problem I have now."

"I'm willing to risk it for our friendship," she said solemnly.

I shook my head. "I really wanted to keep it for my Halloween costume."

She laughed again. "It sounds to me like Davis wouldn't let you wear any costume that wig was a part of for very long."

"Maybe I should forget the costume idea and just ditch the wig." But I wasn't so sure that that would solve my problem. If I got rid of the wig, would I be throwing out our renewed sex life along with it? How could I keep the fire in our love life without having to compete with a hunk of fake hair?

Two days later, during a thunderstorm, the power went out. Davis was attending a late meeting at the office and I was home alone, so I groped my way down into the basement, looking for a flashlight. As I felt my way to the laundry room cabinet where I'd stashed the flashlight, I couldn't believe how dark it was. Even after I'd been down there for five minutes, I could hardly see a thing. I felt like a blind person, having only my senses to rely on.

A light went on in my head just then, even though the ones in the basement were still out. Maybe this was a way to make Davis focus on me again, instead of that wig. Once I'd found the flashlight and switched it on, I went about setting the stage for the next "surprise" I'd cooked up for Davis. I only hoped that this one didn't backfire the way the wig had.

When Davis got home from his meeting, he found a note waiting for him on the kitchen counter. *Meet me in the basement*, it read.

I heard Davis at the top of the stairs, flipping the light switch up and down. I'd removed all the bulbs from the basement lights, so nothing happened. "Hannah, are you down there?" he asked.

"I'm over here on the old futon," I called. We'd been meaning to donate the old thing to charity for months, but hadn't gotten around to calling anyone to come pick it up. I was glad we'd waited, since it was bound to come in handy tonight, if things went according to plan.

"What are you doing down there in the dark?" he asked. I wasn't sure, but I thought maybe he'd come down a few steps into the basement.

"I'm waiting for you," I said seductively.

"In the basement?" Davis asked.

"I don't have any clothes on." I smiled, imagining how he'd react to that news. I was pleased that he didn't argue, or question my sanity. He just started moving toward me. But I'd forgotten to warn him that the futon was unfolded into a bed, and he ended up banging into the end of it. As Davis muttered curses, I crawled toward him. "Are you okay?" I asked, reaching for him.

He grabbed my hand. "I'm fine. But what's going on, Hannah?" Davis crawled up onto the futon beside me and stroked my face. "I can't see a thing."

"That's the whole idea." I unfastened the top button of his shirt. "I want us to forget about appearances for a while, and concentrate on our *other* senses." I undid the next button.

His hands traced the lines of my shoulders. "I think I like this idea." He bent and kissed my neck. "You smell good."

"You feel good."

We made love right there in the darkness, guided only by the senses of touch, taste, smell, and hearing. In a way, it was like we were new lovers, getting to know each other's bodies. We explored with our hands, tasted each other's skin, and breathed in the scents unique to each of us. I lay my head against Davis's chest and listened to his steady, strong heartbeat and fell in love with him all over again.

How we looked, the color of our hair, and even our less-than-perfect bodies didn't matter there in the darkness. The only important thing was how we felt about each other, and how we made each other feel.

Later, we snuggled together—wrapped in the old blanket that I'd thrown over the futon. "Now tell me what this is *really* all about," he said.

"Did you enjoy it?" I asked.

"You know I did." He rolled over to face me. Now I wished I could see him, to read the expression in his eyes.

"I just wanted to remind you that it's not how we look—or whether I'm a blonde or a brunette—that matters. It's how we feel about each other."

"You think I don't know that, Hannah?" He kissed my cheek. "Hannah, you *know* I love you. Why are you worried?"

"Because you acted so different when I was wearing that wig."

"Because you were different."

"That wig didn't make me different."

Davis chuckled, and stroked my hair. "In a way, it did. You were more—I don't know—uninhibited. You weren't dressed like your usual self, so maybe that gave your subconscious permission not to act like your usual self."

Was he right? Had dressing up like another woman made me act like someone else? Someone not as bound by convention and habit as

I'd always been? I had to admit that Davis had a point.

"But what about you?" I asked. "You acted differently, too. Like you were making love to another woman."

He rested his cheek against mine, and I felt his smile. "So maybe I indulged in a little bit of fantasy. Is that so wrong? You're still the woman I love, only this time, it was a more exotic version of you."

I frowned, still not convinced. "I'm not sure what to think. Aren't I enough for you anymore? Just the way I am?"

"Of course, you are. But don't you think after twenty years, we'd gotten . . . I don't know. A little stale?" He caressed my shoulder. "That wig freshened things up again. It made sex fun again."

My frown relaxed a little. We *had* been having a lot of fun in the past couple of weeks. "You're right. It did. I just didn't want it to go too far."

"I'll admit maybe I went overboard, insisting you wear it all the time. I just liked what it did for us. It made us both a little more willing to experiment."

I shook my head. "I don't know if that was the wig."

"Before you bought it, would you have ever thought to meet me in the darkened basement—naked—and have passionate sex on the old futon?"

I laughed at his teasing tone. "You're right. I wouldn't have." I turned to face him. "So, what does this mean?"

"That you're never too old to learn new tricks?" Davis suggested.

"Or, maybe it means that every relationship needs a little variety sometimes."

"That we should play more." Davis patted my bottom. "All kinds of play." He drew me close once more. "Anytime you want me to wear a costume for you, just say the word."

I laughed. "Okay. But sometimes—plain old sex in the bedroom is okay too, right?"

"Anytime. And I've been thinking. . . ." Davis snuggled closer.

"About what?"

"Maybe we shouldn't be in such a hurry to get rid of this old futon."

His kiss smothered my laughter. I had a feeling that things were going to be a little different for us from now on. We wouldn't be so quick to accept dull routine as part of a long-time commitment. From now on, I had a feeling we'd both be looking for ways to keep things new between us.

As for the wig, I intended to put it away for a while—just to keep it from becoming routine, also. But maybe it was time to go shopping for some sexy lingerie. Who knows? The next twenty years could bring the best sex we've ever had! THE END

DANCE OF SEDUCTION

The first time my neighbor saw me naked was caused by Trouble with a capital T. The darned cat darted out the door with me calling for him before I realized I was wearing nothing but my birthday suit.

"Trouble! Damn it, Trouble!" I looked up to find Kurt, whose backyard shared a fence with mine, staring up from his morning cup of coffee. His jaw dropped, and the newspaper he'd been reading floated to the ground.

The first thing I noticed when his coffee cup clattered against his patio table was that he was wearing the tight red shorts I loved seeing him in when he mowed his lawn. The second was that I, however, wore nothing.

Shrieking, my knees buckled, and I almost fell to the ground in my hurry to retrace my steps. I was so flustered that I didn't know what to grab—I had two hands and three places that needed covering. I snatched Trouble mid-air as he jumped to avoid me and hastily back-peddled toward my house, with Trouble yowling in protest and clawing my arms.

I felt my bare butt hit the screen door, groaned, and dove inside— this time showing Kurt my backside because I sure wasn't risking tripping and giving him a full frontal view of my southern hemisphere, should I sprawl backwards with my feet pointing toward the sky.

I slammed the door and leaned against it, cursing the cat that one of my kids had dragged home. My face felt hot enough to fry an egg on it. *What must he think?* For all he knew, he had a naked neighbor with one arm folded across her ta-tas and the other hand on her crotch, and she was shouting "Trouble, Trouble!"

He probably thought I'd lost my mind.

He had to be asking himself what *trouble* meant to a naked woman who lived alone.

The whole neighborhood surely knew that I was single. I'd been divorced over a decade, and all three of my children had graduated high school. My son occasionally crashed on the couch when he was between jobs and roommates, but both of my girls shared an apartment across town. One was a full-time student and the other a nurse at one of our local hospitals. If my house had a revolving door, it was for my kids and their buddies—*not* for single men.

And I was as predictable as neighbors came. Same six a.m.-to-one p.m. job for five years. My only pastime other than gardening—and that, only during warmer weather—was power walking, which I did every afternoon from two to three. I worked on my own cranky automobile, which the kids had christened "Christine" after the demonic car in the horror novel. I grew my own vegetables. I read, watched television, or slept after dinner.

I was boring.

And I'd disgraced myself in front of Kurt, the coolest man in my neighborhood, who'd lived behind me the past three years. We'd never met, but we waved when we saw one another. He lived next door to the biggest gossip on Elm Street, so I was sure Trish or her husband, Walter, had informed him of all the *eligible* women in the neighborhood, including the neighborhood divorcée.

While I was about as exciting as dry toast, Kurt drove a new sports car, wore clothes that made him look like he'd stepped off of the pages of a men's fashion magazine, and had the nonchalant demeanor of a man used to getting his way in a board meeting or having women fawn over him—whether he was in a professional atmosphere or not.

I peeked through the blinds at the window above the kitchen sink. He was still there; sitting quietly, as if he'd not witnessed my humiliation.

Why was he even out there? I asked myself. *It's too early in the year for him to be mowing, and it's too cold for him to be wearing those shorts.*

Even though we saw each other almost every day, we hadn't talked, but thanks to Trish, I knew he left for work promptly at seven-thirty every morning and he got home around five. His little whippet, whom I'd heard him call Wilson, always bolted out of the pet guard in Kurt's patio door and barked joyously every time Kurt left or came home.

I finished getting ready for work, my face still flaming with embarrassment. All day, I wondered what my hunky neighbor had thought when he'd seen me.

That night, I stole glances out my window, seeing if I could spot Kurt going through his usual routines—which included playing catch or fetch with Wilson, checking his immaculate flower beds, poking through his storage barn, which sat at the edge of his property line against our shared fence, or sipping a beer on his patio while he read the newspaper or flipped through a magazine.

My older daughter, who had come over to do her laundry, caught me staring out the window and questioned me. I blew her off, telling her I was just being nosy, seeing what the neighbors were doing.

"Neighbors. . .plural?" Stacy snorted. "Whatever."

I looked up from preparing our evening meal. "What does that mean?"

My daughter gave me a knowing look. "He is good looking. Why don't you ask him over for dinner some evening?"

I dismissed her suggestion. "Yeah, right." I was horribly shy anyway, and good-looking men had always made me duck for cover. Just the thought of what I'd done that morning made me blush, and Stacy mistook my embarrassment for shyness.

"Mom, you're attractive, you have a nice job, and the house is always clean. Go for it."

I looked about. *Clean house? Mine?* There was laundry piled on the sofa, and the floors had dog and cat hair all over them. My kids were as bad as I was about taking in strays, and by now we had three cats to our one dog. Even though none of my children really lived with me, any time they rescued an animal, I was the one who usually wound up taking care of it until they came and offered it a permanent home.

Then I looked at myself as I passed through the bathroom to deposit clean linens. Clear skin, but tired blue eyes, lips that would never have the plumpness of Michelle Pfeiffer's, and dishwater blonde hair in need of a good trim. *Attractive?* I shook my head. *I don't think so.*

As for my job as a cook for one of the local high schools, I enjoyed my work, but it was hardly anything to dangle in front of a man. It certainly would never compete with Kurt's job. I didn't know what he did for a living, but whatever it was afforded him a new vehicle and clothes that looked tailor-made.

Men I'd met casually seemed to want either a sugar mama or a woman who could match what they earned. I could sympathize—my own son had been burned more than once by a girl flirting with him just to have a date for prom or a party. Then she'd leave him for the next best thing that crooked a finger at her.

Men also seemed to prefer skinny, tanned bodies—not overworked, underpaid food service workers who didn't visit a gym three or four times a week. I sported what my mother called a farmer's tan; one that suggested whatever healthy, sun-kissed color my body had came from resting arms on the driver's side door during frenzied trips to and from work. Not from twenty-dollar-a-session tanning beds and expensive cocoa butter creams, neither of which were within my budget.

Nevertheless, Kurt with the red shorts, hyperactive dog, and coffee fetish made me tingle in places that usually weren't even awake. . .much less communicating with me.

I'd forgotten that my birthday would be that following week, when we'd all be off work due to spring break, but my coworkers hadn't. They surprised me with a birthday cake and vase of early spring flowers.

"Surprise!" they yelled as I walked into the large cooking area. They stood in their aprons and hairnets, grinning like maniacs.

Of course, when the kids saw the flowers on my table as they came through the line, waiting for me to collect their money or punch their lunch tickets, they added their best wishes. The morning flew, and before I knew it, our supervisor told us to eat.

Sasha, my best friend at work, cornered me as we took our lunch break together. "You seem distracted today, and not just because we sprang an early birthday surprise on you. What's up?"

I relayed to her what had happened and wasn't amused that she took so much pleasure in my discomfort.

"I can only imagine what he's thinking right now." I stirred my soup.

"Donna, you act like a man has never seen you naked." Sasha winked.

"Well, *he* hasn't!" I avoided looking at her.

"How do you know?" Her question seemed innocent enough.

I set down my spoon and stared at her blankly. "What do you mean?"

Sasha shrugged. "Just what I said. What if that's not the first time he's seen you without your clothes? Maybe he was outside because you've been giving him a peepshow all this time and weren't aware of it."

I couldn't have finished my soup then if she'd fed me intravenously.

"Hey!" she called as I rose to deposit my tray. "Where are you going?"

"Outside to smoke."

"But you don't smoke!"

I held the tray with one hand and waved at her with the other. "I'm starting now."

I reflected upon what she'd said the rest of my shift and all the way home. I thought back to all the times I'd meant to buy curtains for the kitchen window but thought the expense unnecessary. I liked the early morning sunlight that filtered through that southern window, and I figured the window was angled so nobody could look inside my house. I was short and could barely see over the top of the sink without tiptoeing, so I assumed nobody else could see me either.

The living room had thick drapery, as did the bedrooms that faced north, but the windows on the opposite side of the house all had sheer curtains or nothing at all.

"Move." I nudged Trouble aside as I entered the house. I couldn't wait to deposit my purse, change into my jeans and a pullover sweater, and walk around my backyard to see if I'd been making a fool of myself or if Sasha had just been ribbing me.

Before I unlatched the back door to let the dog and cats wander about, I placed a bright red sweater on the kitchen countertop and a vase of yellow and white daisies, pink tulips, and pale lilies on top of the dish drainer, using them as focal points for when I was outside. I stood close to both, measuring where they hit my body.

I looked around warily to see if anyone was watching me, even though the thought was laughable. Kurt was at work, the geriatrics in the neighborhood were watching their afternoon soap operas, and the rest of the folks were at work or school.

You are overreacting. Nobody is watching you now, and Kurt wasn't watching you before today. You're just imagining that he's interested.

I walked to the edge of the property and stood at a trajectory angle where he might see something if he peered around the blue pine, past the bed of bulbs that would soon be blooming, and over the scraggly looking lawn furniture that I'd had for years.

A clear shot of both yellow and red assaulted my disbelieving eyes. I could easily see the red and all of the pastels in the vase, which meant that Kurt could see me from my navel to my throat. . .and that was if I was at the counter. He could most likely glimpse more if I stood further back.

I covered my lips as a small cry escaped. *Sasha was right.* I closed my eyes, then lifted my lids slowly. It was all still there.

I raced back into the house and phoned my friend, tripping over my words as they tumbled from a scattered brain to my trembling lips. "How did you know? What made you guess that? I don't understand why he didn't say something to let me know!"

Sasha laughed raucously. "What's he gonna do, ask you to please stop showing him your girly parts?"

"I'll never be able to look up and wave at him again." I shook— partly from laughter, mostly from nervousness and shock.

"Oh, come on. He's the one who should be blushing. Look at what he's been doing!"

I rushed to Kurt's defense. "We don't actually know that."

"Donna, get real. He's a man. Of course he's been watching you."

"Well, I'll have to stay inside the house until this blows over."

I worked to keep from stammering. "I'll just not go outside for a while."

"You have pets, you have kids, spring is coming, and you love gardening—staying cooped up isn't an option for you." Then she laughed. "Of course, there is one other thing you could do."

"What?"

"You really are naïve, honey. He's watching, so give him some entertainment."

I heard the laughter again and blanched. "I don't get it. What entertain—? Sasha!"

"Oh, don't act so shocked. You'd be inside your own home. It's just innocent flirting."

"Not if I'm stripping for him! That's not flirting—that's an invitation to trouble."

This time she cracked up. "So you *do* have hormones. I was thinking about what you'd be wearing, not that you'd be performing." She howled again. "Funny you'd say *trouble*, considering it was that cat who started this whole thing."

"You are such an evil witch," I said lovingly. "You set me up."

"Want to borrow my belly dancing DVDs?" she teased.

"I do not." I paused as I reconsidered. "Are they any good?"

"I'll bring them right over."

I haven't laughed so hard in years. There we were, two middle-aged women—albeit ones in fairly good shape—gyrating to slow, seductive beats meant to entice, not just entertain.

We wore the leggings we usually wore when we walked in our respective neighborhoods, and we topped them with thin, baggy T-shirts tied at our waists in knots.

Learning belly dancing moves was much like playing the old floor game, Twister. About the time I thought I had a dance move down pat, one of us would either bump into the other one, we'd get a catch in our sides, or we'd fall to the floor laughing.

She didn't leave to go home until late that night, and by the time I woke up, I panicked for a moment, forgetting that school was out for the week. No work. Still, there were chores to be done, schedules to be kept if I wanted a stress-free life.

I hauled my trash to the curb since it was trash day for our street, and I heard a voice sing-songing, "Yoo-hoo! Don-naaaa!" I looked up to see Trish walking towards me.

What on earth is she doing walking here? Her street is busier than mine, so it makes sense. Still, I'd lived here for years without seeing the woman move from her yard to the street.

I brushed off my hands and placed them on my hips, hoping I looked stern and unwilling to chat. Then I felt ashamed. The poor woman thrived on gossip, and although we hadn't chatted in ages, perhaps she was just lonely. This was Trish, though, and Trish always had an agenda.

She got straight to the point, using her hands to help illustrate her words, pointing from my backyard to Kurt's. "I was talking to Kurt the other day, and he pointed out that you have that old mattress beside your storage barn."

I grimaced. I knew my shed wasn't as well-constructed or pretty as everyone else's, but it was sturdy and served its purpose. As for the mattress, I'd hauled them out to the side of the shed when my mom found a bargain at a garage sale. She and Dad had brought over the wrought-iron bedstead and a fairly new mattress and told me they thought Matt could use them. I'd agreed. "Big Trash Day" wasn't for a couple of months though, so I had to store the old bed and mattresses somewhere. There was no room inside the shed, only outside.

"Yes?" I tried keeping my voice steady, hiding the anger building inside me.

"Well, I saw this tiny little mouse running from your barn, so I asked Kurt if he could help."

So *that* was it. Kurt hadn't had anything to do with this scheme. "I see." Again, I kept my voice reasonably low and devoid of emotion.

"So he offered to haul it off for you." She pointed to his house and the empty driveway. "I mean, he drives that fancy sports car most of the time, but his dad has a truck. Have you seen it in his driveway before?"

"Yes, I've seen it." I felt embarrassment flush my face.

"Well, Kurt said he'd be over this week or next since you're out of school for spring break, and. . .you two can work out the details. I told him that I doubted you'd mind if he just went into your backyard and took it, but. . ." She shrugged and offered a sheepish smile that I doubt held sincerity.

"That's fine." I nodded and bit my lip. I couldn't believe she had the audacity to approach him and ask if he'd help clean my frickin' yard. Nosy old bat! Why couldn't she stick her nose into somebody else's business?

I kept to myself the rest of that weekend, praying he wouldn't show up. Every time I passed that window, I considered buying some cheap curtains to hang, just to make certain he couldn't see me.

Sasha came again, and we made a pitcher of margaritas and practiced our dance moves. Somehow, Kurt moved to the back of my mind and I was able to simply enjoy myself, learning something new, feeling exhilarated after the dance workout. I found myself listening to music more often—radio, old cassette tapes, CDs, whatever was around. With each rhythmic beat, I discovered I liked to dance. I enjoyed the feeling of freedom that dancing provided.

Then I lost my mind.

I got a glass of water Sunday afternoon after a full day of working the flowerbeds in front. I'd showered, wrapped my hair in a towel and my body in another, and put on my favorite CD—a slow, seductive jazz piece. I drew the water and when I looked up, he was there in his backyard—sitting at his patio, petting Wilson, and staring straight at me.

I nearly dropped the glass of water into the sink. Everything blurred visually, but I could still hear—and feel—the music playing in the background. Instinctively, I began moving to the music, my hips grinding, even though I was sure he couldn't tell.

I set the glass down, careful to make sure it was out of reach should my self-control slip and I send my drink crashing to the floor.

A slow smile curled my lips, and my breathing became deeper, more concentrated. I lifted my arms slowly above my head and fell into the dance trance, as I called it, oblivious to anything but my body and the sounds coming from the stereo.

I closed my eyes and stretched, reaching for some invisible, intangible object above me. My head lolled back as I swung it slowly in a circle. I felt it pull at the muscles in my neck and ached to work every atom in my body if possible. I removed the towel on my head, feeling a slight breeze that both chilled and warmed me as heat from my body met the cold air in the room.

My hair touched my shoulders, and the feel of clean, satiny hair against my skin felt soft, sweet, and seductive. I lifted my arms as high as I could reach, lowered my chin without looking out the window, and dropped the towel.

It was as if releasing the towel also freed what was left of my imprisoned inhibitions. My now unrestricted emotion embraced the music, became one with it, and I danced as if I hadn't a care in the world—because I hadn't. I didn't care if anyone else watched; I didn't care if they noticed. I danced for me.

I ran my fingers through my hair and felt myself smiling. I heard the sounds of my laughter mingling with the music, and unrestricted emotions zipped up my spine. My hips thrusted and retracted, bumped and twisted, and the muscles in my belly tightened, constricting then releasing. It was as if I could feel every minute tug and pull. My body became a well-oiled, synchronized machine whose parts moved in unison to create an expression of joy that I hadn't felt in ages.

I was alone in my own house, a primal wild woman, queen of her own jungle, my own beauty and my own beast. . .and it felt wonderful to be alive.

Then the music slowed, and I became acutely aware that it would soon be over. I turned my back and unhooked the towel fastened at my breasts. Pulling it slowly from my body, I let it slip from my fingers onto the floor.

Turning to face the window, I boldly looked back at him. . .and smiled.

I have no idea whether or not he smiled back. As soon as the music stopped, I picked up the towel and ran for my room, bursting into stifled giggles.

"You did *what?*" Sasha was flabbergasted when I told her what had happened. "Donna! You didn't look back? Didn't peek from your bedroom window or anything?"

"Are you kidding?" I collapsed onto my bed, staring at the ceiling. "I have no idea what came over me—all I knew was that I was tired of playing mouse to his cat, so I turned the tables on him and did as you suggested. I gave him something to watch."

I giggled again. "That poor man."

Sasha chuckled. "Oh, please. He's a man. He's used to switching channels if he doesn't like what he's watching. Nobody made him sit through the show—he could have gotten up and left at any time."

She laughed outright this time. "One thing's for sure. You'll soon find out if he's interested or not. You'll either have that stupid mattress propped up against the barn until your dad or brother can come over and haul it off, or you'll have a neighborhood clean-up party with Kurt in charge."

"Oh, whatever. He's no more interested in me than I am in you."

She sniffed in disagreement. "I think you've lost your mind. That's what I think. And if he's not interested after watching that little show, you need to concentrate on somebody with a stronger libido anyway!"

I suddenly sobered. "I wonder if he'll tell Trish what I just did."

She scoffed again. "Donna, if she's as nosy as you say she is, you have to realize that she's probably the one who suggested to *him* that you needed that mattress hauled off. I mean, c'mon. He's never said anything before about your backyard."

"Yeah, but it *is* an eyesore. I need to put more effort into mowing that area and keeping it picked up back there."

"Well, not like a single woman has much choice. You're not the one with a truck and the muscles to work that yard. Let me know if you hear from him. I don't care if it's one o'clock in the morning."

I told her that I would and hung up, tired but pleased for some weird reason that I'd finally done something shocking. My life seemed to have taken on a new dimension. Granted, it was a rather perverted one, but it beat thinking of myself as boring.

The weekend passed, as did Monday, Tuesday, and Wednesday. I didn't see Kurt outside or at his window during that time. I still kept busy doing what I enjoyed—the little gardening I could do considering the chilly weather, practicing belly dancing, and reading. I walked every day, grocery shopped, cooked. . .the usual.

On Thursday, Sasha and I went to a movie. When we got back, she pointed from the driveway to my backyard. "Donna, that mattress is gone."

When we walked through the gate, sure enough, no mattress. Not only that, my yard had been cleaned. The shrubbery had been trimmed as if someone with a chainsaw had been in my backyard.

I looked around. Against the house was a large pile of kindling wood, sticks, and fallen branches from the oak trees in the backyard. Someone had stacked it carefully, and had bagged some of the debris and set it next to the rack of wood.

"Think your dad or your brother may have done this?" she asked.

I shook my head. "Neither one of them has a chainsaw, and there's no way this wood was chopped, sawed, or whatever without one. Wow."

"Kurt." She looked at me knowingly. "Had to have been him, Donna."

"No." I shook my head again.

"Well, it sure wasn't ol' Trish."

I sighed. "Doesn't look as if they'd taken anything besides the mattress. Nothing seems disturbed except, of course, the dead branches." I couldn't believe what I was seeing. Someone had to have worked the solid two or three hours I'd been gone to accomplish this.

I stared into the yard behind mine. Kurt's car was gone. Perplexed, I turned back to Sasha. She'd walked to the woodpile and was pulling something from it—a small package.

"Looks like he left you a present. He even wrapped it."

I stared at the brown paper encasing it and the crudely fashioned bow made of twine. With shaking fingers, I untied, unwrapped, and peered inside the paper. It was a CD of tribal music from around the globe.

I burst into laughter and handed it to her.

Sasha peeled a note from the package and read aloud: "Got called to a meeting in Boston, back on Sunday. I'll provide dinner if you'll dance for me again. Kurt."

"No way!" I grabbed the paper and read for myself, blushing furiously.

Sasha sat on the steps of my back porch and pulled me down beside her. "You can't say he's not interested now. What will you wear?"

I held out the twine and giggled. "Wonder if this would cover the situation?"

Before either of us could comment again, we noticed Trish staring from her kitchen window behind us. She was smiling broadly, and she waved.

"Cupid comes in many forms, I guess," Sasha said quietly.

"I'll have to do something for her." I smiled and waved back at Trish. "Bet she'd like to learn how to belly dance for Walter." THE END

INDECENT PROPOSAL

I walked toward the gorgeous dark-haired man perched at the bar. *He would do it for me.* I was not the type to pick up guys in a bar. I didn't even go to bars that often. It wasn't my scene, and it certainly didn't seem like the kind of place to meet a nice guy. But I couldn't miss Ally's bachelorette party. And I wasn't exactly looking to pick this guy up. No, what I was going to ask him was possibly even worse. *What if he says no?*

I reminded myself that tall, curvy blondes always get their way when they walk through a bar in the movies or on TV. And I was a tall, curvy woman with medium blonde hair, so I could do this, right? *I can totally do this. I just have to act the part.* I straightened my shoulders as I moved towards him. He watched me with interest as I wove through the crowd.

I swallowed the lump in my throat. Sure, I was dressed to kill and had spent an hour on my hair and makeup. I'd noticed a few heads turn when I first walked into the bar. But I wasn't exactly overflowing in the confidence department. I just was not the party-girl type. Even if I was, this particular request might be pushing it, even if I had been the most confident and curvy blonde. I looked back at my friends as they giggled over their drinks.

They shooed me on, waving their hands. "Go Joanna!" they shouted across the bar.

I walked over and stood beside the man, taking a deep breath. "I need to ask you something," I said.

He looked at me, and his pale blue eyes almost knocked me over. The girls all agreed that he was hot when we checked him out from across the bar, but up close he was lose-your-breath gorgeous. He was exactly the kind of guy I'd never have the courage to approach. Unless I'd been forced to, as was the case in this hot bar on a humid summer night.

I smiled as he took in my curves, and his gaze settled on my chest. The legend of the curvy blonde in a bar was proving itself to be true. I'd never tried it myself, and I liked the feeling of power it brought.

He must have realized he was staring because his eyes snapped back up to look at mine. "You've got a question for me? Go ahead, ask," he said, taking a sip of his beer.

I nibbled on my bottom lip, twisting my hands in front of me. "Can I have your underwear?"

He choked on his drink and laughed. "Why don't we start with a drink first? What would you like?"

I gripped the bar with one hand. "A beer. Actually, I could really use a shot." My heart was pounding, and I blew out the breath I'd been holding.

"I'll get you both." While he was signaling to the bartender, I spied my friends bent over their table, laughing.

He pushed the shot toward me and I downed it, coughing as the fire raced down my throat. I chased it with a swig of beer and immediately felt a little calmer.

He crossed his arms and stared at me. "Now, why do you need my underwear, and why should I give them to you?"

Oh yeah. The underwear. "Well, I know it sounds crazy, but I need your underwear because I'm out with my friend for her bachelorette party. We're on a scavenger hunt."

He raised an eyebrow. "And you need some guy's underwear?"

I nodded. Ally's maid-of-honor, Jules, handed out a list of items we'd need to collect for a scavenger hunt. We pulled slips of paper out of a bag to determine what we'd each need to get. Caitlin only had to score a pair of shoelaces from a guy, and Mare just had to find someone to buy us a round of shots. She found a willing guy on the first go. I definitely got stuck with the toughest item on the list. Jules was totally the type of girl to ask a stranger for his underwear. We'd always butted heads. I was friends with Ally from high school. We were in orchestra together and had the same homeroom each year.

Ally met Jules in college, and the two of us had never gotten along, but we played nice for Ally's sake. I knew she was loving every minute of my humiliation.

"Yep, a pair of underwear," I told him. "But it has to be the underwear of the hottest guy in the bar." I looked down at the floor. "And a picture."

"Of what?"

I could feel the music pounding through the soles of my platforms. "Of me taking them off you."

He laughed, shaking his head. "And I'm your guy, huh? Was it because you thought I looked hot, or because you thought I looked easy?"

I shrugged. "Hot and understanding, I hope." He was very hot, and so was the bar. I lifted my hair off my neck and started fanning myself. My dangly earrings grazed my shoulders.

He drummed his fingers on the bar. "What makes you so sure I'm even wearing underwear?"

I felt myself turning red. "Oh, I um. . .I just thought. . .well, are you?"

He chuckled. "You're cute when you blush." He took a swig of his beer. "Don't worry, I'm wearing them. Boxers. Were they specific about the type you needed to get?"

"Fortunately, no."

"So you want my underwear." He tapped his chin. His cheeks were bronzed, and his black hair hung to his shoulders. He looked more gorgeous by the minute. "I've been called understanding, but I'm no fool. I'm a businessman." His voice was deep and sexy. Everything about this man was perfect—except for his unwillingness to pass over his unmentionables.

"What do you mean, you're a businessman?"

"I mean, I'm not just giving up my underwear *and* my dignity," he said with mock outrage.

"So what do you want, money?" I was going to kill Jules when this was all over. I should've made sure the guy we picked was good and drunk. That would've made things much easier. Not that I minded being so close to this beautiful man. He was the kind of guy I only dreamed about.

He laughed. "Money would be a little too easy. No, I want something in return, something of fair value."

"Like what?" I tapped my foot impatiently.

He cocked his head. "*Your* underwear. An even swap." He leaned back with a satisfied smile.

I felt myself turning red again.

He threw up his hands. "Come on, quid pro quo and all that. Fair is fair."

I shook my head. "No. No way." *Give this guy my underwear?* I was voted Most Shy in high school. I'd never had a one-night stand or even gone out with a guy from a bar. I was always the good girl. And I was going to have to take my underwear off for a stranger? That wasn't part of the deal. *What did I get myself into?*

My chest tightened, and I felt my shoulders slouching. I was morphing back into the quiet girl who went through high school without ever being kissed. The girl who spent most Friday nights at home, watching a movie. But I forced myself to stand up straight. This was not the way confident, sassy blondes acted on the big screen. They could flirt with anybody and be as coy as they wanted. *Compose yourself. You can do this.*

"No, of course I'm not giving you my underwear," I told him. "I'm wearing my favorite Brazilians. No way!"

"Your favorite? Sounds like you have quite a few of them. Why can't you part with this one?"

I stared at him. "Like I said, they're my favorite. Plus, they're brand new and cost a small fortune as far as underwear's concerned." I shook my head. "No deal." It was true that I was wearing Brazilian-cut undies, but they were my only ones. I usually wore cotton briefs, but I didn't want a panty line showing through my clingy skirt.

He shrugged. "Fine. No deal. No undies for you. You'll just have to find another guy." He turned back to his beer.

I sighed. "We already decided you were the hottest guy in the bar." I pointed to my table of girls who waved at us.

He smiled and waggled his fingers back at them. "They're going to be very disappointed in you."

I planted a fist on my hip. I was twenty-seven years old and had never done anything wild or crazy—I always just *heard* about stories like this. Like Jules' friend who met a B-list actor at a bar in New York and went home with him. Or the time my college friends went out and danced on the bar. I was grateful to be in bed with the flu for that. Jules probably rigged the whole scavenger hunt thing to force me into this. Well, I wasn't about to let the girls down. They probably had bets on whether or not I'd go through with it. I could do this. Maybe it wasn't too late for me to be a wild party girl. Maybe this was the beginning of a brand new me.

I looked him in the eyes—those beautiful baby blues. "Fine. We'll swap underwear."

He stared back at me. "Oh, and I want a picture, too. Fair trade."

I closed my eyes and nodded. "Get me another shot of tequila first. And no putting the picture up on Facebook, either."

"It's a deal." He signaled to the bartender, and I tried to compose myself. *Whoa. Am I really doing this? Really?*

He pressed the shot in my hand, and I threw it back.

"So, where's the exchange going down?" He was right next to my ear, holding my wrist. His rock-hard bicep pressed against my chest.

I had to swallow hard before I could answer. "We've got a limo outside."

"Perfect. Lead the way." He held out his arm, and I took it as we headed for the door.

We walked past my party, and they hooted and hollered as we left the bar. The warm summer air cooled my skin a bit, but my cheeks still felt flushed, and I was feeling woozy.

"Whoa, maybe you've had one too many shots." He set his hand against the small of my back to steady me. "Are you all right?"

I looked up at him under the glow of a streetlight. How wonderful it would be to be out on a date with this guy instead of swapping underwear with him. Oh well. At least I wasn't going to let the girls down. I needed a wild story to tell if I was to join the ranks of Jules and her crew.

He kept his arm around me as we walked to the limo. The driver hopped out and opened the back door. I kept my eyes on the ground, unable to look at him as he held the door for us. I slid across the seat and pressed the button to raise the tinted divider window, giving us some privacy.

"This is a first," I said. I poured us each a glass of wine and took a long swallow.

"It's a first for me, too. I can honestly say no one's ever asked for my underwear before," he said. "I'm glad my mother always told me to put on a clean pair every day." He smiled and raised his glass to me.

I clinked mine with his. "Here's to being a good sport," I said.

"You too. I can tell you really aren't the party type."

"What do you mean?" I said, a bit defensively. I thought I was pulling this off pretty well.

"For one thing, you can't hold your liquor. And you just seem sweet. You definitely aren't the typical barfly. That was my type, but not anymore."

"So, what're you doing at a bar then?"

"Came out with my friends. They were playing darts in back, otherwise I would've introduced you."

I squirmed in my seat. He was making this a lot more difficult. He was clearly a nice guy, the kind I'd love to go out with. And here I was, guaranteeing I'd never have a shot with him by giving him my underwear. "Hey, I don't even know your name."

"It's Costa. Costa Miarcos." He held out his hand.

I shook it. "I'm Joanna Avalon." *There, at least I wouldn't be giving my undies to a total stranger.*

He finished his wine and leaned towards me. "So who goes first?"

"You," I said in a thick voice.

He leaned closer. "And if I understand this correctly, *you* have to take them off of me?" he whispered.

I nodded. "Take your pants off, and I'll do the rest." I reached for my cell phone as he undid his jeans. Trembling, I fumbled with the phone and dropped it.

"A little nervous?" he asked.

I opened my mouth but couldn't find the right witty words to recover. "Yeah, I am a little nervous. You're right. I'm not really this kind of girl. I don't normally do this kind of thing." I fiddled with the hem of my skirt.

He stopped what he was doing. "You don't have to do this, you know," he said.

I forced myself to look at him. He still had his pants on. "No, I do."

He watched me for a moment and then shrugged. "Then let's get started." He took his time wriggling out of his pants, shaking his hips until only striped cotton boxers remained on his thick thighs.

A gasp slipped from my lips, and I slapped my hand over my mouth, embarrassed.

"Won't you at least kiss me before you strip me?" he asked, one side of his mouth curling up.

I nodded and leaned forward, pressing my lips against his, letting him take me in his arms. I ran my hands along his muscular back until I got down to his boxers.

"I better get these off you," I said quietly. But I couldn't bring myself to slide my fingers under the waistband.

He grabbed my hand. "Listen, I know you don't want to do this. Let me take them halfway down, you reach over like you're pulling them off, and I'll take the picture with your phone. You don't even have to look."

"Really?" I asked. I looked into his eyes for any trace of mockery, but there was none—just kindness and understanding.

He squeezed my hand. "Really."

I handed him my phone and closed my eyes. I heard the rustle of fabric, and he reached for my hand.

"Grab here," he said, guiding my hand to his undies.

I grabbed a handful of fabric and heard the click of my cell as he took the picture.

"Pull them off," he said.

Keeping my eyes closed, I tugged on the boxers until they pulled free from his legs.

"Hang on a minute and let me get my pants back on," he said. "Okay, you can open your eyes now."

I opened my eyes and looked down at my shoes. "Thanks," I whispered. "I don't do things like this. My friends kind of put me up to it, and I felt like I had something to prove." I set the boxers on the seat next to me and looked up at him.

"No problem," he said quietly. "And I was kidding about the swap. You don't have to give me your underwear. I was just having fun messing with you. I'm sorry if I made you uncomfortable."

"Don't be sorry. You really helped me out. The girls would've made fun of me forever if I didn't come through on this."

He reached for my hand and pulled me to him. I sat on his lap and took his face in my hands. I kissed him, and he ran his hands through my hair.

"I've never hooked up with someone from a bar before," I told him.

"Really? I'm happy to be your first," he said. He kissed my nose. "Can I get you some more wine, or have you had enough?"

"Sure. I'm gonna be hurting in the morning anyway," I laughed. I sat back so he could pour us another drink. I was having fun. This was the craziest thing I'd ever done. I took the wine from him and took a long swallow of the golden liquid. I couldn't believe I was in a limo drinking wine with a stranger. I closed my eyes, trying to make sense of the night. *Why not make this a story to remember? Why not be totally out of character? Why not be a bad girl for the night?*

I set my wine down and looked at Costa. "I hope I didn't give you the wrong impression."

"No, I understand. Really."

"No. I mean, I hope you don't think I'm not a woman of my word. I said I'd give you my underwear for yours. I feel like I need to hold up my end of the deal."

He held up one hand. "Joanna, you don't have to. I told you that."

"Yes, I do." For some reason, I really *did* have to do this. For me. Forget Jules and everyone else, I had something to prove to myself. I slowly worked my skirt down over my hips, watching Costa watching me, until it dropped to the floor.

"Wow," he whispered. He ran his hand up my leg and slipped one finger underneath the silky lace of my Brazilian. "Very nice," he said. "I can see why you didn't want to part with it."

I felt goose bumps sting my flesh.

He worked his hand along the leg opening and cupped my behind. He moved his other hand up my back and kissed my neck. "You're right," he whispered in my ear. "I can't take these from you. It's far too hot *on* you. I'll settle for something else instead."

I turned to look at him. "What?"

He smiled. "Your number."

I smiled and closed my mouth over his. "Yes," I said through my kiss.

He kissed me back, hard, and nibbled his way over to my earlobe and down my neck. I dropped my head back and held onto his shoulders, hoping I wasn't moaning too loudly for the driver to hear. I'd never done it in a limo. How impetuous was I willing to be? Would I really hook up with a strange guy outside a bar? I pressed myself against him, wanting more.

Costa broke off from our kiss. "This shouldn't happen, not here outside the bar. I want more than that."

I sighed. "Are you sure?"

He tucked my hair behind my ears. "Yeah, I really want to see you again. Like I said, I'm done with the party scene."

I rested my head against his shoulder and laughed. "And here I was ready to join the party scene. What timing."

He ran his finger down my cheek. "Don't change. I like you just the way you are. Even if you did steal my underwear."

I swatted his arm, and he kissed me again before opening the limo door for me.

I got out and handed him my card.

He looked at it and smiled. "Now that was a very good trade. I'll call you this week."

I walked back into the bar, twirling his boxers on one finger.

Ally high-fived one of the girls next to her. "I knew you'd do it!

You owe me five bucks, Jules."

Jules looked at me doubtfully. "Let's see the picture."

I pulled out my phone and showed her the photo.

Jules crossed her arms and pouted.

The other girls giggled and chattered as I sat down at the table.

"He was so hot. You guys were out there for a while," Ally said.

I could feel the blush spreading across my cheeks.

Ally's eyes grew wide. "Oh my. . .did you guys hook up?"

I put a hand on my hip and grinned. "You're talking to Joanna Avalon. What kind of girl do you think I am?"

Ally raised a toast to me. "I just don't know anymore."

But I knew, and so did Costa, despite my best intentions to be a bad girl. THE END

THE SEXY SUMMER GAME THAT SAVED A MARRIAGE
A *Naughty Confession!*

"What's bothering you?" I asked, slipping my well-worn, cotton nightie over my head. I didn't bother asking my husband *if* something was wrong because after twenty years of marriage, a wife instinctively knows when her man isn't himself.

Granted, it had been a long day, but the kids were sleeping and we finally had a few hours of private time to ourselves—time we looked forward to each evening, time when we could relax and, *hopefully,* delight in each other's company.

But that night was different. That night, Sean seemed distracted and distant.

"Nothing, really," he said, flipping through an old, well-worn copy of *Sports Illustrated.*

"Don't tell me nothing," I said, smiling softly. "Have out with it. Tell me."

He tossed the magazine onto the bedside table, swung his legs over the side of the bed, and began pacing the room. "I'm just feeling a little restless, that's all," he said softly.

"I've got the cure for that," I whispered seductively, rising to wrap my arms around his narrow waist.

"I know you do, babe," he said, and then kissed my lips. He held me close and ran his hands lingeringly over my bottom. "But have you ever thought of, well . . . of sleeping with another man?" he asked out of the blue.

I pulled back and his hands slid from my body. "What kind of crazy question is that?"

"A *really* crazy one, I guess," he said, blushing a little. "But the truth is, well . . . I've been thinking . . . well, actually, it's something I read about on the Internet . . . I guess some married couples get a charge out of, well . . . swapping."

"Swapping what?" I asked, but I already had a pretty good idea of what he was getting at.

"Partners."

"You mean like—switching husbands and wives?"

He blushed more and grinned a little, mischievously. "Yeah, sort of."

I walked to the window and rested my elbows on the sill. I leaned forward and took a deep breath of warm, moist spring air. A sudden, unbidden jolt of arousal was quickly stifled by the realization that Sean might be growing tired of me.

"What brought this on?" I asked.

He came up behind me and rested his hand on my shoulder. "I didn't mean to upset you, Julia. I just thought it sounded kind of, well—sexy—and I wanted to tell you about it."

I turned to face him. "Are you getting tired of me?"

"No! Why would you think that?"

"Jeez, Sean. Twenty years of marriage. Three kids. Stretch marks. Saggy boobs. Gee, Sean, I'm not a fool, you know. I know what I look like and I sure as hell don't look like the woman you fell in love with all those years ago." I turned away.

Sean turned me around and smiled into my eyes. "And look at *me*. I didn't have these love handles when I met you; you're not the only one who's changed, Julia. Besides, I'm happy with you and I love you. I was just thinking about it, that's all. We don't have to act on every thought or idea that comes into our heads."

I shrugged and turned, putting my arms around him. "I know, but you really caught me off guard with that one. Are you sure we're okay?"

He kissed my neck and I sighed when his tongue flicked

lightly over my throat while his hands slowly traveled beneath my nightgown. "We're better than ever, babe. If we weren't so in love and so comfortable with each other, I'd never be able to ask you about this kind of stuff."

"I love you, too, Sean," I said as he pushed me back onto the bed and fell beside me.

"Now I'm going to prove just how desirable you are, Julia," he murmured against my lips as he slowly raised the hem of my nightgown above my knees.

It wasn't until a few days later while I was paying bills online that I thought again of what Sean had said about partner swapping—or "swinging," as he'd told me it is also called. When I finished with the business at hand I had a few minutes before the kids would be getting home from school, so I decided to do a bit of "online research" on my own.

Eager and admittedly more than slightly intrigued, I typed *swinging* into the browser. A long list of websites devoted to this practice quickly flashed onto the computer monitor. Indeed, I quickly realized that there was more information online about husband and wife swapping than I could ever digest in the short amount of time available. Apparently, swinging is far more widespread and common than I ever realized.

I clicked on what looked like the largest and most organized site and bookmarked it. Then I scrolled through the choices. They had everything from heterosexual couple sharing to gay-and-lesbian partner sharing; there was even a special section for people who shared the same fetishes and unusual sexual practices—as if partner swapping wasn't unusual enough!

Finally, after about fifteen minutes of scrolling through the site, I found a message board where interested parties could provide a general idea of where they lived and then email each other to actually meet. The board was quite busy; there were over one hundred requests on that day alone, and over twenty pages of previous messages.

I started scrolling casually—not really looking for anyone in our area, but whenever I stumbled across someone who'd written that

they were from the Northeast, I'd stop and read their request. Some
were too far out, while others sounded dangerous and just plain *weird*,
but finally I found a couple who seemed rather . . . "normal"—under
the circumstances, of course. They'd written that they were from the
tri-state area—about two hours away from us—and they were looking
for a married couple, preferably a well-educated, working couple with
children who'd want to have a friendship, and possibly "more."

Well, I knew darn well what that "more" was all about. My first
instinct was to criticize them—even look down on them for having
such an odd sex life—and then I realized that I was on that website
doing *the exact same thing*. The only difference between them and me
was that I hadn't posted my request . . . yet.

I chided myself for thinking that I was superior to that couple. After
all, I have to admit that the idea of partner swapping—even though I
didn't tell my husband—was quite intriguing to me at that point. So
I clicked on their email address and before I could change my mind,
I wrote them a quick note describing Sean and myself, detailing how
long we'd been married, and giving them a brief description of our life
together, followed by a short explanation as to why I was interested
in a possible friendship with them. By the time I finished the kids
were pouring in the door, clamoring for snacks, requesting help with
homework, and begging for rides to the mall. My clandestine Internet
adventure was quickly forgotten as I switched into "Mommy Mode"
and spent the rest of that day tending to my family.

"Hey, Julia?" Sean called from the family room the following
Sunday morning.

"Yeah? What is it? I'm cleaning the oven!" I called back, turning
my head away from the acrid fumes inside the soapy oven.

"Do we know anyone by the name of C. Troyer from New York?"

"No, not that I know of."

"Well, you have to come and see this, then."

"Jeez, Sean—I'm up to my neck in oven cleaner right now! Can't
it wait?"

"Yeah, I guess it can, but this is a strange coincidence. Remember
what we were talking about last week? About the—" He hesitated

for a moment, and then lowered his voice. "The swapping, sharing—whatever you call it. You know what I mean."

I pulled off my yellow rubber gloves, hurried to the family room, and looked over Sean's shoulder at the computer screen. "What is it?"

"Look," he said, pointing at the name listed in our email account. "C. Troyer, in reference to 'sharing.' "

"Oh, my gosh—I bet I know who that is," I said, rubbing his shoulder and giving his neck a soft squeeze.

"Oh, yeah? What have you been up to?" he asked, winking at me.

"Nothing," I said, smiling. "Well, maybe I *have* been up to a *little something* . . . but not much." I pushed his hand away from the mouse and clicked on the email. "One day I was bored and I just did a little Net surfing."

"Looks like you did more than just surf."

"Yeah, a bit more, I guess. I found a partner swapping website and took a little look around."

He gave me a look of surprise. "Oh? And what did you see? Anything you liked?"

"I don't know; there weren't any pictures," I teased. "But this couple, Christian and Ava Troyer . . . they seemed pretty nice—and normal—so I emailed them, just for the heck of it."

"What'd you tell them?"

"Not much. Just that we had discussed swapping and we're both curious."

"We are?" he asked, grinning excitedly as he pulled me onto his lap.

"Well, aren't we? I mean, *you're* the one who brought it up in the first place!"

"Yeah, but I didn't think you were interested. In fact, I thought you were dead set against the whole idea; that's why I haven't mentioned it again."

"I gave it some thought," I said, sliding my arms around his neck.

"Tell me," he whispered huskily.

"Well, after some consideration, I thought that *maybe* it would be kind of a good idea. A sexy-good idea."

"Really?" he asked, more than a little shocked. "You want to sleep with another man?"

"Sean! All of this was *your* fantasy; I just followed through on *your* idea. Do you have a problem with it now?" Truthfully, I wasn't all that surprised that Sean would balk at the idea. While the idea of sleeping with another woman was surely appealing to him, I knew that the idea of sharing his wife with another man would make him uncomfortable.

"No, no, babe—I'm cool with it. But, well . . . are you?"

"I honestly don't know. But I think I'd like to explore the idea a bit more."

"What do you mean, 'explore' it?"

I settled into his lap and rested my head on his shoulder. "Well, we've been together for twenty years, and in all that time, we've been faithful to each other, you know?"

"Mmm-hmm," he murmured.

"So, here we are in our forties and, well, aren't you a bit curious about what it'd be like to have a little 'adventure'?"

"Sometimes I am. But I love you and I would never be unfaithful to you. You're too important to me, Julia; you and the kids are my whole life."

"And you're mine. I still love you more than anyone, Sean, even after all these years, but this *could* be an opportunity for us to explore other aspects of ourselves, and yet still maintain our marriage bond." I hesitated, and then tentatively asked, "Would it bother you to see me making love with another man?"

He was silent for a moment. "Would it bother you to see me with another woman?"

"It might, but I'll be honest: The thought of you watching me with another man turns me on *immensely*."

"It does?" he asked, sliding his hand between my legs and gently fondling the zipper of my jeans with his thumb.

"Yeah," I whispered huskily.

He kissed my lips gently, but I could tell from the tenseness in his arms that he was holding back. "I'm afraid I'd go nuts watching you with another man. I might get too jealous," he admitted.

"You want to find out?" I asked seductively.

His hand slid upward, beneath my blouse, and he deftly unclasped my lace bra. "You know what I think?"

"What?" I whispered against his mouth.

"I think we should go upstairs and 'discuss' this some more."

I wrapped my arms around his neck as he lifted me and carried me toward the stairs. "You always have the *best* ideas," I said, unbuttoning his shirt.

Later that evening after considering what we were about to embark on, Sean and I carefully composed an email for Christian and Ava Troyer. We didn't really expect a response—especially not the very next day—but to our surprise the next morning there was an email from the Troyers waiting for us in our email account. They offered to meet us for dinner midway between our home in Pennsylvania and theirs in New York.

We met the following weekend at a swanky restaurant in an upscale hotel, where we made room reservations for the weekend.

"This hotel is absolutely stunning," I said, looking around and admiring the finely appointed dining room. Our waiter hovered close by, eager to cater to our every need.

"What are you going to have? I hear the Chesapeake-style chicken is out of this world," sultry, dark-haired, Ava said, pointing to the description of the crab imperial-stuffed chicken breast described in the leather-bound menu.

"Oh, that does sound good. I think I'll have that and a salad," I said, smiling, and then giggling slightly.

"What's so funny?" Sean asked pointedly.

"Yeah, you have to share it with the entire class, missy," wickedly handsome, blue-eyed, raven-haired Christian teased, sipping his champagne.

I shifted nervously in my chair and giggled again. "I was just thinking that we're probably the only people in the restaurant this evening who met on the Internet and will be going to a hotel room together after dinner."

Ava looked around and arched a dark eyebrow, smiling so that her glossy, pink lips curved into a devilish bow. "Maybe that table, over there?" she said, nodding to a corner booth where four elderly ladies dined on shrimp cocktail.

Christian and Sean laughed and I joined in. "No thanks," Christian said. "Personally, I think we've got a better deal right here."

Before I knew it dinner was over and we were having luscious, decadent dark-chocolate mousse for dessert. "This is a fitting end to our meal," Sean remarked, smiling contentedly.

"Yes. Or a wonderful appetizer for pleasures to come," Ava purred.

A soft blush crept over Sean's cheeks—so soft that I was the only one who noticed. However, I knew instinctively that Ava's comment made him uneasy, so I slipped my hand in his beneath the table and gave it a soft squeeze.

"We can still make a run for it, you know," I whispered to him minutes later as we left the dimly lit, intimate restaurant and crossed the plush lobby toward the hotel elevator banks.

He stopped in his tracks and pulled me close, placing his hands on my hips as his blue eyes searched mine. "Have you changed your mind?"

"No; I'm okay if you are."

He smiled and took my hand and led me over to a velvet sofa; he sat on the soft, cushioned bench and pulled me down beside him. "Tell me the truth, Julia. Is this really what you want? It's not too late to turn around and forget the whole thing, you know."

"Do you want to?"

He sighed. "I'm asking you. I want to know how *you* feel, and I want the truth. I don't think we should go through with anything unless we're both in absolute agreement about the whole arrangement."

"I love you, Sean," I said, clutching his hand and resting my head on his shoulder. "I think we should go upstairs and . . . see what happens. Ava and Christian are nice people; I like them."

"All right, then. It's decided; for better or worse, we're in this together. But remember, Julia: If you change your mind at any time, just give me a sign and I'll pull the plug on this entire adventure."

Upstairs at their room on the tenth floor, I was slightly unnerved when Ava answered the door wearing nothing more than a filmy, black negligee with skimpy, provocative-looking, leopard-print lingerie underneath. Behind her, lounging on the black, leather couch, Christian wore a pair of black, silk pajama bottoms and nothing else. If it hadn't been before, it was now abundantly clear that they had far more experience with this sort of thing than Sean and I.

"Come in and make yourselves comfortable," Ava invited, taking my hand and leading me over to the small, graciously appointed bar set up in a corner of the spacious suite.

"What can I get you to drink?" Christian asked, rising from the couch to play bartender.

"I'll have a glass of red wine," I said, setting my purse and jacket over a chair.

"I think I'll just have a Diet Coke. I need to keep my wits about me this evening," Sean teased.

"Aww," Ava purred softly. "But you need to *relax*, Sean. At *least* change into something a bit more comfortable."

Sean nervously eyed our overnight bag, which the porter had earlier brought up to Christian and Ava's room, and then glanced at me. I smiled and shrugged, took a sip of my wine, and then picked up the smallish bag and carried it into the luxurious bathroom.

Before long, Sean and I were wearing our pajamas; while they were silk, they were nowhere near as revealing or as provocative as Ava's and Christian's. By the time I finished my second glass of wine Christian had turned the lights down low and popped a few sultry-sounding CDs into the stereo.

"We usually start by playing a little game," Ava said, retrieving a kit from her Louis Vuitton suitcase and opening a box that contained what appeared to be a board game.

"I've never seen a game like that before. What do we do?" I asked.

"It's easy," Christian said. "All you do is roll the dice and move your game piece to the appropriate square. Now, see—on each square," he said, pointing to the board, "there are instructions you must follow."

"Everyone ready?" Ava asked, her ample grin broadening devilishly as she laid out the board game on the mahogany coffee table and we all took seats on the leather couch and facing loveseat.

Sean and I nodded and Ava tossed Sean the dice.

Sean rolled a seven and landed on a square that read: *Gently kiss and caress the breasts of the woman sitting farthest from you.*

He looked across the game board at Ava. She smiled and gave him a playful, "come hither" look. "Come on over," she said, slowly unbuttoning her silk-covered buttons. All at once she undid the front-closure clasp on her bra and without so much as a millisecond's hesitation, bared her full, surgically augmented breasts.

I was breathless as Ava stood and approached Sean. I sat still and did not say a word, watching as she took his hand and led him over to the edge of the room's California-king-sized bed. I put my hand out weakly when Ava's husband, Christian, leaned across the coffee table and reached for me, his eyes full of erotic intent. Even in my slightly tipsy state, the very idea of another woman having sex with my husband unnerved me, but I said not a word.

Sean and I agreed to this, I repeated to myself. *I will see it through.*

Still, as I watched Sean with Ava, a fine sweat broke out on my brow and my hands grew damp. I shut my eyes and took several deep breaths in an attempt to calm myself. When I reopened my eyes, though, I had to stifle a gasp. Sean was holding Ava in his strong, well-muscled arms. He was fondling her bare breasts while he gently took her nipple into his mouth.

I sat stock-still, unable to take my eyes off the scene playing out before me, and when I felt Christian's hand on my shoulder, I nearly jumped out of my skin. "Oh, you startled me!" I gasped.

"Sorry. I didn't mean to," he answered softly. "How about if you and I sit over there?" he suggested, nodding toward the other California-king-sized bed.

I felt myself turn hot all over as I swallowed nervously. "I guess the board game is over, then?"

Christian smiled indulgently. "It's really only intended to break the ice."

"And I guess the ice is broken, huh?" I looked pointedly at my husband and Ava.

"I'd say so. Come on," he said, gently taking my hand. "How about you and I sit over there together?" He nodded again toward the unoccupied bed.

I took another look at Sean and Ava and shrugged. "Sure. Why not? After all, those two certainly seem to be enjoying themselves; we might as well, too."

"That's the spirit, sweetheart," he said, grinning as he led me over to the other bed.

The sheets felt cool against my hot flesh and if I closed my eyes I could almost pretend that I was at home, in my own bed with Sean. But that night I was living out a fantasy for the first real time in my life, and I finally decided to let myself enjoy it.

I relaxed as Christian slid my chemise from my shoulders. I sighed when he caressed my breasts and I ran my hands though his thick, black hair when he kissed my lips, but for me, the most erotic moment came when I stole a glance across the room at Sean making love to Ava on the other bed. Seeing my husband with another woman made me jealous, but it also aroused me to a fever pitch.

Ava caught me watching and grinned at me from the other bed. Then she shot her husband a naughty smile. "So, you guys want to see a little girl-on-girl action?" she asked.

Sean's eyes widened. He did not expect this, but I'm sure he was pleased. Both men settled onto the sofa and waited. Christian poured himself another glass of champagne from the bottle of Cristal chilling on ice in the silver bucket.

"Are you okay with this?" Ava asked me in a whisper as she somewhat tentatively approached me.

While the idea of being with a woman doesn't turn me on, it doesn't totally repulse me, either. And I figured that even if I didn't enjoy it, I could always pretend and fake it for Sean's sake.

"Sure. Why not?" I said, smiling at Ava.

"Then lie back, girlfriend," she whispered to me. "Don't be nervous; we won't do anything that you're not completely comfortable with."

As I reclined on the huge bed, part of me wanted to flee—or, at the very least, protest. But I have to be totally honest with you and admit that my curiosity was overwhelming, and as I parted my legs for Ava, I caught Sean's eye, and the intense arousal I saw there urged me on. What began with me planning to feign sexual pleasure from a woman quickly escalated into pure ecstasy as I focused my senses on the woman between my parted thighs and the man who held my gaze. I rested my head back on the pillows, grasped the bed sheets in my fists, and let the warm, exquisite sensations ooze through me like hot lava. Before I realized what was happening I felt Christian's mouth close over mine, his hands running through my hair, and I wrapped my arms around his neck as white-hot pleasure racked my body.

Rain splashing on the windowpanes woke me in the early morning. The candles had burned down hours before, the stereo was quiet, empty wineglasses littered the tables, and the suite was lit by only the cool, gray cast of a dreary day.

I raised my head from my pillow and shimmied out from beneath Christian's arm, which he'd carelessly slung over my back during the night. Sean and Ava were lying sound asleep in the next bed, snuggled in each other's arms, her head on his chest and his arm around her shoulders.

They look good together. In fact, they seem to belong together, I thought, feeling my gut twist with powerful jealousy, far different from the wine-soaked, erotic feelings of the night before. I watched them for a moment, and then quietly rose from the bed and made my way silently to the bathroom.

I flipped on the light, stared at my sallow, mascara-streaked face in the mirror . . . and realized I'd made a huge mistake.

I've opened Pandora's box and my marriage might never be the same again, I thought with dawning fear.

"Babe, you in there?" Sean called softly as he knocked on the door.

"I'm here," I answered softly, quickly drying my tears on a washcloth.

He opened the door and let himself in, gently closing it behind him so as not to wake Christian and Ava. "What's wrong, Julia? Have you been crying?"

"No," I lied. Then I sighed and decided to tell the truth. "Yes. I hate this, Sean. We made a mistake."

He looked at my reflection in the mirror; our eyes met there. "Don't worry, honey; it didn't mean a thing."

"But I saw you! You held her all night! If it didn't mean anything, then why did you have her cuddled in your arms?" Against all my forced resilience, I started to cry. Sean came to me and immediately took me in his arms, kissing me gently and rubbing my shoulders for comfort.

"I didn't even realize, Julia. We honestly just fell asleep like that, and . . . I don't know, babe, but I didn't hold her in my arms on purpose."

I pushed him away and crossed my arms over my chest. "So you say. Why should I believe you?"

Sean's eyes opened wide as he looked at me with disbelief. "What? You don't trust me now?"

"How can I? You slept with another woman!"

"And you made out with another guy—and fooled around with a woman!"

"But I'm not a lesbian—I slept with her to please *you*! My gosh, Sean—I don't even know now if I can ever trust you again!"

"Don't even go there, Julia," he snarled, his blue eyes suddenly like cold, hard flint. "You enjoyed yourself—don't you lie to me!"

"And so did you! I stood there watching while you screwed another woman!" All of a sudden I reached for my makeup bag and threw it at him, hitting him squarely on the side of the head. Sean flinched as his face darkened with anger.

"Now you just hold on a minute here, Julia, damn it! Are you going to let jealousy over this ruin twenty good years of marriage?"

Tears streamed down my face. "Maybe—because I can't trust you anymore!" I sobbed. "Oh, God, Sean—this is the biggest mistake we've ever made!"

Tentatively he reached out and placed one hand on my arm.

"Honey, calm down for just a second, now. After all, we both agreed to this; in fact, you set the whole thing up, and—"

"And that was my first mistake!"

"What are you guys doing in there?" Ava called cheerfully from the other room. "I've ordered breakfast from room service."

"I want to go home, Sean," I told him in a hard, cold, steely voice. "*Now.*" I was no longer trying to keep our conversation private.

"Wait," he urged quietly, his voice barely above a whisper. "Just have breakfast and be polite. Then we'll leave. We can discuss all of this when we get home this evening."

"But we booked the room for the weekend!" I hissed.

"So what? That doesn't mean we have to stay. We'll just tell them we need to get home."

I went over and weakly, dismally rested my head on Sean's chest and finally nodded. "Okay. But let's get out of here quickly."

Ava and Christian both turned to look at us as we exited the bathroom. "Everything all right, folks?" Christian asked, smiling pleasantly.

I gave a weak smile and held on tightly to Sean's hand, waiting for him to extricate us from this excruciatingly uncomfortable situation.

"This is insane," Sean finally said quietly.

"Maybe," Ava allowed easily enough, "but it's harmless. We're all adults here, Sean. Don't worry about it. We'll have a nice breakfast, go out on the town, have dinner, and get 'reacquainted' with each other this evening."

"I'm not worried, Ava, I. . . .," he hesitated. "I guess I'm crazy, but I've realized I don't want my wife screwing another man . . . or woman, and I'm not comfortable being unfaithful, either. It's not that I don't find you attractive, Ava, because I certainly do, and I feel I have to be honest about that. It's just that I love my wife very, very much, and if we do this again, I'm afraid I'll ruin a damn good thing."

Christian smiled and shook his head. "It's okay, man. I know where you're coming from."

I reached for my clothes and slid my sundress over my head, and then slipped into my sandals. "You okay, babe?" Sean asked me, smiling tenderly.

I managed a smile for him. "I've never been better. But I'd really like to go home now."

You might find this hard to believe, but as we drove home we held hands like teenagers. "I only want you, Julia; I don't want anyone but you. What we did was a huge mistake," Sean surmised as he drove.

I leaned over and laid my head on his shoulder.

"I'm so glad you spoke up because, honestly, I felt the same way. Sleeping with Ava really freaked me out. I don't think our marriage could withstand that sort of thing again. It's just blatant adultery." He slid his right arm around my shoulders. "I guess we're just meant to be mated for life, babe."

"But what about . . . what Ava did to me?"

"What about it?" he asked as he slowed the car to turn into our tree-lined driveway.

"Did it bother you? Do you think our marriage will suffer because of it?"

"Well, do you want to leave me and be with Ava? Did you like it?"

"Honestly, it felt good, but it's not something I want to do again. It's just not me, Sean."

He leaned over and kissed my lips tenderly. "Good, because I don't like sharing my wife with anyone—not even Ava. But I'll tell you something."

"Oh? What?"

"Seeing you with her was really exciting."

"You wanted her?"

"Hell, no. I wanted you and only you. Watching her with you made me jealous and aroused. It made me remember why I fell in love with you in the first place all those years ago."

"Why?" I asked him softly.

"Because you're the most sensual, loving, desirable woman I've ever had the pleasure of laying eyes on and from now on, it's just going to be you and me, babe. No more 'experiments,' no more messing around. What we have together is rare and precious and we cannot ever risk it again. Nothing's worth the risk."

We'd been together for twenty years at that point and in that moment, I knew in my heart that even though we had our share of troubles, Sean and I would be together for life.

My husband and I decided to take a road seldom traveled by married couples. We put our love and trust in each other on the line to explore a controversial, seductive, dangerous avenue where anything—including the destruction of our marriage—could have occurred.

There are so many things that happen in a marriage. Sometimes it's hard to tell if you're coming or going but one thing I *can* tell you is that trust and true friendship are the only keys to marital bliss. If you don't have those two things firmly established between you, you might as well throw in the towel and walk away.

I should know. Because two years ago my marriage was put to the ultimate test and the only thing that saved it was knowing that my husband will always be my best and most loyal friend. Even when we played that sexy—and risky—game, I realize now that deep down in my heart, I always knew that we could never be parted. THE END

DELECTABLE DELIGHT
My Lunchtime Rendezvous

"It's already ten minutes before noon?" I asked, looking at my watch. "I've got to get home for lunch. Now!"

I pushed away from my desk and Alexis grabbed my arm. "Dara, you've gone home for lunch every day this week. What's going on?" She narrowed one eye at me.

I could feel the smile unfurl on my face. "Bring your lunch and find out."

She snatched her purse and lunch. "I'm always up for an adventure."

"Trust me, you won't be disappointed," I told her, as we walked out of the office.

She begged for more information the entire ten-minute ride to my house, but I wouldn't tell her a thing.

When we got there I grabbed two sodas from the fridge, and led her out to the back deck. We settled in a pair of lawn chairs with our lunches.

Alexis looked around. "So, what's the big deal?"

I threw up my arms. "What? The scenery and this beautiful, sunny day isn't enough for you?" I teased. "Then look up, girlfriend, into the beautiful blue sky next door where you will see the hottest guy in the world working on Mrs. O'Malley's roof." I pointed across the yard.

Alexis shielded her eyes with one hand and gasped. "I can't believe you've been keeping this a secret. What a hunk!" She turned to me. "But wait—I thought you were through with guys as of last week and that horrible blind date. Remember? You complained about it for days."

I rolled my eyes, trying to forget the guy my Aunt Tilda set me up with. He insisted we split everything on our date: the dinner bill, the movie tickets, even our popcorn. "I said I was done looking for a boyfriend. It is not in the cards for me." I shrugged, convincing myself this was the right decision.

Boyfriends had brought me nothing but heartache. Any time I fell for a guy, I ended up falling hard, and getting hurt. Hookups would be nothing but fun. I was fast approaching thirty and determined not to fall victim to the ticking clock reminding me I should be married with kids. No, I had a new motto to live by: too many guys, too little time. That was a totally different clock to live by.

"No, really, Alexis. I'm glad I can finally accept the fact that I am not meant to be in a relationship and start having some fun instead. How can I resist a hot guy right next door? It's perfect timing, like it was meant to be. He'd make the perfect summer fling." I looked up at him and his taut muscles pulling against his tanned skin as he worked.

Alexis looked over at him and shook her head. "I don't know. He looks like a keeper to me. And I don't believe you for one minute. You aren't the type of girl who just hooks up. You want to settle down. Admit it."

I shook my head. "Nope. And I'm going to prove it with him. He's the first guy on my Project Hook Up list."

"Dara Miller, always the marketing whiz. I can't believe you've even got a campaign name. But trust me, you don't know your own brand. You're a romantic, not a bed hopper." She crossed her arms and looked very satisfied with herself.

I pointed up at the guy. "I'll let you know in a few days."

The guy looked down at us and waved.

Alexis snapped her head away from him and scrunched down in her seat. "He saw us," she whispered.

"Yeah, we're not exactly being subtle. I figure he's only going to be here two or three more days. The time for being subtle is over," I said quietly. I stood up and took off my blazer, and hung it off the back of my chair. I held my hair off my shoulders and pressed the can of coke against the back of my neck.

"You are a piece of work," Alexis said, laughing. "I guess I've forgotten how to flirt after four years of marriage."

"It's easy when you don't care about the end result." I looked up and the guy had stopped working, and was watching us. I held up the can of Coke. "Want one? It's really hot out today."

"Sure," he called down. "It's just about time for lunch, anyway."

He set down his tools and climbed down the ladder. Unfortunately, he put his shirt on before he walked over.

"Act very married," I told Alexis. "He's mine."

She rolled her eyes and set her left hand on top of her knee. "How's that?"

"Perfect."

The guy walked up on the deck and my stomach flipped. He was even more gorgeous up close, with pale blue eyes, and dirty blonde hair. He was at least six-foot-three. "So you're the woman distracting me for an hour each day. And today you've brought a friend," he said.

I held out my hand. "I'm Dara Miller. I like to come home for lunch, you know, to get out of the office. My friend Alexis came with me today."

"I'm Mike Madison," he said. He had a strong handshake.

I wondered what those hands would feel like wrapped around my waist.

Alexis popped up and shook his hand, too. "Alexis Pietraz. I wish my husband were handy. I doubt he could even make it up a ladder," she said.

I looked back at her. "Subtle," I mouthed.

"Aww, cut him some slack. Maybe he just doesn't have the right tools," Mike said with a laugh.

"You look like you've got the right tools," I said.

He stared at me and raised an eyebrow. "Absolutely."

I heard Alexis choke on her drink.

I leaned against the deck railing. "Well, you'd never get me up there, I'm afraid of heights."

He folded his arms. "Then I guess you aren't interested in the roofing position I've got open."

"Oh, is it your company?" I asked.

"Yep. It's our family company. My brother is out here with me. But I'm looking to spend more time on the sales end of the business."

"So you won't be up on the roof anymore?" I asked.

"I'll be finishing this one up. If I can hire someone, it'll be my last one." He popped open his soda, and drained it in one gulp. "Well, unfortunately, I've got to get back up there. Gotta work while the sun's shining, you know? Thanks for the drink."

I raised my can of soda. "No problem. We'll see you tomorrow!"

We watched him walk back and take his shirt off again before he climbed back up the ladder.

Alexis sighed. "I wonder if we need a new roof. I'm going to ask Bill tonight."

I whacked her arm. "You just built your house last year. You don't need a new roof."

She gazed over at my neighbor's house. "You're right. I just need a dreamy home improvement guy . . . with the right tools."

We fell into each other laughing like we were sixth graders spying on the football team in the locker room.

I wiped the tears from my eyes and sighed. "Well, I suppose we should head back to work. If I time it right, I might be able to get home before he's done."

The day flew by and I touched up my hair and makeup before I returned home.

"Want some company for dinner?" Alexis asked, as we walked out together.

"Yes, but not with you," I said, winking at her.

"Who are you kidding? You're not looking for dinner—you're just after dessert."

I crossed my fingers. "Here's hoping!"

I slipped into a casual sundress and took a bottle of wine and two glasses out on my deck. Mike and his crew were still on the roof and probably would be for a while; the sun wouldn't be setting for another few hours. Hopefully Mike was thirsty—and interested.

He looked over and waved. I held up the bottle of wine and he held up his hammer. "I'll be finished up soon," he said.

"I'll save some for you," I shouted up to him.

He gave me a thumbs-up sign.

I closed my eyes and leaned back in my chaise lounge. I must have fallen asleep, because I woke with a start when I heard a chair being dragged across the deck.

"I'm the one who should be conked out." Mike sat in the chair next to me and slumped back.

"Hey, I was working today, too. Marketing can really tire a girl out. Would you like some wine?"

"Absolutely," Mike said. "Although, I wish I could change. I'm hot, sweaty, and dirty."

I tilted my head and smiled. "I know. I like it."

He laughed, and took the wine from me. "Mrs. O'Malley did say we could use her pool while she was away."

"Oh, that's right. She told me that, too. She's on vacation." I pictured the new bikini I had upstairs. "Do you want to take a dip? I'm sure she'd want her hired help to be comfortable and cooled off."

"You know her better than me. But I'll be swimming in my boxers," he said, gesturing to his dirty jeans.

I smirked. "To start with." I couldn't believe the flirty comments just falling from my mouth. Maybe my inhibitions were down because I had already decided Mike would be nothing but a fling. I wanted to hook up and nothing more. The whole thing felt very freeing, actually.

"And what will you be wearing?" Mike asked, sipping his wine.

"Let me go change and I'll show you." I went upstairs and changed into my tiny bikini, and grabbed two towels. *I'm really going through with this, aren't I?* I looked at myself in the mirror and shrugged.

Mike whistled when I stepped out on the deck. "Good thing you weren't wearing that when I was up on the roof. I might have fallen off."

We walked over to the pool and Mike pulled off his T-shirt and dropped his pants. His thick thighs were white compared to the rest of his darkly tanned body. He looked down and laughed. "Kind of like a farmer's tan in reverse."

"It's cute," I said.

He took a running start and did a cannonball dive into the pool. I shrieked as the water splashed me.

"Bet you can't beat that," he said.

"Give me a chance." Grateful that I had taken six years of gymnastics when I was a teenager, I walked toward the edge of the pool, and slowly turned over into a handstand. I pushed off into the water and swam up next to him.

His golden skin sparkled with drops of water in the setting sun. "Okay. You win," he said.

"What do I win?" I stepped closer to him.

His gaze swept over me. "Whatever you want."

I pressed my body against his and our lips met. He grabbed my shoulders with those strong hands and kissed me hard. My head spun; I couldn't believe I was doing this. I barely knew this guy and we were making out, half-naked in my elderly neighbor's pool.

But that didn't stop things from progressing. He found the hook to my bikini top and quickly took it off. He took my breasts in his hands. "Mmm. You are so hot," he breathed into my ear.

"So are you. I've wanted to do this since I first saw you. Luckily, I had to come home during lunch that first day."

"I thought you came home every day?" he asked.

I shook my head. "Only on days when gorgeous men are walking overhead."

He laughed and picked me up in his arms. "Now that we're cooled off, wanna move things inside?"

I caught my breath; *am I ready to do this? This is what I wanted: A hot summer fling, free of any commitments or expectations.* "Yes, let's go back to my house."

We climbed out of the pool and wrapped ourselves in towels. He took my hand and we ran across the grass to my deck. I opened the sliding door to my family room. We stepped inside and immediately fell onto each other on the couch, kissing and groping. I couldn't stop myself if I wanted to.

He stripped off his boxers, and worked his hands under my bikini bottom. He slid it off of me, and we found each other, clinging to one another as we kissed and moaned and finally collapsed in ecstasy.

"You're just as hot and sweaty as when you first came over," I said, panting.

He laughed. "We might have to take another dip in Mrs. O'Malley's pool." He took me in his arms and spooned behind me, resting his head on my shoulder. I could feel his heart beating against my skin. We fell asleep in each other's arms.

I woke at seven in the morning, surprised to find us still on the couch.

"Mike," I whispered in his ear, "do you want to come up to bed?"

He sat up, and looked at the green numbers of the clock glowing on the cable box. "The guys are going to be here in about an hour." He rubbed his face with his hands. "I've got an extra set of clothes in my truck. Mind if I shower here?"

I leaned over to kiss him. "Only if I can join you."

He laughed. "Even after last night? You are too much."

I took him by the hand and led him to the shower. We kissed under the warm spray and lathered each other up. *This fling thing is pretty nice,* I thought. *Maybe I can turn it into a two-day fling.*

Mike kissed me good-bye, and we headed out the door for work. But we stopped in our tracks when his crew pulled up, ready to unload the supplies and tools to finish their roof job.

The blood drained from Mike's face. "I am going to be hearing about this all day."

"Don't worry," I whispered. I held out my hand for him to shake. "Thanks for meeting me so early, Mike. I'll let you know if I'm going to go ahead with the renovations or not." I had inherited the house from my grandmother and it could stand to undergo a few updates. So, it wasn't out of the question he might be here giving an estimate. Still, I had to bite my lip so I wouldn't collapse into a fit of laughter.

"You're very welcome. I can stop by during your lunch break if you have any more questions." He winked, before he turned to leave.

Alexis popped up from her desk when I came in. "Well?" she asked. "How was your night?"

The look on my face must have been enough to answer her question.

"Shut up! You did not."

I knew I was blushing. "I did. And it was just as perfect as I imagined a fling would be."

"Are you going home for lunch today?" she asked with a sly smile.

I looked at my watch. "I'll be walking out the door in three hours and fifty-eight minutes."

I rushed home for lunch, but this time, Mike rang the doorbell out front when he came over. "I'm just trying to make this look like an official visit," he said.

"Certainly, come right in." I closed the door behind him, and we started kissing right in the living room. We didn't get much farther into the house than that.

I sighed, as I lay on top of him on the couch. "Take your time finishing Mrs. O'Malley's roof. I'll miss you around here."

"We've only got another day, I think. You're lucky. It was a long job. A total strip down, right to the rafters."

I laughed. "Sounds like what we just did."

He kissed my nose. "You are like, the perfect woman: successful, hot, funny and sexy. You're not inhibited at all. I love that. Can I take you out to dinner tonight?"

I traced my finger along his cheekbone. "Will your boss let you leave the jobsite early?"

"Let me ask him. Okay, the answer's yes. I want to go home and change. Can I pick you up at seven?"

"Sure. And now, we better get back to work."

He reached for my hand and kissed it. I ignored the goose bumps brought on by his sweet gesture. My fling didn't need to be kind and romantic, just hot and available. That's all I wanted.

We dressed and I showed him to the door. "Thanks for the estimate!" I called after him.

He looked at me and shook his head, laughing.

We lingered over dinner and talked about everything: our favorite pets growing up, our worst teachers, and our failed relationships.

The waitress stopped at our table. "Can I get you dessert?"

I looked at Mike. "No, we're having dessert at home."

He bit his lip trying not to laugh.

It was amazing how easy it was to be sexy and fun, just like Mike had said I was. But when there were no expectations, there was no reason to be reserved. This fling thing really was a great plan.

We drove home, holding hands, and I lead him to my house.

"No, come here with me," he said.

I followed him to Mrs. O'Malley's house. "Another swim? This time it'll have to be skinny-dipping. I don't have my bathing suit on." I started sliding off the straps f my sundress.

"No. Follow me." He walked over to the ladder. "Come up with me."

I took a step back and shook my head. "I told you, I'm afraid of heights."

"Go up first. I'll be right behind you. I promise, you'll be fine." He put his hands on my shoulders. "I won't let you get hurt."

I snapped my gaze away from his wide, sincere eyes. I set my foot on the first rung of the ladder.

He set his hands on my hips. "You can do it," he whispered into my ear.

My heart was pounding as I climbed to the top and stepped onto the roof. I sat down and hugged my knees.

Mike hopped onto the roof and sat down next to me. He put his arm around me. "You did it! See? Isn't this great up here?"

I shook my head, no.

"Don't look down. Look up at the stars. We're right up here among the treetops. I actually love roofing. It gives me a different perspective on things being up here." He kissed my head, and I leaned against him.

We looked for constellations and watched fireflies dance in the fields beyond. We chatted, laughed, and kissed.

"Now, what about that skinny dip you were talking about?" he asked.

We climbed down, stripped off our clothes, and slipped into the pool. Mike held me against him, kissing me and running his hands over my skin. I felt like a naughty version of Cinderella, who knew she'd have to leave her prince soon enough. But that's what I wanted, right?

Mike stayed the night again, and when I woke the next morning in his arms, my heart tightened, realizing this fling was coming to an end.

I replayed the night for Alexis, who "oohed" and "ahhed" over all the romantic parts. "Tell him to give my husband some pointers," she said.

I dashed home for lunch, this time a few minutes early so I could make us both something to eat. As I pulled up to my house, I saw Mike in front of Mrs. O'Malley's front yard. I smiled and felt my heart flutter just thinking about being in his arms again.

But my smile died on my lips as I parked along the curb. Mike was leaning against a car in front of Mrs. O'Malley's house talking to a young woman—a very beautiful young woman, with long red hair, and even longer legs. She held out a lunch for him, and pressed her other hand against his chest.

That was all I needed to see. A fling is one thing, but to be with someone who was hooking up with several girls at once made me sick. I started my car back up and sped down the street. *Why do I feel so horrible? How did I get hurt by a fling? Wasn't that the point—that a fling didn't mean a thing? So why am I crying?* I was too upset to even stop anywhere for lunch, and I drove around town until my lunch break was over, wondering why I was crying if Mike really was just a one -night—okay, a two-or-three-night stand.

I was quiet when I got back to the office, and got right to work on my latest project.

"What's wrong?" Alexis asked.

I forced a smile and rubbed my temples. "I'm just tired. This fling business can wear a girl out. Luckily, he's done with the roof later today so I don't have to see him again."

She set her hand on my shoulder. "You know, just because you said you didn't want to get serious with anyone doesn't mean you can't. It sounds like you found a great guy."

I shook my head. "Nope. He served his purpose." But my heart felt hollow as I said those horrible words.

I went shopping at the mall after work so I wouldn't have to see him again. It was dark when I got home, and there was no sign of the roofing crew next door. But I found Mike's business card taped to my front door.

"Call when you need another estimate," it read.

I tossed it in the garbage and sunk into a hot bath. *It will be good to sleep alone tonight*, I told myself.

I slept in late the next day, later than I usually do on Saturday mornings. I woke to a knock at my door. I threw on a robe and went downstairs.

"Mrs. O'Malley, what are you doing here?"

She held up a tiny strip of material. "I'm guessing this is yours. I'm glad you used my pool, I'm just not sure how you could have forgotten this. I hope you weren't distracting the construction crew I had over here."

I shook my head. "No, ma'am. Although they were pretty cute."

"I've known the Madisons since they were little kids. It's great all of them took over their father's business."

"What do you mean, 'all of them?' I thought it was just the two sons."

She shook her head. "Oh, no. Their sister helps in the office. Pretty little thing, with long red hair."

I took the bikini top from her and tried to turn down my smile. "You don't know how much I appreciate this, Mrs. O'Malley."

I waited until after lunch to call Mike. "I need an estimate," I told him over the phone.

"I was hoping you'd call. I missed you last night. You busy tonight?

I could help you with a number of different home improvement projects," he said in a sexy voice.

"Just being here with me is the best way you could improve my home." THE END

LOVE ON THE MENU
Never Stop Feasting On Each Other With Absolute Relish

I strapped on the brand-new, black, four-inch-stiletto mules and wobbled like a klutz across the bedroom floor.

Well, this is going take some practice, I thought to myself. It'd been ages since I last wore high heels and it looked like I might break my neck before I mastered the skill again.

"Mommy, you have pretty shoes!" piped up Cara, my three-year-old. "Can I try them on?"

"Here you go, baby girl," I said, handing her an old pair of pumps.

"But, Mommy," she protested, "yours are prettier!"

I dug a little deeper in the closet and found a pair of old, silver slippers. "Look what I found!" I exclaimed. "They look like princess shoes!"

"Oh, Mommy, can I be a princess?" Cara clapped her hands with glee.

"You're *my* little princess," I told her, giving her a big hug and a kiss. "Try these on, too," I said, handing her some bright scarves and buying some time. Cara sat in front of the mirror, enthralled, wrapping one scarf around her neck, then dropping it to the floor to try another.

Picking up a tray, I went back to practicing walking in the mules. *I've never been a very good waitress,* I remembered, *but at least one good thing came from it. Were I at least a competent waitress, I never would've met Jason. . . .*

I smiled to myself, recalling that fateful night when Jason brought his girlfriend to the restaurant I was working at. It was my first week and I was still *very* nervous. . . .

Jason and his date, Morgan, were seated in my section. I took notice of how he pulled the chair out for her while she batted her long, thick eyelashes at him. Morgan was drop-dead gorgeous, decked out in a slinky, low-cut, red dress. He, too, was so handsome, though dressed more casually. They looked every inch the perfect couple.

My hands shook as I took their drink orders and told them the specials. They say when animals sense fear, they go straight for the kill. Well, that's basically what Morgan did to me. She zeroed right in on my panic.

"What soups do you have this evening?" she asked in a condescending tone.

"Broccoli cheddar and French onion."

"And what salad dressings?"

She was looking right at the list on the menu. *Is she testing me?* I wondered, but nevertheless I ran through the entire array of dressings that I had memorized.

"Poppy seed—do you have a poppy seed dressing?" She peered over the menu, glaring at me.

Of course. The only one I forgot. "Yes, we do have a poppy seed dressing, actually. Would you care to order now?"

"I haven't decided yet," she snapped.

"Take your time; I'll bring your drinks right out," I answered politely.

Jason just smiled sheepishly at me. *He's got his hands full with that one,* I thought. *She certainly looks high maintenance.*

I turned in their drink orders at the bar and went to my next table. I recognized the older couple seated there as regulars. They greeted me like an old friend.

"You took such good care of us last time, we asked for you again, Sienna," the gray-haired lady greeted me.

I smiled warmly. "It's always my pleasure to serve you."

I returned with drinks in hand. Morgan was cooing at Jason with her pouting, glossy lips, her acrylic fingernails running up and down his muscular bicep. I felt like I was intruding on a private moment.

"Have you decided, yet?" I asked timidly.

"Yes." Her tone quickly changed. "I'll have the New York strip steak—rare; a baked potato, sour cream on the side; a salad with the house dressing—on the side, no onions; and another gin and tonic," she rattled off faster than I could write. I only prayed that I would remember it all.

"And you, sir?" I turned my attention to Jason.

"Porterhouse, well done; a loaded baked potato; and the salad with blue cheese dressing. Another Heineken for me, also, please." He smiled as he handed me back their menus.

By this time the restaurant was starting to fill and I could tell it was going to be a busy Saturday night. As it was, I was hoping for good tips that weekend I already had almost enough extra saved for the deposit on an apartment. My best friend, Natalie, and I had found a small two-bedroom that we could easily afford and I could hardly wait to escape the constant battling at home between my mother and stepfather.

Was it no tomatoes? I vexed as I plucked the bright, red cherry tomatoes off Morgan's salad. I loaded a basket with fresh-from-the-oven rolls and headed back to their table, but as soon as I set the salads on the table, I could feel a chill in the air.

"No onions, I *specifically said, no onions,*" Morgan said tartly, clipping each word.

"I'm sorry," I apologized, quickly snatching up her salad. "I'll get you another one." I rushed back into the kitchen.

"Sienna, your order is up," the kitchen manager called out.

"Be right back," I answered, grabbing another salad and carefully removing all of the red onions from it.

"I'm so sorry," I told Morgan, practically begging forgiveness when I returned to their table with her corrected salad. I got a cold stare in return, so I hurried back to pick up my other orders.

By this time, I had more tables and I was rapidly losing track. *Did I drop off warm rolls at table six? Did table four get their dirty martinis?* Nevertheless, I just kept smiling working away, dropping off drinks and picking up empty dishes. Finally, I carried the tray to Jason's table and served them their dinners. "Is there anything else I can get you right now?" I asked graciously.

Jason looked lovingly across the table at Morgan. "Do you need anything, baby?" he asked her.

She was cutting into her steak and examining it with all the careful scrutiny of a county coroner investigating an unsolved murder. "This isn't *rare*," she announced, staring up at me in disgust. "I want another one."

Once again, I apologized. *Even though the steak is pink*, I thought, forcing a conciliatory smile, *the customer is always right*.

Back in the kitchen, though: "This steak is *rare!*" the chef barked at me. "What? Do they want the damn thing still bloody and mooing?"

My other orders were backing up as I dealt with this crisis. "I'm sorry, but the customer—she insisted on sending it back."

I grabbed another tray to deliver and rushed back out to the dining room. As I glanced over at Jason's table, I could see the mounting tension. Morgan's hands were waving and Jason was getting red in the face. I dashed back into the kitchen and mumbled a quick, anxious thank you to the chef.

"Here you go. Please accept our apologies," I told Morgan and Jason moments later, and then rushed off before she could find fault again.

I am such a coward, I thought miserably.

Finally, things started to settle down and I had time to stop by the table with my regulars, just to chat. "Are you folks celebrating anything special tonight?" I asked them. I'd noticed they were more dressed up than usual.

"Call me Edna, dear, and this is Bill," she said warmly. "Actually, I'm glad you noticed; this is one year free of cancer for me!" she told me proudly, positively beaming.

I fought back a tear. "Oh, I'm so happy for you, Edna! Congratulations! That is wonderful news, indeed!"

"And now, I would like to order a very special dessert for my lady," Bill said, reaching out across the table to take Edna's hand in his.

Back in the kitchen, I told the manager, "I want to pay for their desserts."

"You're too nice," he remarked. "You'll never make it in this business, doll."

A few minutes later I dropped off the bananas Foster and turned to check on Jason's table, asking them politely, "Can I get desserts for you two this evening?"

"I'll have another gin and tonic," Morgan snapped.

"The strawberry shortcake sounds good to me—and some coffee, too, please," Jason requested.

Back in the kitchen, I dressed Jason's dessert plate with extra whipped cream and fresh strawberry slices. *I'll make a tip from that table in spite of it all,* I vowed.

I went back down and set their drinks down carefully at their respective places, but Morgan was raising her glass just as I reached forward with the plate of strawberry shortcake. As luck would have it—I caught her elbow, causing her drink to spill down her front.

She leaped from her chair, her voice shrill and obnoxiously loud from too much drink. "How *dare* you?" she shrieked. "Jason—*do* something!" she sputtered in a viciously indignant rage.

He stood immediately, trying to wipe down the front of her dress with his white, linen napkin. "It was an accident, Morgan. Sit down," he told her calmly.

The manager, alerted by the screech, rushed to the table as I stood by helplessly. "Please forgive this service, folks. Your evening is on the house. I only hope you'll come back again soon so we can make this up to you," he implored, his face beet red.

"Accidents happen," Jason said graciously, nonetheless looking very embarrassed, indeed. I suppose because—

Morgan was *still* making a *huge* scene in front of the *entire* restaurant.

"Believe me, mister—we'll never set foot in this dump again! Come on, Jason!" she barked as she stormed out with all eyes on her.

Jason hesitated. "It was an *accident*, Morgan," he told her once again, this time with even more patience. "Let me pay the check, please; I insist," he told the manager.

"That's not at all necessary, sir," the manager reiterated. "It will come out of the waitress's pay. It's her mistake, after all. And if it should turn out that there's a cleaning bill for the dress, we'll gladly take care of that, too."

"I don't want anyone to get into trouble," Jason said, pointedly making eye contact with me as he dropped a wad of twenties on the table. "It wasn't her fault; it was a complete and total accident."

I retreated to the kitchen with the manager at my heels, practically foaming at the mouth. "We can't tolerate such ineptness here," he told me hotly. "I'm sorry, but you're just not working out. Jackie will finish your tables."

I just stood there, absolutely dumbfounded. "Am I—am I—*fired?*" I stammered, horrified.

The manager nodded firmly. "I'm afraid I have no other choice."

I will not cry, I swore to myself. *I absolutely will not cry.* But all at once I felt so low that I could've dangled my legs off a dime. *Another setback toward finally moving out and sharing an apartment with Natalie,* I realized miserably. In fact, she was picking me up that very night after my shift—in two short hours—and we planned to catch a late movie. Head hanging low, I trudged back to the break room and dialed her cell, only to get her voicemail.

"Sorry, Nat, but I have to cancel tonight," I said after the tone. *I'll just walk home,* I thought. *It'll give me time to think.*

I hung up my vest and splashed some cold water on my face. Too embarrassed to even say good-bye to the staff, I snuck out the back door. I was barely out the door, though, when Jackie caught up with me.

"Wait a minute, Sienna," she called. "Here's part of your tips." She shoved two twenties into my hand.

"Where did this come from?" I asked, surprised.

"That old couple saw the whole thing and they think you got a bum deal—which you totally did, by the way. Anyway, that guy left more than enough to cover his bill, so I guess the rest is yours. Hey—you should've *heard* the argument he and that bitch had in the parking lot! He sure told that bimbo a thing or two! Anyway, look, sweetie—I've got to get back in there, but I'll make sure you get the rest of your tips, okay? In the meantime, you take care."

It was late October and already there was more than a hint of winter in the air; needless to say, I was having second thoughts about walking home. Still, too proud to call for a ride, I pulled my jacket tightly around me and set off. We lived on a farm two miles outside of town, so I knew there was a long stretch ahead of me without streetlights, but I've never been afraid of the dark.

Of course, at that point, the dark was the least of my worries. I still had to get home in one piece and then—find another job.

With my frozen hands stuffed into my pockets, I kept up a brisk pace. I was just about to turn off the main highway and onto our dirt road when a car slowed as it passed me by. It made a U-turn and pulled up alongside of me. I was ready to bolt through the cornfields when I recognized the driver as the man from the restaurant: Jason. I have to admit—it'd be *very* hard to forget *his* handsome face!

"Can I give you a ride?" he asked. "It's really cold out."

"No, thanks. I'm almost home," I lied, quickening my pace.

He was out of the car then, running to catch up with me. "Please—at least let me apologize for tonight," he begged. "I'm really sorry you lost your job."

I stopped, let him catch up with me, and shrugged, my breath coming out in a puff of misty vapor. "Don't worry; I'm sure I'll find another job."

"Well, at least let me buy you a cup of coffee, then," he implored. "You look frozen."

I had to admit—a cup of coffee did sound pretty tempting. Plus, I really did *not* want to go home and face the music.

"Okay," I finally agreed.

He held the car door open for me as I climbed in. *None of my old boyfriends ever held a door open for me,* I thought, feeling kind of special all of a sudden. *Then again—maybe he's just taking pity on me.* Regardless, I was grateful when he turned the heater on high.

"My name is Jason," he said, and after our introductions, we made small talk as he drove.

He pulled into a twenty-four-hour diner on the interstate. The place was quiet, only a few truck drivers seated at the counter. The waitress handed us some menus as we settled into a cozy booth.

"Just coffee, please," I told her.

"Coffee for me, too," Jason said. "What kind of pie do you have?" We both ended up ordering slices of cherry pie.

"I never did get to finish my dessert," he stated matter-of-factly.

I lowered my eyes. "I'm sorry," I murmured, remembering all the trouble I caused him with his girlfriend. "Is she still mad?"

Jason broke out with a laugh. "After what I said to her, I should think so! I'm certainly not going to call her to find out." He winked at me. "My mother never liked her, anyway."

Changing the subject, Jason told me about his job working at a recreation center, his family, and his favorite sports teams. Jason's also a very good listener and I found myself sharing my plans for the future with him, apartment hunting with Natalie, and life on the farm. Before we knew it, we'd gone through several coffee refills each.

"It's getting late," I said finally. "I better be getting home."

He drove me there, pulled into our driveway, put the car in park, and reached for my hand. "I really enjoyed talking with you tonight," he started. "Would you consider a real date sometime soon?"

I smiled. "I'd like that." He handed me a pen and paper and I scribbled down my phone number. "Thanks for the coffee and the ride," I said, making a quick getaway.

I wonder if he really will call? I asked myself later as I lay awake.

He *did* call, two days later. "Hello, Sienna," he said. "How's your typing?"

"It's adequate," I answered. He gave me the address of an insurance company that was looking for help.

"Would you like to go out to dinner Friday?" he asked.

Ah, Cara, you are a princess, because your daddy has made me feel like a queen, I thought dreamily, watching her play dress-up.

Needless to say—I landed the job at the insurance agency—where I *still* work part-time. Natalie and I moved into that apartment right on schedule and although I really loved the independence of living on my own, when Jason asked me to marry him a year later, I didn't hesitate.

Since then, never for an instant has Jason compared me to Morgan—though it did take me a few dates to get past my self-consciousness. I just couldn't help but recall how beautiful she was and the fancy clothes she wore, but luckily—Jason only has eyes for me. Every day he makes me feel special; through him, I've learned to love, laugh, and not to take life too seriously.

"Sounds like Daddy's home," I announced, hearing Jason's car pulling into the driveway. I quickly tucked the spike heels back into their shoebox and set it on the top closet shelf. *More practice tomorrow,* I told myself.

I took hold of Cara's hand as she made her way gingerly in the oversized shoes. "Look at me, Daddy! I'm a princess!" she called out excitedly as her daddy walked in.

Jason picked her up and twirled her around in his strong arms and gave her a big kiss. "A princess? Since when did you turn into a princess?" he teased.

"Mommy says I'm a princess," she stated emphatically. "And Mommy has new shoes, too!"

Jason turned his head to give me a kiss. "You go shopping today?" he asked.

Out of the mouths of babes. Please don't spoil my surprise, I prayed. "There was a really good sale; I couldn't resist," I fibbed. I didn't have the nerve to tell him how much I *really* spent, but I had a feeling that it was going to be worth it. It was all part of a special dinner I had planned for Jason's thirtieth birthday celebration the following evening. With any luck, I fully intended to knock his socks off!

"You don't have any surprises planned for tomorrow, do you?" he asked warily, giving me a devilishly knowing grin.

"Maybe," I teased. "You'll just have to wait to find out!"

The next day, I shot an email to Jason at work: *Happy Birthday, sweetie! Come straight home after work. XXXOOOXXX!* This was his late night; he'd be home by seven-thirty and then the fun would begin.

I got off work at two that afternoon and made a mad dash for the supermarket, and then rushed to pick up Cara from the babysitter's. "You're going to spend the night at Nana's," I told her. "Nana has some new kittens." So far, Cara had only spent a few nights away from us, but she loved the farm and special times with Nana.

"Can I bring my bear with me?" Cara asked.

"Of course, honey. In fact, you can help me pack your overnight bag." I even tucked in extra toys to safeguard against a late-night call.

"Thanks again, Mom," I said half an hour later as I was dropping off Cara at the farm. "If you need to get a hold of me, just call my cell, okay?"

"No worries, sweetie. You kids just enjoy your night out. Tell Jason 'Happy Birthday' for us!" she said.

"I will—and *we* will!" I assured her playfully, keeping most of my plans secret. "Don't forget, now: cake and ice cream on Sunday for the family celebration," I reminded her.

After that I rushed straight home, pulled down all of the shades, and set up the CD player with a selection of soft, romantic CDs before jumping into the shower. Freshly shaven, lathered, and shampooed, I slipped into the alluring French maid's outfit I'd kept hidden for the past week. I pulled on the sheer, black, thigh-high stockings and slipped my feet into the ultra-sexy stilettos. I brushed out my glossy hair, letting it fall gently to my shoulders. Feeling quite naughty, indeed, I applied more mascara and ruby-red lipstick. Then I checked myself carefully in the mirror—adjusting, lifting, and tucking. I even made *myself* blush!

Oh, Jason, this is going to be a birthday you won't ever forget! I thought delightedly.

Steadying myself in the stilettos, I checked the time. With only minutes to spare, I went through the house, lighting candles in every room. As I heard Jason's car pull into the driveway, I hit the play button on the CD player. His eyes popped when he opened the door and saw my barely-there, risqué getup.

"Oops! Do I have the right house?" he asked, grinning.

"Oui, monsieur! Welcome to Chateau Sienna," I cooed in a French accent. "Tonight, your pleasure will be my pleasure."

"I can hardly wait," Jason said, already loosening his tie.

"First, you must be properly dressed. We have a very strict dress policy here, you know."

I took him by the hand and led him into our bedroom, where I'd laid out a new, crimson, silk robe for him, complete with matching boxers. I toyed with his chest hair as I unbuttoned his shirt, rubbing my hands seductively over his stubble as my fingers traveled up the length of his neck to graze his full lips.

"Your razor awaits," I said, turning for the kitchen. "Dinner will be served shortly. Don't be late."

While he was shaving and dressing/*un*dressing, I quickly put together a tray of cheese, smoked oysters, crackers, and frozen grapes. Jason met me in the living room, where I'd set up a small table complete with candles, red, red roses, and champagne.

"For your dining pleasure," I said, handing him the menu I wrote out with my calligraphy set on parchment. Our fingertips barely touched as I passed it to him, but the sensation was electrifying. "May I interest you in an appetizer?" I asked, pouring him a glass of Cristal.

"Maybe something small . . . something that won't spoil my *appetite*." He winked at me, grinning with devilish delight.

"Just a nibble," I teased, pulling my top down and revealing my bare breasts.

His tongue licked hungrily as I inhaled the intoxicating aroma of his cologne. Right then and there, I could've easily succumbed to his desires, but there was more loving on the menu, so I reluctantly pulled back, catching my breath.

"Here—try these," I invited, pushing the tray of hors d'oeuvre in front of him.

He laughed. "Do you really think I need oysters?"

I slowed the pace down a bit, allowing him to snack and sip champagne as I took off his robe and rubbed coconut-scented massage oil into his bared, muscular shoulders. "Are you ready to order your entrée?" I asked after a delicious while. "I have some sizzling-hot specials to offer. . . ."

"Oh, I'm ready," he groaned, reaching for me.

"First, could you unhook these for me, please?" I lifted one leg and delicately placed my foot on Jason's groin. He ran his hands down the length of my stocking, his fingers titillating me as I opened up for his touch. His finger slid into me as I moaned with pleasure.

"The shoes," I reminded him.

He slipped them off, tossed them aside, and then pulled me onto his lap. Wrapping my arms around his neck, I gave him a long, slow, open-mouth kiss as his hands pushed my top down again, baring my shoulders as he nuzzled my breasts. My legs spread apart, inviting him to explore as I stroked his manhood, hard and firm through the silkiness of his boxers.

"I'm ready for dessert," Jason groaned.

"Dessert will be served in the bedroom," I whispered into his ear while running my tongue around its rim. "I'll be right in to join you."

Jason was reclining against the pillows on our bed when I carried in the tray of strawberries and whipped cream. I set the tray on his nightstand and slowly removed what remained of my costume.

Straddling Jason, I dipped a berry into the cream and held it to his lips. With his eyes on me, his tongue licked the cream from the berry. I dipped a finger into the cream and let him lick it clean. Then I dipped into the cream again, this time dotting it on my bare nipples as he hungrily licked them clean. . . .

Hours later, holding each other tight in the flickering candlelight, I murmured, "Happy Birthday, baby." THE END

STORM WATCH

"Where are you, Allie?" My Aunt Rosie's voice sounded distant through the cell phone connection though she was only twenty miles away.

"I'm leaving right now. I—"

"You haven't left the island yet?"

"I'm starting the car now," I explained and turned the ignition key.

"Oh child, it's too late now. They've closed the bridge to the mainland. Why didn't you—"

My cell phone clicked off just as a huge bolt of lightning split the sky and thunder rolled down the beach like a rampaging monster.

I punched the re-dial button and got only a steady beep. *Uh-oh.* The lightning may have taken out the cell tower and severed my communication with the outside world.

I tuned in to the local radio station to see just how much trouble I was in.

"*—storm is producing winds of ninety-five to one hundred miles per hour.*"

I was in deep trouble. Daylight was fading Sunset Island sat in the path of a hurricane, and I was stuck.

I slapped my palm against the steering wheel. *Why hadn't I left when management had evacuated all the guests?* Of all days to become more conscientious about my job. I'd restocked my work supplies and caught up on two weeks of paperwork.

I worked at Costa del Mar Spa Resort as a massage therapist and assistant spa manager. It was my dream job. The flexible hours let me lounge on the beach and enjoy the island where I'd grown up. As a teenager, I couldn't wait to get away. The island wasn't a hot spot for the younger set—it catered to an older demographic—and I wanted to escape to the big city, especially after the business with Sam.

I'd majored in accounting. Companies could always use someone to keep track of their money, couldn't they? Then after three years at an accounting firm, which included three brutal tax seasons filled with fourteen-hour days, I knew I had to do something else or risk burning out before I was thirty.

I'd been having weekly sessions with a massage therapist and out of curiosity one day, I asked her about her job. By the end of my session, I'd found a new calling.

I cashed in my 401K, moved back to Sunset Island, lived with my Aunt Rosie to save on rent, and started my training at the local vocational college. By the time I finished school, the island's hotel changed hands and was turned into a spa resort—a spa resort needing licensed massage therapists.

Now I was happier than I'd ever been. My folks were retired and living in Arizona and Aunt Rosie had let me buy her older beachfront cottage for a song when she moved into assisted living on the mainland.

With any luck, I'd still have a house if the island took a direct hit. Sure, many of the old-timers rode out hurricanes with regularity. It was some sort of badge of honor for them. But I'd seen the havoc even a Category 1 could cause, and I wanted no part of it. This storm was a weak Cat 2, but it could change in a heartbeat.

I killed the engine and shouldered open the door. The wind and rain lashed at me as I pulled my laptop case from behind the driver's seat, and I still had to retrieve my suitcase from the other side.

An unfamiliar car pulled behind mine, and I wondered who on earth was as dumb as me and still here. I could see a man's shape through the tinted glass. A *lost tourist?* But why come to me?

I hurried toward my front door, unwilling to stand in the rain any longer than necessary, especially to wait for a stranger.

As I stood under the small overhang by the front door and fished in my pocket for my keys, I heard a car door slam and turned to look.

Sam Trent. The boy who'd once been a part of my wildest dreams and who'd only recently disappeared from my nightmares. The boy I'd spent graduation night making love with, first in the backseat of the car I'd just exited and later under the stars on the beach. The boy who had been my friend for as long as I could remember and who disappeared the day after graduation and never called again.

Only he wasn't a boy anymore. This was the grown-up version, and my traitorous pulse fluttered at the sight of the only man I'd ever loved.

Whoa! Don't go there.

He had a duffel slung over his shoulder as he rushed up the walk and crowded next to me under the awning.

"Why didn't you leave your key out when you got out of the car?"

I gave him a surly look. "Hold your horses. It's here." Triumphantly, I produced the key and shoved it in the lock. Sam followed me inside and bumped the door closed with his hip. I flipped the wall switch and nothing happened.

As he dropped the duffel on the tile floor, his gaze swept the room. "Nice," he said as he took in the cozy bungalow. He'd visited when my aunt owned it, but I'd completely redecorated. Instead of floral print wallpaper and uncomfortable antique furniture, the walls were pastel and overstuffed furniture invited guests to linger. Bright artwork decorated the walls, and seashells and beach glass dotted the tabletops and shelves.

But the focal point of the room was a picture window, which afforded a spectacular view when the sun dropped into the Gulf of Mexico and bid each day a fiery farewell.

"Why didn't you board up this window?"

"I'd planned to, but I was busy at work and lost track of time." I placed my purse and laptop on the coffee table.

"You always were the responsible one."

And Sam would have been, too, except for his horrid home life. How many times had the motherless boy come running to our house after one of his father's drunken rages? Only he'd never shared the whole story. He'd told me once that he often wondered if beatings wouldn't have been better than his father's insults. Bruises would fade, but John Trent's heartless words had irreparably gouged his soul.

"Too late now. Where's an inside room? We need to get away from this glass."

I planted my hands on my hips. "Still bossy as ever, I see."

"Only when my life is on the line, babe. You, uh, better get out of those wet clothes." I followed his gaze and it lead straight to my chest, where my puckered nipples strained against wet fabric and made me look like a contestant in a wet T-shirt contest.

"My suitcase! It's in the backseat. . ." My voice cracked as I blushed. Sam cleared his throat nervously and looked everywhere but at me, apparently remembering sex venue number one of graduation night.

"Unless you packed everything you own, I'm not going back outside."

When I moved toward the door, he grabbed my wrist. "And neither are you."

A tingle traveled up my spine as he touched me, and I gasped softly.

"Where can I change?" he asked, picking up the duffel.

I pointed to the rear of the house. "The guest bathroom."

As I stood in my bedroom and stripped off my drenched clothing, I imagined Sam doing the same. I pictured him as he'd looked that night—long and lean and oozing sexuality. We'd both been high on hormones and the excitement of graduation, and the only thing that had stopped us from having sex a third time was a torn condom. In his haste, Sam had put a finger through his last one, and a small island wasn't the best place to discreetly buy condoms after midnight.

The shrill wind yanked me from my thoughts. This was no time for daydreams. Mother Nature was raising a ruckus and all hell would soon break loose.

I found Sam in the bathroom wearing cut-off jeans and a Bahamas T-shirt. *Had he visited there? Alone, or with another woman?* I brought myself back to reality and watched him splash bleach in the tub.

"Do you do windows too? Because if you do—"

"Dammit, Allie. We'll need water after the storm is over."

I blinked but couldn't stop the tears. In two strides, Sam was beside me, pulling me into his arms.

"I'm sorry," he whispered, and I felt his heart pounding next to mine. For one crazy moment I wished he'd kiss me and add my bathroom to our lovemaking venues, but there wasn't time to re-live high school fantasies.

"Me too. The noise from the wind is driving me crazy."

I stepped back and wiped my eyes with the hem of my T-shirt. "I think my bedroom closet will be the safest place. It's a walk-in with no windows, and there'll be plenty of room."

Sam nodded. "I'll be there soon. Put my bag in there. It has a flashlight and radio."

Minutes later I helped him wedge a mattress against the door, and he settled his large frame into the closet, pulling his long legs out of the way to make room for me.

"If you don't mind the dark, I'd like to save the flashlight for later," he said, setting it and the radio on a plastic bin.

Actually I wouldn't mind at all. Then I wouldn't have to look into his eyes.

"This is it, huh?" I watched shadows dance across his face as I burned nervous energy by rearranging pairs of flip-flops.

Sam took my hands in his larger ones, and I shivered.

"Come here." He tucked my body next to his and with a flick of his thumb, he killed the beam of light.

Outside, the storm intensified. Rain hammered the windows, and branches scraped the roof as the wind howled relentlessly. Leaning against Sam, I was aware of every breath and felt his body warmth seep into me, just like ten years ago.

"Why did you leave?" My voice was little more than a whisper.

"I knew you'd ask sooner or later. I'd just hoped it would be later. Much later." He released a long breath. "I left because of my father. When I got home that night, he was waiting for me, drunk. He did most of the talking and told me I'd never amount to anything."

"Why'd you come back?"

His laugh had a hard edge to it. "I thought the next question would be 'Why didn't you call me?'"

"I'm getting to that." My tone was clipped. "Why did you come back?"

"He called me. He said he's changed and wants another chance." He shifted against me and I could feel his muscles flex. "I want a chance, too. To show him he was wrong."

"Sam. . ." My voice was barely audible.

"I've wanted to do this since I saw you standing in the rain," he said. "We'll have plenty of time to talk later." He pressed his lips to mine, nibbled gently, and I surrendered to ten years of memories.

Sam nuzzled my neck and a tremble quaked through him. A fine sheen of perspiration covered his skin. Hurricane Betty created an inferno outdoors, the heat rose in my closet, and I feared the damage not only to my island home, but to my psyche as well.

Seeing Sam again, drenched from the rain and standing in my living room, had left me scrambling to gather my composure. Lying in his arms in the dark with his hard body pressed to mine had shattered what little composure I had.

As suddenly as he'd kissed me, he stopped and put space between us.

"I didn't mean for our first meeting in ten years to be like this—me all over you like a randy bull. I'd planned to call you and invite you to dinner, and I'd prayed you wouldn't tell me to do unpleasant things to myself."

I choked back a giggle. Had we met again under different circumstances, would I have told him off?

"Then this storm developed and threw a hitch into my plans. Seeing you again—standing on your porch looking like a drowned kitten in beachwear—did me in."

He nibbled my earlobe and my lungs filled with the scent of him. All sexual. All sensual. All Sam. I had an explanation about why he'd left so suddenly, basic as it was, but right now all I wanted was to get reacquainted with Sam's body.

Heat pooled between my thighs. *Venue number three, coming right up.*

"You okay?" he asked. A hint of desperation tinged his voice as if he needed to be sure I was at ease.

"Yeah."

"Good," he replied. "We're going to be okay."

Ten years away from him had done absolutely nothing to dampen his appeal, but I had to wonder if he felt the same. *Should I just come right out and ask?* After all, once the storm was over and he left, I might not have another chance.

Sam made the decision for me, only I didn't have to ask.

His whisper broke the silence. "I've suffered through a decade of wondering about you. Ten years of regret and long nights filled with dreams about us and that night."

So I wasn't the only one who dreamed. Maybe there was hope after all. I'd dated since Sam, but he was the benchmark against which I measured all men, and none had come close.

"I've done pretty well with my life. I've proved my father wrong and achieved things beyond my wildest dreams. But I've been thinking a lot and came back to Sunset to re-think and re-group. I helped my dad batten down the hatches, but I knew you hadn't left yet."

"Spying on me?"

"No," he answered, perhaps a little too quickly. "Well, not exactly spying. Right place at the right time."

I couldn't control my laughter. "It's okay. I think it's kinda sweet you'd care after all these years."

"Well, yeah."

Sam might be tough on the outside, but inside there was still a very vulnerable soul.

"We should turn on the radio and check the storm." I figured a diversion was called for. I groped for the radio. Instead, I groped Sam.

I heard him groan.

"I'll do it," he said and brought the radio to life.

"*—leave low-lying areas. Seek shelter immediately in an interior room with no windows. The eye is located—*"

Over the crackle of static and the howling wind, we heard a sharp cracking noise, then the sickening crunch of metal and the sound of shattering glass.

"My car." The words were a choked whisper from the lips he'd kissed just moments ago and were quickly followed by a sob.

"Don't cry, honey. My rental was parked right behind yours. It could have been that. And it's just a car. You can get a new one."

But it wasn't *just* a car. It was the car where I'd given him my virginity. The car where I'd fallen head over heels in love with him even though we were supposed to be just good friends. I tried not to cry, but a sob broke through anyway. Sam flicked on the flashlight and illuminated my face.

"It'll be okay." He swept his thumb across each cheek, gently wiping away my tears. Then he pulled me close again. Despite the oppressive heat I shivered, just like I'd done the night he'd made love to me and left me gasping in the wake.

"What happened to Juan?" Sam asked, changing the subject, apparently in an effort to take my mind off the storm. Juan was the tiny Chihuahua I'd owned as a teenager.

"He's in doggie heaven, proudly wearing that little sombrero you bought for him."

"He was a character, wasn't he?" Sam clicked off the flashlight, satisfied he'd stopped my tears.

"Yeah," I answered, raising my voice over the wind's increasing fury. "We had fun, didn't we? Growing up on this island?" I relaxed into his embrace.

Another roll of thunder vibrated the house as if some giant hand had grabbed it from above and shaken it. I sank even further into his arms as he dropped a kiss onto my hair.

"I couldn't imagine any place better," he whispered in my ear.

"Me either." *Any place was heaven as long as it was with you.*

"You have to believe me when I said it was hard to leave. That night rocked my world. I've never forgotten it. But I couldn't take the abuse anymore. I had to leave before he pulled me into hell along with him." He released a long, audible breath. "I didn't leave you in trouble, did I?"

"No. My parents were okay with me coming in after curfew since it was graduation."

"That's not what I meant. You didn't get pregnant, did you? I mean, I used a condom, but well, sometimes they don't work."

I could feel my mouth forming a perfect "O" as the realization hit. "Nope, no trouble on that front."

"Good," he said as he lowered me to the carpet. "I've felt like enough of an ass for the past ten years. If I'd left you pregnant. . ." His words trailed off, lost in the roar of the gale-force winds that battered our shelter.

Once again he pressed his lips to mine. I arched and pushed my body forward, eager to feel his muscular chest against me. And as he insinuated one knee between my thighs and settled between them, I realized the wind speed wasn't the only thing that was rising.

I ground my hips against his, oblivious to everything around us. Oblivious to the years between the last time we'd been together and the present. Unless his body was lying, he wanted me, and I damn sure wanted him. And it appeared nothing was going to stop us.

I arched upward again, dizzy in a haze of pleasure. Aching to have Sam inside me. Ready to pick up right where we'd left off that starry summer night.

Suddenly Sam spit out a curse word that perfectly described what I wanted him to do to me.

"It's okay. I'm on the pill. You don't have to worry—"

In one swift move, Sam stood up and pulled me with him. Within seconds I repeated the expletive as a stormy cocktail of salt water, sand, and seaweed flooded our safe haven and swirled around our feet. Only moments before I'd been ready to consummate the renewed attraction between us; now I was wrenched back to the reality of riding out the storm.

I grabbed the flashlight and radio while Sam shoved the wet mattress aside. He carefully opened the door and we prepared to face the wrath of Mother Nature. In the dim glow of the flashlight I gave him a questioning look.

"Bathroom!" he commanded and pulled me across the bedroom. He paused to gaze at the bed dominating the room. The frilly comforter and pillows were like an inviting oasis, and if it survived the storm, I had no doubt we'd comfort each other right in the middle of it.

"No, this way," I yelled above the roar. "My bathroom. You'll see."

"The supplies," I yelped, remembering the snacks in his duffel. I turned back toward the closet.

"They're ruined. Come on." He took another look at the bed and grabbed the comforter and blanket, quickly rolling them up and shoving them under his arm.

Hurrying along, I prayed that Plan B worked. He ushered me into the tile bathroom and shut the door behind us.

"I'm not too thrilled about that window," he grumbled. But then he noticed the décor, looked skyward, and mouthed a silent thank you.

"Put this in the bottom to cushion the tub," he commanded, shoving the wadded blanket toward me.

I shot a slanted look toward him, ready to comment again on his bossiness, but decided against it. Sam was only trying to save our necks, and I shouldn't complain, especially because I should have left the island, and he wouldn't be in this mess too had he not been worried about me.

He pulled a stack of towels from shelves lining one wall. "Catch," he said, tossing them to me. Then he helped me into the antique claw-foot bathtub. The deep porcelain fixture sat on a raised platform that just might keep us above the rising water.

Sam stepped in behind me and sat, stuffing a rolled-up towel behind him and spreading the thick comforter across us as he leaned against the end of the tub. I settled against him, facing away.

"Nice and cozy, huh?" he joked as he pulled me closer. A shiver zinged through me again, and I remembered the last time I trembled in his arms. But a hurricane was anything but nice or cozy.

The intimacy of our position in the tub was contrasted by the ferocity of the storm. And Betty wasn't the only storm. My emotions were in turmoil over Sam's return, and I wasn't quite sure whether to say anything.

Should I just enjoy a brief respite from my less-than-stellar social life and enjoy whatever Sam might have to offer in the way of a short fling? Or should I step up to the line and admit my feelings—that I'd been in lust with him when we were teenagers, that the lust had changed to love after we'd had sex, and that he'd shattered my heart when he left.

"I've never forgotten that night," he said.

I opened my mouth, but no sound emerged. I sat, stunned by his announcement, the small bathroom intermittently illuminated by streaks of lightning. *Had he read my mind?* But more importantly, did I want to bare my soul to the one man with the power to shred my heart?

I twisted in his arms, and in the dim light I pushed back his damp hair, then traced the strong line of his jaw. He trailed his fingers down my neck until they rested just above my breast. I knew he was waiting for a signal—some sign to continue.

"I waltzed out of your life ten years ago without looking back, but I've changed. I won't make another move unless you agree."

I placed my hand on his cheek and gave him a barely there kiss before sucking his lower lip seductively.

I'd given him the sign. If his body's reaction was any indication, need was slamming him with a force stronger than the hurricane. He nibbled back, gently at first, then hungrily like a man who'd been without nourishment for weeks.

To my disappointment, he turned me away from him again and pulled me back against his chest. He drew lazy circles on my arm with one hand while the other slipped under the waistband of my shorts.

My breath caught in my throat as he stroked his finger back and forth over the damp silk between my thighs. As the rising water eddied around the base of the tub, he took me higher and higher toward my release. He whispered to me and told me a combination of remembrances from the past and promises for the future. And when I shouted his name and trembled in his arms, my voice echoed in the silence of the tiled bathroom as the eye of the storm descended.

Sam gave me a few minutes to regain my equilibrium before throwing off the comforter and announcing we had to leave.

"I saw a concrete block building a few blocks inland. It's two-story and should withstand the wind better. We need to get there before the eye passes."

I knew the building. It housed a computer repair shop on the first floor, and the second floor was storage. Sam's rental car had survived with a few scratches, but as I'd feared, mine lay crushed under a fallen palm tree. Sam drove as fast as the wet streets would allow.

He used the flashlight to break a small pane of glass in the back door, reached in, and unlocked it. We'd ask forgiveness later. This was survival, and a bit of broken glass was negligible compared to human lives. We navigated our way upstairs, not sure how much time we had before the storm descended again.

The storage room was amazingly organized with boxes of parts stacked around the perimeter and a battered sofa in the middle. A large-screen television dominated one wall, and a state-of-the-art game system sat on a mini-fridge beside it.

"You need to get out of those wet clothes," Sam said matter-of-factly when I began to shiver.

"I'm o-k-k-kay," I replied, my chattering teeth indicating otherwise.

"Here," he said, pulling a blanket from the sofa. "Wrap up in this."

I can do this. I can do it. The mantra repeated in my brain as I stood behind the blanket Sam held in the air. The thought of us huddled naked under the thin coverlet sent a jolt of electricity through me. That alone should have warmed me up.

I stripped off my soaked T-shirt and shorts and let the soggy material fall to the floor. There was no way I was going to undress completely, so I left my bra and panties on. They would dry soon enough and provide me with at least a modicum of modesty, although heaven knew why I was concerned about modesty considering our past. He'd seen me naked and touched the most intimate parts of my body.

A hot blush crept up my neck as I remembered the pleasure Sam had given me in my bathtub. And just as swiftly I remembered the hurt that had consumed me when he left town. Hurt that had not completely subsided over the years.

"I should have beaten you with the flashlight while we were still in the closet," I mumbled, angry with myself for giving in to his charm and those soulful brown eyes that reminded me of a bottomless pool of rich, sweet choc—. *Stop it now.*

I should be furious rather than lusting after him. I should be incensed that he had left me alone after the single most wonderful night of my life, wondering what I'd done so wrong that he not only left but forgot how to use the telephone or email. He'd broken my heart, and if he thought he could just waltz back and pick up the pieces, he was mistaken.

"What was that, babe?" The wind had begun to pick back up and strong gusts whistled through the palms outside.

"Umm, I asked if you think we'll need the flashlight since we're not in the closet." I rationalized the lie. If he could abandon me, I could lie. "I'm done," I said, standing helplessly in the middle of the room. "Want me to hold the blanket for you?"

I grabbed the soft material and held it as high as I could, but I heard the rasp of his zipper and the splat as his shorts hit the floor.

Boxers or briefs? I wondered. *Or perhaps he was going commando tonight. . .*

"Now what?" I released an exasperated sigh. "We can't stand like this forever."

"Sure we can," Sam teased. "We'll take turns holding the blanket up until the storm is over." His laughter danced through the air.

I rolled my eyes and imagined a long night of playing "Swap the Blanket" and trying not to play peek-a-boo with Sam. But before my imagination could dream up any more games, Sam grabbed the blanket and draped it around me.

"You need it more than I do." His voice grew husky and reminded me of dark nights and smooth whiskey. I closed my eyes as I pulled the blanket around me, wrapping myself in its warmth. Warmth that felt almost as good as Sam's embrace.

"We should turn off the flashlight," he said. "And you can open your eyes, sweetheart. I'm decent."

"That all depends on your definition of decent."

"Dammit, woman. You are determined to drive me crazy, aren't you?"

I blinked, knowing that the answer was yes, but not willing to admit it. And his navy silk boxers were doing a pretty good job of driving me crazy, too.

"Don't think I don't remember that you wore black lingerie that night, too."

He'd peeked.

And I remembered enjoying every moment while he took it off and made love to me.

He spun me around and captured my lips in a fiery kiss. When I gasped, he took advantage. Our tongues met and he groaned as I threaded my hands into his hair and pulled him closer.

The damp boxers hanging low on his hips couldn't disguise his arousal. He slid his hands under the blanket and ran his fingers under the elastic band of my panties. At this point, permission was mine to give and pleasure was mine to receive—if I wanted to take that chance again.

I ended the kiss, flattened my palms against his chest, and pushed away. "No. I can't do this. I won't let myself fall for you again because I don't know if I can survive when you walk away and break my heart." I choked down a sob and blinked back the scalding tears that threatened to betray my vulnerability.

"Who says I'm going to break your heart?"

"It's inevitable, Sam." I pulled the blanket closer around me, cold in spite of the humidity and heat. "You'll go back to wherever you came from, back to your job and your life there, and I'll be left again with memories. Just like before."

Sam bracketed my face with his palms, tilted it upward, and looked squarely at me.

"Who says I'm leaving?"

"But your job—"

"I wasn't completely honest with you earlier, Allie."

Uh-oh. Here it came. The painful truth that probably included a wife and kidlets back home somewhere.

"Oh?" I said, willing my emotions to remain calm and not give away my disappointment.

"My job stinks, Allie. I'm burned out. When my father called last month and asked me for another chance, I realized it was the opportunity I'd been waiting for."

"Sam—"

"Let me finish. I told you I came back because my dad asked me to. But the truth of the matter is, I came back for you too. When I called my dad to arrange my visit, he mentioned you still lived on Sunset. I figured you'd settled down by now. I mean, what guy in his right mind wouldn't scoop you up in a minute? You're smart and fun and—"

"Did you really come back for me?" I sniffled as my heart pounded in my chest like the entire percussion section of an orchestra.

He whispered his one-word affirmative answer and added another word. "Beautiful," he said. "You always were the most beautiful girl on the island. Only now you're a beautiful woman." He nuzzled my neck. I wriggled against him, rubbing against his arousal and causing him to release a sound that was part groan and part growl.

"I'm ready to give my father another chance. Are you willing to give me another one, too?"

As Betty's fury swooped in again, we sat in our commandeered shelter, catching up on the years we'd been apart and consuming the owner's supply of sodas and cheese crackers. Sometime in the middle of the night, the winds calmed and we were left with only the sound of rain tapping steadily on the roof. Once the immediate danger was over, my body's adrenaline surge stopped and I fell asleep spooned against Sam's body, his breath warm and steady against the back of my neck.

I awoke shortly after dawn. Sunshine streaked in through the small windows. I turned my neck carefully, working out the kinks from sharing a too-narrow, too-lumpy sofa. A soft kiss on my shoulder let me know Sam had awakened too.

"I'm sorry," I said. "I didn't mean to disturb you. It's just that I'm stiff."

He rocked his hips against me and chuckled. "You're not the only one."

The tingling in my stomach wasn't hunger—at least not for food. I was hungry for Sam. I wanted him to devour me and feed the flame smoldering inside me.

"We could finish what we started in the closet," he murmured.

I responded with a loud yawn.

"Or not," he said, stretching and pulling away from me.

"Come back here, mister." He rolled onto his back, and I crawled on top of him, my breasts pressed against him, his arousal pulsing against my belly.

I wiggled and heard his breath hiss between his teeth. "Just in case you're wondering, this is my way of saying I'm willing to give you a second chance."

The beginning of a smile curved the corners of his mouth. He cupped my breasts in his large hands, expertly tending to my body, and my senses reeled.

"Please," I begged, one word communicating my desire. He understood completely. With one hand, he released the front clasp of my bra. I removed my panties, then his boxers, and at last we were flesh to flesh, woman against man.

He grasped my hips and I welcomed him into my body, then matched his rhythm until we reached the peak of delight together. As I tumbled down from the whirl of sensation, I slumped against him, our naked bodies damp from our lovemaking.

"Thank God for second chances," he murmured as his fingers trailed lightly up and down my back.

"I'd be more than happy to go for a third any time you're ready," I replied, surprised by my boldness.

"As tempting as that sounds, I'm not too eager for the owner of this building to come checking on storm damage and find us naked and basking in the afterglow."

"Well, you have a point." My head understood the logic of the situation, but my heart and body definitely wanted more.

We cleaned up in the tiny bathroom, dressed quickly, and left a note for the owner to contact us about the broken window. Then we drove to my house to assess the damage. All over the island, people were emerging to look at the aftermath.

My home was uninhabitable but repairable. Cell phone service was soon restored, and I let Aunt Rosie know I was okay.

"Can we drive by to check on my dad? The stubborn old fool refused to leave."

"You left him alone to stay with me?"

"When he wouldn't leave, I decided to stay, too. I was helping him board up his last window when I saw you drive by. I figured I'd invite you to join our hurricane party. But I liked ours a whole lot better." He wiggled his eyebrows and winked. "Once I check in with him, what do you say we check into a hotel—Costa del Mar if they're open and have a room—and see if we can brew up another storm?"

I nodded. That was the kind of storm I didn't mind. THE END

A SCANDALOUS CONFESSION!
What Happened In Suite 1529

Most women would kill to lead the life I led. Most women would kill me for thinking about ending my marriage of twenty-plus years. Instead of feeling lucky, I defined myself as nothing more than a forty-five-year-old housewife and a stay-at-home mom. Whatever the term, it still means one thing—I was bored with my life and wanted a change.

My husband, Carlton, was wonderful—and dull. Nothing exciting ever happened to us. He had his work as an investment banker, and with a new accounting or investing scandal on TV every other day, his attention was always diverted.

I can't even say that Carl let his body go over the years. At the age of fifty, he has the body of a very athletic man of thirty. His smooth, pecan skin is as clear as the day I met him almost thirty years ago. Most of my friends describe him as striking—which he is, no contest—and women still find him attractive. I would have been jealous—if I still were attracted to him.

See, the thing is, I didn't let myself go, either. I work out at the gym every morning and I still turn a head or two. That was my biggest chore each day, since the last of our three children left home for college just a few weeks earlier. Carl usually ate breakfast downtown near his office. He always claimed he didn't want me to go to all that trouble of cooking for just him. My friends thought that was sweet; I thought it sucked.

Since our baby girl, Aneesa, went off to Princeton University two years ago, mealtime was the only time I was assured a little of Carl's attention. But after a while, I didn't even see him on most days until dinnertime. He always had some client to meet, and then he went to work out at the gym. By the time he finally dragged himself home, I was in bed, asleep.

Which left me with nothing but free time. What's that old saying? "Idle hands are the devil's tools." It's so true.

It happened so slowly I didn't realize what was going on.

I met him one day as I was having lunch at my favorite restaurant in downtown Arlington. I ate at Javier's Mexican Eatery at least three times a week. I was having my usual lunch of taco salad and a frozen margarita when someone interrupted me.

"Why are you eating all alone?"

The question was innocent, but I knew better. I looked up into beautiful, dreamy, brown eyes. His skin was golden brown and he looked all of thirty—if he was that.

"I just stopped in for a bite to eat," I said shyly.

He stood by the table, attempting to show me his good manners. Finally, I relented and asked him to sit down.

"My name is Jerome Dunston." He plopped down on the hard chair. "I was taking a little break myself." He waved for the waiter.

Once the young man appeared, Jerome ordered a beer and some fajitas. Soon, the waiter was gone.

"I'm Rachelle." I took a sip of my margarita. "What do you do?"

He played with the salt shaker as he answered my probing question. "I'm an attorney. A divorce attorney. I met with a new client at her office near here."

"Oh," was all I could manage to say. *Is this a sign from God, telling me to get out while I still can?*

He pointed at my three-carat wedding ring, smiling. "I see you don't need my services. How long?"

I didn't smile. Carl's face immediately came to mind. "We just celebrated our twenty-fifth wedding anniversary last month," I said dryly.

"Are you happy?" He asked, nodding to the waiter as he returned with his food.

"Who's really happy these days? Don't most people just make do?"
He smiled, finally placing his left hand on the table. A gold band
shone on his third finger on the left hand. *He's also married. Maybe he
just wants conversation.*

"Not necessarily," he answered frankly. "I think happiness is where
you find it. I just usually don't find it at home."

I watched him take a long drink of beer and pondered his
statement. *When was the last time I felt truly happy?*

"Why are you still married? After all, you're a divorce attorney;
you can just represent yourself," I teased.

He took my question seriously. "Yes, I can divorce her, but we have
children and that makes a sticky situation. And besides, I don't want
to. We both do our own thing and we like it like this."

It didn't seem like a marriage to me. *At least Carl doesn't sleep
around, or at least I hope he doesn't. Nothing is absolute these days.*

I saw his lips curving upward in a smile. He was asking me
something. "I'm sorry. . . ." I said.

"I was asking you what you're doing after this." He leaned back in
his chair, assessing my attire of a Donna Karan linen dress. "Let me
guess. You're going to hit the mall, before rushing home to get dinner
started for your husband."

"Then you'd be wrong."

"Picking up the kids from school? Then on to something Mom-
like?" He smiled at me, thinking he had me figured out.

I shook my head.

"You're going to meet your husband for a quickie in a motel room.
You know, for that role-playing thing." He leaned across the table,
whispering, "You know that's not very effective."

Again, I shook my head, not having enough nerve to admit that l
had nothing on the agenda. Nothing at all. It wasn't even the day for
my manicure, pedicure, or massage.

He finished chewing the fajita that was stuffed in his mouth, wiped
his lips, and threw the cloth napkin on the table. "Okay, give."

"Nothing," I said. "I'm doing nothing." I signaled the waiter for my
check. "But that doesn't mean I'll cheat on my husband."

He smiled as if he had won the Master's Golf Tournament. "I never suggested that you should cheat on your husband."

I could already see the wheels turning in his head. Maybe my subconscious was speaking for my brain. "Good. I want to make sure that point is clear."

The waiter returned with my check. I reached for it, but Jerome grabbed it out of my reach. "I'm glad we agreed that you're not going to cheat on your husband. Let me get this for you." He reached inside his jacket pocket, retrieved his wallet, and plopped down his American Express Gold Card on top of the two bills.

"That's really not necessary. I can pay for my own lunch."

"Yes, I'm quite aware of that. I just thought you were nice and wanted to repay you for letting me sit with you."

"Thank you, Jerome," I said, hoping he would leave, or at least let *me* leave. I rose, thanking him for paying for lunch, but he insisted on walking me to my car.

As he opened the door to my Mercedes, I thought he was going to make his move and I would have to find some way to turn him down. But he didn't.

Maybe I imagined all those sexual undertones at lunch. Maybe he really did just want conversation.

He placed my keys in my hand. "It was a pleasure, Rachelle. You're a very beautiful woman. Any man would be proud to have lunch with you. Perhaps we will meet again."

I nodded like an idiot. I started my car and drove away, all the while thinking about my marriage and how my dreams were chased away with the onset of motherhood.

Later that evening, I was fixing dinner when I heard the back door opening. I immediately grabbed the heavy, LeCruset skillet and headed for the nearest door to hide behind, thinking a burglar was entering the house.

"Baby, I'm home."

It was Carl. I stepped out of the pantry and breathed a sigh of relief. "I thought someone was coming to rob the house! What are you doing home so early?"

"I came home to see you. I think we need to talk."

He knows. Somehow, he knows I had lunch with a man—one of his many clients probably saw us. What was I thinking?

"Carl, I can explain."

He looked puzzled. "Explain what?" He took off his jacket and threw it on the back of the chair. "I was talking about *us*."

Oh, my God; he does know about my having lunch with Jerome. I tried to blink back my tears of disappointment.

Carl sat at the table, watching me and approving of the sundress I was wearing. "You look nice, baby. I know I've been neglecting you lately by working so much. Why don't we go out to eat tonight?"

"We're not celebrating something, are we? Did you close that deal?" I asked him, but in my mind, I thought, *Is he really going to ask for a divorce in a crowded restaurant?*

"Yes, we're celebrating something. We're celebrating finally being free of children! I just realized today that we haven't done anything exciting in a while."

Contemplating divorce today was pretty exciting, I thought. I turned off the stove, put a lid on the skillet, and turned to face my husband. "Dinner would be fine."

He stood and walked toward me with a confident gait that said he owns the world. He wrapped me in a tight embrace that let me know he was still very much a man and that Viagra would not be needed any time in the near future. He leaned down and kissed me gently on the lips. The kiss was so tender I almost swore he was taking lessons from someone else.

"I'll just go take a shower and get changed." He grabbed his jacket and headed upstairs.

I paced the width of the kitchen, wondering where my husband was. Surely, this man was not he. Nothing about him seemed familiar after all these years. That kiss was not like his usual, chaste kisses— when he remembered to kiss me, that is. This was something new. But I didn't have long to ponder anything.

Carl was back downstairs in less than thirty minutes, dressed in blue, cotton, walking shorts, a red and white cotton shirt, and some leather, slip-on shoes. He looked like an ad for a magazine. The shorts showed off his muscular legs and the shirt showed off his wide expanse of a chest.

"You look nice, Carl."

He smiled, walking toward me. "Well, if you're looking like something off the cover of a fashion magazine, I have to do something to scare off those other men, don't I?"

"What other men?"

He motioned for me to head to the garage. "I know, Rachelle," he said in a quiet voice.

My heart started hammering, but then I realized I didn't really do anything—yet. "What on earth are you talking about?"

He didn't respond.

I walked into the garage. "Which car?"

"I'll drive," he said. He walked to the Range Rover and opened the passenger door for me. "I know about all those men ogling you at the gym."

I smiled at him as I stepped up into the truck. "I have no idea what you're talking about," I teased as he closed the door.

He slid behind the steering wheel, laughing. "One of my clients works out in the mornings and he's always telling me how so many men are always checking you out."

I should have known he couldn't be this romantic on his own. "So you decided to take me out to dinner to show me what?"

Carl laughed and started the Rover. After we were on our way to the restaurant, he answered me. "I realized today that we don't really do anything together anymore. Remember all those plans we made years ago? When we're finally free of children, we were going to travel and finally see Europe. What happened to those plans? I guess I can be pretty anal about work."

Anal isn't the word I would use to describe a man who'd rather watch CNN Money Matters or read the Stock Market Report than make love to his wife.

He was watching me, waiting for a reply to his statement.

"You're not *that* anal, Carl. I can't remember the last time we had a meal out together, but that means *nothing*," I said sarcastically.

He put one of his large hands over his heart and moaned. "Oh, that hurt," he said playfully.

I was about to say that I was sorry, but he was laughing. He was messing with me. "You know it's true," I said instead.

"Yeah, it is—and I'm going to change that, starting now."

After we were seated at the restaurant, Carl was as charming as he was in the early days of our marriage. He ordered a bottle of champagne for us to help celebrate our newfound "whatever." He toasted us and I glanced around the crowded area.

I noticed a familiar face staring back at me.

Jerome sat at the table across the room with someone who had to be his wife. She isn't drop dead gorgeous, but she's pretty. She's willowy, tall and thin, and her caramel skin actually glowed under the dimmed lighting.

I couldn't understand why Jerome was flirting with me so fiercely earlier when his wife looks so good. But then again, why was I flirting with him when my husband looks so good? "The pot calling the kettle black," as my mother would have said.

"Well, I'll be damned," Carl said, interrupting my selfish thoughts. "I can't believe that man has the nerve to show his face in public."

My eyes followed Carl's gaze and to my surprise, they landed on Jerome. I had to say something. "Who is it, Carl?"

He leaned across the table, whispering to me. "It's Jerome Dunston, a divorce attorney. One of the guys at the office is going through a divorce and the wife hired Dunston. He's a shark in the courtroom. No man doing battle with him in divorce proceedings ever comes out with much."

I tried to remember which one of his partners at work was separated, but did it really matter? Did I really care?

"I didn't know you know him."

Carl shook his head. "If I had my way, he wouldn't be walking right now. Brian is going through a hard time and Dunston had the nerve to show up at work and *threaten* him. I told him he's not welcome on our property."

Never in our marriage did Carl ever act like this. The raw passion that he exuded at that moment definitely left our bedroom years ago, and it was then reflected in his brown eyes.

"I didn't know you could do that."

"When it's interfering with our work, I can do anything I damn well please," Carl said with an assertive voice.

Who is this man sitting across from me? Not the lump of coal I usually sleep with! This man has a pulse.

We enjoyed our meal and headed for home. As he drove back to the house, he tuned into a classic jazz station. Jazz is my favorite kind of music! Usually, all he listened to was the news stations and talk radio. The sexy sounds of the saxophone lulled both Carl and me into silence. He almost ruined the mood by wanting to travel down memory lane.

"You know, what Brian is going through reminded me of when we were first married. Things were tough in the beginning, but we stuck it out, didn't we? It's a shame people don't try harder these days, isn't it? Brian has only been married a few years and they're already giving up."

He had this melancholy memory of the early days, but I didn't understand why. *I'm* the one who had to deal with diaper changes, sick children—and a husband who was always working. He never had time for kids or me. Even with all that, I stayed.

After we got home and settled in for the night, I just knew we would have sex. Carl wasn't overly amorous on the ride home, but it was just a feeling I had.

That feeling was wrong.

I came out of the bathroom, lotioned down with Marc Jacobs, smelling like seduction and dressed in a sheer, lace nightshirt a blind man could see through, ready to continue on the path to passion.

Carl was sprawled in the middle of our king-sized, four-poster bed, sound asleep.

A few days later, I was enjoying my lunch again, when I ran into Jerome. He's definitely a persistent man. He approached my table, dressed in a suit that had to be tailor-made for his tall, lean body.

"May I?"

I nodded and motioned for him to sit down.

"I didn't know Carl is your husband," he said in an almost accusatory tone. "I was at his office the other day."

"I know; he told me."

"Well, what's on tap for today?" he asked suggestively.

I signaled for the check. "I think you're assuming an awful lot. I told you before that I'm not interested in cheating on my husband."

"What if he's cheating on you?" He leaned back in his chair with a confident, cocky smile. "You know all the signs are there. He works late, he's always out with clients—or so I hear."

"Well, I guess you haven't heard the best part. Yeah, he's cheating on me, but it's his *job* that's his other love, not another woman." I regretted the statement as soon as it left my mouth; it wasn't as if Carl *never* showed any affection to me. I could see the wheels turning in Jerome's adulterous mind.

He leaned toward me, whispering. "You know, you are one beautiful, black woman and any man would be proud to be with you. Your husband is a fool. Why don't you let me show you how big of a fool he is?"

I knew what he was asking, but I remained silent.

"We could meet at a hotel and I could show you how beautiful you are." He ran a finger gently over my clammy hands.

Even his touch was electric and sent all kinds of shivers through my body. I wanted to say, "Yes," but I knew I shouldn't. I was, after all, married to a wonderful man—who took me for granted.

Over the next month, Jerome began popping up at all the places I frequented. He was trying to wear my defenses down; I knew that. But it didn't stop me from enjoying the attention and feeling needed, even if he was someone else's husband and I was someone else's wife.

I knew better, but I decided to meet Jerome at the hotel one day.

All of my senses were telling me that Carl would come around and realize that he was driving a wedge between us. But he didn't mention it, and nothing changed. So if there was going to be a problem between us, I might as well make it worth my while.

Jerome and I scheduled to meet at two, but I wanted to do it right.

I took a shower and dressed in my favorite Anne Klein, strapless, linen dress. I looked in the mirror at my appearance and twirled around like I was going to the prom.

The phone rang, disrupting my giddiness. I picked it up, thinking it was probably Jerome, wanting to confirm I was still going to be there. Thank the Lord I only said, "Hello."

"Hey, baby," Carl purred into the phone.

"Carl." I sucked in a deep breath. "Is something wrong?" He very seldom called during the day, unless it was pertaining to the kids or something business related.

"Nothing. Can't I just call you in the middle of the day? Maybe I just miss hearing your voice."

"Maybe." He used to call me at least three times a day. But that was a long time ago, when making love nightly until we were exhausted was the order of the evening. "You haven't called me in a long time, unless something was wrong. Is that it?"

He took a deep breath. "I just called to say that I love you and I miss you."

I had to sit down for that one. "Well, Carl, I love you, too."

I heard someone come into his office. Carl covered the mouthpiece, muffling the conversation, then came back on.

"Look, baby, I gotta go. We'll talk later." He cut the connection.

"Yeah, we'll talk later," I mimicked, knowing that time would never come. I stared across the room at the oval-shaped mirror and watched the woman staring back at me. The dress fit in all the right places and in my opinion, looked really great on me. I took off the diamond necklace Carl gave me on my last birthday. It didn't feel right wearing that when I was going to commit adultery. I grabbed my purse and headed out the door.

As I drove to the Arlington Hilton Hotel, I thought about what I was doing—or was about to do. *What am I thinking? Did I really think this through?* But I was tired of thinking, tired of being the good wife. And I was tired of being lonely. Everyone else in my family was achieving something in life. I just wanted to feel needed.

Carl didn't even need me anymore.

I pulled into the hotel parking lot and was met by a young man. He opened my door, offered his hand to help me out of the car, and then handed me a valet ticket. I watched him drive away in my Mercedes. With a deep breath, I headed inside to the scene of the crime.

I walked inside the hotel lobby, heading straight for the bar. After I ordered a sour apple martini, I called Jerome's cell phone. He answered on the second ring, and then quickly told me the suite number and disconnected the line. I took a sip of the cooling liquid, wondering where the "kind" Jerome disappeared to. The man on the phone sounded very business-like. I finished my drink and headed to the elevators.

I exited the fifteenth floor and walked to suite number 1529. How odd it is that those numbers are the last four digits of my cell phone number. And those numbers just happen to be a combination of both Carl's birthday and mine. Something in me began to snap. I don't know what. As I raised my hand to knock on the door, I trembled. *Just last minute jitters*, I thought.

I knocked.

The door opened and Jerome was already dressed in the hotel bathrobe. He invited me inside the suite. It was quite nice. A grand living area led to a lavish bedroom, where a large, king-sized bed stood waiting, the plush covers already pulled back. I could see a bottle of chilled champagne sitting on the nightstand.

"Hello," Jerome cooed, as I took it all in.

"Hi," I somehow pushed out of my mouth. "Sorry I'm late."

He closed the door behind me, forcing me farther into the room. "It's okay, baby."

Why does he have to call me that? That's Carl's pet name for me. Jerome stood behind me, wrapping his arms around me and kissing my neck. "Why don't you have a drink of champagne and get comfortable?" He pointed to the other hotel bathrobe.

I noticed his suit hanging neatly in the closet. I nodded, trying to hold back the tears that were threatening to spill out of my eyes. I was determined to go through with this. I *needed* this.

The bed was soft, but it didn't yield to my weight as I sat down.

Maybe if I had another drink, my nerves would settle down. Guilt is such a powerful emotion; there isn't enough liquor to kill that feeling. I watched as Jerome sat beside me with that silly grin on his face—that's what did it for me. I stared at his devilish smile and I knew what I had to do.

I rose from the bed and faced Jerome. "I can't do this."

He rose and grabbed me. "What do you mean, Rachelle? We made plans. Now you're saying you don't want to have sex. What the hell is this?"

"I changed my mind." I wanted to give my marriage one more shot.

"Well, I haven't changed my mind," Jerome countered. "I can call your husband and tell him you came on to me and begged for it."

"I have no doubt that you will." I walked closer through the living area to the door, trying to make my escape.

Jerome caught me before I could open the door. He pinned me against it with his hungry body. His erection was very evident, but instead of making me want to give into passion, it only made me want to give my marriage one more try.

Jerome was breathing hard in anger. I knew he wasn't letting me out of the room willingly without having sex first. He was in the prime position for a kick to the groin, as Carl taught me in the early days of our marriage. He always wanted me to be able to protect myself. Not many men would be willing take a kick to the nuts for demonstration purposes, but Carl was. As Jerome started gyrating his body against mine, I made my choice. I raised my knee ever so slightly, making sure he didn't realize what I was about to do. I moaned for dramatic effect, trying to fool him.

"I know you want me," he breathed in my ear. "Women like you always want a man like me."

"A woman like what?" I moved my knee into position.

He grunted, slowing his movements against me. "You know, you've been married a long time, didn't have the good stuff for a while, and you want it bad."

He was only half-right. When I walked into the hotel, I was prepared to go all the way, just to satisfy my yearning for someone to need me. But this man didn't need me, either. Well, he needed me for a physical reason, but not a spiritual one. I moved my leg then and kicked him—hard.

"Ow!" Jerome fell to the floor, writhing in pain.

"Sorry!" I made my getaway and ran out of the hotel, digging inside my purse for the valet parking ticket. I shoved it at the attendant. "Please hurry." I just wanted to get out of there and back home as fast as I could.

Soon, I was in the car and driving, but I didn't go home—not directly. I drove around town, thinking of what I could possibly do to right the situation. I would have to confess, of course, and then Carl would be furious with me. And he had every right to be. I drove home to face the music.

I was surprised to see Carl's truck in the garage when I pulled in. *What is he doing here?* The back door opened and he emerged, smiling at me. *I really do have a special man.*

He opened my car door, helping me out. "Hey, baby." He leaned to kiss me. "I didn't like how our conversation ended, so I decided we can talk now."

I nodded, knowing the end of my life as I knew it was over.

Why does it have to be like this? The minute I decide I'm ready to give our marriage a second chance, he's probably ready to end it. I walked inside the house like a prisoner walking the last fifty feet to the electric chair. I sat at the kitchen table and he sat across from me.

"Carl, I would like to explain about today."

He shook his head. "Rachelle, it's not important. Not to me. Is it something l should know?"

"Not really. But I want to tell you, anyway." I wanted to make a clean slate of things. I wanted to share with him the feelings I felt for him, but something in his eyes told me that he already knew.

He reached across the table and grabbed my hand. "Honey, where you were and what you almost did aren't important. The fact that you didn't and that you're giving me another chance is enough for me."

"How did you know. . . .?"

"Jerome called me."

I couldn't stop the tears. I should have kicked Jerome harder and rendered him unconscious, so he couldn't have called Carl. But that would have only deterred him momentarily. I released Carl's hand, but he grabbed it back.

"I knew he's a bastard. But if that made you realize what we have, I'm thankful. I wish you told me before. You know what they say about old fools."

"But," I started, "I want to be honest with you about everything. I don't want anything to shatter what we have."

Carl shook his head. "I don't want to know. Let's just use this as a lesson learned and move forward." He stood and took my hand, leading me to the living room. We didn't stop there. He took me upstairs, straight into our bedroom.

We stood in front of our bed, less than a foot apart from each other. He smiled, reaching around to the side zipper of my dress and unzipped it slowly. He eased it down my body and it fell to the floor. My Carl, who never believed in the art of seduction, was putting the moves on me!

He gazed at me as I stood in only a mauve, strapless bra and matching panties. "Baby, you look as good as the day I met you, if not one-hundred percent better." His large hand grazed my flat stomach, igniting a sensation I hadn't felt in years.

His lips touched mine in a feather light kiss and we fell on the bed. I melted in his arms as he wrapped me in a tender embrace. For the first time in too many years to count, I felt his erection against me. "Carl, are you okay?"

He moved against me. "Better than I've been in years."

He kissed me again, deepening it as my mouth welcomed his tongue. We kissed like teenagers in the backseat of a car. He unsnapped my bra and slipped my panties down my legs, all the while not breaking our kiss.

"Carl," I panted. I pulled at his shirt, ripping the buttons, and finally, it struggled free of his body. His chest looked as magnificent as ever.

"Hey, if I didn't know better, I'd think you've never been made love to." He turned on his side, unbuttoned his pants and slid them down his muscular legs, along with his boxers.

He lay next to me, naked, his tall, lean body silently crying out to me. I ran my hand up and down his chest, loving the feel of hard muscle under his skin. I gazed down between us and smiled. His erection stood proud and at attention.

I massaged him, listening to him moan in surrender. He lay on his back, pulling me on top of him. Reluctantly I let him go. He entered me in one smooth motion. He slipped inside my body so easily and so completely, I was at a loss for words. The feeling of love and contentment I was feeling at the moment can't he described in mere words. I gasped as he moved against me. He grabbed my waist on both sides, sliding my body back and forth, back and forth.

"Carl!" I screamed, not able to hold back my climax any longer. He crushed my body to his and kissed me in rhythm to his strokes.

"It's all right, baby," he purred in my ear. "Just enjoy the ride." He wrapped his arms around me and surged deep inside me one last time, before I felt him climaxing inside me.

"Oh, Carl," I moaned, not wanting the most intense intimacy in our marriage to stop. Apparently, neither did my body as I had another orgasm. As it washed through my body like a Texas tornado, I kissed Carl wantonly. My tongue danced with his as his hands caressed my butt gently.

Finally, my body calmed down and I lay atop Carl's chest, panting like a marathon runner. I listened as his heartbeat also calmed down. He chuckled.

I raised my head so I could look into his eyes. "What's so funny?"

"Me." He kissed my forehead. "Today was the darkest day of my life. I thought our marriage was over and I didn't know how I was going to go on without you. But, like every other day of my life, you made it bright again. I love you. I'll do whatever it takes for you to be happy."

"Even if that includes working fewer hours?"

"Even that, baby. You are the most important thing in my life. I learned that today."

I couldn't believe what my ears just heard. "Carl, I'm not asking you to give up all your clients. I just want to be able to take a vacation together and actually spend some time with each other."

"No problem. I hammered out a new schedule today. I realized what we have is worth keeping. I won't go into the office on Fridays and that will be our day, okay? And I promise to be home by five on the days I work. And no more client dinners."

It was what I wanted all along. Just a little attention from my husband, but I didn't want him to give up what makes *him* happy to make *me* happy. "Carl, I know how important your job is to you. I'm sure there's a happy medium for us."

He turned toward me, his hands gliding over my sweaty body, caressing me in places that made my heart race with anticipation. "I'm ready to slow down. The business is doing great. I have a capable assistant. And I want to be with you."

He kissed me on the lips, teasing my lips apart. *God, that man can kiss.*

I raised my head and stared at the man who just made love to me. It was so different, and yet more fulfilling than any other time we made love. Words just didn't seem necessary, so I showed him how much he means to me—over and over again.

Love isn't gone. It was just in a recession. THE END

TOO DARN HOT

I glared at the glowing green numbers on the clock beside my bed. It was two a.m. "I give up," I moaned into the hot, sticky night. I tossed my pillow across the room. "It's too hot to sleep." The ceiling fan whirred at top speed, and the two window fans brought no relief. I did the depressing math: I had to be awake in four and a half hours to go to work after zero hours of sleep. That equaled one long day ahead of me, but at least my office was air-conditioned.

I rolled over and sat up. Max was asleep, of course. I poked him in the ribs, but he didn't even move. He'd been living with me for a week, and boy, could he snooze. I kissed his gorgeous red head and slid from the bed. I stood in front of the fan and let the air blast my skin, blowing the soft material of my cotton baby-doll—the perfect, barely-there outfit for such a sweltering night.

I crept out of the room and looked back at Max. "No really, you sleep. I'm fine." I shook my head. *Typical male.* I cracked open the refrigerator and lingered in front of it, enjoying the crisp shot of air. I poured a glass of wine, dropped in a few ice cubes, and stepped out onto the deck.

"So, you can't sleep either?"

I jumped at the sound of a deep male voice. "What're you doing up here, Jack?" I slid the door closed behind me and took a long swig of my drink to slow my heart. We'd been flirting since I moved in five months ago. Jack was six-foot-three and full of muscles from head to toe. His curly brown hair grazed his shoulders, and he insisted his bright green eyes weren't the result of contacts. If I were casting a model for the cover of a romance novel, he'd be my first choice. And there he was, lounging on my hammock like a gift from the gods. So, of course my heart was hammering at the sight of him.

I shot a glance back at my sliding glass door. Or, maybe my heart was racing because of my secret hidden inside the bedroom. I didn't want Jack to know about Max. I hadn't exactly asked whether it was okay to let him move in with me. Not that I knew if Max was really going to be around for long. This was a first for me, and I didn't know how long he wanted to stay, either. He seemed like the type who needed to roam. But I liked having him around. What can I say? I hate being lonely.

Jack sat up in the hammock. One corner of his mouth curled up in a delicious grin. (I forgot to mention how gorgeous his lips were. I could imagine them doing several different naughty things to me.)

"I'm doing the same thing as you, Kate. Trying to beat the heat. You said I was welcome up here anytime." He shrugged. "And technically, it *is* my deck." He winked and those lips curled into a full smile as his eyes swept over me. "Are you sure it's legal to wear that outdoors? I'd hate to have to call the authorities for indecent exposure." He grabbed his beer from the floor and tipped it back, never taking his eyes off me.

"So, make a citizen's arrest." I held out one hand. "Why don't you handcuff me?"

He shook his head and laughed. "Don't tempt me."

I grinned at the moon, knowing it glowed through the sheer pink fabric that grazed my hips. I walked over to him. "My landlord leaves me no choice. If he would put in an air-conditioning system, maybe I would cover up with more suitable clothing."

"Hey, your landlord priced an air-conditioning system for this old double, and it's rather expensive. Besides, I like this unsuitable clothing." He tugged at the hem of my sheer nightgown, just covering my lacy panties.

I shivered, wondering if he could see the goose bumps on my arms. I sucked in a gulp of humid air.

Jack wasn't wearing much either, just his boxers, showing off an impressive set of abs. I sat next to him on the hammock and fanned my hand in front of me, trying to catch my breath. "It's not much cooler out here, is it?" I pulled my long black hair off my neck and leaned back. I took another sip of my wine and dipped my finger in the cool liquid. I slowly ran the tip of my finger along the glass' rim, watching Jack.

His gaze settled on my cleavage, and his mouth parted ever so slightly. I thought I heard him groan.

I stared at him and smiled, pleased with the effect I was having on him. I'd come a long way from the quiet girl in high school who couldn't even get a date for prom. I'd spent most of my time studying or practicing the cello for orchestra. The librarians knew me by name, but the football players never gave me a second look. Neither did the chess club members, for that matter. I figured I was destined for a quiet, lonely life. I'd be the crazy old lady, living alone with two-dozen cats.

But I was just a late bloomer, as it turned out. During my freshman year in college, I had a roommate that was a part-time model from a wealthy family. She decided that she simply had to take me on as her little project. With her unlimited credit card, paid for by Daddy, she treated me to several new outfits and a makeover.

"Your pale blue eyes would really stand out if you dyed your hair darker," Brynn had said when we first met. "Don't you wear any makeup? Not even mascara?" We'd gotten drunk one Friday night, and she got out one of her notebooks to make a list of all the ways we could improve me. She circled me, tapping her finger against her nose. "Don't get me wrong, you're nice and sweet and all that, but I swear, you'll be a totally different girl once we wax those eyebrows."

By the time we were finished with the new hair, makeup, and wardrobe the next day, her friends thought she'd gotten a new roommate. Then we spent time practicing the fine art of flirting at local bars. I always left with a few numbers scrawled on cocktail napkins. But rather than settle down with one boyfriend, I had a blast dating all sorts of cute guys: jocks, computer nerds, artists, and musicians. Two guys had even proposed to me before college was over. But I had big plans for my life. I wanted to see the world and really live.

I almost flunked out of college my second semester, I was having so much fun. I could've gotten a degree in flirting instead of marketing. And my skills were serving me well on the hammock with Jack. *Wait till I call Brynn with all the juicy details!*

But sitting next to Jack, fingering a wine glass (a surefire seduction trick Brynn had taught me), something felt different. At age twenty-nine, I wanted something more than just a fling. Jack had a successful construction business rehabbing old houses. He was funny and kind. He tucked my mail under my door for me and helped carry up my groceries. And best of all, I hadn't seen him bring home any women in a long time.

Even though we'd spent hours talking and flirting over the past few months, I'd been reluctant to make a move. He was my landlord, and I loved my apartment, plus the rent was very reasonable. But there he was, in front of me on my doorstep. It was like the stars in the inky sky had aligned for me. It was a sign. There was no way I could resist my impulses on such a sultry night with a half naked hunk grinning at me. I'd been wanting him for too long to resist.

Jack ran his hand through his hair. "No, it's not much cooler out here," he said. "In fact, I swear it's getting hotter." He raised an eyebrow and nudged his knee against my hip.

I felt heat rush across my cheeks. "Yes, it definitely is." I plucked an ice cube from my wine glass and sucked on it for a moment. I set the glass down. "Maybe I can help." I took the ice cube out of my mouth and leaned next to him, hovering over his body. I ran the cube up his abs.

He sucked in his breath and closed his eyes.

I worked the cube up his stomach and across his chest until it disappeared, melting on his tan, taut skin. Drops of water clung to the dark stripe of silky hair that disappeared under his boxers.

His Adam's apple bobbed as he swallowed. Then, he grabbed my hand and licked off the cold water dribbling down my wrist.

I ran a cool finger along his lips, and he bit it playfully.

"That's not nice," I cooed, enjoying myself.

"Neither are you. Damn, Kate, you're killing me," he said, his voice low and husky.

I drained my wine and took the last ice cube between my teeth, leaning over him again, running it across his nipples until it disappeared. I looked up at him. "Does this help?" *If my high school self could see me now!*

"You are wicked." He stared at me with those twinkling green eyes.

I don't know if it was the heat, the full moon, or the sexy lingerie, but I made the move I'd wanted to make since I moved into Jack's upper apartment. I straddled his gorgeous body and kissed him.

His mouth answered back and he took my hair in one fist, pulling my head back. He grazed my neck with his teeth as I pressed against him, my voice caught between a moan and a squeal.

"I'm surprised I haven't seen you bring any guys home," he said, sliding the strap of my baby-doll off my shoulder with his teeth, his breath warm against my skin. He traced his finger along my breast. "I figured you'd have 'em lined up at your door."

I tried not to think of Max sleeping inside. Jack hadn't seen him, or had he? Was he waiting for me to 'fess up? *What did Brynn advise me in college? "When you're trying to keep a secret, keep quiet. Only open your mouth if it's for a kiss."*

So, I just smiled and drew him back in for another kiss. "Well, I found *you* at my door, didn't I?"

"I guess it's my lucky night," he said. He traced his fingers down my throat to my breasts and took one nipple in his mouth, teasing it with his tongue.

"Very lucky," I moaned.

He kissed me again and ground his pelvis against mine, gripping my bottom with one of his huge hands. "You've been driving me crazy since you moved in." His hands explored my curves, and I sighed.

"I knew I was going to rent your apartment the moment I saw you," I admitted.

He rubbed the tip of his nose along my cheekbone until he reached my ear. "Why do you think I offered the rent so cheap?" he whispered with a laugh, pressing his mouth against mine.

Then Jack's kiss died on my lips. "Where'd he come from?"

Max was standing in front of us.

I sat up. I'd forgotten all about him. "What're you doing out here?"

He blinked at us, then crawled into my lap.

I smiled nervously at Jack. "Don't tell my landlord. I didn't exactly ask if I could have a cat." I started petting the big tabby and felt him purr in response, butting his head against my arm. I peeked back at the door. I'd left it open a crack. *Damn!*

Jack frowned at me. "You can have a cat in your apartment, just not that one. He's mine. I thought he ran away!"

I laughed. "This is *your* cat? He just showed up at my door last week."

Jack glared at Max. "What a bad boy you are," he said, rubbing his hand roughly down Max's back.

"I guess he gets that quality from you," I said, tickling Max's chin.

"Very funny."

Max batted Jack away with his paw.

Jack narrowed his eyes at the cat. "You ungrateful. . ." Jack turned to me. "Let me guess. Were you wearing that? We have the same taste in women. Can't say I blame him for dumping me for you. I'd do the same thing." He crossed his bulging arms.

I tapped my chin in thought. "Actually, that night I was wearing a cute satin baby-doll. I'm not really a sweats and T-shirt kind of gal."

Jack's eyes went wide. "So you have more stuff like that?"

Max rubbed against my leg.

"Maybe I'll show you more someday. I'll have to check with Max." I picked the cat up and hugged him, then set him back on the floor. He ran inside and stood in the doorway, waiting for me. He meowed loudly at me.

"Tough competition," Jack sighed.

"He's quite the snuggler in bed."

"Hey, don't be so quick to judge. You haven't snuggled with me yet," Jack said, looping his arms around my waist from behind. He rested his chin on my shoulder. "I don't imagine he'll ever be happy to come back and live with me now."

"You can always come upstairs to visit. . .both of us." I pulled away and went to the door, crouching down to pet Max.

Jack smiled. "How about I come in to visit tonight?"

I closed the door, leaving Max inside. "Let's stay out here. Might be cooler." I looked back at Max. "And more private." I stood in front of Jack and pushed him back on the hammock, giving him a good view of the lace on my panties. "Or, maybe it'll be even hotter out here."

He blew out his breath. "Newsflash, Kate. It's going to be hot wherever you are tonight."

I took his hand. "It's not like we can sleep anyway."

He pulled me down to him as a chill chased its way up my spine.

"Meow," I whispered in his ear.

He laughed and slid off my baby-doll.

"That's better," I sighed.

"Much better," he said, wriggling out of his boxers.

And I finally surrendered to the heat, as the steamy evening turned downright sultry.

It wasn't long before we moved in together, all three of us. THE END

PLEASURE AT THE OASIS

F riday, six o'clock p.m.," the robotic male voice on the answering machine announced.

"Hi honey. This new project is killing me and it has to be finished by Monday. Don't wait up for me. It'll probably be after midnight before I get home. We'll do something special tomorrow. I promise. Sorry I missed you. I love you, Miranda."

I stabbed the delete button, dropped the mail on the kitchen counter and released a long sigh. I'd spent the entire afternoon at work daydreaming about a night with my husband, and now it didn't look like it would happen after all.

In my head I understood the late hours he had to work. Tim was working to make our dreams come true, and our biggest dream was to buy our own home. We were tired of cramped apartment living and wanted more space. We wanted to own a little piece of land and a house that was all ours. We'd both grown up with fathers who served in the military, and between us we'd moved too many times to count. More than anything we wanted to put down roots, and eventually we wanted to start a family.

After making myself a ham sandwich and grabbing a soda from the fridge, I settled into the recliner in our tiny living room and tugged a fleece comforter around my shoulders. It smelled like Tim's aftershave—spicy and sexy—and the aroma sent a tingle through my veins along with the reminder of another lonely night at home.

Our schedules had been so hectic lately that it was only by sheer coincidence we even saw each other some days. A night out for dinner and a movie was non-existent. When we were home together, we usually fell into bed too exhausted for much more than a few hugs and gentle kisses.

After eighteen months of wedded and bedded bliss, I missed my husband. I missed our passionate nights and the long, lazy afternoons that left me breathless and sated. I'd never bought into the story that men absolutely "needed" sex; it was an excuse to justify whatever means a man used to get in a woman's pants. Tim and I never needed an excuse to make love. We'd been enormously attracted to each other from the moment we met. I felt a stirring deep in my womb just thinking about the last time he'd pinned me to the bed with his muscular body. A wave of disappointment slammed against me, because the days since we'd made love numbered in the double digits.

I grabbed the evening paper from the coffee table and hoped it would distract me. If it didn't, I might have to dig out the battery-operated boyfriend and take matters into my own hands.

I read the headlines and then scanned the movie listings, thinking a nice action-adventure film might do the trick. Something with blood and gore would take my mind off of my sexual frustration. Then I spotted the small ad on the last page of the entertainment section.

The Oasis Has Re-opened Under New Management
Located in the Historic District
Performing Tonight through Sunday: Sabrina James
Join us for drinks, dancing, and the best jazz in town.

Sabrina and I attended the same small college in Georgia and lived in the dorm together. While I studied business administration, courtesy of the college fund my parents had set up along with a couple academic scholarships, Sabrina worked her way through school singing at local restaurants. Once she turned twenty-one, she switched to jazz clubs and bars. She came from a single-parent home where money was tight, and her mother insisted she get a college degree so she'd have a profession to fall back on. But I always knew her true love was music and performing for a live audience. Listening to Sabrina perform would be the perfect distraction from my missing husband.

The historic district was advertised as the "Art and Soul" of the city, and it featured antique shops, intimate bistros, and trendy nightspots. The Oasis was supposed to be the latest "in" club and was a place where folks could enjoy good music and a relaxing atmosphere. Everyone said it was an oasis in the desert of a long work week. Sabrina would shine in this venue.

I circled the ad and glanced at my watch. I had time to take a shower, change clothes, and still make the show. A night out would be just what I needed to take my mind off my sex life—or lack of one. I let the folded newspaper fall to the coffee table and hurried to the bathroom.

After my shower, I slathered my damp skin with cucumber and melon scented moisturizer. I fixed my hair and makeup, and slipped into my favorite black jeans and a black-and-white print baby doll top. Chunky silver earrings, a matching necklace, and red Cuban wedge heel sandals completed the outfit. I stuffed my credit card, a couple of twenties, and my ID in one pocket, my house key in the other, and I decided to call a taxi rather than fight Friday night traffic and search for a parking place.

The Oasis was packed and the only available seats were at the bar, but the tall stool gave me a clear view of the stage. Sabrina was between sets when I arrived, so I ordered a glass of club soda and leaned against the barstool's high back, observing the crowd and taking in the renovations made since I'd last visited the club.

The atmosphere was much more intimate now and catered to a more sophisticated clientele. No more grungy rockers and blaring music.

"Great place, huh sugar?" I turned toward the slurred voice and saw a heavyset man who had to have been at least fifty years old. He swayed in place next to me. Maybe if I ignored him he'd go away.

"You like jazz, baby doll?" He stretched one arm across the back of my stool, and the stench of his beer breath made my nose itch. So much for my plan of ignoring him.

Just as I was ready to give him a piece of my mind with words that would make my mother blush, the bartender, whose nametag identified him as Jake, arrived with my drink.

"Roscoe, why don't you go back to your table and leave this nice lady alone? Or do you want me to have to call your wife again?"

The older man rushed away faster than a racehorse out of the starting gate.

"Thanks," I said, sighing with relief.

"No problem. He's pretty harmless, but you just look too nice to be hit on by an old, sloppy drunk," he explained. "And besides, that ring on your finger makes you off limits. I wouldn't want him bothering my wife."

"Your wife is a lucky woman," I said, taking the glass from him.

It was nice to know there were still some good guys left in the world. I took a sip of my club soda and as I grabbed a handful of peanuts from the bucket on the bar, my diamond wedding band twinkled in the light. Tim would love this place. He listened to jazz morning, noon, and night, and he owned stacks of CDs by all the great artists past and present.

"Ladies and gentlemen," the announcer began, "please put your hands together and welcome back Sabrina James."

Hearty applause filled the room as three men moved into position on the low stage. One sat behind a full set of drums, the second began tuning an electric guitar, and the last man raced up and down the scale on a tenor sax. The lights dimmed and a spotlight shone on an elegant woman sitting at the piano keyboard with a microphone angled toward her mouth.

Sabrina was even more beautiful than I remembered. Her blonde hair was parted on one side and hung past her shoulders, and multi-colored chandelier-style earrings twirled and sparkled from her earlobes. A turquoise and silver tank top and dark wash jeans hugged her curvy frame, and bright pink toenails peeped from a pair of high-heeled sandals.

She nodded to the drummer and he tapped out an opening beat. The club soon filled with upbeat, lively music. A few couples stepped onto the wooden dance floor and swayed to the melodies. Others sat hand-in-hand, losing themselves in the spell cast by the talented musicians.

After several songs, I became aware that someone new occupied the barstool beside me. But Brad Pitt himself could have sat down and it would have made no difference. I was here to relax and enjoy the music. Nothing else.

The band finished the set as I drank the last of my club soda, and I motioned to the bartender. As he approached, I felt a tap on my shoulder and heard a man's low, sexy whisper in my ear. "Ask him to bring me a Mirage, would you? And order one for yourself too. It appears you need a refill."

A Mirage, the club's signature drink, was a mixture of champagne, orange schnapps, and cranberry juice. Like its counterpart in the desert, it was intended to create an illusion, but this illusion was one of sobriety. The drink was so smooth most patrons didn't realize they were tipsy until they stood and the room began to spin.

I turned quickly and stared into the face of a drop-dead gorgeous hunk of a man. His dark brown hair was short and spiky on top, and his jaw was shadowed with a day's growth of beard. Eyes as blue as sapphires stared back at me, and with one wickedly raised eyebrow, he challenged me to refuse his request.

He was dressed in jeans that hugged his six-foot-plus frame like a second layer of skin. A black T-shirt stretched across his broad shoulders, thick biceps, and strong pectorals, and over that he wore a leather vest with an embossed design. Thick-soled leather boots added an inch to his already impressive height.

He definitely stood out amid the yuppier and trendier group that patronized The Oasis. Maybe he was a holdover from the previous ownership. Maybe he hadn't heard yet that this was no longer Outer Limits. Maybe I'd tell him when my vocal chords decided to work again.

"Cat got your tongue, babe?" he asked. "Or maybe I have something in my teeth and you're just too much of a lady to tell me?" A broad grin split his face and showed even, white teeth.

"Uh. . .no. It's just. . ." I stammered. I'd been hit on more than a few times in my life, and a few times I'd taken the bait. *After all, what was the harm in an innocent drink?*

But dear Lord, once I looked beyond the jeans, tight T-shirt, his full lips, the hint of a bulge in the front of his jeans. Horrified, I became aware of my body's reaction to him, and a zing went straight down my spine and settled between my legs.

"Well it must be the cat has your tongue because I checked my teeth in the mirror before I came in." He laughed heartily at his own joke.

The bartender stopped in front of my stool. "You want another drink?"

"No, uh. . .Jake," the hunk beside me replied, squinting in the dim light to see the bartender's name tag. "Bring us two Mirages." He reached into his back pocket and pulled out his wallet, which stretched his pants even tighter across his crotch. He pulled out several bills and laid them on the counter to cover the cost of the drinks plus a hefty tip for the bartender.

Jake shot me a questioning look and when I nodded, he left to fill the order. Minutes later, he returned with the drinks in their specially designed glasses with deep green stems and bases.

"You got a name, babe?" the man asked, leaning just a little closer.

"I . . .uh . . ." My gaze wandered again to his sculpted chest and a tattoo that peeked from beneath the edge of his left sleeve. "Miranda. My name is Miranda," I stammered, the words emerging with a high squeak that reminded me of Minnie Mouse.

"Miranda." The name emerged from his lips with a low growl. "That's a real nice name, but I think I'll call you Randi. It's sexy just like you are. And I'm feeling a little bit randy tonight myself." He chuckled and then grew quiet, staring blatantly as his gaze started at my painted toenails and worked upward, leaving a tremor of excited uneasiness in its wake. "I'm Chase," he added, raising his glass in a toast and taking a generous sip.

"Chase," I squeaked again. I sipped from my glass and hoped the cool liquid would soothe my parched throat.

"Have you been here before?" he asked, cracking open a peanut with one hand and offering it to me.

I nodded my head, marveling at his long, thin fingers. "I came with some friends a couple times when it was a rock club, but I'm not really the club type. I just came tonight for the entertainment." I waved my hand in the direction of the stage. "Sabrina and I have known each other since we were in college together, but I haven't seen her in a few years. I saw the ad in today's paper and well, I thought I'd come down tonight since I didn't have other plans and she's really great and . . . what?"

Chase stared at me with an amused grin turning up the corners of his full lips.

"You're cute when you babble like that," he explained.

"I wasn't babbling. I was answering your question." I took another sip of the flavorful concoction. "I was *not* babbling."

"Like a brook, babe. Like a cool, bubbly mountain stream."

I opened my mouth to protest but he interrupted. "It's part of your charm. I like it."

"Oh." I squirmed a little on the barstool, silently cursing my traitorous body and its reaction to this intriguing man. I found myself wondering how his hands would feel on my skin, how his lips would feel against mine.

"So you came tonight for some hot licks?"

Was my attraction to him that obvious? Was he able to read my mind? A blush crawled from my chest to my face, and I was certain I glowed in the dim light. Chase obviously noticed my embarrassment.

"Jazz licks, sweetheart. You know—improvisation," he explained.

I tried to respond but before I could form a coherent reply, the lights dimmed a little more and Sabrina's voice purred over the sound system. "Okay folks, we're going to slow things down a little bit, so grab your sweetheart and have some fun on the dance floor."

The piano sounded the opening bars of *The Way You Look Tonight*, and when Sabrina began to sing, her throaty voice created an atmosphere that inspired lust and need.

"I love this song," I said without thinking.

"Then you should be dancing to it."

I twisted my hands in my lap, shredding a cocktail napkin into tiny pieces. *Just one dance wouldn't hurt anything, would it?* I'd keep him at a respectable distance and no one would know.

Chase slid from the barstool and placed his hand against the small of my back. Slowly he ushered me toward the sea of swaying bodies and we stopped in the shadows at the edge of the dance floor. Clasping my right hand in his left, he pulled me toward him and then wrapped his other hand firmly around my waist. Gradually we began to move together to the slow and sensual rhythm of the music, and as the saxophone wailed, the notes bound us together.

His scent intoxicated me—leather, mint toothpaste, and something musky that was definable only as a hot-and-bothered man. The smooth leather of his vest was a sharp contrast to the rough stubble that darkened his jaw. I moved my hand higher on his shoulder. Absentmindedly, I wondered if his skin felt as smooth as the leather vest and then took a mental step backward.

"This is nice. Very nice," Chase murmured, sliding his arm further around my waist and tugging me closer. "You're a great dancer. Did you know that?"

I swallowed hard, feeling our bodies touch. My neglected libido was awakening and begging to concede. Lust called my name and even over the music, I could hear it loud and clear.

"I'll bet you're good at a lot of things," he suggested and nudged his pelvis against mine. His body throbbed against me, further fueling my need. I stopped in my tracks and swallowed a moan. If I stayed on the dance floor with Chase, I might give in and wave the white flag of surrender. I pushed against his impressive chest and began to back away.

He held on tight and leaned in to whisper in my ear. "Randi, you can't leave me out here like this. I'm turned on, and right now you and I are the only ones who know. If you walk away, the whole room will know."

And this was my problem because . . . ?

Maybe I'd led him on and let him think there might be more to this evening than a dance? Hopefully, he knew that wasn't going to happen. The least I could do was save him from a huge embarrassment. And was it ever huge.

I remained in his arms and we resumed our dance. But I was overly aware of him against me, his heart thumping underneath his T-shirt, his scent stimulating me and making my femininity respond.

I willed my body to relax and began reciting multiplication tables in my head to divert my attention from Chase and his effect on me.

Two times two equals four. Four times four equals sixteen. Sixteen times sixteen equals . . . .

I needed a calculator to go any further. Maybe if I went through the alphabet and named words beginning with each letter.

A is for apple. B is for balloon. C is for cat. D is for...

His tattoo was a devil. I needed to find another distraction.

I looked up and saw him staring down the front of my blouse where my black bra peeked from behind the low neckline.

"Is something wrong?" His voice was low, with a note of longing and danger.

"Yes!" I blurted.

My cry captured the attention of the couples around us, and I quickly tried to explain myself to him. "No, not really wrong. Well, sort of . . ." My voice faded and my cheeks grew warm.

"Randi, if you're worried about that ring on your left hand, I promise I won't tell if you don't. I'll do my best to keep your old man out of the picture, because I really don't want anybody with a bad attitude and a gun knocking on my door looking for a fight."

I glanced at the thin gold-and-diamond band, and my heart ka-thumped in my chest. It had been so long. My whole body was screaming with arousal. And Chase was so handsome and so . . . available.

"If you're thinking what I'm thinking, I know a back room where we can solve this problem real quickly."

I gave him a puzzled look. Then the band segued to an even slower blues number.

"I know the guy who owns this place."

"Yeah, right," I countered. "And I know David Letterman."

He couldn't control his laughter. "Come on," he urged, placing one large hand at the small of my back and nudging me through an open doorway in the corner of the room. "It's quiet, it's dark and it's secluded," he said. "It's perfect."

"I can't. My husband—"

"Won't know if you don't tell him. Sweetheart, I'm not taking you to a bedroom, so we're not talking about a romp between the sheets. Just a little hand and mouth coordination. Some pressure release, so neither one of us explodes."

"You're making this hard for me," I said hesitantly.

He nuzzled my ear. "Randi, honey, you've already made it hard for me."

I allowed him to lead me down a long corridor to a door marked "Manager."

"Right where I remembered." He reached overhead and pulled a key from the top of the doorframe, then twisted it in the lock. The door swung open with a squeak, and in one smooth move Chase hustled me inside, flipping the deadbolt and sealing us in the dimly lit room alone. Before I could catch my breath and begin to rationalize my uncharacteristic behavior, he put both hands around my waist and backed me against a cold metal desk piled high with papers. With a deep growl, he pressed his body firmly against me and brushed his knuckles down the side of my face and throat.

I snaked my arms around his neck as rational thought surrendered to pure lust. He ran his tongue along my bottom lip, and then nibbled gently, asking me to invite him in. I parted my lips ever so slightly and he slipped his tongue between them.

His right hand moved to my chest before lifting my top and flicking open the front closure on my bra.

My entire body was charged and sensitive, and it was screaming for action. A moan interrupted us, and annoyance filled me until I realized the sound came from me. Low, passionate moans filled with longing.

Chase dropped his hand from under my blouse, prompting me to complain with a whimper. His hand connected with my thigh, traveled upward, and flattened against my rear. I laid my forehead against his shoulder to balance myself.

No sooner had I regained my equilibrium than Chase's hand moved to the seam of my jeans and lingered over the thick material, fueling the inferno raging inside.

"More," I begged him. "Don't stop." I could sense the heat licking at my body and soul, but his hand quieted before the heat gave way to total combustion.

"Later, baby," he said. "I promise."

Determinedly, I unzipped his jeans and pushed them down. When he whimpered in response, I simply smiled. "You like that Chase?" I asked, hissing the last letters of his name, shocked at my own boldness and bravado. I could still walk away. I could leave his earthy smell, his rugged appearance, his touch, his tongue, and his caressing hands.

In reply he kissed me deeply, and I knew that leaving was impossible.

"I bet you'll like this even better. Yes, Chase, you're going to like this a lot."

In the light of a single sixty-watt bulb, we pleasured each other until we both soared and crash-landed again. In silence, I righted my clothing while he disappeared into the adjoining bathroom to clean up.

"I'll leave first," he said re-joining me in the office. "Wait a few minutes and then slip out. If anyone sees you, tell them you got lost looking for the bathroom." He crushed his mouth against mine for one last soul-deep kiss.

Then he turned abruptly and strode out of the room, closing the door behind him with a gentle snick, and leaving me against the desk with my heart still racing.

As I waited, I counted off one hundred heartbeats and then slipped out of the office. Fortunately, I saw no one in the hall, and I made my way to the restroom where I washed my hands, finger-combed my hair, and planned my escape, hoping Sabrina had not seen me leave the dance floor with a leather-clad man.

I skirted the lights and hurriedly walked to the front exit where I asked the valet to call a taxi. During the ride home I relived the feel of Chase's talented hands on my body and his urgent kisses, and I wondered what he would have felt like lying naked beside me in bed.

After paying the taxi driver and tipping him far too much, I quietly let myself in the house. Tim's suit coat and tie hung from the rack in the front hallway, and his leather briefcase sat against the wall. Walking toward the bedroom, I could hear water running and the sound of him singing in the shower.

By the time I reached the shower door, I was naked. Slipping under the spray behind him, I wrapped my arms around his waist and kissed his shoulder softly.

"How's the project coming along?"

"Good," he replied lazily. "How about you? Did you have a nice evening tonight?"

I nuzzled his shoulder and then nipped the skin gently. "Very nice."

He rinsed the soap from his body and whispered. "Thank you, sweetheart."

"It was my pleasure. And yours too, if I remember correctly. I'd forgotten about your biker persona. Your grandfather would spin in his grave if he knew what you did tonight Timothy Chasen Holmes III." I waggled a finger at him in a mock reprimand. "I was surprised but definitely not disappointed to see 'Chase' at the club tonight. He was the perfect touch, no pun intended."

Tim laughed softly and turned to face me. "Chase had a hunch about getting lucky at The Oasis tonight, especially after you circled the ad and left it on the coffee table. Of course it didn't hurt that our computer system went down at work and the club manager was one of my fraternity brothers at the university."

"Ah, yes. I wondered how you knew about that office. You're a sneaky little devil. And I had no idea you'd kept that leather outfit."

"I packed it away after last Halloween," he explained. "A guy never knows when leather might come in handy," he added and wiggled his eyebrows.

"And speaking of devils, the tattoo was a nice touch too." I tapped his arm where the skin was reddened from his efforts to scrub the temporary tattoo off. "You should have left it on."

He shook his head, worked up a rich soapy lather in his hands, and began to wash me, paying careful attention to the sensitive areas he'd pleasured earlier. "I don't want Chase around you anymore. Besides, there's no telling what this 'old man' might do if he caught some hustler messing around with his wife." He winked at me as his hands roamed my body.

"Well, I still like the tattoo." I kissed the spot on his arm for emphasis. "It completed the look perfectly."

"You do have a point there," he agreed.

"No, baby, *you* have a point." I giggled as I reached out and ran a finger along his aroused body.

He kissed me gently and then spoke softly against my lips. "So it seems. But this time I want you with me all the way, sweetheart. Our other adventure was a little one-sided. I'll keep that promise I made earlier."

"I like the way you think," I said as I pressed against him.

We switched places under the spray of water and he rinsed my body free of soap, his talented fingers arousing me to a fevered pitch. He twisted the knob to shut the water off. He dried me and then himself with a large fluffy towel, and then scooped me into his arms and carried me to the bedroom, lowering me to the king-sized mattress and stretching out beside me.

Tim lowered his head and pressed his lips to mine, slanting his mouth first one way and then the other. He nibbled as he ran his hands up and down my sides before settling them on my breasts.

"Did Chase cause that?" he asked, lightly rubbing a spot of beard burn at the base of my throat.

When I nodded in the affirmative, he kissed the spot tenderly. "I'll make it all better." Then he began to knead and massage my flesh until I squirmed about on the smooth cotton sheets and said his name over and over.

"Make love to me, Tim. Now," I begged. "I want you so much."

Within minutes he was on top of me and we were both racing toward explosive release.

As I floated back to earth, my husband sweaty and breathing

heavily beside me, I glanced at the digital clock on the nightstand. The numbers showed twelve thirteen. I remembered his message on the answering machine earlier: *We'll do something special tomorrow.*

It *was* tomorrow. My loving husband had made our home an oasis, but it harbored no mirages. I was safe and secure in his love, and I knew that our marriage would last forever. THE END

THE BEST THING THAT EVER HAPPENED TO OUR SEX LIFE!
Separate Beds, Separate Bedrooms

"You look like hell," Marcia declared as she sat down beside me in the break room.

"How sweet of you to notice," I replied sarcastically. I sighed. "No sleep again. I just dozed off while taking a customer's order. One more complaint and I'm toast."

Thank heaven it was just the two of us in the break room that day, because I was very close to tears. Marcia has seen it all in her lifetime. Closing in on retirement, she's been with the company from the beginning. Along the way she buried two husbands, had four kids, and God knows how many grandkids. Most people think of her as a blue-haired, old busybody, but she's always been supportive and kind to me. At my wit's end and with no one else to turn to that day, the dam burst and it all came tumbling out.

"I love my husband, but I can't stand living with him anymore!" I poured my heart out as Marcia calmly sipped her coffee. "He gets up at four a.m. to work out. Then, when I just get back to sleep, the shower wakes me up. I've had no sleep since he started working the early shift. My nerves are shot. We get into fights over the smallest issues. We don't make love anymore. Our bedroom has become a battleground!" There was no stopping the tears.

Marcia put her motherly arms around me. "Sally, you're exhausted. Rob is no doubt exhausted, too. Patience gets mighty scarce when you get run-down. It's not easy dealing with two different schedules in one household."

"What can I do, Marcia?" I wailed.

"Don't you have two bedrooms? Problem solved," she declared.

"But, but—" was all I could utter. I just sat there, dumbfounded.

"Separate bedrooms doesn't mean you're giving up on your marriage; they might even save it. You're entitled to a good night's sleep." Always the mother hen, Marcia checked her watch. "Four o'clock, Friday afternoon. Get out of here before the rumor mill gets a look at those red eyes. I'll clear your desk and tell Dorothy you had an emergency. Now, scoot!"

All the way home, I kept running the bizarre concept of separate bedrooms through my mind. No, Rob would never go for it, I decided. I tried to dismiss the idea, but it was starting to make sense to me. I needed and deserved a good night's sleep. My life was in chaos because I was always tired. My job was on the line, and worse yet, my marriage was deteriorating. By the time I turned into the driveway, I'd made up my mind to at least talk to Rob about separate bedrooms.

Rob had been home for two hours already. He was sacked out on the couch with a beer. He sat up when he saw my red eyes. "You're early. What's wrong, honey?"

For the second time that day I became a blubbering idiot. He held me in his arms as I repeated my conversation with Marcia. "I'm just so exhausted!" I wailed.

"Marcia sounds like a smart lady. Sure, let's give it a try," he said.

I pulled back to arm's length. "What about us?" I asked, not quite believing that Rob was actually buying into the concept. "Separate bedrooms? Hon, don't you want to be with me?" The tears began once more.

"Just because I'll be in the room down the hall doesn't mean you can shirk your wifely duties." Rob winked. "You still have to do my laundry."

I gave him an elbow to the ribs. "Get me a beer and we'll talk it over."

"Okay, but I want this in writing. Let's set some ground rules,"

Rob announced. "I don't mind the back bedroom—there's less traffic noise— but I want to know what my 'options' are."

"Well, we can divide up the nights. Whoever's bedroom we use can set the rules," I suggested. "Who gets the odd day?"

Rob grinned. "Even God needed a day of rest."

"Are we just doing weekdays?" I asked while grabbing a notepad. "I'll take Mondays and Thursdays."

"There goes my Monday Night Football." Rob feigned a groan, which earned him another elbow to the ribs. "I guess that leaves me with Tuesdays and Fridays. Wednesdays can be our day of rest, but all bets are off on the weekends."

Well, that was easy, I thought. But I still had my doubts. I just hoped. . . .

Rob woke me later. I'd dozed off mid-thought. My sweetheart had fixed dinner; well, he'd ordered pizza and lit candles.

"How long was I out?" I mumbled, rubbing my still-swollen eyes.

"You're totally exhausted, Sally," Rob said, kissing my forehead. "I really had no idea how bad it's been for you since my hours got changed. I nearly always grab a nap in the afternoons before you get home. I'm ashamed that I didn't see what this was doing to you sooner."

"I love you, sweetie. Things will work out," I said, melting into his arms. I'm going to miss these arms around me every night, I thought sadly.

That weekend we fixed up the back bedroom. On Saturday, we shopped. We found a manly bedspread and curtains to match. While wandering through the department store, we walked through the infant section. Rob spotted a baby monitor and looked it over.

"Not for a few more years," I reminded him with a nudge.

"No, silly—for us. So I can say good night without putting on my slippers," he said, adding it to the cart.

Back at home, my mood soared when I saw all the extra space that was left for me when Rob's clothes were moved into the second bedroom. Finally, I wouldn't have to sort through storage bins to find the right shoes. Getting dressed in the morning would be so much easier because my wardrobe could now be better organized.

Sunday night Rob kissed me good night and announced, "See you tomorrow night."

For the first time in ages, I watched a movie that night to the end without feeling compelled to follow Rob to bed. There was no guilt later on, either, as I read in bed with the light on; I was disturbing no one. I pressed the baby monitor button and whispered, "I love you," as I turned off the light.

I woke up when my alarm went off the next day feeling refreshed and energetic. My morning flew by.

"You look pretty chipper today," Marcia remarked.

"We took your advice," I sheepishly admitted. "Separate bedrooms. Last night was the first good night's sleep I've had in months."

"Now you have to make it work," Marcia advised. "You're young; you'll figure it out." She winked at me before turning away from my desk.

This has to work, I vowed silently. I wasn't giving up on my marriage just for a little sleep. I shot off an email to Rob: My place at seven-thirty. Jungle attire. Plan on one hour.

I stopped at the supermarket on my way home for some quick dinner fixings and fresh fruit. Rob made no mention of my ambiguous email during dinner. He looked at the clock while helping tidy up the kitchen. "I've got to find some jungle attire before seven-thirty. Any suggestions?"

I laughed. "A loincloth will do. See you later."

I arranged the fruit on a platter and headed for the bedroom. I had time for a leisurely bath before getting into a skimpy, leopard-print teddy. I put "nature sounds" on my alarm clock and dimmed the lights.

There was a knock on my door. Rob came in dressed only in Hawaiian shorts. He glanced around. "I love what you've done with the place," he murmured.

"Welcome to the jungle," I said, pulling him in and closing the door. I led him to the bed. "Make yourself comfortable."

I fed him grapes, pineapple, and melon chunks as he reclined on the bed. Then I took coconut-scented oil, seductively warmed it in my hands, and rubbed it into Rob's broad shoulders. "You can get in on this, too," I suggested.

Straddling him, I transferred the oil from my palms to his. Looking deep into his gorgeous brown eyes, we shared a passionate kiss.

His strong hands rubbed oil on my shoulders as he slipped my teddy down. He cupped my breasts as he nuzzled my neck. With oily hands, he slipped my panties off, applying more oil to my tender inner thighs.

I pulled the drawstring on his shorts and let them fall away. I gently caressed his manhood and watched his face; I could see all the stress being replaced by relaxation and pleasure. We made hot jungle love that night.

Afterward, we lay holding each other. "Take a shower with me before we say good night?" Rob asked.

We playfully lathered each other and we stayed in the shower until the hot water ran cold. By then, we were squeaky clean, to say the least.

I woke the next morning to the sweet scent of coconut. I smiled as I recalled the fun from the night before. That thought stayed with me all day; needless to say, it was a very good day.

I arrived home that afternoon to find a note from Rob: Pizza coming at five-thirty. Leave a good tip. Will be home later.

I panicked as I dug through my purse. I had a measly $6.42—not enough to cover the cost of the pizza, let alone the tip. It was five minutes before the pizza was to arrive and I had no time to run to an ATM. I was still rummaging through my purse when the doorbell rang.

"I hope you'll take a check," I said to the guy behind the pizza boxes.

"Sorry, lady, I only take cash. But if you're short, maybe we can work something out." It was Rob behind the boxes.

I played along. "All I have is $6.42, but I'll throw in this lovely lamp."

"No, no, that won't do. That's a pretty sweater you're wearing. Is it worth $18.39?"

I seductively removed my sweater and we exchanged the pizza for the sweater. "Thank you, lady," Rob said as he turned for the door. "I have other deliveries."

"But wait, you forgot your tip," I said, setting the pizza down. I reached behind him, threw the deadbolt, and took him by the hand. I led him to the bedroom and all the while he played the part of the teenage delivery boy.

I closed the bedroom door and slowly removed my clothes. Then I unbuttoned his shirt and unzipped his pants. "Quick, before my husband gets home." I lay back on the bed and let him take me while he was still wearing his pizza delivery cap and with his pants down around his ankles.

"That's the best tip I've gotten all day," he said, zipping up. "I wish I had more customers like you."

We ate cold pizza that night. Let me tell you—it was a very satisfying meal.

Rob was long gone by the time I was up the next day. There was a note by the phone: Plan on dinner out tonight. How about Jimmy's? Pick you up at seven-thirty.

Jimmy's is our favorite restaurant. It's where Rob asked me to marry him seven years ago, but I couldn't remember the last time we'd dined there.

Nothing could pry the smile from my face that day. I was in such a good mood that even my customers picked up on the pleasant vibes and most of them increased their orders. At ten to five, I was finishing up the last of my filing when Marcia stopped by. "I've got a date tonight," I said cheerfully.

Marcia smiled. "Who's the lucky guy? Oh, by the way—the boss noticed the extra sales. Good job." Before leaving she winked and said, "Have fun tonight!"

Maybe, I thought to myself, I have time to stop and pick up that dress that I've had my eye on for weeks.

Two weeks before, I'd actually tried it on, but I'd put it back, not wanting to have to justify the cost to Rob. But that was two weeks before when Rob and I were fighting about every little thing. The tension seemed to be disappearing as we got more sleep. So, I went and quickly found the dress, happy to discover that it was now twenty-five percent off. Can this day get any better? I wondered.

At home, I blew Rob a kiss as I made a beeline for my room to get ready for our "date." I took extra time to curl my normally straight hair, pulling it softly back with clips. It sounds silly, but I was actually nervous, almost like it was a first date. Will he like the dress? Is my hair going to hold up? All these dumb questions were running through my mind.

"You look beautiful!" Rob exclaimed, kissing me gently so as not to smear my lipstick. "That dress is the perfect color for you—it matches those pretty blue eyes of yours."

The restaurant wasn't especially busy. The hostess informed us that we could have our choice of tables. Rob directed her to a small table near the kitchen. "But there are so many better tables. Are you sure?" inquired the puzzled hostess.

"Positive," Rob firmly stated. "This is the table where this beautiful lady agreed to be my wife."

Tears started to fill my eyes; I was so touched. Rob isn't usually the sentimental type.

We were holding hands across the table when the waiter brought out a bottle of wine. "Compliments of the house," he said.

We had so much to talk about over dinner. I hadn't realized how little meaningful conversation we'd had over the past few months. Our schedules had been controlling our lives and now it seemed like we were finally regaining control. It felt pretty good.

Normally we forego dessert, but that night we both wanted to prolong the wonderful evening. We ordered decaf coffee with our desserts and savored every bite.

I still had so much to tell Rob. "You look so handsome. I used to resent your working out because it took time away from me," I confessed. "Could I come to the gym with you on the weekends?"

"I would really like that," Rob said, kissing my fingers. "Saturday, we'll get up and go together."

We were quiet on the ride home, content to just hold hands. Rob walked me to my bedroom door and kissed me good night.

"I love you," I whispered.

"I love you, too," he said as he disappeared into his room.

I had an empty feeling in my heart as I was preparing for bed. This was one night when I knew I would miss Rob's presence in my bed. I was just lying down when Rob's voice came over the baby monitor.

"Good night, sweetheart, I love you."

"I love you, too, sweetie," I replied. After that, I could sleep.

Thursday night was my night to set the rules. I kept Rob in the dark all through dinner. We chatted about our days at work, keeping the conversation light. As we were finishing the dishes, Rob came up behind me and nuzzled my neck. "What's the plan for tonight?"

I playfully smacked him with the dishtowel. "Give me a half-hour to get set up. It's naked karaoke night. You bring the beer."

Exactly thirty minutes later, Rob knocked on my door. He was wearing nothing but a smile and holding a six-pack.

"I almost forgot we had this thing," I said, pointing to the karaoke machine. "It's been so long since we used it."

I put in a country disc as Rob popped open a beer. "I'll go first." I didn't have all of Shania Twain's moves as I did Come On Over, but I could definitely tell that Rob was enjoying it.

Handing the mike over to Rob, I sprawled out on the bed as he fumbled with the machine, finally selecting Achy Breaky Heart. He has a beautiful singing voice, even while hamming it up. I was choking on my beer and laughing as he got into the act. He played air guitar as he belted out Billy Ray Cyrus's hit.

Then Rob dimmed the lights and lowered the volume. He got very serious and sang Vince Gill's You And You Alone. His eyes were locked on mine with every word he sang. He took my hand and went down on his knee. At the end of the song, he simply laid the mike down and took my face in both of his hands. Staring deep into his brown eyes, I had never felt closer or more in love. As he kissed me, he gently pushed me back on the pillows. His kisses started at my lips, continued down my neck, and lingered on my breasts. His hands gently seduced me as I opened up to him. His tongue sought to bring me the ultimate pleasure and I climaxed again and again.

Later, we cuddled, sipped beer, and talked. "You're remarkable," Rob insisted.

"I'm nothing without you," I murmured, snuggling closer.

Rob stayed another hour just holding me and talking before saying good night. Had we been sharing the same room, he would've simply rolled over and gone to sleep. It was nice; we were bonding after sex.

I sought Marcia out at lunchtime the next day. "Everything's working out so well! Even though we're in separate bedrooms, we seem so much closer," I confided. "Thank you so much for your great advice."

"Yeah—who would've thought separate bedrooms could save a marriage?" Next, Marcia confessed, "My Gary, bless his heart, snored something awful. We slept in separate bedrooms for years. No one knew."

Rob had dinner started on the grill by the time I got home. "Get out of those work clothes and sit out here," he said.

We sat on the patio, enjoying the pleasant breeze as we ate. "You really don't mind this new arrangement?" Rob questioned.

"It seems to be working," I admitted. "I had my doubts, but I feel so well rested and I have more energy now."

"Me, too," Rob agreed. "And I'm not bruised from you kicking me all night long!"

We sat and talked, discussing our plans to landscape the yard and upgrade the house. We were making plans for the future when a month before I'd thought we had no future.

"If we cut down that maple tree, we can put in a flowering cherry," I suggested.

Rob shook his head. "No way. That tree is perfect for the tree house I plan to build for our kids."

Finally, the chill of the night drove us inside. "Meet me in my room in a half-hour. Wear that long, white nightgown," Rob instructed.

I took a quick bath and slipped into the white negligee. It was one of my favorites—long, lacy, and very romantic. I gave my hair an extra brushing, fanning it out on my shoulders. I added a spray of perfume and then I was set.

Timidly, I knocked on Rob's door. Rob, dressed as a gladiator, opened the door. He pulled me into his arms and gave me a passionate soul kiss. My knees were shaking as he handed me a book. On the cover was a picture of a gladiator holding a maiden in a white gown.

"I know how much you like to read and sometimes I even get a little jealous. I want to be your hero."

"You are my hero!" I exclaimed, melting into his arms. THE END

IT HAPPENED
ONE NIGHT

"I'm sick and tired of relationships that don't go anywhere," I lamented to my friend Justine during our lunch hour one day. "You know what I'm talking about, that total all-encompassing euphoria that wraps around your heart at the start of a new love, only to crash and burn when things don't work out."

"So why not have a one-night stand?"

"What? Are you crazy?"

She swiped a French fry through a dollop of ketchup on her plate and shrugged. "You need to get laid, I realize that. A one night stand is the perfect solution. There are no worries about becoming emotionally attached, and if you're not emotionally attached, you won't get your heart stomped on."

"A one night stand?" I wasn't sure I was the kind of person who could jump from bed to bed, yet the more I thought about it, the more it made sense. I'd get physical relief but would keep my heart out of the firing line. "How will I know I'm not sleeping with a maniac?"

Justine shrugged. "How do you know you're not sleeping with a maniac after going out with someone for a while? You know as well as I do that some guys pretend to be something they're not and then when you fall for them, they turn into monsters. Just make sure you use protection."

We finished lunch and went back to our respective work places. Justine is a florist; I work in a bar. I thought about her words long into the evening, weighing the pros and cons. I really didn't need a man to fulfill my physical needs. There was a store just down the street that specialized in sex toys . . . but I'd never had the nerve to go in. Then again, nothing could compare to a flesh and blood man.

As for safety, you don't work in a bar if you can't take care of yourself. I have my black belt in karate and can protect myself if the need arises.

It was a busy night and I had enough to do without thinking about our conversation, but the trouble was that most of the people who came in were couples. A lot of them were all over each other, unknowingly rubbing it in my face that I had no one. There was even a customer at the back of the bar who was fondling his date under the table.

The boss had put a stop to that quickly, not wanting the bar to get that kind of reputation, but the damage had been done to my libido. The couple left immediately, and I could just imagine what they were doing right now.

I needed a man.

The thought knocked repeatedly in my head, keeping time with the windshield wipers as I bumped along a deserted, black-as-night back road. My whole body ached with need. But instead of being laid out in some guy's bed, I found myself in the middle of Mother Nature's wrath as lightening stabbed the night sky and the car literally shook with the force of the wind.

"Damn."

I cursed my co-worker for telling me about this "guaranteed" shortcut home. I swear this road hadn't seen blacktop in years. My car lurched. The distinctive flub-flub of a flat tire was the icing on the cake.

I muttered a string of curses that would have made a sailor proud. I'd been having problems with that tire and had an appointment to get it replaced at the garage, but I'd been so focused on my lack of a sex life that I'd totally forgotten about it.

My cell phone was dead and I wasn't going to stand out in the pouring rain with no light to change it, so I maneuvered my way into the backseat, prepared to spend a frustrating night there. Maybe if I indulged in a little self-satisfaction, I could relax enough to sleep.

As I was getting comfortable, a light through the trees caught my attention. It hadn't occurred to me that there might be someone living in this God forsaken area, but if I could use the phone to call the garage, it would save me an uncomfortable night.

I opened the door against the wind and stumbled through the rain, keeping that light in sight as my lifeline. When I broke through the trees into a clearing, I saw the small log cabin. I hoped that a Hannibal Lector type didn't live here.

I knocked. The door opened seconds later. Shock made my mouth drop open. There was a God after all.

A gorgeous example of man opened the door wearing nothing more than unsnapped jeans. He smiled, his teeth flashing white against the backdrop of the fireplace. "It was a stormy night and I was hoping for an angel to put me out of my misery. Here you are."

"I . . . I have a flat tire. Cou—could I use your phone?" His sheer masculinity had me stuttering like a sex-starved fool. If there was ever a time for a one-night stand, I'd just found it. The guy was enormous, easily 6'4. I wondered if his manly attributes were proportionate to the rest of him.

"Sorry, the storm knocked out the power. How about a glass of wine instead?" He stood to one side of the door and ushered me in.

"I didn't know anyone lived here."

He poured some wine and handed it to me, his gaze roaming over me. It wasn't the discomfort of wearing wet clothes that made my body stand at attention; it was the look on his face. I'd never experienced a hungry look like that in my life.

"I'm just renting the cabin for a week, hoping to lose a bad case of writer's block."

I took a sip, planning my strategy. I was determined to get into this guy's pants. From the looks he kept giving me, I wasn't going to have to work too hard at it.

"What do you write?"

He grinned, and without waiting for an invitation, he lifted my shirt over my head.

"Erotic romance for a men's magazine."

I barely registered his words because his hot mouth was at my breast, doing delicious, torturous things.

I couldn't talk; I could only feel.

He walked me backwards toward the fireplace, then slowly lowered me down onto the Navaho rug as he kissed his way up to my mouth. The man knew how to kiss. In fact, the man knew how to do everything right. In no time at all, we were lying naked. The warmth of the fire bathed our skin with heat, and then it wasn't just the fire that was making things hot. I never knew someone could be so talented in the art of sex. I lost count of the number of times I climaxed.

A long time later, I tried to find my breath as the perspiration dried on my body.

He tenderly kissed my cheek. "This was the most fun I've had in a long time," he murmured. "I think my muse has returned. You're incredible. Will you stay for the night? It's not safe to be driving in this storm."

"We've shared the most intimate act two people can share, and yet we don't even know each other's names."

He smiled and held out his hand. "I'm Dylan."

"Hi Dylan, I'm Chrissy. And yes, I'll stay for the night."

We reached for each other two more times and I'd never known such satisfaction.

"I've never been so uninhibited in my life," I confessed later when we were relaxing with a drink of wine. "I wonder why that is."

"That's easy," he said, running a finger along my collarbone. "I'll bet you've been in a few relationships that went from dull to boring in a big hurry. You wanted excitement. That's why you're here with me, knowing it will never go anywhere."

I was stunned. "How could you possibly know that?"

He shrugged and took a drink before answering. "People are afraid of being ridiculed. It's human nature. When you're intimate with someone you're in a relationship with, you leave yourself open. By having a one-night stand with no emotional attachment, you can let your true wants and needs rule because you're never going to see that person again. They can't hurt you."

A complete stranger summed up my sorry excuse for a love life in one sentence. It was liberating and depressing at the same time.

Dawn was breaking when he walked me back to my car. It took only ten minutes for him to change the tire.

"That should do it. Make sure to get that tire fixed."

He gave me a lingering kiss goodbye and settled me in my car. I was on autopilot all the way home and I fell into bed, exhausted beyond all belief. When I woke up, I wondered if the whole interlude had just been a dream. But my body was throbbing with the kind of satisfaction only a bout of solid, continual sex could produce.

I learned something really important about myself that night. I began to realize it wasn't the lack of sex that was bothering me, it was the lack of emotional nurturing that I needed. I'd spent the night with a virtual stranger, and yet, he'd made me feel like the only woman in the world. That hadn't happened in any of my other relationships, and I made a vow that from now on, I wouldn't just look at what I could get sexually, I'd look for emotional fulfillment as well.

A couple of months later, I saw an adult magazine on the newsstand. A cover line caught my attention: "It Was A Dark and Stormy Night."

I flipped to the page and smiled at the first sentence: "An angel arrived at my door to fulfill my erotic fantasies." I smiled as I put the magazine back on the rack. I didn't need to buy it. I had my memories.

I thought that was the end of it, but I was wrong. A couple of weeks after the magazine came out, I was serving drinks at the bar when I felt as if I was being watched. I set the drinks in front of my customers and turned.

There, at a back table, watching me with a smile on his face, was Dylan. He crooked his finger at me and I walked to him.

"Fancy meeting you in a place like this," I said. I was all in a dither having him so close to me again. I'd never felt like that with anyone else. "Are you here for a drink or did you have something else in mind?"

He chuckled. "Both. Most importantly though, I wanted to see you again. I've spent the last two weeks checking out every bar in town looking for you. I don't know what I would have done if I hadn't found you."

"So, you found me. Now what?"

"We need to talk."

Uh-oh. The worst phrase in the English language: *We need to talk.* My knees trembled as all sorts of different scenarios crossed my mind. Did he have health issues? We'd used condoms so that shouldn't be a problem. Maybe he was married and his wife had found out. That would be a big problem.

I glanced at the wall clock. "I have a break in ten minutes. Can we talk then?"

"No, a few minutes isn't enough time. How about dinner tonight? At the cabin. I rented it again for another week. I'll do up a barbeque. Do you like steak?"

I nodded. "Okay, but I don't get off work until nine tonight."

"That's okay. I'll see you just after nine then."

He pushed away from the table and gave me a very thorough kiss goodbye. Justine was sitting at another table having lunch and she clapped as he went out.

"All right, spill it. Who's the hunk?"

"The hunk's name is Dylan. He's . . . well . . . what I mean is—"

"Out with it, who is he?"

"I had a one-night stand with him a few weeks ago," I blurted out in a rushed whisper, smoothing the hair away from my burning face.

Justine looked toward the door. "Well, you certainly know how to pick them. What's he doing here?" She grinned. "Did he come back for more?"

"I have no idea. I'm meeting him for dinner tonight. He said we need to talk."

"Oh, the famous 'we need to talk' line." She grinned. "Maybe he's pregnant."

Justine fell silent for a few minutes then looked at me with a smile. "I think he knows a good thing when he sees it. Maybe he wants to jump your bones again."

"No way," I denied. "A one-night stand is just that, there's no coming back for seconds."

The rest of my shift dragged on, and I swear the hands of time were going counter-clockwise. Finally, ten minutes after my shift ended, I was on my way to the cabin. I pulled to a stop behind Dylan's jeep and turned off the engine.

"What am I doing here?" I muttered to myself as I walked up the deck stairs. "I was never supposed to see him again. This kind of defeats the whole concept of a one-night stand."

"Talk to yourself much?" Dylan stood at the door, watching me with a smile on his face.

"Hi," I said, hoping my face didn't reflect the embarrassment I was feeling.

He leaned forward and kissed me, then ushered me into the cabin. "I'm glad you agreed to come out tonight."

"Well, I must say my curiosity is getting the better of me," I replied, moving to sit on a stool at the breakfast nook.

Dylan had already made a salad, and I picked a piece of cucumber out while I watched him make garlic bread. The man had a physique that would rival Adonis. He turned and caught me staring at his butt.

"Like what you see?" he grinned, leaning across the counter and stopping three inches in front of my mouth.

"As a matter of fact, yes."

"Good. Maybe later you can see it more up close and personal."

"I guess that all depends on what this talk is all about."

He tapped the end of my nose but didn't say anything. I watched as he went out the back door and flipped the steaks. A few minutes later, he came back in carrying a plate with the best looking steaks I'd ever seen. My stomach grumbled.

Within minutes, we were sitting on the couch in front of the fireplace. Although I was really hungry, my stomach was tied up in knots in anticipation of our talk. So far, Dylan hadn't given me any hints.

He watched as I pushed the food around on my plate. With a sigh, he took my plate and set it to the side.

"Your heart's not into dinner tonight, is it?"

I shook my head. "No, I'm too nervous about this talk you want to have."

"Okay, I'll tell you why you're here." He stood up and went to stoke the wood in the fireplace, then turned to me. "I kind of lied to you."

I *knew* it—it was going to be bad. He was married. "Go on."

"Remember how I told you that with a one-night stand, you can let go and fulfill all your wants and needs because there's no emotional attachment?"

"Yeah."

"Well," he cleared his throat, "I've become emotionally attached—to you. Now I know," he said, holding up his hands when I opened my mouth to speak, "I'm breaking all the rules of a one-night stand, but the way I figure it, the worst is behind us."

"The worst is behind us? You're going to have to clarify that for me."

"What I mean is, I know all your secret sexual desires, wants, and needs. And," he said, sitting down beside me and putting an arm around my shoulders, "they match my own. So you see, it's a good thing we opened up with each other because now we know what we need to keep each other happy. And we've gone way past that 'should we or shouldn't we' stage."

I knew somewhere in that garbled explanation, there was a message. It sounded like he wanted to have a relationship with me.

"All right, Dylan. What exactly is it you're trying to say?"

"We know each other sexually. Let's get to know each other emotionally. I'm tired of relationships that don't work out, just as you are. But I think we have something good going here. I'd like to explore it further and see what happens."

Did I dare take a chance with my heart again?

Yes.

Having one-night stands isn't something I'd recommend to

everyone. It can be downright dangerous. I took a chance, and fortunately, it worked out for me. Dylan and I have been together for over a year now, and my heart still pitter-patters every time he comes into the room, and he says the same goes for him.

This life I have with Dylan is my happily-ever-after. THE END

THE CONFESSIONS OF CANDY APPLE
I Lived In Shame . . . Till A Special Guy Made Me Proud To Be Me!

No one grows up *wanting* to be a stripper—
Least of all me.

As I sat inside that giant, faux birthday cake, waiting to jump out after a hearty, probably drunken round of "Happy Birthday To You," I couldn't help but think of the path I took in life.

I had to think about it or else I'd go crazy inside the cake. I learned the hard way that I'm claustrophobic. My first cake-o-gram was a nightmare. Since then, I'd learned to cope. Usually by thinking about why I was there. And why I wasn't selling lingerie at Victoria's Secret or hawking cell phones at a mall kiosk. The answer was always the same:

Money.

My legs cramped as I crouched low. I massaged the muscles beneath my custom-made, black, satin tuxedo pants. I hoped I'd be able to dance once I popped out to surprise the birthday boy on his twenty-third birthday.

Twenty-three. I was almost there, another two months. I had to wonder how different our lives were—me, and this man I was about to strip for. There I was, smashed into a hollow, plywood cake, ready to jump out and bare my body to a roomful of strangers. Who was he? Where was he in his life?

"Almost time, Candy," Randi said.

My real name is Barbara Kays, and believe it or not, I grew up a normal, happy only child in a middle-class family. Candy Apple is my stage name, given to me by my boss at Strip-o-Grams, because of my red hair. Since then many men have told me I look good enough to eat. I try to ignore people like that, but it's hard.

All the assumptions that go along with stripping are hard to ignore. Stereotypes are hard to break. No one wants to hear about my 4.0 GPA. Or my collection of Boyd's Bears. Or the fact that I love hot cocoa year-round and read anything written by Agatha Christie.

They want to know if I'm a natural redhead, or if I will go out with them after the party. Specifically, they want to know how much it will cost for me to go home with them.

At first these propositions repulsed me. It took a while for me to understand that people rarely look beyond a stereotype. Barely looked beyond the fact that I take my clothes off for a living. They don't care about me. They only care about my body.

I've accepted that. I really have no other choice. I have to either recognize it, or live my life in shame and enraged. I refuse to do either. There is no way I'd go around and announce that I work for Strip-o-Grams, but I wouldn't deny it.

I do what I have do, and no matter what some might say, it is honest work.

My top hat bumped against the top of the cake, the door I'd pop out of in just a few minutes. I wished Randi would cue the music already. Crouching in high heels is never fun. I just hoped my cherry-red garters were still attached beneath my pants.

It's times like these when I wonder if I should have stuck to the conventional route in life.

"You okay in there, Candy?" Randi asked. She knows about my phobia.

Randi is actually her given name. Randi Lesko. Her stage name is Randi-Licious. The other girl rounding out our threesome that night was Sammy Sizzle. We were all graduate students at UFL.

Randi and I were in our second years of med school, Sammy in law school. One day I plan to be a plastic surgeon. All I have to do is pay for my education, which is why I strip.

Finally, the partygoers launched into "Happy Birthday." The cake lurched forward. My stomach did, too.

I was nineteen when my parents died in a horrible car accident, leaving me broken-hearted and penniless. I maxed out my credit cards to stay in school and took out every loan I could. I'd tried regular jobs. None paid nearly enough to support my college education.

It's Randi who pointed me in the direction of Strip-o-Grams. She's been doing it since her freshman year of college, not for the money, but for the attention.

I took a deep breath and jumped up, gloved arms raised, with a bright smile firmly planted on my face.

After being in the dark for so long, it took me a few moments to adjust to the light of the room.

Sammy hit the play button on the CD player.

I began to move and sway, thrusting and bumping and grinding. It was a routine I'd done at least a hundred times. I could do it blindfolded—and I did a time, or two.

The music was sexy, sultry, a mix of R&B and rock. I kept up with the up-tempo as I climbed down from the top of the cake, slid down to the floor, completely aware of how my body looked—tanned and toned, thanks to the many hours I spend in the tanning bed and at the gym at the university.

I know how to play to the crowd: to shimmy, shake, and pose for the maximum cleavage.

My vision cleared and I finally dared to venture out into the room to seek out the birthday boy. He wasn't hard to find. Sammy and Randi flanked him, their arms lingering over his torso.

I caught his gaze, and with a start, realized I recognized him. His eyes grew wide as recognition apparently hit him, too. Either that, or he liked the way my breasts bulged from my too-tight vest. In my distress, I flubbed my routine, missing my split and a leg kick. I tried to catch up to the song, to ignore the fact that Brandon Preston was the birthday boy. To pretend I was somewhere I wasn't—*something* I wasn't.

It was hard.

Even harder, was the fact that I liked Brandon Preston—liked him a lot. We'd been flirting since the start of the year, since we'd been paired in anatomy class. For the past two semesters I'd been trying to work up the courage to ask him out—and hoping beyond hope that he'd finally notice my intentions and ask me out, instead. This wasn't at all turning out the way it was supposed to.

We were supposed to date like normal college students. Go to dinner, movies. Eat takeout Chinese food while watching reality TV in my off-campus apartment. Even that fantasy had a glitch, though. Eventually, I knew I would have to tell him about my job as a stripper. Then my little dream world with the perfect guy, the perfect relationship, would shatter, anyway.

If I was honest with myself, isn't that why I'd kept my distance from him all that time? Because eventually, I knew I'd need to tell the truth? And what man would want me then? Certainly not boy-next-door Brandon Preston.

So, I figured if this was to be the only time I'd ever have with him, I was going to make the most of it. I was going to give it my all.

I was actually fully dressed—for the moment. Layers are the key to a successful Strip-o-Gram, at least according to my boss, Beverly. And she would know since she was a stripper named Busty Bev for ten years before she went independent, opening Strip-O-Grams.

The song slowed, and I used my hips to bump and grind with the rhythm of the song. My hair was coiled inside the top hat, and as I flung the hat at Brandon, my red hair tumbled free, falling around my face, tickling my back.

I watched Brandon as I moved my hips in circles, a sexy belly-dancing type of move Beverly taught me early on. Brandon's eyes were as big as Frisbees.

I smiled, but kept my eyes hooded enough to keep up the sexy look. I even licked my lips, something I'd thus far refused to stoop to do. For once, I found that I was having fun dancing. I loved watching Brandon's reactions—the bobbing of his Adam's apple; the parting of his lips. The way he shifted uncomfortably in his chair. I knew I was getting to him—and I was glad. I was the center of his attention, right in the very place where I'd longed to be for almost nine months. I *almost* wanted the moment to last . . . forever.

Because suddenly I realized I was never going to have a shot at everlasting love with him. Not *now*, when he knew what I did for a living. I made a decision, then and there—as I swung my leg over his head, straddled him, and pulled off my black, satin gloves, a little bit at a time. I wanted him to always remember me with . . . fondness. No, with *longing!*

Within a minute, I'd danced away from him, just out of reach, and had taken off my rhinestone-encrusted vest, revealing the matching bra beneath. As the song reached its crescendo, I whipped off my tuxedo pants to reveal barely there panties, a garter belt, and sheer, shimmery, red stockings.

The cheering in the room went silent for a moment, men gaping, but then they cheered wildly, slapping Brandon on the back—hooting and hollering for me. Some waved money, and usually I'd take it from them, but not that night. That night was all about Brandon.

Smoothly, I danced my way over to him. Sammy and Randi danced around the room, eagerly collecting the money I ignored. I focused on Brandon. I shimmied, I shook; I teased.

Brandon stared.

"Do you want to see more?" I whispered into his ear, my voice husky and deeper than normal.

As he nodded, I licked my bottom lip.

All he could do was nod. The crowd hollered their encouragement.

Slowly, I reached up and unclasped my bra. I swayed in front of him, tempting him to touch me.

I was breaking the rules then. Beverly would've had a fit. There is absolutely no touching allowed, and there I was, practically begging Brandon to reach up, caress.

Bev must've stressed this to whoever hired me, too, because though Brandon's hand twitched, much to my dismay he didn't raise it.

The cheering in the room almost drowned out my music, but I paid little attention. I was in my own world, a world that consisted of just Brandon and me.

My bra fell to the floor. I danced around it, careful not to snag my stilettos on it.

I recognized the closing strains of the song and realized I was almost done.

"How much more?" I asked, bending over him, my breasts practically served to him on a platter.

Still, he didn't touch.

"More," he croaked.

Slowly, I slipped my finger into the waistband of my panties and tugged. The fabric gave way—as it's supposed to—and I carefully tucked the panties into Brandon's shirt pocket.

I danced around, watching his hungry eyes follow me. Never before had I felt this kind of power. Stripping had always been a job, a way to make money. But that night it was about me . . . and Brandon.

The song ended, and as the crowd cheered, I broke Beverly's number one rule. I leaned in and kissed Brandon on the lips. "For the birthday boy," I whispered, before pivoting on my four-inch heels. I strutted to the bathroom, where I'd placed my bag earlier.

I quickly changed; Sammy and Randi would take care of the cake and my discarded clothing. It would cost me fifty dollars to replace those panties, but it was money well spent.

Three men were waiting for me outside the bathroom door with their phone numbers. I took them—as I always do to avoid trouble—and quickly left the apartment, waiting for Sammy and Randi outside.

It was one thing to dance for Brandon, but I knew even then that it was going to be completely disconcerting to see him in our usual setting, with clothes on. What would he do? Say?

I guessed I'd find out the next day.

I almost skipped classes that day. My stomach was in knots; I changed clothes four times.

In the hallway outside chem lab, I paced. I didn't want to go in early and have to face Brandon any longer than I had to. Chimes echoed down the hallway. I stepped into the room, kept my head down, and went right to my station without meeting anyone's gaze.

Near the end of class, I felt a tap on my shoulder. My stomach tightened. I looked up.

Brandon.

Oh, God. Why do I feel more naked now, fully clothed, than I did last night?

"Hey," he said.

"Hi."

"I, um, was wondering if I could buy you a cup of coffee after class."

My mind spun. *Coffee? Why?*

"Barbara?" he said. "Did you hear me?"

I looked deep into his blue eyes. The hunger from the night before was gone. All I saw then was the desperate need not to be rejected. "Okay," I said stiffly, daring to smile. "I'd love a cup of coffee."

After class we walked together to Starbucks and settled in at a table. He drank vanilla lattes like I do. I wondered what else we might have in common—and if I'd ever have the chance to find out. I didn't know what to say, and apparently neither did he. We'd already exhausted the weather and the chances for UFL's football team next season.

"Maybe I should go," I said, starting to rise.

Brandon's broad shoulders stiffened. "I'm sorry. Am I that boring?"

"What? No!" I sat back down and hoped that my nerves weren't showing.

"Then why go?" he asked, spinning his insulated, paper coffee cup in his hands.

I took a quick sip of my latte, burning my tongue. It took all I had just to look him in the eye. "I'm not sure why I'm here—why you wanted to see me."

I'd been thinking about it since he asked. A part of me really hoped he wanted to get to know me—my inner self—despite my job. However, I was really worried that he only wanted to get to know me *because* of my job. Strippers have reputations of being easy. I'm not. I never have been. I simply take my clothes off for money. Is it immoral?

Probably. But *I* am not immoral.

But Brandon had no way of knowing that!

So why did Brandon invite me here? What does he want from me? A friend? A girlfriend? His own private lap dance every night?

Shoving his cup aside, he said, "I've wanted to ask you out for a long time."

My eyes widened. "Well, I guess I broke the ice last night, huh?"

He laughed.

"Why didn't you ask me before now?" I asked, trying to sort this mess out, and my confusion.

A piece of dark brown hair flopped onto his forehead as he gazed up at me from lowered eyes. "You're so . . . so beautiful, Barbara. What would you want with me?"

It's funny, but I don't consider myself pretty. My hair is too red, my skin too pale. I have a decent body, but beautiful? I'd never describe myself that way.

I answered him as honestly as I dared. "I'd want a lot with you, Brandon."

"Really?"

I smiled. "I've been hoping you'd ask me out for months."

He reached out, touched my hand. "Why didn't you say anything?"

I pulled away from his touch, knowing that if this was going anywhere, we needed to have this out. "My job," I admitted.

"Are you not allowed to date?"

He was so serious, I tried not to laugh. "That's not it, Brandon. I . . . well, there aren't many guys who want to date a stripper."

"I'm not one of them," he said—so firmly that I had to press him on it.

"Really? And what will you tell your friends or your parents when I meet them? What will you say when they ask if I have a job?"

Mentally, I cringed. *Way to scare him off, Barbara. Why not just run out and pick up wedding invitations?*

"I'd tell them that I'm dating this incredible girl who lost her parents her freshman year of college and worked her butt off at conventional jobs to pay for school, but it wasn't enough. So she finally took a friend up on her offer to come work with her. She makes a mint taking off her clothes at parties, and probably makes more money now than she will when she becomes a topnotch doctor."

My mouth had fallen open. "How—how do you know all that?"

"Sammy's my roommate."

Why didn't I know this? Sammy and I were friends—I'd been to Sammy's a few times—I'd never seen Brandon there. I definitely would have remembered that!

Did I ever mention my crush on Brandon to Sammy? I didn't think so—I didn't even know she knew him, what with her being in law school. "I don't know what to say."

"Say you'll go to dinner with me on Friday night."

"Oh, Brandon, I don't know."

He laughed. "I am boring, aren't I?"

I couldn't help but smile. "You're not. Honest. I'm just—I'm just worried."

"Worried? About what?"

"After last night—"

"Last night was *incredible.*"

My cheeks heated. "That's just it. I don't want you to get the wrong impression, Brandon."

"Like?"

"On the whole, I'm a good girl." My *goodness, did I just say that?* There I was, a twenty-two-year-old woman describing myself as a "good girl."

"I know that, Barbara," he said softly.

"Do you? Do you really? Because even though you've seen me naked already, I'd want to take it slowly with you. I'd *need* to take it slowly."

"Darn. I was hoping for a repeat performance tonight."

It took me a second to realize he was joking. I let out a sigh of relief.

"Why'd you kiss me last night? Sammy said you never did that before—that it's actually against the rules and that you could get fired for it."

My cheeks had to be bright red. I took another sip of my latte; I was glad it was cooler by then. "Honestly?"

"Of course."

"Because I wanted to. Because I figured that once you saw me as a stripper you'd never want to date me. Because if that was going to be the only time I was ever going to be able to kiss you, then I was going to do it."

His eyes softened; the blue deepened. "I didn't think it was possible."

"What?"

"To like you more than I already do."

My heart melted. "You barely know me," I whispered.

"I'm realizing that I'm going to enjoy getting to know all of you."

I raised an eyebrow.

He laughed. "I mean that in a purely non-physical way."

Amazingly, I believed him.

"Since we're being honest," he said, "there's something I should probably tell you."

"What's that?"

"About last night . . . ."

I held my breath.

"You—"

"What?"

"I set it up with Sammy. I'm the one who hired you."

"What? Why?"

"First off, look at you. You're the best birthday present I've ever gotten."

I couldn't help my embarrassment.

"Second," he said, "I couldn't just walk up to you and say 'Hi, Barbara; I know you're a stripper, will you go out with me?' You probably would have run screaming in the other direction."

He was right. I would have.

"But if you knew I knew . . .?"

I saw his point and smiled. "What time on Friday?"

He smiled. "Seven?"

"You're not going to have a problem with my job?" I asked. I still needed the money.

"Are you going to be kissing anyone else?"

Feeling somewhat shy, I shook my head.

"Then, no. I can't say I won't be jealous of men looking at you, but I'll be proud, too."

"Proud?"

"Yes. Proud of how hard you work to get what you want."

I realized then that it was going to be hard to take this relationship slowly, considering how I was feeling for him. "Okay, then. We can give it a shot."

"Can I walk you home?" he asked.

I nodded.

As we walked out of the coffee shop, he said, "I know you want to take things slowly, Barbara, but do you think you'll ever . . . you know—do that for me again? What you did last night? Because it *really* was amazing."

I smiled at him, gazed into his eyes. "I'm sure that by your next birthday, Brandon, you'll get . . . a second kiss." THE END

SEX WITH A STRANGER
Was He My Husband Or Not?

If only I had known. My God, if only I had known!

But I didn't, and when I pulled into the parking lot that day, I had no idea my life was about to be irrevocably changed. The course of events that unfolded was so unexpected, so unbelievable, so bizarre, that to this day I still have a hard time understanding it. I didn't know. Honestly, I didn't know! If I had, things would have been much different. Nothing seemed out of the ordinary except the motorcycle parked on the lawn, right beside the "Stay Off The Grass" sign. The big Harley Davidson Chopper with its high handlebars, the jet black paint job with orange and white flames on the side, the little plastic Virgin Mary dangling from a key chain—everything about it seemed out of place, but how was I to know that the man who owned it would play such a pivotal role in my life? No one could have known. Except him. And he wasn't telling. He was just waiting. Stalking. Preparing to pounce.

I said hello to a neighbour as I fumbled for my keys. Everything seemed normal until the door opened unexpectedly and my husband, wearing only his bathrobe, greeted me with a beaming smile.

"Daniel!" I said with surprise, putting the keys back into my purse, "I didn't expect you home this early. You usually work until eight on Fridays."

He smiled again and suddenly produced a bouquet of flowers from behind his back.

"Oh!" I exclaimed, accepting the flowers and kissing Daniel on the cheek. "You haven't given me flowers since before we were married. What a pleasant surprise!" I kissed my husband again. "Have you been fooling around on me, or something? They say flowers and candy are signs of a guilty conscience."

He smirked and I could tell his feelings were hurt.

"I'm sorry," I said. "Just joking."

I felt terrible at having upset him. Especially as we had been going through some rough times lately. Daniel and I had fallen madly in love, dated only three months, then gotten married a year and a half ago. From the start, we both wanted a family and made love frequently without protection. After the first few months, we started "trying" to have a baby: charts on my cycle, thermometers, even lovemaking whenever he could - but no luck. Eight weeks before I set my eyes on that motorcycle for the first time, we went to a fertility expert and were informed that because of a problem with Daniel's reproductive system, we might never be able to have a child together. The doctor said that even with the most up-to-date technology, there was still only a "slim chance" we could conceive. He did, however, not rule out the possibility that it could happen, even without any kind of medical intervention.

Daniel was devastated! So was I, yet I tried not to show it.

I told Daniel we could adopt and that, ultimately, there was a chance, no matter how slim, that we could do it ourselves. Daniel was not appeased. He withdrew into a shell, avoided lovemaking and became more distant. Even though he always protected his privacy to a degree, it got to the point where he literally did not touch me, make eye contact or speak about anything but the most mundane matters. That went on and on. I got frustrated, we had a major argument, and he slept on the couch for the last three weeks. Now, when I saw the flowers, I knew he was extending a peace offering. I accepted gladly and made a big deal over it by putting the flowers in my favorite vase and sitting it on our bedroom dresser, right beside our wedding picture.

"Can we make love?" I blurted out, desperately wanting to be close with my husband and to forget, in our thoughtless dance of passion on the marriage bed, words like "infertile," "lazy sperm," and "slim chance."

"Make love to me, Daniel!" I said, opening up to the man I loved. I kissed him and he seemed stiff, as if debating whether or not to accept my offer. "Talk to me!" I exclaimed, irritated that he had not spoken a single word since I came home.

He raised his right index finger into the air, then walked into the living room and returned with the notepad and pen we kept by the phone. He wrote something and handed it to me.

I read the words: "Can't talk."

"What?" I asked, staring at him. "What do you mean you 'can't talk?'"

He took the pad, wrote on it, then handed it to me.

I read his words: "Phil at work bet me fifty dollars that I could not go one full day without saying a word. He says it's impossible for a car salesman to keep quiet that long."

I laughed. "You can talk to your wife. I won't tell."

He wrote: "But I would know. That would be cheating. Nothing I hate worse than a cheater."

I never heard him say that he specifically disliked cheaters before, but I accepted that he wanted to win the bet fair and square, particularly since Phil usually took his money at 9-ball when they played on Tuesdays evenings.

"By the way," I asked, smiling, "if you agreed not to say a word, are you still allowed to write words? Seems like a grey area."

He wrote on the pad: "He never said anything about writing."

"Okay," I said, "I guess we'll have to get on without you speaking." I paused. "Alright, Mr. Strong and Silent, it's time for you and me to make a little whoppie." I hugged him. "Honey, I know things have been a little tough lately, but I love you very - "

He put his index finger over my lips and shook his head so that I would speak no more. Then he led me into the bedroom. He wanted to make love, and I was more than willing. Daniel unbuttoned my blouse and folded back the silky red material. With uncharacteristic smoothness, he unhooked my bra in the back and slipped the soft white lace upwards, releasing my heavy, excited breasts. Then his mouth was on me, ravenously kissing me until the pleasure was a torture from which I had no desire to escape. Each kiss and touch were like little shocks that swept through me and transported my body on a magic carpet ride of sensual delight.

"Stop!" I finally said, pulling away, my bosom damp and tingling. "What's gotten into you? You're an animal tonight!"

Daniel ignored my words. His warm, soft eyes melted me to the core and I did not resist when he pulled me close, peeling off my blouse and bra. In a flash he was behind me, kissing my neck, nibbling my arms and fondling my breasts. I groaned and hardly noticed his hands slide down, so strong was the erotic fog into which I had been willingly swallowed. I stepped out of my slacks, then felt him kissing down my back as he liberated me from my panties. Never had I been so keenly aware of my own nakedness, and never had I so deeply enjoyed the drunken lust surging through my smouldering body.

"I don't have any clothes on," I said flirtingly, stepping back, facing him and covering myself with my hands.

He pulled my hands away and devoured me with his eyes, seeking out every curve and hidden crevice.

I put my hands back over myself. "You're usually too shy for this," I said. "We always do it with the lights off or under the blankets."

To my surprise he stripped naked and stood in front of me. No shame or embarrassment crossed his face. He was brazen and immodest. I wasn't use to that behaviour, but I liked it. And I liked looking at him, his firm body oozing masculinity and sexiness. He sat on the bed and his manhood showed strong and powerful, ready for any adventure its owner might embark upon. I found myself extremely aroused. Of late, I had been fantasizing about being an exotic dancer, writhing on the floor and driving men to drink. But those were only fantasies and I never imagined I might one day act like a stripper. Never until now. Daniel encouraged me with his gestures. I danced hot and sexy, gradually loosening up in the bawdy foreplay. Soon I was the queen of sex, showing no inhibitions or modesty as I moved in a way that I thought would make Daniel blush. But he didn't. With his fiery eyes he encouraged me to go further and further. It was scaldingly erotic and I let myself go.

Just looking at me drove him to distraction, but whenever I moved, his eyes half-closed and he could not turn away. Now I remembered what it felt like to be lusted after by him, to be wanted with such an aching need that his energy stood painfully rigid and ready to erupt during the dance of love. The moment had arrived, so I ran with it. The more I whirled and twisted, showing off every inch of my steaming body, the more he groaned and stared with hypnotic attraction. It was so liberating.

Finally he could stand it no longer and pulled me against himself, touching me all over and exploring me until the pleasure became so intense I thought I might explode like a bomb in his lap. Then he laid down on the bed, pulling me on top and thrusting forward until we were joined in union, driving each other to the edge of a cliff, only to retreat momentarily before again surging in a mad, intoxicated dance of body on body, woman on man. Suddenly the song, *One*, by Metallica came on the radio. Daniel disliked heavy metal, but instead of turning it off, he reached over and turned it up. That shocked me, but after months of no surprises, I was ready for all my husband could dish out. We danced rhythmically and the music raged on. When the hard-driving guitar solo played, Daniel took me like an animal, a sex machine. He reminded me of The Terminator. I rolled over, pulled him on top of me, wrapped my legs around his slender waist and we mated in shameless ecstasy. He stiffened, paused momentarily, then pulled me hard against him and held tight. I accepted his tremendous man energy. We clung like lovers in a dangerous time until he, spent and exhausted, uncoupled and rolled off with a groan.

"You were great!" I said, feeling like a beautiful woodland nymph. "I loved it! That was the best ever."

I put on my long red housecoat and walked out to the kitchen for a drink. Suddenly I noticed the phone off the hook. I put it back on and a minute later heard it ring. I was going to answer it when Daniel, still naked, waved me off. At first I thought nothing of it, then I remembered his vow of silence. I turned to go back to the phone when he suddenly spoke into the receiver.

"Hello," he said in a voice I had never heard before.

It was not my husband's voice. It was deeper, huskier. Absolutely without question, Daniel's voice was different! I froze, unable to understand what was going on. My mouth drooped open and my heart seemed to pound irregularly.

"No, she's not here yet," said my husband in a voice not his own. "You tried to call and the phone was off the hook? Sorry. Must have put it back on wrong after I called you today." He paused and looked me in the eyes. "I'll have her call you the second she arrives, Danny. Oh, wait! I think I hear something. Yes, she's at the door. I'll tell her you want her. Can you hold? . . . Good."

He waited about thirty seconds, then passed me the phone.

"Hello," I said in a confused voice, feeling as if I had just awakened from a vivid dream.

"Susan!" exclaimed my husband on the phone. "I know you're a little shell-shocked. It was wrong of me to keep this secret, but as you can see, my twin brother is paying us a visit."

My jaw dropped, and the world stopped turning. I felt drunk, as if things were happening too quickly for me to comprehend them. It all started making sense. The bike—it belonged to him, the brother. My "best ever" lover. This stranger stood naked not ten feet from me, picking his tooth in the mirror. What to do? Scream? If Daniel found out another man touched me, he would leave. I knew him too well to doubt it. He was a good man, but possessive. He often told me that if another man kissed me, and I kissed back, he could never touch me again. If he felt that way about a kiss, how would he feel about the track meet I had just experienced with his brother? I had to keep it secret.

"Susan," he said sharply, "are you there?"

My body still glowed from the wild sex. "Yes," I said, my head spinning so much that I nearly fell over. I tried to sound humorous and nonchalant. "This is quite a shocker, Daniel! H-e-l-l-o. Not a couple minutes ago I never knew you had a identical twin brother. Any other minor details you forgot to mention? Not wanted by the FBI or anything, are you?"

"Listen," Daniel said, "I have to tell you something."

"Yes," I murmured, still hardly making sense of what was going on before me.

"You alright, Susan?" he asked. "You don't sound too well."

"I'm fine." I cleared my throat. "Just overwhelmed."

"I should have told you this before, but somehow the right time never arose," he apologized. "There's no avoiding it now, though. My brother called today and asked if we could talk."

The brother casually walked into the bedroom, his tight butt slowly disappearing around the corner.

"Why didn't you tell me this?" I asked.

"Ten years ago my brother and I had—how shall I say it—an abrupt parting of the ways. We haven't spoken since. I thought we'd go to our graves without making up, but apparently he wants to reconcile."

This madness was starting to make sense.

"And you never had a chance to tell me about him?" I asked incredulously, feeling a hot flush of anger at the omission. "Never told me he was coming here?"

"He just phoned today," Daniel explained, "no more than two hours ago and asked if he could stay the weekend while passing through. I called the super and told him to let Mark in, then I called you at work, but you had already left. Mark rang me after he got into our apartment, but when I called back later to talk to you, I kept getting busy signals. I wanted to come home, but Phil's at that seminar and Ted the prick wouldn't let me go."

Suddenly, in a flash, such as when you wake up from a terrible dream and begin to orient yourself, I realized that Mark had intentionally left the phone off the hook. He didn't want us to be disturbed! Disturbed? Us? I had just made animal love with a complete stranger! With my husband's own brother! I felt sick to my stomach.

Keep it secret at all costs! I ordered myself.

"Susan, talk to me."

"I don't know what to say." I paused. "I only just met your brother, but he seems like a nice guy."

"We used to be very close. But . . ." He hesitated. "Anyway, I've got a feeling things may turn out for the best. Mark seems more grown up now. He's got a good job as a welder and even earned some kind of degree in media. Apparently he wants to go work in the oil fields of northern Alberta, Canada, save enough money, then come back south and open his own radio station. He's got balls, you gotta say that."

Yes, you're right there, I thought.

"I want him to stay the weekend."

Mark came out of the bedroom wearing black leather pants, high black boots and no shirt. He walked up and stood beside me, light from the window on his perfect body. A tattoo was clearly visible on his back, on the left shoulder blade, near the spine. I looked more closely. It was a fake wound and a bloody knife with the word 'Revenge' scrawled on the handle. After awhile, he slowly put on his white t-shirt in front of me, his tired muscles rippling.

"Seems like a real gentleman," I said into the phone while biting my lip. "We haven't spoken more than a few words yet, but I'm sure he is the finest kind. He is your brother, after all."

"Right," said Daniel. "Susan?"

"Yes."

"He's the only blood I have left. Be nice to him, okay."

If only you knew how nice I've been, I thought.

"Be nice to him for my sake, alright," Daniel requested. "I'll be home soon as I can."

"Okay," I said, trying to sound upbeat.

"Love you."

"Love you, too."

The moment I put down the phone, I turned to Mark and felt like killing him. "You son of a bitch! Who do you think you are?"

He gave me a cocky grin. "Your lover."

"You're no lover of mine. I could charge you with rape."

He smirked. "You liked it."

"That's not the point."

"It certainly is the point. And I have videotape proof that you loved it."

"What!" I exclaimed, feeling faint. "What the hell are you talking about?"

He walked into the bedroom, then returned a couple minutes later carrying a metal carrying case and a video camera. "Before you came, I set up this camera behind the curtain and taped our whole tryst." He grinned like a Cheshire cat.

"Oh, my God!" I exclaimed, realizing he was telling me the truth. I tried to grab the case from him but he was much too big and strong to overpower. "Give it to me!"

"I already did."

"You bastard!" I snapped, snarling at him. "Give me the freakin' tape!"

"No." He put the camera in the case and locked it.

I stepped back. "I can't believe this. Why have you done this to us? Daniel will never forgive me."

"Never tell him."

"I can't lie to my husband."

"If you say nothing, that is not a lie."

"It's a lie by omission."

"Well, do what you have to do. But we both know Danny has always been a possessive man. If you tell him, he'll divorce you so fast your head will spin. Guaranteed, he will never touch you again because you're sloppy seconds now. He won't talk to you, he won't be in the same room with you, he won't even allow himself to think about you. You will be spoiled goods. Yesterday's news . . . But do what you have to do, Susan."

"Damn you to hell!"

"You are damned too, my dear. We committed this sin together."

"This would not have happened if you had told me who you were, or even if I knew you existed."

"That is your husband's fault. He should have told you about me and how he stabbed me in the back."

"I didn't do this willingly!" I insisted. "You tricked me!"

"You loved it."

I felt like screaming at the top of my lungs, but I just wanted this over with. The only thing in the way was that tape. It could come back to haunt me. I suddenly lunged at the case, grabbed it, but it was locked with heavy clasps and Mark wrestled it away from me. He laughed in my face.

"Why did you tape us if you didn't plan on telling him?" I asked, my hair a mess as I tried to regain my balance and breath. The world was crumbling before my eyes. "Why?"

"Leverage. If you don't do as I ask, I will give it to him. Maybe an anniversary present."

"What do you mean? 'Leverage' for what?"

"You must do as I ask or . . ."

"This is blackmail," I asserted. "That's a felony."

"Open your housecoat," he said, stepping back to get a better view.

"No."

"Strong willed. I like that." He stared into my eyes. "Open your housecoat."

"I don't take orders from you."

"Honey," he said with a grin, patting his case, "you were a cat in heat on this tape. Daniel won't give a damn what you say. All he'll see is his dearly beloved doing the dirty with his own brother. You'll be history. Out on the street." He lifted his eyebrows. "Open your housecoat."

"I love my husband. He needs to know the truth. I can't allow you to hold this over my head. I'll tell him when he gets home."

"He will hate you. Your marriage will be over. But it's your decision, Susan. You can ruin your life if you wish."

"Who are you trying to convince, you or me?" I leveled a hard look at Mark. "Is this some kind of sick joke to you?"

He shrugged and headed to the door. "I'll send him the tape on your anniversary. I swear it." He touched the door knob. "Good bye."

"You're a real bastard!"

"That means your husband is a bastard too." He looked at me very sternly. "Make an informed decision, Susan." He paused. "Open your housecoat and show me your naked body."

"I think you've seen more than enough already."

"I'm not playing games with you anymore," he threatened. "Do it or else."

"Or else what?" I shot back in a challenging tone. "You've already ruined my life."

"No one needs to know. This is our secret."

"Oh, I get it. You want more. Not going to happen!"

"I just want to see you, darling. You already wore me out in bed."

"Yeah, right," I said with a sneer, turning my back to him and walking towards the bedroom.

"Good bye, sis."

I quickly turned. "I really don't think you're leaving."

"Good bye, sis. It's been a pleasure."

"Fine," I said, steaming. "Like I care."

He suddenly started laughing, walked into the living room and sat on the couch. "Actually, I think I'll stay for awhile and enjoy more of your hospitality. Daniel invited me for the weekend and I wouldn't want to be unfriendly."

"Now I know why he never mentioned you."

"No, actually you don't know."

"Well, I know enough."

"You know nothing."

"I know it will take a long time for us to get over this situation, but he loves me and in the end he will hate you even more." I glared at him. "You know, I really don't care what happened to your relationship, but it must have been bad for you to do this to him, and to me."

"Your husband, my brother, stabbed me in the back and ruined my life, that's all." He smiled falsely. "No biggie."

"So, you thought you would return the favor?"

"Precisely."

"Thanks alot, brother-in-law. Nice meeting you, too."

"Do you want me to leave?"

I thought about it for a short while and knew what had to be done. "Daniel will know something is wrong if you're not here when he gets home. You'll have to stay, at least to say hi and that you've been called away on business or something. Then leave."

"Think he'll know you just gave me the ride of my life?"

My eyes narrowed and I could feel my blood pressure rising. "If I had a gun, I might shoot you right now."

"That would look good," he said. "Tell the truth and I can see it now, camera crews from CNN and the big networks setting up outside your apartment twenty-four/seven. 'Woman has wild sex with twin brother, then kills him.' It's *Movie Of The Week*. You'll be on all the talk shows, covers of tabloid magazines. You'll be one of those celebrities like Darva Conger and Rick Rockwell from *Who Wants To Marry A Millionaire* . . . And don't forget the tape. The question of what actually happened here will take fourteen years and the Supreme Court to decide. You know how Daniel loves his privacy. You'll never have privacy or freedom again. You'll be rats in a cage."

The description surpassed dreadful. "What do you want?"

"Open your housecoat."

"Not that again." I knew he was determined, and that he held all the cards. "If I do, do you just want to look and not touch?"

"Yes."

I hesitated and thought to myself: Why am I even considering this? This is crazy!

"Come on, honey. It's the right thing to do."

"It's a pile of bullshit!" I cried angrily.

"Do it."

"You're a pervert."

"Do it."

"I'm not going to do you any favors. If you want it, come and get it yourself." Mark walked up to me and reached out to untie the belt securing my housecoat. He was oblivious to everything around him as he touched the belt. I reared off and slapped his face. He jumped back, eyes flashing, then smiled insidiously. "Bitch!" he said.

"I take that as a compliment coming from you."

He continued to rub his cheek. "That settles it, sis. I'm definitely staying the weekend now."

"I don't care what you do, just stay away from me." I paused when a little gremlin, lurking somewhere in the back of my brain, asked me if there was time to have sex with him again before Daniel got home. I was mad at myself for even thinking such a despicable thought. "What happened can't be changed," I told him, "and you do have me over a barrel, but you can't stop me from hating you."

"Want to hear something really incredible?"

"What?" I asked with aggravation.

"As we stand here, my little Olympic swimmers are having a race up the Susan River to a little egg hiding in your nest. Isn't that a comforting thought?"

"Oh, my God!" I thought.

"I went to a fertility clinic ten days ago," he said, "and had my seed tested. The technician said I was 'rich.' She joked that a woman could get pregnant by standing downwind of me. You probably have a race going on down there between five hundred million athletes, but only one," he paused dramatically, "will win the gold medal."

"Oh, my God!" I shrieked, almost feeling them inside me. "I'm ovulating right now."

"I know."

"What?" I asked, shocked by his words. "How do you know that?"

"I know everything, Susan. For the last three months I've had a private investigator watching you and Daniel. Your schedules, your routines. I knew Phil went to the seminar and Daniel would have to cover for him. My man even hired a hacker to get your records from the fertility clinic. Right now, you are in your most fertile period."

My heart literally seemed to miss a beat. "I am done talking with you," I stammered. "You are the biggest pig I ever met."

I walked into the bedroom, locked the door and changed into fresh clothes. When I finished, I came out half-hoping Mark would be gone, but half-fearing that if he was, I would have to check the mail everyday for that damned tape. He sat on the couch drinking a beer with his feet on the coffee table. He ignored me and I was about to lose it, to scream and tell him to get out and never come back when the door opened and Daniel rushed in, his face brimming with life. Mark seemed shocked. He jumped off the couch, paused a split second, then put out his hand. Daniel pushed it aside and hugged his brother hard, their faces on each other's shoulders. They tried to talk and look at each other, but then put their heads back down on each other's shoulders and started whimpering. Tears welled in their eyes. They hugged for a long time, whispered things to each other, then stepped back, both looking at the floor before glancing into each other's eyes.

They apologized for having taken so long to mend their differences, then they shook hands and patted each other on the shoulder. Looking at them side by side, I was amazed at how identical they were. It was impossible to tell them apart. They made small talk for a few minutes and then Mark turned to me.

"I just met your lovely wife," he said. "She's a fine woman."

"Yes, she is," Daniel agreed, gazing at me with pride. "I have always been able to count on her through thick and thin."

"So," Mark said awkwardly, "where should I stay, Danny?"

"Looks like couch duty," he said.

Mark laughed. "Hey, I've slept in worse places. Remember the time we went rafting and stayed overnight at that religious commune?"

"The weird music!" Daniel said excitedly, his smile returning after being gone for weeks. "Six o'clock in the morning. Woke the damned roosters up!"

Mark laughed heartily. "The sand flies were the worst. They bit all night." He looked at me. "Did my brother ever tell you about that?"

"No," I said listlessly, turning my back to him.

"Susan," said Daniel, "try to be more civil. Mark is just being friendly."

I bit my tongue.

Daniel moved towards the kitchen. "Cold one, brother?"

"Make it two and you got a deal," he said.

Daniel got the beers and spoke to Mark for twenty minutes; I wandered away to do chores. When Mark went to the bathroom, Daniel bore down on me.

"Try to open up a bit," he whispered.

"I don't really like your brother," I said back in a hushed voice.

"What! You don't even know him."

"Something about him gets on my nerves."

"Well, for my sake, try to be friendlier."

No sooner had he spoken those words than Mark came out and started packing his things.

"What's going on?" Daniel asked, hurrying to him.

"I better leave."

"You just got here."

"I know, Danny, but I don't feel welcome." He looked at me. "It's no big deal. I'll grab a motel room for the weekend, but maybe we could have a game of pool tomorrow."

Daniel was visibly upset and pulled the bag out of Mark's hand. Then he grabbed the carrying case with the tape inside and put everything in a closet. "My brother is not sleeping in any motel. You're staying here with us."

"I don't want to intrude," Mark said with an imploring look. "It's not a problem, really."

"You're staying!" Daniel insisted, leaving no room for dispute. "You're my brother, for God's sake!"

Mark looked at me. "Only if it's alright with her."

Daniel looked at me.

"Alright," I agreed, "he is welcome here if you want him to stay the weekend."

Daniel sighed. "Good. That settles it."

"I'll stay if you make me one promise," Mark said to his brother.

"Anything."

"You have to work tomorrow, don't you?"

"Yep. Phil is out until Monday."

"Okay," Mark said, "I will stay, but to prove there are no hard feelings on anyone's part, I want to take Susan for a ride on my bike tomorrow while you're at work. If she agrees, I will stay."

I was going to tell him to forget it, that I would not ride with him if he were the last man on earth, but I could instantly tell that Daniel not only wanted me to accept the terms, he needed me to agree. For some reason, beyond the fact that he had been estranged from his brother for ten years, it was crucial to him that I go for the ride with his brother. He looked at me and I knew what he wanted. Mark looked at me. I felt like the girl in Michael Jackson's Thriller video who suddenly notices herself surrounded by ghouls with nowhere to run.

"Alright, Daniel," I said, faking a smile, "I'll go for a little ride on his bike if it means so much to you."

Daniel kissed me and Mark thanked me. I went out shopping for the evening and gave the brothers time alone, but I could feel Mark's swimmers heading towards their destination. Or, being Daniel's identical twin, was it possible he too had "lazy sperm" and had lied to me about his virility? Would there be no repercussions from our bedroom romp? Those thoughts swirled in my mind and totally distracted me. Only when I realized it was late did I go home. The brothers were still talking, discussing old times, having a beer and enjoying each other's company. I had the impression that Mark was sincerely drawing closer to Daniel, though I didn't stick around and went to bed. Late at night, when Daniel crawled in beside me, I kissed him and told him I needed to make love with him. I couldn't bear knowing his brother was the last man to take me. He was reluctant, particularly since Mark was just outside our room on the couch, but he eventually came around and we quietly made love. After harvesting his seed, I kissed him and rolled over. My mind raced and I couldn't shut it down, but I eventually fell asleep in the early morning hours..

When I awoke, it was 9 am and Daniel had already gone to work. I smelled coffee, bacon and eggs. After putting on a long, loose dress, I went into the kitchen and found Mark hovering over the stove.

"Good morning," he said pleasantly. "I made you breakfast."

"Please give me the tape," I pleaded.

Without a word, he retrieved the locked case, took out the tape and handed it to me. I was shocked at the easy exchange. To verify it was in fact the tape, I went into my bedroom, locked the door, and played it on the VCR. Within seconds there was no doubt. I almost didn't recognize the wanton, sex-crazed woman who performed like a porn actress. To my dismay, I watched the tape longer than I needed to, then ejected it and proceeded to the basement where I threw it into the incinerator. I waited until the thing was melted into nothingness.

"I didn't think you would give it up so easily," I said to Mark when

I returned. "Why the change of heart?"

He placed a plate in front of me with bacon, eggs and toast. Then he poured me a cup of coffee. "You promised to go for a ride with me today. Do you keep your promises?"

"I always keep my promises to Daniel."

"Good. We'll leave after breakfast, okay?"

"As you wish," I said flatly.

After breakfast, Mark did up the dishes while I, for some unknown reason, put on my make-up and tried to look my best. We didn't speak as we left the apartment or as we approached the big Harley Davidson. Mark climbed on first, fired up the motor and I stepped back, shocked by its low and aggressive pitch, its animal rumble, its almost lifelike presence. But I had promised, so I climbed on behind him in the "bitch seat." Within seconds we were moving forward and I was impressed by the machine's power and how it vibrated beneath me like a living creature. Mark handled the strong beast with ease, controlling it like John Wayne rode his horse in old westerns. We reached the highway and he opened it up. The wind in my hair, the speed, the freedom, my arms around his waist everything combined and mingled into a feeling of intensity, of excitement, of unspoken sensual heat. This man, identical to the man I had fallen in love with at first sight, could turn the heads of women. He was the best lover I ever had. But he had tricked me and I would not forget, not forgive.

We drove to a quiet lake in the countryside and he brought his big machine to a stop. I climbed off, the vibration of his mammoth steed still reverberating in my loins. Would he try to seduce me again? I had loved the sex he gave me, but I would die before submitting. I would never tell Daniel what happened that day, but I would be faithful henceforth. Truth is, even though I had not purposely cheated on my husband, I felt an overwhelming and unremitting sense of guilt. I had enjoyed the sex. Loved it. Even now, after knowing, I still felt warm inside and was aroused by memories of Mark's heated passion. But like an addict who gives up that which attracts her the most, I would never taste the drug of his love again. Never. No matter what he tried or what course he took, he would never have me that way again.

"Walk with me?" he asked, looking into my eyes.

"If it's just a walk you want."

"Just a walk," he said.

We walked along the lake's edge and stopped to watch a duck swimming with her ducklings. He sat at a picnic table; I sat on the other side.

"I always wanted a family," he suddenly said, watching the ducks.

"I find that hard to believe. You look like a rebel."

Mark shook his head. "Not a rebel. Loner, maybe, but not a rebel. I'm a welder and pipe fitter. I go to work everyday, pay my bills, never look for trouble. Even went back to school and got a certificate." He paused and took a deep breath. "I loved a girl once." He turned to me. "She was the only woman I ever loved."

"What happened?" I asked, feeling his depth of emotion swelling forth.

"Daniel and I lost our parents early," he began, turning back to the lake, "and granddad raised us. All through our young lives we had only each other and I loved Daniel as my brother and my friend; I would have died to save his life. But then Kate came along and stole my heart. I loved her so much it hurt." Tears glistened in his eyes. "Before he died, my granddad built a bed for me with his own hands. I slept in it every night. One day, after my grandfather died, I caught Daniel and Kate in that bed together. They were kissing, making love."

My heart raced at this news, but I let Mark continue.

"Not only had she betrayed me, so had Daniel. He was my brother, my blood, my friend, my twin. But he stabbed me in the back. And in that bed! I could never sleep in it again. So he laughed nervously I lost not only the one woman I ever loved, I lost my brother, my best friend, and the last thing granddad ever made for me. I left and it took ten years for us to meet again. The rest is history, all of which you are keenly aware." He paused. "Do you understand how I hated him?"

I looked down at the ground. "I think I understand."

"Revenge is a mighty force, Susan. It is overpowering, all-consuming. For these last ten years I have boiled, waiting like a coiled snake for the moment to strike."

"And how do you feel now?"

"Once tasted," he said, a tear rolling down his cheek, "revenge is not always so sweet."

"Let's not talk about it any more. It's depressing."

"Thing is," Mark said, ignoring me, "that the lust for revenge drove me all these years. After I tricked you, I still felt angry - like he owed me something more, a pound of flesh maybe. But once I saw him, I remembered all the good times we had and how we had depended on each other. I found myself wishing we could go back in time." He took a deep breath. "I'd like to have a relationship with him again and I think I should tell him what I did to you."

"No!" I snapped. "It must be a secret forever. Must be!"

He looked at the duck and ducklings. "I wanted to marry Kate and have a family with her, but that dream died on the bed granddad made for me. Revenge, it's a funny thing. Instead of trying to find another woman to raise a family with, I ended up trying to destroy yours."

"You didn't destroy it. I still love him. I will always love him. Only him."

"I envy you."

I felt compassion for this man even though I hated no man more. "What will you do?"

"I'll work in Alberta a few years, save every cent I can, then come back someday. Maybe me and Daniel can be friends again." He looked at me. "Would you mind if I came back someday, or do you want me to stay away forever?"

I did not answer for over a minute. "I want my husband to be friends with his brother again. I would like to see you come back someday."

"Sorry you got caught in the crossfire, Susan."

"Take me home now, Mark."

We drove back to the apartment. Mark called Daniel on the phone and told him something came up and he had to leave right away. I watched out the window as he pulled out of the parking lot and headed north. A few weeks later, he called from Alberta and asked if Daniel could fly up and come fishing with him for a few days, apparently his new company offering to cover all costs.

"I'd love to!" my husband said with undisguised enthusiasm. "But we'll have to do it soon. Susan and I just found out today that we're going to have a baby! A baby!" He paused. "Mark, I've never been happier in my life. I want you to be the godfather."

"I would be honored," he said to his brother. "Congratulations, papa." THE END

CURSED BY CUPID?

Everything was absolutely perfect.

I'd rushed home from the office, cursing the heavy traffic all the way. I spent an hour in the kitchen, sweating over a hot stove. Then I hurried through showering and changing into my favorite dressy-casual outfit—black leggings, ballerina flats, and an oversized jade green tunic. With a few minutes to spare, I'd carefully set my tiny dining room table with Grandma Jackson's creamy linen, gleaming silver, and Queen Anne china. Then I added a small nosegay of red rosebuds in the crystal vase she'd given me for my twenty-fifth birthday, and flanked it with two white tapers in the matching candlesticks. I checked on the thick, juicy steaks and baked potatoes keeping warm in the oven, tossed a crisp green salad and put it in the fridge next to the chocolate mousse I'd prepared the night before, and I was done.

By six o'clock, I was subtly made-up and perfumed, my long brown hair loose on my shoulders, waiting.

There was just one tiny problem—my boyfriend, Will, was nowhere in sight!

By six-thirty, I was worried. At seven-fifteen, I started to get a bit upset. Will was the nicest guy I'd ever dated, by far. Had he waited until our third Valentine's Day together to let his inner jerk shine through?

I couldn't believe it, but by eight o'clock, it seemed pretty likely.

I blew out the candles, tossed the ruined steaks into the garbage, washed my face, and changed into my usual attire for a night alone at home—comfy purple sweats and the battered bunny slippers I'd had since college. I was going to pop a movie into the DVD player, put my fuzzy feet up, and finish the chocolate mousse—let's face it, no one knew how to do Valentine's Day solo better than I did. I'd had lots of practice before I met Will. For a long time, I'd actually believed I was cursed by Cupid.

It took a while for me to notice the message light on my answering machine flashing.

Will must have called when I was in the shower!

My relief lasted all of ten seconds.

"Hi, Suzanne," Will's recorded voice said. "I'm running a little late. Gwen called, and she's having problems with her computer again. I promised her last week that I'd fix it, so . . . I'll try to finish fast and be there by seven. Bye."

Gwen. Again.

"Nice going, Mr. Romance," I muttered.

Will was a computer technician, and pathologically unable to ignore anyone's PC-related distress call. Normally I didn't have a problem with it—except when it came to the clingy woman who lived across the hall from him. How many times had Gwen spoiled our plans in the years I'd been with him? I started to count as I hunkered down and dug into the chocolate mousse.

Not just with computer woes, either. There'd been the leaky faucet in Gwen's bathtub while the superintendent had been on vacation. That had made us late for my parents' thirtieth anniversary party. Then there was the time she'd sprained her ankle and Will had to drive her to the emergency room. On *our* anniversary. Gwen's now-deceased cat had escaped from her apartment two or three times, always on Saturday night, and she seemed to have more spiders and other bugs in her place than any other ten single women I'd ever met.

There have been way too many little mishaps, a nasty voice in my head sneered. *She's out to steal your man, if she hasn't managed it already. Grow a backbone and do something about it!*

I ignored it and kept eating, refusing to cry over something I should have seen coming. There was simply nothing like chocolate to ease the pain of rejection, was there?

Will plainly preferred Gwen. He'd just taken his time letting me know it, that was all. I'd have to accept it sooner or later.

It was going to be sooner. I'd learned something from the handful of brief, rotten relationships I'd had in my early twenties, hadn't I?

Will loves you, another voice insisted. *You know he does.*

"That's why he sounded so funny," I said aloud. "He couldn't just come out and say he doesn't want to see me anymore."

The slimeball!

Sure, he could have, snapped the nastier voice. *But he didn't.*

I polished off the last of my second portion of mousse, licked the spoon, and sighed. There were two more servings in the fridge, but I already felt ill. "Easy come, easy go."

There was nothing easy about it, remember? Get off your butt and go over there, you wimp!

"Shut up!" I exclaimed. "Not an option."

Planning to spend Valentine's Day alone for the rest of your life?

"Not going to happen."

It could. You know it could. How could you forget what it used to be like for you, pre-Will?

I stared at the pair of empty parfait glasses on the coffee table and contemplated watching *Sleepless in Seattle* for about the fiftieth time.

Then I got up and started looking for my car keys. Though I traded bunny slippers for boots, I didn't stop to change the rest of my clothes.

Maybe Will was done with me. But he was going to have to tell me so—to my face.

Will's apartment was nearby, and even in the light snow that had begun to fall, driving there didn't take long. All the way, I rehearsed what I'd say and how I'd say it. Imagined myself asking Will if he was proud to be responsible for the newest crack in my often-broken heart. Pictured the look in his gentle blue eyes when I said the hurtful words.

"Take that, Will Murray!"

Then I swore to myself that I wouldn't cry, no matter what—knowing full well that it was a promise I was going to break before the night was over.

The fear I might do just that kept me sitting in the car for a while when I arrived. The snow was coming down much more heavily, swirling in an icy wind off Lake Ontario, cloaking the landscape in a thick, sparkly carpet of white.

Hiding everything ugly in the winter-bare world, making it beautiful again.

Just as my happiness with Will had made the gaps in my self-esteem invisible for a while. I'd almost forgotten they were there.

"I can't do this!" I said loudly.

What else are you going to do? Sit here and freeze to death? Gwen would love that. Ice sculpture, that's you.

I growled, snatched my keys out of the ignition, and headed inside.

I hadn't taken two steps out of the elevator before I heard Will's voice. Followed by a woman's—rich and smoky, with a faint British accent.

I froze, cursing softly.

About to turn tail and run, I hesitated for a second too long.

A petite, platinum-blonde woman in snug black jeans, gold kitten-heeled pumps, and a baby-blue cashmere pullover came out of the apartment across from Will's.

"It's working," she called.

"Great. I'll be right there," Will said.

That was when the blonde turned toward me, and I got a good look at her.

She was slim, perfectly made-up, and her silvery hair was styled in a becoming, swingy bob.

But she was also seventy-five years old if she was a day!

I felt my mouth drop open.

I was still standing there, unable to move or speak, when Will came out of his apartment.

Naturally, he saw me right away.

"Oh, thank God. I was so worried about you! I just called again." As his boyishly handsome face creased with concern, Will rushed over and pulled me into his strong arms. "Where were you?"

"Nowhere special," I said stupidly.

Will kissed me lightly, but with enough heat to steal my breath. I could see the effect the kiss had on him when he lifted his head again. His slow smile and the gleam in his eyes promised more to come, but his words were calm and measured. "Sorry, Suz. This took so much longer than I expected. But I'm glad you're here now. You can finally meet Gwen."

Slightly hysterical laughter bubbled up inside me. Along with something else—relief, joy . . . love. How could I ever have doubted him or what we had together?

"I'd like that," I said, taking the lady's hand as he made the introductions.

"You have a special young man here," Gwen told me. "A true gentleman."

"I know." I slanted him a glance as the hand Will had resting on my hip strayed a bit lower. "He's one of a kind, that's for sure."

Will grinned and led the way into Gwen's apartment. It was a mirror image of his, decorated in an eclectic blend of antiques and modern pieces. I discovered it suited her as we chatted over a cup of Darjeeling tea while Will finished working his magic on her computer. Gwen was a widow, and she'd traveled widely both before and after her marriage. Despite her age and imperfect health, she still managed to get back to England once a year to visit her son and his family, and she was quite apologetic about her continuous need for Will's help.

"I impose on him shamelessly," Gwen confessed, as he announced that he was finally finished.

"You don't impose at all." Will bent over and kissed her pale cheek. "Call me if it acts up again."

"Just not tonight," she said with a wink that made Will chuckle.

Blushing, I stood up and held out my hand. "It was good to meet you," I said.

"You too, dear. I hope we'll see each other again one of these days."

With his apartment door finally closed behind us, Will reached for me without a word. He kissed me slowly and thoroughly for a very long time, and then confessed, "I'm starving. What about you?"

I laughed and thumped his chest. "Since all I had for dinner was chocolate mousse, I could eat."

Will groaned. "You cooked?"

"I did. Now you are ordering in."

"Pizza, Thai or—?"

"Thai sounds good." I kissed him lightly. "Just don't forget the *Lahb Gai* or the sticky rice."

Will loved the spicy chicken dish as much as I did, so he nodded as he went in the kitchen to make the call.

I wandered into his living room and made myself comfortable on his couch. Idly changing channels on his big screen TV, I wished I still looked as good as I had earlier, but I doubted Will had even noticed my disreputable appearance.

If he had, it certainly hadn't affected his physical response to kissing me, which I got to experience again when we were curled up together after our meal.

"You smell nice," Will murmured, nibbling on my neck.

"I smelled—and looked—even better," I said, beginning to unbutton his shirt, "At about six o'clock."

"Stop reminding me." Will slipped one big, warm hand under my baggy sweatshirt, made an appreciative sound when he discovered my lack of bra, and curled his fingers gently around my breast. "I'm sorry, Suz. I had a big night planned, too."

"Quit apologizing and take me to bed, why don't you?"

Will bit my earlobe. "What's your hurry?"

"I've been thinking about this. . .about you. . .all day." I pulled his shirttail free of his pants and went straight for his belt buckle.

"Me too," he said in a low voice as I continued undressing him, caressing each part of his body that I uncovered with hands that shook. "Oh, Suzanne. . ."

I laughed, pleased by his unguarded response to my touch, to the slide of my lips along his bare shoulder. And I shivered in delight at the deft, no-nonsense way he reciprocated, getting me out of my sweatpants and lacy white thong in record time.

"Love me," I said quietly, as he rolled on top of me.

"I do," Will said, pulling my sweatshirt over my head and tossing it on the rug.

Joining our bodies made both of us gasp with pleasure.

I ran my fingertips slowly along his spine, savoring the shudder that rippled through him. "I love you back," I told him, wrapping my legs around his hips.

Assailed by raw sensation, I forgot everything but the sweet, sensual man in my arms for a long, long time.

After we'd finished making love, we crawled into his big bed. Will fell asleep at once, and I wasn't far behind.

I woke just before seven. Will still slept, snoring softly. I slipped quietly out of bed, retrieved my sweats and thong, and took a shower. When I was dressed, I decided to surprise my lover with coffee in bed.

I was the one who got the surprise.

I found a gift-wrapped box of white chocolate truffles, a really wilted bouquet of lavender roses, and a small blue velvet box on Will's kitchen table.

I had a big night planned, too, he'd said.

Oh my.

Was it a ring? Or just a pair of earrings?

I couldn't make myself look, even though I was desperate to know. Instead, I put the coffee on. I was cleaning up the mess from dinner the night before when Will put his arms around my middle and kissed the side of my neck.

"Good morning," he whispered.

I turned to face Will, leaning back a bit so he could kiss me. Which he did, with a lot of enthusiasm. "Oh, scratchy," I said, lifting a hand to touch his stubbly cheek as he straightened again. We rarely spent entire nights together because our schedules didn't always match up well, so I didn't get to see him stubbly very often. It was a look that made my pulse rate kick up.

"I was afraid you'd left." Will kissed me again, taking his time about it. "You're not running off, are you?"

"I'm staying for coffee." I smiled at him. "And eggs, if you want some."

Will nodded. "But I have something to ask you first."

"Does it involve serious thought?" I asked lightly.

"It might."

"Okay. I'm ready."

"I hope you are." And then, just like that, Will dropped to one knee. Right there, in front of the sink in his kitchen. From the pocket of his bathrobe, he produced the little box I'd seen on the table. "This is for you, if you want it," he said, lifting the lid.

Inside was a gorgeous, brilliant-cut, solitaire rose diamond ring. "Oh, Will," I whispered.

"I'm ready to take the next step," Will said, taking my hand. "Marry me, Suzanne?"

"Yes. Whenever you want."

"Is next Saturday too soon?" Will took the ring out of the box and managed to get it on my finger somehow. It was a perfect fit.

"Probably." I wanted to cry.

"As soon as we can." Will stood up and lifted my chin, just as my eyes brimmed. "What's wrong, love?" he asked.

"I. . .oh, Will!" I sobbed.

"I messed up again, didn't I? I knew I should have waited. Taken you someplace romantic and then asked you. Oh, Suz, don't." Will thumbed the moisture from my cheeks. "I wanted it to be special, and this was—"

"It was special," I said fiercely. "Because it was you. Asking me to be your wife. That's good enough for me."

"Then why are you crying?"

"Because I don't deserve you."

"What would make you think something like that? As far as I can tell, it's the other way around." Will looked genuinely puzzled.

"You don't understand. I was jealous. Of Gwen. I thought you were having. . . an affair with her."

"Because I kept letting you down."

I looked away. "Yes."

"She needs me. You know that."

"Yes."

"And you're going to be okay with me being late once in a while, from now on?" Will persisted.

"Of course."

"So what's the problem?"

"The problem is I came over here last night to smack you silly. . .and then take down a senior citizen!" Even as I said the words, I was starting to laugh.

Will snickered. "Really? You were going to fight her for me?"

"After I kicked your butt." I stroked his rough cheek. "I couldn't just let you go."

"Good to know, should I ever be tempted to stray."

I lifted an eyebrow. "Will you be, do you think?"

"With you at home? Never." Will kissed me. "Promise."

"Really?"

"Really. See, the thing is, most women would have freaked out over how much time I was spending with Gwen two years ago." Will kissed me again, even more slowly than before. "You're the only woman in the world for me, Suz. I've known it since the day I met you."

I believed him. The sincerity in his eyes and voice was unmistakable. I also realized then how right I'd been when I'd told Gwen that Will was one of a kind. My little crisis hadn't been about him, or Gwen, at all.

Thankfully, it was over, and our life together was about to begin.

But did I deserve him? Was he right?

As Will went off to shower and get ready for work, and I started making our breakfast with his pretty pink diamond winking on my finger, I had to wonder.

But clearly, Will thought we were perfect. . . and I couldn't argue with that! THE END

LOVE ON A DARE

His lips softened over mine, teasing and cajoling, seducing me with promise. He tasted of wine and desire. He pressed me closer, molding me to his taut frame. Fire swept up my spine and I curled my arms around his neck, lost in his heat, wanting more. Tiny sounds of pleasure I barely recognized as mine escaped me. An ache built deep inside and I forgot everything but the feel of his lips and his body. He cradled the back of my head with his hands, burying his fingers in my hair. I'd never before been kissed like this, with an urgency and expertise that turned my insides to liquid and made me forget everything but the man who held me in his arms.

Suddenly the sounds of clapping and shouts of "More! More!" rose around us, releasing me from my sensual haze. Embarrassment swirled through me and I jumped back. My breathing harsh, I stared at the man in front of me. His ragged breathing matched mine. The intensity in his deep brown eyes made me shift uncomfortably.

"What's your name?" he asked.

"I'm sorry," I managed on a shaky breath. My face burning, I hurried over to the table where my friends waited—laughing and leading the crowd into even louder claps and cheers. Calls for more kisses reverberated through the bar, filled with patrons eager to get a start on the June weekend.

"Danielle, that was great," Amy said when I reached the table. She wiped tears from her eyes. "I can't remember when I laughed so hard."

I scooped my purse from the chair where I'd left it and sent a narrowed-eyed glare around the table. "I can't believe you made me kiss a stranger in a bar."

"Stop pretending," Maddie said with a laugh. "You've been ogling him since we got here. It's your thirtieth birthday. Let loose. You wanted to kiss him. And you know you can never turn down a dare."

My friends and I had been together since kindergarten. They knew me well. Unfortunately for me, they knew I'd always been competitive. Maybe it was being raised with three brothers, but I've never met a challenge I didn't accept. And I never lost. Taking on whatever dares my brothers threw at me, I'd gotten myself into lots of scrapes growing up, to the chagrin of my parents. But I was thirty now, and kissing strange men in bars was too much, even for me.

Amy stopped laughing and looked beyond me. "I think he's going to come over."

Heart thumping, I turned around. At the bar, his friends, all part of a bachelor party, laughed and egged him on. I thought I saw money exchange hands. The jerks were placing bets! The handsome stranger walked toward me.

Despite my embarrassment, I couldn't help appreciating his good looks as he strode closer. His black T-shirt stretched over his muscular chest, and his wide shoulders tapered to a narrow waist. Black jeans rode low on his slim hips and encased his long legs. Having been in his arms, I knew he towered over me by at least a foot. His hair was cut short, but the shadow of a beard on his chiseled face gave him a dangerous look and saved him from seeming too "corporate."

He smiled when he reached me, a wide smile showing even, white teeth. My traitorous heart did a little flip. I felt another flush creep over my face.

"You don't need to be sorry," he said in a deep voice with a trace of a soft Southern accent. Humor shone from his brown eyes. "I've never had a beautiful stranger come up to me and start kissing me. I liked it."

He stood a whisper away. I inhaled his scent of spice and male and the lingering notes of the wine he'd been drinking. I was never at a loss for words, but his raw masculinity made my words stick in my throat.

Behind me, Amy snickered. I silenced her with a glare, and then turned back to the handsome stranger. "I do need to apologize," I said, finding my voice. "My friends dared me to kiss you. I'm sorry I used you like that."

"You can use me anytime," he said in a smoky voice.

His voice, his words, the appreciation in his eyes, all made my insides heat up. *What had I gotten myself into?*

"Our friend is suddenly shy," Alice said, moving closer to him. "That's not like her."

He laughed, his gaze still on me. "You didn't tell me your name."

I shook my head, squirming under his attention and the stares I felt from everyone in the bar. I hated being the center of attention, especially for pulling such a stupid stunt.

"My name isn't important," I said, clutching my purse.

"You're not married, are you?" Maddie asked him. "We didn't see a ring. We checked before we sent her over."

He shook his head. "I'm free as a bird."

"There you go," Amy said with a self-satisfied look at me. "You're both single." She turned to the handsome guy. "Since my friend isn't talking, I'll talk for her. Her name is Danielle."

"Danielle." His soft accent made my name sound beautiful, almost musical.

Heat coursed through me. Disturbed by my reaction to him, I jerked my gaze from his and looked around at my friends. "I'm out of here."

"You can't leave," Maddie said. "I'm the designated driver."

"I'll wait by the car." Grabbing my purse, I practically raced out of the bar.

The pediatric office where I was a nurse hummed on Monday morning. It seemed as if every kid in our practice had gotten ill over the weekend. My humiliation over my actions Friday night in the bar had dissipated. I wouldn't admit it to my friends, but I'd enjoyed kissing the handsome guy, and I had to acknowledge the whole incident was rather humorous. But I'd run off like some scared virgin.

I consider myself reasonably intelligent and attractive, but I've never had a long-term relationship. No man I'd dated had ever excited me very much. I usually ended up being buddies with them, like my brothers.

The guy in the bar Friday night sure didn't give me any brotherly vibes. My face heated now, remembering the sizzling kiss and my wild response.

"Danielle." Our receptionist's voice drew me out of my daydream. I turned to see the elderly woman standing by the doorway to the small office the nurses used.

"There's a guy outside with his nephew," she said. "Claims the little boy has a bad sore throat. Sounds like strep. The doc is stacked up to the rafters with patients. Do you think you can do a throat culture?"

"Sure, I'll be right out."

I tapped keys on the computer to enter the report I'd been working on, and then went out to the waiting area. A man knelt in front of a small boy I recognized as one of our patients, six-year-old Nicky Foreman. His mother, a widow, had recently remarried. The man with Nicky was wiping tears from the little boy's face with a tissue.

There was something familiar about the man's short hair and his wide shoulders. My gaze scanned him, admiring the way his white T-shirt stretched taut across his muscled back.

"Can I help you?" I asked.

He stood, jamming the used tissue into his jeans' pocket, and turned to face me. I stared into dark brown eyes. Familiar eyes. The surprise on his face turned to humor.

His full lips quirked in a grin. "We meet again, Danielle."

"Oh. My. Gosh." *How did this happen? Fate? I don't believe in fate, yet the last time I saw him we were in a bar in Philadelphia, thirty miles from my home here in Delaware. What were the chances of seeing him again? Very good, I guess.*

Nicky clung to the man's hand. The little boy looked ready to start crying again.

I quickly came around the desk and knelt in front of the frightened child. "It's okay. Don't be afraid." I straightened and turned to the man who'd brought in Nicky. I had a job to do and a little boy to take care of. "You're his uncle?"

He nodded. Worry flitted over his rugged features. "Will he be okay? I'm not used to kids. His mother, my sister, got married Saturday and I'm babysitting while she's on her honeymoon. I called her and she said Nicky gets strep throat a lot and I should bring him here."

"We'll take good care of Nicky. Don't worry. I'll check his throat and do a culture."

The tension left the handsome guy's face and he smiled. "I'm supposed to give you this." He dug into his pocket and produced a folded sheet of paper. "Here's a note from my sister giving permission to treat Nicky for any medical problems while she's away."

I took the note from him, unfolded it, read it, and then handed it back. "So you're Tara's brother?"

He nodded and held out his hand. "Adam Delancey. You know my full name. What's yours?"

"Danielle McAllister." I took his proffered hand. As we touched, something electric passed between us. I quickly pulled my hand free. He gave me a surprised look and I knew he'd felt the same kind of electricity.

"Now you know why we had the bachelor party Friday night."

At the mention of Friday night, my face heated up again. I looked away from Adam and held out a hand to Nicky. "Come on, sweetie. Let's get you fixed up." The three of us went back to the exam room.

A little later, Adam, armed with a prescription for antibiotics, held Nicky in his arms, comforting the scared little boy. "You'll be okay, big guy. We'll call your mom when we get home and you can tell her what a good boy you were at the doctor's." Nicky buried his head in Adam's neck.

"We'll have the results soon," I said. "We'll give you a call."

I turned to leave the room.

"Danielle," Adam said, stopping me.

Turning, I met his eyes. "Is there something else?"

He smiled, a bone-melting smile I felt all the way to my toes. "There is. I'd like to see you again."

"I don't know."

"You're single, right?"

I swallowed. "Yes."

"We're not exactly strangers," he said, leaning closer. "Can I call you?"

His nearness sent a delicious shiver through me. There was no reason for me to say no. But it had been only three months since I'd parted ways with the last guy I'd dated. I wasn't sure I was ready to start dating again. And Adam scared and excited me. No man had ever made my insides liquefy with such heat and need.

"Afraid?" he asked with a soft laugh.

I bristled. "Of course not."

A mischievous light came into his eyes. "I think you're a woman who likes a challenge. I dare you to go out with me for two weeks and not kiss me." He grinned. "I'll do everything I can to make you want to though. I double dare you."

My competitive juices stirred. I couldn't turn down the dare. I lifted my chin. "You're on."

It was my last date with Adam. According to the terms of our bet, if after two weeks, I'd resisted kissing him, he owed me dinner at one of Philadelphia's best restaurants. Then, he'd walk away from me. If he won, he'd have his kisses and my commitment to keep dating him. Tonight would decide the winner.

As I fixed my unruly curls into a ponytail, I thought back over the last two weeks. I'd enjoyed spending time with Adam. A lawyer, he'd left South Carolina to take a job with a Philadelphia firm to be closer to his sister, his only family. While he waited for his new apartment in Philadelphia, he was living at his sister's in Wilmington.

What would happen tonight? My insides knotted with anticipation and I studied myself in the bathroom mirror. *Ponytail looks good, makeup okay.*

As I applied a coat of soft coral lipstick, I felt the familiar pang of need whenever I thought of kissing Adam again. I wanted to kiss him. I wanted to do a lot more than that. I'd never lost a dare. But my resolve to resist him wavered with each date. He was charming, funny, and sexy. He knew what his nearness and his touch did to me and he tempted me every chance he got.

We'd waited until his sister returned from her honeymoon before going on our first date, to a trendy bistro in Philadelphia. Adam took me to Atlantic City another time, to a Phillies game, and to dinners at upscale restaurants and neighborhood diners. He'd brought me flowers and candy every time.

The doorbell rang and my pulse raced. I patted my hair and took a deep breath, then went to the door. Adam stood before me, looking gorgeous and sexy. *Not fair*, I thought, my gaze sweeping him. Dressed in tan slacks and a black T-shirt, he vibrated with a sensuality that enveloped me and made heat gather deep inside me.

He held out a bouquet of yellow roses, my favorite. I could never resist yellow roses. He was good all right. He knew how to play.

"If I could have found blue roses to match your eyes, I would have bought all they had," he said, his voice husky. His hot gaze trailed over me.

I squirmed under his close scrutiny, and looked down at my black Capri's. They were okay. No stains. *Did I have a stain on my green tank top?* I resisted the urge to run my hands down my clothes.

I raised my gaze to Adam's. His eyes lit with a sexy gleam, a gleam that met an answering awareness in me. Desire curled in my stomach. I wanted him. And he knew it. Well, I'd show him. I'd win this dare.

As I took the flowers from him, our fingers touched, sending jolts of pleasure through me. I stepped back. Holding the flowers close, I inhaled their sweet perfume, willing calmness into my body, fighting a losing battle.

I moved aside to let Adam into my apartment. My cat, Topper, sleeping on the sofa, roused from his nap and opened his green eyes.

"Hey, Topper, old boy." Adam went to the cat and stroked his head. I heard Topper's purrs across the room. He really knew how to pour it on. He even liked my cat. Gotta love a man who likes cats.

Adam had pulled out all the stops, taking me on a dinner cruise down the Delaware River. The popular cruise ship, known for its romantic lunch and dinner cruises, was crowded this July Fourth. Once darkness fell, fireworks would start in Philadelphia. We'd have a front row seat from the ship's deck.

We sat at a table in a secluded corner of the glass-enclosed dining room overlooking the river. The setting sun lit the still waters of the Delaware, bathing the usually murky river in a golden glow. The ship cut smoothly through the water, past the New Jersey shoreline, visible in the dying rays of the sun. The double spans of the Delaware Memorial Bridge loomed ahead, as if beckoning the ship closer.

Candlelight flickered on our table, the light reflecting on the white tablecloth. The shipboard buffet featured rosemary beef, smoked ham, chicken stuffed with cheese and spinach, macadamia-crusted salmon, and pasta—all worthy of the best restaurants in Philadelphia. The waiter poured us each a glass of wine from a vintage bottle of Pinot Noir, then left.

Adam picked up his wine goblet. His eyes sparked with gold fire in the candlelight. "To the most beautiful woman who ever took a dare." He grinned. "And to my winning."

I touched my glass to his. "Oh, you think so? I've never lost a dare in my life. And I don't intend to start now."

"We'll see about that," he said with a chuckle.

I picked at my food, my appetite gone. I'd resisted Adam's considerable charms for two weeks. If I won the dare, he'd be out of my life. I hated to lose, but I couldn't let Adam walk away. I needed time, but had none left.

Adam set down his fork and touched my hand where it lay on the table. "You're not eating much," he said, looking at my plate. Then he smiled, a wicked, knowing smile that raised my pulse a few beats. I'd never before felt this kind of passion with any man, or this need to know Adam better, to have him in my life. *Was this what real love felt like?*

"I don't have much of an appetite." I pulled my hand from his and picked up my wine glass, taking a sip, letting the rich liquid slide down my throat, hoping it would dissolve the confusion that wound through me. It didn't.

"Could your not having an appetite have anything to do with losing our bet?" Humor tinged his voice.

I glared at him. He threw back his head and laughed.

Our dinner over, we walked outside to the deck and leaned on the ship's railing. Water lapped the sides of the ship as it cut through the water. Pale moonlight shone a path over the water and drenched the stars above. On the other end of the deck, an orchestra played a slow, romantic tune.

"Shall we?" Adam asked, turning to me and holding out his arms. His lips quirked in a sexy, lopsided smile.

I put my hand on my hip. "Oh, you're good, you're really good. We can dance all you want, but I won't waver. I'm winning this dare."

He leaned closer. "I don't think so. Let's dance, unless you're afraid."

"I'm not afraid of you," I said with more bravado than I felt. I couldn't tell him I was more afraid of my feelings for him.

He took me into his arms and held me close. My traitorous body melted against him. I inhaled his scent—coffee, wine, mint, and Adam. I leaned my head on his firm chest. His heartbeat vibrated through me, sure and steady.

"Danielle," he whispered. He ran his hand slowly down my back. A sensual knot tightened low in my belly.

The music ended, but we continued holding onto each other, swaying gently to our own music. We finally pulled apart. Despite the warm night, a chill went over me. I missed Adam's touch.

"Are you cold?" he asked, putting an arm around my shoulders.

"I'm okay."

He touched my chin with his fingers and tilted my face toward his. He bent his head, his eyes dark and mysterious in the moonlight. "There's nothing in our dare that says I can't kiss you," he whispered.

Oh, how I wanted him to kiss me, but I knew if his lips touched mine, I'd be lost. I pulled away. "No fair."

"Why is that?" he asked, failing miserably at looking innocent.

"You know why."

He laughed.

The first boom of fireworks pulled our attention to the Philadelphia shore. We ran to the railing as fireworks lit the sky, brightening everything around us. Adam put his arm around my waist and pulled me against him. His touch provoked a rush of pleasure. I'd seen fireworks my whole life, but this night there was something special in the air, something that made the fireworks more colorful, more exciting than ever before. Maybe it was the man next to me. The man who made me feel more alive than ever before.

Suddenly, I knew. I'd waited my whole life for Adam. My relationships with other men were tepid compared to the excitement and sensual energy that coursed through my veins when I was with him. I wanted to keep seeing him, to become a part of his life, and he mine. But I'd never lost a dare. I would figure out a way to win both the dare and Adam.

Forty-five minutes later, the fiery display was over.

I looked up at him. "That was amazing."

He kissed the top of my head. "You are amazing."

Desire flared deep inside me, burning me like hundreds of fireworks going off at the same time.

We made small talk as we drove back to Wilmington. Contentment stole over me, along with confusion. Our date and our dare were coming to a close. Who would win?

The usually thirty-five-minute drive took close to an hour and a half with the traffic leaving Philadelphia on the holiday night.

When we got to my townhouse apartment, Adam walked me to the door. I dug in my purse for my keys, and then slid the key in the lock.

"Danielle." Adam cupped my shoulders and drew me around to face him. "The two weeks is up."

I blew out a breath and nodded.

His jaw tightened and anger flashed in his eyes. "Seriously, Danielle? I really care about you. I can't believe you're going to let me walk away. Don't you care at all? Is this silly bet worth more to you than a relationship with me? Don't you want to see what we might have? Take a chance on me, on love. I dare you."

I looked into the dark eyes of the man I was coming to love. No way could I let him go. I dropped my purse and moved close to him. I skimmed a finger over his full lips, and then stood on tiptoe to kiss him with all the pent-up desire I'd held inside for the past two weeks.

With a small groan, he pulled me closer, deepening the kiss. I clung to him, pressing against his firm body. Who cared about a bet when I had Adam?

He released me, holding me in the circle of his arms. His eyes shimmered in the dim light from the street lamps. "Danielle," he whispered.

I wrapped my arms around his neck. "My friends and my brothers will never let me forget I finally lost a dare. I don't care. I've won a lot more."

"I think we both won." He bent and kissed me again, a possessive kiss that dared me to love him—a dare I gladly accepted. THE END

WHERE THE BOYS ARE—2011!
You'll Find Them Down In Lake Travis, Texas!

*E*strogen, *tequila shots, and half-naked men don't mix,* I thought to myself about a nanosecond before my terminally stupid brain commandeered my tongue.

That thought vanished—along with an ounce of tequila—sometime *after* I licked a patch of salt from a half-naked beach boy's neck and *before* I bit into the lime wedge he held in his mouth.

Lick it.

Slam it.

Suck it.

Given the quart or so of Australian beer I'd swilled beforehand, my head started swimming after three shots. The fourth I did just because I liked licking the beach boy's neck. Actually, I didn't do the shot itself. After flicking the salt with my tongue, I pointed out across the lake like, "Hey! Look at that!" and tossed the tequila over my shoulder. Even in my inebriated state, I felt reasonably certain that the swimming sensation I felt was *not* a direct result of the motion of the boat deck beneath my landlubber legs.

My married friend, Amber, sashayed toward The Neck and pasted on a pretty pout. "Me want some." Alcohol rendered Amber speechless. Except for baby talk. *Yecchh.*

Shouldering me aside, she salted the wet spot I'd already slobbered all over. My tequila shots partner didn't miss a beat, but in fact offered his inviting expanse of salted, suntanned neck to Amber, as KC and The Sunshine Band insisted,

Do a little dance,
Make a little love,
Get down tonight,
Get down tonight

Slut, I thought, watching Amber in action. *She'll probably do just that.*

My eyes narrowed for a couple seconds. But the idea of her getting my sloppy seconds pleased me and *that* made me smile. My amusement overpowered the cavewoman urge I had to yank her ponytail and tell her to find her *own* neck.

The latter didn't seem to be an overly friendly way of settling matters, considering that the switch didn't seem to bother The Neck. He dragged his eyes away from me (okay, so he didn't exactly drag them) and gave Amber a wolfish once-over.

"I *so* need to get some air," I announced to nobody in particular, since by that time Amber was all over The Neck like a cheap suit and The Neck's eyes were glued to her ample cleavage.

I looked down at my own chest. No cleavage to speak of. With a shrug and a tiny grope of the beach boy's swim-trunked ass, which I hope appeared accidental, I slipped away, walking a-little-to-the-left, a-little-to-the-right. In other words—I was essentially staggering.

I don't think they noticed, though. Nor did either of them appear to be interested in the fact that we were outside in the open air— therefore *no reason* existed for me to leave to "get some air."

Peering from under my lashes—so that I didn't appear to be peering—I surveyed the crowd for somebody to hang out with who looked cute and fun. Although I enjoy my alone time, I was on vacation and I felt like I should make an effort to be social. Sidling over near a group of fellow twenty-somethings, I eavesdropped outside their circle hoping to join in on an interesting conversation and maybe make some new friends. From what I could tell, one of the girls was actually *describing an antique church organ* that had been the focus of a recent newspaper feature story.

"It's a magnificent organ!" the girl gushed.

"*I'll* show you a magnificent organ," one of the guys responded.

My eyes rolled so far back in my head that I'm pretty sure they turned a complete circle. Don't get me wrong—I'm all about humor. But an exaggerated avowal of masculinity from a simple minded braggadocio always seems colossally immature to me. In fact, that particular remark sounded like something my latest ex-boyfriend would say. Plus, in my experience, guys who talk big—aren't (if you get my drift).

So clamping my teeth together to keep from popping off with a rude retort, I beat a hasty retreat.

By this time I was getting *really* bored. I looked around to see what my friends were doing.

Mimi held court from a hammock, pushed to and fro by two bronzed, sun-bleached, cookie-cutter beach-boy types wearing designer sunglasses and low-slung, palm tree-bedecked surf shorts. I hoped she had a beach towel close at hand to wipe off all of that drool.

Dylan flirted with a group of similar beach-boy dudes whose attention was simultaneously being demanded by their female counterparts: a handful of emaciated, suntanned, belly button-pierced Paris Hilton look-alikes in designer sunglasses and low-slung bikinis. According to Mimi, the male and female look-alikes were regulars on the houseboat party circuit at Lake Travis.

Melora made a wobbly, drunken attempt at a headstand. One of the guys stuck out a hand to spot her and I immediately thought, *Great. She'll probably break her neck and we'll get to explain that to the school board.*

Savannah occupied a wicker chair set apart from the group, her arms crossed over her chest, her expression sullen. Everyone seemed to be having a good time except her. In fact, her eyes positively *glinted* with contempt. I blinked and looked again. Or maybe not. Maybe she was just tired.

Understandable. I was tired myself. We'd had a long-ass drive through the night before arriving late that morning.

As the brilliant Texas sun emblazoned its last rays on the horizon, the luxury condo-on-the-water rocked gently. I gripped the handrails, padded barefoot down the spiral staircase that led away from the frenzied top deck, and walked the length of the docked houseboat to the aft deck in search of a few moments alone.

One pair of stolen underwear and the pressure would be off. But, the way I figured it, stealing underwear required making out. And not only was I not thrilled about the prospect of a one-night stand, but I felt more like throwing up than making out at that moment. Not to mention that I didn't have a partner.

Dropping onto a cushioned chaise, I stretched out and closed my eyes. The rhythmic rocking of the boat and the sound of the water lapping against the hull lulled me into a totally relaxed state. A soft breeze floated across my skin like a lullaby as the sultry perfumes of a lakeside Texas summer enveloped me.

Just as I was close to drifting off, a loud horn sounded, causing me to jump. I headed to the side of the boat to see what was going on, caught my foot on a deck chair, pitched forward, and grabbed for the railing to catch myself. My momentum was too great and I flipped over the railing and into the water.

I swallowed half the lake (well, it felt like it, anyway) when I went in, which made it kind of hard to scream for help. In a panic—because I couldn't breathe and also because I was fearful that a five-foot catfish or some other hateful lake creature might think I was lunch—I started hollering and splashing madly. In light of my drunken stupor and exhaustion, it didn't take long for my energy to ebb, even though my clothing—a white, lace halter and white, hip-hugger shorts—was lightweight. I coughed the water out of my lungs and started screaming, but no one heard me and my voice weakened fast.

I went under, but managed to kick myself back to the surface. By then, my muscles had minimal strength left; I floated and desperately dog-paddled and waited for my life to flash before my eyes. Then, using my last reserve of energy, I propelled myself headfirst back to the houseboat. A lot of good that did me—there was no magical way to get up onto it in sight.

Although it was June, the sun was almost down and the water felt chilly, which had the effect of numbing my muscles further. I started to go down again as sick dread surged through my veins. A feeling of helplessness swept over me as I realized that I couldn't save myself. Briefly, I thought about how devastated my parents would be when a cop knocked on their door to tell them I drowned.

The last thing I remember is spiraling into blackness as the water closed over my head.

A pair of strong hands held me as water spurted out of my mouth. I choked and gagged for a while, which I'm sure was *really* attractive. When my coughing was spent, the strong arms attached to the strong hands lifted me. A pair of intensely turquoise eyes bored into mine.

"Wh-who? Wh-where?" I spit out before a sexy voice interrupted me with a brusque—

"Don't try to talk."

The arms pulled me onto a cozy lap and my rescuer held me against him, rocking me like a baby and smoothing my sopping curls. I had the strange and overwhelming feeling that I belonged in those muscular arms; I felt safe, protected. And his stud-in-the-sunshine scent—ohmygod—it was enough to make a girl *swoon*.

I must've groped him (I mean, after all—I wasn't in my right mind) at some point because I quite clearly recall him saying in a honeyed drawl, "I'm not one of your little boy toys, darlin'. Like that dude you were playing grab-ass with on board."

Did he see me licking that dude's neck? I wondered. And that's the last coherent thought I had before the dark place beckoned again and I surrendered to its allure.

When I awoke, I was befuddled at first. I lay in a king-size bed in the most gorgeous bedroom I'd ever seen in my life.

I sat bolt upright. *Where the heck am I?*

That sudden frisson of fear was chased away by a rush of memories. I realized I was in an opulent stateroom aboard the Mimi, a huge houseboat more lavish than anything I could conjure up in my wildest dreams. I thought I *knew* what a houseboat looks like before the Mimi—but The Mimi makes Buckingham Palace look like a double-wide trailer.

I'd come to Lake Travis, Texas with my friends. We'd arrived late in the morning, toasted Dr. Seuss with pricey champagne, and kicked off the merriment. Numerous neighboring houseboaters and stray partiers meandered aboard to party with us.

But why am I at Lake Travis?

Then my mind drifted back to the day when I agreed to this summer-vacation-in-Texas fiasco . . . and I remembered the whole story.

It was a frigid day in the dead of winter back in Colorado. I was the first to hit The Sanctuary that day. Then one by one, my friends flooded in. The Sanctuary, otherwise known as the teachers' lounge, was our island of sanity amidst the teeming hysteria that was life inside Wildman Senior High School. There, we relished private moments away from the high school students who made us crazy on a daily basis. There, we analyzed the problems of the world. There, we shared secrets and dissected each other's sex lives.

After the six of us had settled around the table, chattering animatedly and unpacking our respective lunches, Mimi the Drama Queen silenced us with a long, hissing, "*Shhhhhh!*"

Five mouths shut. Five pairs of quizzical eyes trained on her and all at once, Mimi was in her element. For effect, she dipped her chin, widened her eyes, and flared her nostrils like a witch about to cast a spell. After glancing over both shoulders as if to assure herself that no eavesdroppers lurked in the corners—although clearly we were the only people in the room—she eyed each of us meaningfully: Dylan, twenty-five, art teacher—the fast-and-loose hippie who loved tie-dye and allowed any and all men to walk all over her; Amber, twenty-nine, psychology teacher—the nymphomaniac whose boring and inattentive husband drove her horizontal with our principal, among others; Melora, twenty-five, drama teacher—the unhappy preacher's daughter who had alcohol issues and sad eyes; and last but not least, Savannah, twenty-four, music teacher—the plump, artsy, moody, hostile, terminally single girl who had a chip on her shoulder because of her weight and because she was sure that no desirable man would ever like her for what was inside, not outside.

Mimi was twenty-seven and a science teacher. She was a poor-little-rich-girl who'd do it with any guy who'd lift up his head because her parents gave her things instead of love. As for myself, I was twenty-three at the time and a language arts teacher—my first "real" job, you might say. I come from an average, middle-class upbringing in a fairly functional family. After graduating from the University of Colorado, I'd reduced my wild partying to weekends only (mostly). Since then, I was in a transition stage, looking to get more out of life, even though I wasn't naïve enough to believe in the fairytale thing. However, I did seem to keep on kissing frogs and hoping that one of them would turn into a handsome prince. Anyway, power dating was fun and nobody got hurt.

To the casual observer, my friends and I appeared to be intelligent, grounded, sensible, all-American women. As educators in a town with a population of 9,000, we had to watch what we did in public. Prim and proper—that was us. Uh-huh. And if you believe *that*—I've got some swamp land in Florida you might be interested in.

Savannah, never one to tolerate Mimi's theatrics for long, demanded, "Dude, what's up? End the suspense already."

Mimi jammed her folded fists onto her narrow waist and glared at Savannah.

Melora threw up her hands. "What's with the big mystery?"

Mimi flashed us all a *look*. "I've got three words for you: Midsummer. Houseboat. Hookups."

We all started talking at once then.

"Hold on, hold on!" Mimi yelled into the hullabaloo.

The racket died down.

"You know what the summer solstice is, right?" she asked.

"The first day of summer," Amber supplied.

"The summer solstice occurs at the precise moment when the sun's power is at its zenith. In other words—it's the day of the year with the longest daylight," Mimi explained, ever the science teacher. "It's all about the seasons of the year, which are caused by the twenty-three-point-five-degree tilt of the earth's ax—"

"We are *so* not your science students, Mimi," Melora interrupted.

"Yeah. Cut to the chase," Savannah insisted.

"Well, then—we're celebrating the summer solstice at the Lake

Travis Fire Festival this year . . . and Daddy says we can all stay on The Mimi for a week!"

"And 'The Mimi' would be what?" I asked.

"A houseboat!" Licking her lips for emphasis, Mimi leaned forward and dropped her voice dramatically. "*And* we're going to throw in a one-night stand thing . . . just for fun!"

I raised my eyebrows so high that they crowded my hairline. "You mean a pickup contest?"

Mimi wrinkled her nose. "Not a *contest*. That would be *beneath* us. Just a little . . . *activity*, to keep us *entertained*. I've had the best sex of my life from one-night stands. Haven't you?"

As if. I'd had one drunken, stupid, unsatisfying single-episode encounter that felt like one too many. But I could pretend to be game.

Savannah scowled. Dylan and Amber grinned. Melora averted her eyes.

"It's all about getting away, relaxing, having some fun, and really letting our hair down," Mimi insisted emphatically. "We're under scrutiny twenty-four-seven here in Wildman. We deserve one teensy-weensy week of summer vacation to do whatever the heck we want—*including* picking up guys and stealing their underwear as proof of our one-nighters."

Savannah balked like a mule on a pack trip. "No. Way."

Judging from Mimi's expression, it was clear that Savannah's thought processes were transparent to her. "We'll talk more about the one-night stand element later," she said to Savannah.

She proceeded to explain that the summer solstice is also referred to as Midsummer because it's roughly in the middle of the growing season in Europe. The reason for the fire festival thing, she said, is that ancient pagans celebrated Midsummer with bonfires.

"Midsummer was the night of fire festivals and love magic. Fire, the 'little brother of the sun,' naturally gains greater power when the force of the sun is at its height. Through the fire's power, maidens found husbands on Midsummer's Eve."

Right, I thought. *Like she's looking for a husband. What she's looking for is fresh meat.*

"Lake Travis is resurrecting the fire festival custom this year. So, who's in?" Mimi asked excitedly.

I surveyed my gal pals' faces. Everyone except Savannah appeared to be captivated by Mimi's idea. Apparently, they found it not the *slightest* bit slimy to be plotting seductions.

Whatever, I thought with a resigned sigh. *After all, this is 2011.*

Dylan, being the doormat that she is, was the first to capitulate.

Savannah was next, with this blunt comment: "I'll go, but I'm *not* doing the one-night stand thing. No one would want me, anyway. No one wants to do a fat chick."

"Savannah," I cut in, "you are *not* fat. Lots of g—"

"You don't have to lie, Jill. It's okay. No big deal."

I knew she was lying and my heart hurt for her. However, she was so prickly that I knew there wasn't a heck of a lot I could do to make her feel better.

Two other arms outstretched and then there were four hands piled on top of Mimi's—everyone's but mine. Five sets of eyes studied me intently, waiting.

A relaxing trip to a lake. Right, I thought. *It sounds more like an erotic journey down the rabbit hole. But, hey—I guess I'm game. I mean, I could do with an* Alice In Wonderland *type of adventure.*

Okay; so I caved. I mean, it was only my second semester at Wildman and I wanted the other teachers to like me. My main concern was that we'd all be crammed into some floating trailer. Some people just aren't meant to live in beehives. Namely, me.

It was all about fun, though, right?

"In the immortal words of Dr. Seuss, 'It's fun to have fun, but you have to know how,' " I finally said, and topped their hands with mine.

Famous last words, I thought.

Words that are starting to sound mighty shallow, indeed.

That attitude almost got me drowned.

I flopped down on my back again. *Ugh.* My mouth tasted like the floor of an elephant pen smells and my head felt like an overripe cantaloupe about to split in two.

I wondered how I'd gotten to my stateroom. *Did the hottie who saved me bring me here?* The comment he'd made about me playing "grab-ass" with the beach boy made me cringe. In fact, it made me feel utterly cheap and shallow. *Jeez! Was he watching me or what?*

I kicked off the covers and looked at myself. The lace halter I'd shelled out fifty bucks for was now a crappy shade of lake water and my hundred-percent-cotton shorts were wrinkled and dingy.

How dumb am I? I wondered miserably.

The clock on the bedside table said, *Time is marching on without you.* The hands ticked toward high noon by the time I'd showered and hit "the salon," which is what Mimi *insisted* on calling it. It looked more like a space-age living room to me, with windows that wrapped around the entire room, rattan furniture, rope lighting, a wet bar, ceiling fans with palm-frond paddles, and an entertainment center that had palm trees etched into the glass and that boasted a flat-screen TV, surround sound, *and* a karaoke system.

Savannah, Dylan, and Melora chatted on a cushy sofa as they munched chips and salsa. I dropped down next to them and dove into the basket of multicolored tortilla chips.

"Jeez. You look like crap," Savannah said.

I gave her a *look.* "If you almost drowned, you'd look like crap, too."

They eyed me like I was an escapee from the local insane asylum.

"You *do* realize that I almost drowned, right?" I asked them pointedly.

"What are you talking about?" Dylan asked.

I explained to them what had happened to me, but they looked no more inclined to believe me than before.

"I don't remember you not being there," Melora said, puzzled, shaking her head.

Like you would, Melora, I thought sourly. *You were three sheets to the wind yourself.*

Savannah dismissed my story with an offhanded, "Dude, you were *drunk.*" Sometimes her bluntness really grated.

"Where are the others?" I asked, quickly changing the subject.

"They're 'otherwise occupied,' " Melora said as she dragged a celery stick through her bloody Mary.

Before long, a rumpled Amber waltzed in, followed closely behind by Mr. Grab-Ass. He checked me out as he walked past, but I ignored him.

Too late, slimeball, I thought. *You had your chance.*

Amber gave him a quick kiss good-bye and swatted him playfully—and dismissively—on the butt before ushering him out the door. When she reappeared, Melora, Dylan, and Savannah immediately started quizzing her, but she dashed off to her stateroom, returning momentarily with a pair of boxer briefs, which she twirled on one finger.

Amber is such an ass, I immediately thought. I couldn't have cared less about the slimy beach boy, but the unspoken codes of friendship require one to abide by certain rules. And hitting on a guy your friend is occupied with—whether she likes him or not—is just *wrong.*

Minutes later, Mimi appeared with her flavor of the night. I wondered if he realized that his shirt was on backwards. *Probably not,* I quickly surmised, seeing as he looked pretty hungover. After she'd summarily ridded herself of him, Mimi disappeared, and then reappeared with a pair of boxer briefs—*her* proof of *her* one-nighter.

My reaction involved suppressing an eye-roll. Dylan looked p.o.'d that she hadn't been successful in her own mission; Savannah looked p.o.'d *in general*; Melora looked more interested in replenishing her Bloody Mary than in one-nighters and their underwear. Nevertheless, Savannah quickly retold the story of my near-drowning incident, making me look like a nutcase to Mimi and Amber, along with the others.

"Wow. Rough night," Amber said.

"What *I* want to know is: Did you do your mystery man?" Mimi asked devilishly.

I touched my temples, and then flung my hands upward and outward. "Did *none* of you even *miss* me?"

They fidgeted uncomfortably. Clearly, they hadn't.

"Sorry," Dylan finally said half heartedly.

"Let's party," Melora said, quickly changing the subject.

A group consensus landed us in a six-seat speedboat that afternoon. One of Mimi's daddy's deckhands dropped it from the houseboat into the water via a state-of-the-art hydraulic launch system.

I was nervous at first with Mimi at the helm, but it soon became apparent that she was an old salt at navigation. I started feeling alive again with the wind in my face and the hot Texas sun beating down on my bare skin. The shoreline rushed by as Mimi gave us a grand tour of the lake, busting a few boat wakes for good measure.

My eyes widened when Mimi buzzed a beach while sitting on the top of the captain's seat with her bikini top off and doing a Queen Elizabeth wave. She reluctantly donned it again before docking at Pelican Pink's, a restaurant on the water that serves boaters in their boats as well as inside a palm tree-themed building on the water.

Following a brief dialogue on hair-of-the-dog and wild summer drinks as our waitress shifted from espadrille to espadrille on the dock, Mimi asked, "Sex On The Beach, everyone?"

Everyone nodded but me. The thought of booze made my stomach turn. "I *so* don't want any booze right now. Safe Sex On The Beach for me, please," I told the waitress.

"Party pooper," Melora said.

"Yeah. You're no fun," Savannah said.

They didn't get it. I'd almost *drowned*, for crying out loud—mostly because I'd been drunk and stupid. Let me tell you—it was one of those life-altering events.

My friends, on the other hand, were into *mind*-altering events. After a couple of rounds, Mimi cranked Jimmy Buffet's "Margaritaville" and the girls began to party hearty. Man magnets that we were, it wasn't long before various and sundry beach boys were on us like flies on honey. As the sun blazed down and the water slapped against the boat and the muggy air clung to us like vaporous cobwebs, everyone else frolicked while I remained subdued. Expectantly, I searched each and every male face, hoping to discover a pair of startling, turquoise eyes. Having no luck, I looked around for an escape route. Not only was the loud, raucous music making my head ache, but the only guy I was interested in was the one who'd saved me from drowning. He wasn't there, so I didn't want to be, either.

This realization was—I must admit—shocking to me. Feeling the need to ponder this further, I decided to head back to the houseboat. Luckily, my getaway came easier than I anticipated. One of the beach boys suggested a game of beach volleyball and the whole group migrated to the adjoining beach. As we passed Pelican Pink's, I slipped away from the gang and stepped inside. More palm trees. Surprise, surprise. I bellied up to the bar and first thing—checked out the color of the bartender's eyes.

Not turquoise. Dang.

Ditching my virgin beverage in favor of a good, old-fashioned, hangover-quenching Coke, I perused a flyer on the wall detailing the fire festival set for the eve of the summer solstice: *Midsummer is the moment when the warmth and beauty of the year are at their height,* the poster declared. *The longest day of the year is a time when the humming fullness of summer seems endless. Fill your darkness with light.* Scheduled events included a day of music, dancing, storytelling, classes, crafts, demonstrations, food, and fun that would culminate with a bonfire on the beach.

After I'd sucked down my Coke I trekked down the beach back to The Mimi, kicked off my flip-flops, pulled off my shorts and tank top, and flopped onto a chaise on the aft deck—the same one I'd tumbled off of the night before. After undoing the catch on my bikini top, I stretched out on my tummy and closed my eyes. I set my iPod to Shuffle Songs and drifted away to David Cassidy telling me that he thought he loved me.

I returned to consciousness when a pair of strong hands started kneading what smelled like suntan lotion into my bare back.

"You're going to fry without sunscreen," a familiar drawl scolded.

My soul lit up when I heard his voice. I started to flip over, but he stopped me with gentle pressure.

"A wet T-shirt in the dark is one thing. But I don't think our relationship is ready for full-frontal nudity."

I smashed my face into the chaise and grimaced. "I'm truly sorry about last night," I said, groaning with hungover embarrassment. "I can't thank you enough for saving me."

He laughed as he eased himself down onto the chaise beside me. "No worries. Anyway, it was fun being a hero for a day."

I wiggled sideways to make room for him. "I have a question for you: Did you bring me back onto The Mimi? How did I end up in my stateroom?"

"Whoa. You said *a* question. That was two."

"Okay; did you bring me back to my stateroom?"

"Yes."

When he offered no further information, I rolled my eyes. "Well, you're a fountain of information."

"'Just naturally blabby, I guess, said the Sundance Kid to Butch Dylan."

"None of my friends saw you. They don't believe you even exist."

Again, that rich laugh. It heated my soul as much as his sensual hands warmed my skin. Everywhere he touched me, my skin caught fire.

"Could I look at you?"

His hands stopped moving on my back.

I hastened to add, "All I remember about you is your extraordinary eyes. I want to see if the real thing matches my memory thing."

With a fast, dexterous motion, he latched my bikini top.

"Oh, brother," I muttered. Guys are such showoffs. "Close your eyes."

He chuckled. "Why?"

He likes laughing, I thought contentedly. *Laughing is a good thing. I'm all about laughing.* "Because getting up from a chaise longue is inelegant, at best."

Leaning close to my ear, he whispered, "Remember, now: I've already seen you at your most inelegant."

My areolas puckered. *Why is he having this effect on me?* I wondered, amazed and suddenly breathless. *I don't know, but it sure pisses me off!* "You just *think* you have," I retorted. "Now turn around so I can get up," I said crossly.

As soon as I felt him lift his body off the chaise, I arched my back and quickly adjusted my bikini top. Just as I raised myself from the chair—as gracefully as possible, mind you, just in case he was cheating and watching—I heard a splash.

I whipped around only to find myself alone.

My heart dropped like a stone. I ran to the starboard side of the boat and peeked over the railing—

No mystery man in sight.

I sprinted over to the portside.

Nothing.

He vanished into thin air.

I am so not a social butterfly, I thought to myself as I watched the sun paint the sky vivid shades of pink and orange the following evening. Just then, a mosquito big enough to carry off a small dog bit into the flesh of my calf and I yelped and reached for the bug spray—a necessity of life in South Texas, where mosquitoes are stork-sized.

Once again, I manned the aft deck while the others partied up top. I figured it had to be a bad sign that I actually missed my life back in Colorado. I mean, it's just *wrong* for a girl to miss home when she's on vacation.

As it was, I knew the others were beginning to think I was downright antisocial. But I wasn't antisocial, really, just, well—fed up. Mimi and Amber were terminally horny, Savannah was terminally pissed off, Melora was terminally drunk, and Dylan was terminally loco. The terminal partying associated with Lake Travis seemed terminally pointless to me, the beach boys were terminally boring, and the terminal motion of the boat—even though it was moored to the dock—made me terminally queasy.

With those thoughts in mind, I marched to the spiral staircase and climbed up to see what the others were doing. As soon as my head cleared the deck, Melora yelled, "Jill! Come play Power Hour with us!"

Walking over to the round table where my friends sat amongst a group of beach boys, I noticed that Melora's hair was disheveled and that she was well on her way to drunk. "What the heck is Power Hour?" I asked.

"Sit down and you'll find out," Savannah said.

Amber flashed me her most winning smile. "Yeah, come on; we were just about to start."

I ignored Amber because I was still pissed off at her. Turning to Melora, I said, "Give me the details."

Mimi, who was draped across yet another beach boy, chimed in, "It involves beer. You'll *love* it!"

Melora pointed to Mimi's beach boy. "He taught us. You take a shot of beer every minute for an hour."

When I immediately declined to participate, they jeered me until I fled below to escape their taunting. Restless and fidgety, I elected to take a sunset stroll along the beach. As twilight settled over the lake like a dark, silken cloak, I strode down the dock, removed my flip-flops, stepped onto the beach, and started walking. The squishy sand felt wonderful beneath my feet; my calf muscles strained against it as I established a quick and rhythmic pace. I'd read that walking in the sand is good for a person's calf muscles.

Couldn't do mine any harm, I figured.

Merriment burst out of Pelican Pink's as I tramped by. On impulse, I elected to go in and check out the local color. The same thing was going on there as on The Mimi—as well as on numerous other houseboats and in cabins and campgrounds along Lake Travis, I was sure. The party scene was pretty much what lake life was all about, I concluded.

Squeezing my way through a throng of sweaty bodies, I spied a lone barstool and bellied up. I'd downed about half a Coke when an arrogant, obnoxious beach boy wearing a captain's cap approached me and asked me to dance. I demurred politely and turned back to the bar, but the jerk wouldn't take no for an answer.

"Don't be a bitch. You're gonna love it," he insisted as he latched onto my left arm and tugged me off the barstool.

I planted my legs, but the floor was slick with spilled beer and he was much stronger than I was and when I locked my knees, I started sliding in the direction he was pulling me. Being a woman of the new millennium, however, I knew I couldn't allow that predator to strong-arm me. I grabbed his wrist with my free hand and swung myself around. When I was in front of him, I pressed close and grasped his forearms.

"Not so fast, Captain," I protested sweetly.

The buffoon had the gall to smirk at me.

He thinks he's getting what he wants. What a dumbass. I formed my mouth into a pretty moue and fluttered my lashes at him. I let him pull me into his arms and then when I was in proper position, I lifted my knee—

And smashed it into his groin.

He dropped to the floor with a moan and rolled around there, holding onto the family jewels for dear life.

I narrowed my eyes. "No means *no*, sailor. Don't you ever touch me again."

I turned on one heel . . . and crashed *smack* into a stone wall with laughing, turquoise eyes.

I raised one eyebrow as I drank in every detail of my Adonis: a wreath of dark curls, the face of a marble angel, and chiseled *everything*. He bowed slightly, and I melted.

Taking my hand in his, he asked, "Can I do this? Or are you going to cold-cock me, too?"

"I'm not up for a title match tonight. I could take you, though," I added with a wink. When he smiled, my guts flip-flopped inside of me like never before. I was entranced; I couldn't drag my eyes from his face.

He pressed his rough cheek against mine, sliding it excruciatingly slowly down to my ear as he palmed my neck and smoothed back my hair with a soft stroke of his thumb. "It's too bad we don't know each other better," he whispered, "because I'd like to kiss you . . . right . . . now. . . ."

His turquoise eyes glimmered with lust. Figuring that what's good for the goose is good for the gander, I stood on tiptoe and nuzzled my head into the soft place under his chin. With my lips next to his ear, I whispered, "You saw what I did to that guy. If you try to sneak off again, I'm going to do that to you." I punctuated my statement by nipping his earlobe.

He encircled me with his muscular arms and pulled me against his hard, chiseled chest. Under my hand, a rumbling started as laughter rose up within him.

"You had me at hello," he joked.

I clasped his hand. The feel of his body, hot and hard against mine, is what drove me over the edge. "Come on," I said, and out the door we went.

Outside, I slammed him up against the palm tree mural on the wall and claimed his mouth with mine. The feel of his lips, soft and demanding all at once, is what undid me as a sexual frenzy the likes of which I'd never experienced overcame me. I licked the seam of his lips with the tip of my tongue, tugged at his bottom lip with my teeth, French-kissed him like we were dying and had no tomorrow.

You know how those soap sluts manhandle their men? That's what was going on. It was sheer joy, sheer pleasure. His lips meshed perfectly with mine and I felt like I'd waited a lifetime for him as my mind raced, thinking, *this is pure, unadulterated lust. I'm playing with fire and I'm going to get burned.*

All at once I pushed him away from me. We gazed at each other in the silvery shards of moonlight, our chests heaving, our eyes locked. I felt like I was sinking into a turquoise sea.

Spinning on one heel in the sand, I dashed off down the beach.

Buttery rays of sunshine spilled into my stateroom the next morning, illuminating the leopard-print curtains drawn back to the sides of the extra-large windows. My friends all preferred air-conditioning, but I love the arousing scent of sultry summer air. Even though the air of South Texas summers is stifling, muggy, and heavy, the cool breezes off Lake Travis make for wonderful sleeping weather.

The sun had climbed high enough by then that my skin felt gross and sticky. I jumped into the shower and then headed for the galley in search of breakfast. Quiet pervaded the salon, which suited me just fine.

A pair of flowered boxer shorts hanging from a lampshade was what I noticed first. Upon closer inspection, I saw a note pinned to them that read: *DYLAN!* in big, black, bold letters followed by a winking smiley face. I rummaged through the cupboards and, finding nothing appetizing, I breakfasted on Nutter Butters.

As I waited for the others to rise and shine I scanned a coffee table book on the works of Michelangelo. Adam in *The Creation of Adam* fresco on the Sistine Chapel ceiling reminded me of my mystery man, although his legs were longer. One of the *ignudi frescoes* reminded me of him, especially his neck and jaw line. The statue of David reminded me of him, particularly the hair. Almost every painting of Michelangelo's reminded me of him. I slammed the book shut in frustration and paced from one end of the salon to the other.

Just when I'd decided to wake the others so I'd have someone to talk to I heard a sharp rap. One quick scan of the wraparound windows and I picked up on a telltale shadow. Sailing over to the window, I lifted the sash and peered out through the screen.

There he was—my mystery man. Miles of sun-kissed flesh extended above faded, denim cutoffs. My blood ignited instantaneously.

"Grab your swimmin' suit and a towel and let's go," he said.

"Go where?"

"Just get 'em. Hurry up."

He grinned and I was a goner.

He waited while I dashed off a note to the others and ran back to retrieve my beach bag and change into my bikini. As I passed Amber's room, I heard noises that I didn't even want to *contemplate*. I felt a rush of sympathy for her husband. *Clearly,* I thought, *he's clueless when it comes to her extracurricular activities. She must be a really unhappy person.*

So was Melora and so was Savannah, I suddenly realized. Come to think of it—Mimi was pretty unhappy, too. And who knew about Dylan? She kind of existed on another plane.

What about you? I asked myself. *Are you happy?*

I am today, came the answer.

Turquoise Eyes watched me intently as I disembarked. As nervous as I was, I just knew I'd trip or otherwise make a fool of myself; I thanked God in heaven when I didn't.

We ambled down the dock side by side in companionable silence.

He led the way to a speedboat tied up at the marina near the gas pumps.

He indicated that I should board the boat first, smiling as he said, "Age before beauty."

I socked him playfully in the gut. "Then *you* should go first."

"Hurt your hand?" he asked.

I rolled my eyes. "Very funny."

He grinned that grin and I melted into a puddle again. Then I just stood there like an idiot, staring at him and thinking that maybe having a serious lover isn't such a bad idea. His grin widened and I dropped my eyes as he helped me down into the boat.

I peeled off my shorts and top and stowed them in a compartment on the side of the boat. That time *he* was the one staring. I grinned; he grinned back.

"Yo, you ready to cast off?" asked the young guy working the pumps. "Or are you two gonna sit there and make eyes at each other all day?"

"Jealous?" Turquoise Eyes asked as he settled himself on top of the driver's seat.

The kid put his foot on the side of the boat and pushed us away from the marina. "You got that right. But I got a date later."

"Behave yourself," Turquoise Eyes advised.

The kid winked. "Aye, aye, Captain Cobalt."

We idled away from the marina and through the harbor. I caught him watching me out of the corner of his eye as I slathered sunscreen all over my body.

"Can I ask you just one question?" I said over the rumble of the engine. "Do you think our relationship is ready for sharing names?" I was, of course, referring to the comment he'd made to me previously when I almost lifted off the chaise without my bikini top.

He studied me for a second before answering. "Yours is Jill. However, today I'm the captain and you're my first mate."

My eyes widened. "How do you know my name?"

He shrugged. And then there was that grin again, only lopsided this time, perhaps to add an air of mystery.

I jumped up, wrapped my hands around his neck, and pretended to choke him. "Tell me right now or I'm going to throttle you and toss you overboard and you are *so* going to be fish food."

He wiggled his fingers at me. "Ooh, I'm scared! I'm going to dangle your feet in the water and the sharks are going to nibble on your cute, little piggies!"

I pressed my fists against my hips. "Yeah, right. There aren't any sharks in this lake."

"So I'll take you down to the Gulf and pull you behind the boat and use you for shark bait."

"Touch me and die," I warned, grinning.

He looked at me with a challenge in his eyes and dragged his index finger slowly down my bare tummy. "It would take more than a threat of death to make me not touch you."

He tucked me into him for a second and then he pushed me down in the captain's seat between his legs and cushioned me with his thighs. A heady feeling rushed over me. It was the best day of my life.

A few seconds later he leaned down and said into my ear, "My name's Silas."

I twisted so that I could look at him. "Then what was that 'Captain Cobalt' thing all about back there at the gas pumps?"

"My boat's a Cobalt. It's a brand name."

When we reached the buoys that signify the end of the no-wake zone he flipped a switch and the engine noise increased to a loud, powerful, sexy rumble. Then he really opened her up and we lit out across the water at Mach 2. With regret, I slid from between his legs and returned to the first mate's chair; I knew I had to experience the moment up high in the wind like he was sitting. Grabbing the top of the windshield, I hoisted my booty up onto the top of the seat and let the wind stream through my hair. I flung my arms up to be buffeted by the wind and screamed, "*Woo-hoo!*"

After awhile the mouth of a cove came into sight and Silas decelerated and turned us into it. He idled over to a secluded spot and shut off the engine; the loping noise was fabulous, but the peaceful silence was great, too. In fact, I quickly realized that it couldn't get any better than that day: Silas, his awesome boat, brilliant sunshine, and warm, easygoing waters. (Okay, so the mosquitoes *weren't* so wonderful, but thankfully Silas came prepared with bug spray.)

Then, after Silas dropped anchor, I discovered that I'd assessed too soon; in fact, it could—and *did*—get better. Much to my delight, he whipped out a picnic lunch he'd had prepared for us courtesy of Pelican Pink's: smoked salmon, peanut butter-and-jelly sandwiches, potato salad, fresh fruit salad, and iced sugar cookies in the shape of sailboats.

After lunch, we sprawled out across the seats in the bow like kitties in the sun. I learned a lot about Silas that day. For instance: He doesn't like salmon (hence the peanut butter-and-jelly sandwiches, in case I didn't like salmon, either). He thinks drinking alcohol is "stupid" because that's how it makes people act. His favorite color is red. His favorite cookies are chocolate chip. His favorite teacher was Mrs. Leigh in the first grade. His favorite movie is *Top Gun*.

Still, he dodged every personal question I asked him, and that definitely made my red flags go up. I was pretty much lovestruck by then, but suspicious nonetheless. Or maybe *hurt* is more like it. The questions he sidestepped included those regarding his last name, hometown, current place of residence, and the type of work he did for his livelihood.

Maybe he's a thug or a dope dealer, I considered.

No way, my female intuition insisted.

Additionally, he refused to tell me how he knew my name and where he'd been watching me from. No matter how cleverly I disguised the intent of my probing, he eluded me every time. Finally, I simply gave up. Also, I guess I figured, like Dr. Phil says, "People who have nothing to hide, hide nothing."

The shadows surrounding Silas didn't ruin the day, though. On the contrary, it was phenomenal. We talked and made out and we even managed to find time for swimming, sunbathing . . . and more making out. And then there was the making out.

And did I mention the making out?

After all that swimming and sunshine we were tuckered out and starving by suppertime. Silas drove us back and we docked at Pelican Pink's and dined in the boat again, which was just fine by me. One thing we'd found we have in common is that neither of us cares much for crowds.

After we ate, Silas moored the boat in his slip at the marina. He raised it out of the water automatically with some hydro-lift thing. I helped him tarp it, taking note of his slip number, and then we walked back toward The Mimi.

As we neared her, we could see the party in nonstop full swing on the top deck. Feeling extremely selfish and not wanting to burst my fairytale bubble by sharing the details of my special day with anyone, I bade Silas farewell at the end of the gangway with a searing, scandalous, scorching French kiss.

"Get a room!" some smartass yelled from the top deck.

I rolled my eyes. "Screw you, beach bum," I said under my breath. To Silas, I said, "Thank you for this unforgettable day. Thank you from the bottom of my heart."

I kissed my first and second fingers and then pressed them against his lips. He kissed them and pressed them back against my own lips and it was the most romantic gesture *ever.*

This guy is phenomenal, I thought. *How can I leave Lake Travis and never see him again?*

The eve of the summer solstice—that's when the you-know-what hit the fan.

Honestly, it's almost like I could feel the impending doom in the air when I woke up that morning, urgent and ominous like a gathering storm. The air was heavy and still, the humidity suffocating, and when I peeked out the window I wasn't at all surprised to find the sky dark as sin. I shut the windows to let the room cool off—plus I didn't want it to rain in later.

I was first in the galley again, which was a relief because that meant no one was there to nag me about power-munching Nutter Butters for breakfast. This time Melora had left a pair of men's Jockey shorts on the solid, granite dining bar with a note attached.

Honest to God, get over yourselves, I thought, rolling my eyes. There I was at Lake Travis, cohabitating with a slut, a doormat, a nympho, a bitch, and a drunk. And the whole trip was about one-night stand underwear. It was all just so sordid and tawdry.

As it was, four of us boasted underwear trophies and two of us didn't. Savannah, at least, had been upfront from the beginning, firmly announcing that she had no intention whatsoever of taking part in the underwear game. I'd gone the passive-aggressive route and acted like I was okay with the concept when in fact, I never intended to participate.

Because of this, I could do nothing but shake my head when I spotted the chart taped to the refrigerator. They were actually keeping score now, and Mimi was in the lead with nine.

Impressive, I had to grudgingly admit to myself, *seeing as this is only our fifth day on Lake Travis.* Amber was close behind her with seven; Dylan and Melora trailed with two and one in that order.

The six of us certainly left our teacher personas far behind, I reflected. *Four days on Lake Travis and our skeletons are already hurtling out of our respective closets! And just how well do we really even know each other, anyway?*

Personally, it hadn't taken me long after reaching Lake Travis to find the conversations shallow and the loud, obnoxious, drunken behavior tedious. Silas was the only bright spot in my whole vacation.

Naturally, once my mouth was stuffed with Nutter Butters, voices wafted in from down the hall. I chewed fast, but it didn't matter; the underwear contest leaders didn't even compute the Nutter Butter thing when they stormed into the galley because they were mired in an argument. They both looked dog-tired and hungover . . . and only one of them carried a pair of men's underwear.

Mimi had a black look on her face. "You *knew* I was working Troy and you still *stole* him from me!" she screeched at haughty Amber.

So. Amber hit on Mimi's guy, I surmised. *Big surprise.*

Amber tossed her hair and hung Troy's underwear next to the others—on hooks in the galley ceiling from which copper-bottomed pots formerly dangled. "Listen, honey—all's fair in love and war. You got that?"

"I'm just saying—"

"Hey. If you can't hang onto your man, it's not my fault, Mimi," Amber said acidly as she pranced over to the leader board, erased her seven—and penciled in an eight.

She's actually proud *of herself, for crying out loud,* I realized, stunned by Amber's brazenness. *In fact, she's freaking trying to* win *this thing!*

Mimi stomped over to the leather couch by the window, dropped onto it, and pouted.

Can you say psycho sluts? I thought, shuddering with inward revulsion. *These two need some* serious *therapy.*

A knock on the door stopped their bickering. My heart skipped a beat, but the corners of my mouth curved into a frown when an unknown beach boy opened the door and stuck his head in.

"Is Troy still here?"

Mimi looked askance at Amber.

"I'll get him," Amber said, exiting the galley just as Melora and Dylan entered.

"Come on in," Mimi said sourly to the dude.

All told, three beach boys piled into the room.

"You guys ready to party?" the short one asked.

"Born ready," Melora told him with a wickedly eager grin that made her look like anything *but* a preacher's daughter.

"Hey, guys, can I ask you for a favor?" Mimi asked.

The chubby one of the three stuck his hand into a bowl of peanuts on the bar, closed in on a fistful, and started shoving them into his mouth. "Depends on what," he said through a nutty mouthful.

"Well, you guys have been partying here for three days now, right? Free beer, free booze, free food—free everything, right?"

"Dude. That doesn't mean we have to do whatever you want," the tall one said.

"Oh, I know. But believe me, you won't mind this much—maybe not at all, in fact. I mean, can I be blunt here? You see, I need one of you to sleep with Savannah."

"The fat chick? No way," the short one said.

Mimi looked pointedly at the hefty one.

He turned red and started shaking his head, begging off with his peanutty hands in the air. "Hey. Dude. Don't look at me just because I'm fat. I don't like fat chicks, either."

"Yeah. We ain't chubby chasers," the short one added for good measure.

"Okay, then; I'll buy you whatever booze you want. You can pound some imported beers, close your eyes, and pretend she's Pamela Anderson. Just be sure and wear underwear," Mimi said.

"So it's true that you girls are screwing guys for their underwear, then?" the fat one asked.

The tall one looked up at the underwear dangling from the hooks overhead and gingerly took down Troy's boxer briefs. "Must be true," he said. "Cuz these are Troy's."

"Don't you touch those!" Amber screeched, running into the galley. "Those're *mine*!"

The tall one dropped the boxer briefs, his eyes widening in surprise. "Guys, let's get outta here," he said to the others. "This is too freakin' weird."

The person who I assumed was Troy appeared in the galley behind Amber looking definitely worse for wear—even though I never saw him before. "Hey, wait up, y'all," he said sleepily to his buddies.

"Hey, Troy—you wanna do a fat chick while you're here?" the short one asked him.

"What're you talking about? And, hey—how did my underwear get out here? I thought I lost 'em."

The tall one pointed at Amber. "She only banged you for your underwear, buddy. These bimbos are running a scam."

The short one pointed at Mimi. "And *that* one will buy you as much hooch as you can handle if you do her fat chick friend and let her have these," he said as he picked Troy's discarded undies off the floor and tossed them to him, guffawing so hard that snot escaped from his bulbous nose. "It's your lucky day, man—you can use these *twice*! Go find the fat chick and get a two-fer."

Mimi shrugged rather meekly. "Fat girls need loving, too, you know."

Troy balked at this concept. "No friggin' way, dude!"

Mimi sighed. "I don't blame you; Lord knows *I* wouldn't do it. I mean, who wants to have sex with a pig?"

Savannah stepped out from the darkened hallway and into the galley just as the thunderstorm broke outside. Her face was contorted with rage and hurt, her eyes wild. The lid was about to explode off the boiling teapot.

I considered running for cover. Melora and Dylan did, scurrying like frightened rabbits across the room to Mimi and flanking her on the sofa.

"I *hate* you! I hate *all* of you!" Savannah screamed, tears streaming down her reddened cheeks. "Every single one of you in this room has flaws, but that's okay! But poor Savannah, the fat girl! Her imperfection is an obvious thing that everyone can see! So she gets made fun of! She gets shunned! While the rest of you go happily about your lives with your secrets hidden so you don't get judged for them! How freaking *fair* is that?"

Violet eyes blazing, Savannah looked straight at the loudmouthed short guy. "You're an *idiot!*" Then she glared at Troy. "You're a *jackass!*" To the tall guy she said, "You're a *dumbass!*" And to the fat guy, she said, "And you're a fat, ugly, pathetic *hypocrite!*"

They stared at her, speechless, and then bolted for the door, falling all over each other trying to be the first one out.

Evil-eyed Savannah only glared at each of us girls in turn as she launched into her tirade with fresh fury. "You know what? I wouldn't have *come* on this miserable trip if I'd known it would turn into a nonstop, senseless, drunken *orgy!* This is *total* b.s., you guys! The six of us have spent no quality time here together whatsoever! This whole damned vacation has been nothing but an excuse for you worthless sluts to get drunk and get laid!" She paused just long enough to nod at first Amber and then Mimi. "You two! You act like *street whores*, pawing and rubbing on everything male in sight! It's disgusting! Especially for *you*, Amber! *You're married*, remember? Or did you conveniently forget that little fact the second we crossed the border and left Colorado? For God's sake, Amber—you took solemn vows to be *mo-nog-a-mous*, you two-timing, backstabbing bitch!

"And as for *you*, Mimi—you think you're better than everyone else just because your cold and unfeeling daddy is rich. Well, I've got news for you, princess—your daddy doesn't love you and everyone can see it just by looking at you, even if you can't! You're nothing but a coldhearted, worthless, *unlovable*, two-faced bitch!"

A deafening clap of thunder punctuated her words. Melora jumped. Amber winced and promptly burst into tears. Mimi looked positively dumbstruck. Huge, fat raindrops pelted the houseboat as Savannah eyed Dylan with disdain. "*You're* nothing but a Mimi wannabe, Dylan! You copy everything she does because you don't have the *guts* to be your own person—much less the gumption to stand up for yourself! You're a pothead loser, Dylan, and that's all you'll ever be!"

Tears slid down Dylan's cheeks as Savannah berated her. Melora looked petrified; she no doubt knew what was coming.

"And *you!*" Savannah screeched, reeling around to spew venom at Melora with every syllable. "You're *pathetic*! You're nothing but a sickening, sloppy *drunk*! Your next stop should be rehab, Little Miss Lackluster! Do *not* pass go! Do *not* collect two hundred dollars! You probably don't even *remember* what you did to get your underwear trophy, you blackout, Baptist bimbo!"

Savannah swiveled toward me, almost unsteady on her feet, her face purplish with rage. I walked over to her and timidly patted her arm in an attempt to soothe her, "Savannah, you need to settle down and—"

"*Why?* Because you don't want to hear what I have to say?" Her spittle sprayed onto my face, so maliciously emotion-packed were her words. Startled, I stumbled backward as she glowered at me with malevolence. "Have you got your underwear yet, Miss Perfect? From that handsome, clueless, *brain-dead* dude you've been spending all your time slobbering over? Have you spread your legs like the *whore* you are to claim your trophy?"

"Listen, Savannah—who made you the repository of all truth?" I challenged, desperate to get a word in edgewise.

She sneered at me in lieu of a reply.

"Revenge isn't the answer, Savannah. I know you're lashing out because you're in pain—because you overhead some terrible, mistaken things said about you that no one should ever have to hear—but no one meant to hurt your feelings; no one set out to betray you. And saying all these nasty, hateful things isn't going to make you feel any better. It's just wrong, Savannah; it's pointless, and you know it as well as I do. Let's discuss this like adults."

"*Adults?*" she hissed, turning on Mimi. "How *adult* is it to make vicious, hateful, *hurtful* remarks about an overweight *friend* behind her back?" She pointed at each one of us with a baleful sneer. "You're going to pay for this, you miserable, pathetic *bitches*! Every single one of you!"

She threw the door open and fled the houseboat in the torrential rain.

In her wake, not one of us said a word. Finally, after several agonizing, silent moments had passed, Melora burst into tears, Mimi turned a sickly shade of gray-green. Amber looked like she wanted to break something—possibly her own neck with a well-hung rope. Dylan stood as still as a statue and I started pacing.

Several minutes later, Savannah returned soaked to the bone, stormed through the galley, and quickly returned with her bags. She didn't look at or speak to any of us. She simply walked out the door.

I was positively sick with shock, horror, and shame. All I could think of was finding Silas.

Clever girl that I used to be, I'd memorized his slip number, so I grabbed an umbrella from the stand by the door, sprinted over to his boat dock in the warm, pouring rain, conned a dockworker into lowering his boat for me, unfastened the tarp, stepped into the boat, and waited for him on the bench seat in the back.

Nothing could soothe me—not the sultry air or the gentle rolling motion of the boat beneath me or the sound of the summer rain. Before long, though, my eyelids grew heavy. Curling up into a ball on the bench, I propped my head on a life jacket and gave myself up to sleep.

I dreamed of Silas. He came to me as Odur, the god of sunshine, swooping in on a winged horse and flying me away to Happily Ever After. I felt him haul me up onto his lap, gently place my head on his shoulder, and caress me tenderly.

"Jill," he said. "Jill, wake up."

I jolted awake. It wasn't a dream. Silas was there and he was holding me on his lap.

I yawned and stretched. "I hope you're not mad that I came here."

He pressed his lips against mine. Several minutes later I came up for air, panting and weak.

He chucked my cheek. "Were you dreaming about me?"

My eyes grew large. *How could he possibly know?* "What do you mean?"

"Midsummer is a magical time. Legend has it that whatever is dreamed this night will come to pass."

If only.

"So? What's up?" he asked.

I poured out the short version of Savannah's outburst, omitting the whole tawdry one-nighter thing.

"You wanna do the fire festival together tonight? Maybe that will help get your mind off all the bad stuff."

I nodded eagerly.

After a bit, he walked me back to The Mimi. Cotton-ball clouds scudded overhead and dark clouds skulked on the horizon, but the rain had stopped. Hopefully, the weather would hold out for the festival.

Silas kissed me good-bye. "Later, cupcake."

None of the others were in sight and curiously, no partying was going on up top. I went straight to my stateroom, took my sweet time getting all tarted up, and then headed for the salon.

Mimi stood near a window, a pensive expression on her face. Dylan sat on one of the sofas looking sad.

"I'm headed to the festival," I announced to no one in particular. I tapped my cell phone, which I'd fastened to the waistband of my miniskirt, and added, "If you need me, hit me on the hip."

Mimi nodded. Though I felt bad about ditching them, I didn't know what else to do. The way I looked at it, the group vacation was pretty much blown. They could sulk if they wanted to, but I intended to have a good time in spite of everything. After all, my time with Silas was drawing to a close.

The crowd at the fire festival was charged. Musicians and dancers performed while clowns fashioned balloon animals and painted children's faces. A plethora of booths offered everything from artwork to Midsummer T-shirts. Silas bought me dinner at the barbecue booth and dessert at the funnel cake booth.

Darkness descended earlier than normal due to the ominous clouds looming overhead, but then the sky exploded with riotous, sparkling, dazzling colors as the fireworks display commenced. My eyes followed the wild movements of the fire twirlers' torches and then flitted to the dancers in risqué costumes thrashing provocatively to the beat of rhythmic drumming. A few festival goers hugging the edge of the dance floor also started moving to the primal drumbeat. Before long, the dance floor was so full of writhing, scantily clad bodies that many people were forced out onto the sandy beach. Indeed, with the darkness of night, the festival transformed into a steamy, pulse-pounding, bacchanalian affair. Primal electricity crackled through the crowds along with the lightning that streaked anew through the sky vault.

Silas pulled me onto the sand. Our bodies tangled together in a slow, carnal motion as we swayed to the endless beat and felt it move deep within our loins. Silas worked me away from the crowd, rubbing his body against mine, demanding more. With his muscular forearms he trapped me against a palm tree and bent his head to kiss me. I licked his fine, full lips and tasted the nectar of the gods. I was ready to have my way with him on the spot, but the elements conspired against me as Mother Nature dampened my plans with a sudden downpour.

Silas's thoughts must've mirrored mine because he said, "Let's go."

"Where?"

"Come on. I'll show you."

He led me to a secret spot where he said no one could see us. Thunder roared as we clamored down a field of stones and under a dock and onto the wet, brown sugar-colored sand. Immediately, I unfurled a beach towel from my backpack and laid it down where it was dry under the dock. Lightning bolts flashed and thunder crackled and boomed overhead as we ripped off each other's clothes. Then Silas pulled me down onto the towel and covered my naked, wet body with his.

Without preamble, he thrust into me. I met him stroke for stroke. We grasped for what we wanted, what we needed from each other. I was crazed to feel him moving inside of me, desperate to feel the weight of his body on mine, and I reveled in his ardent lovemaking. I found him thrilling beyond belief—both solicitous of my needs and masterful at fulfilling them.

Naturally, I wanted to satisfy his every desire, as well. Employing every bit of muscle I possessed, I forced him down onto his back, straddled him, and lowered myself onto his greedy flesh triumphantly, tormenting him into compliant ecstasy.

He pulled my head down and slanted his mouth across mine, whispering as he kissed me, "You're evil, Jill."

Moments later when an odd noise invaded my consciousness, I jerked upright. "What was that?"

He pulled me back down and kissed me again. "What was what?"

I looked over my shoulder into the darkness. "That thump."

"I don't know," he said huskily. "Who cares?"

I shrugged and started to get back to business. However, he took advantage of the distraction, flipping me over and thrusting into me to dominate me once again. Within seconds, I folded beneath his will. He power-stroked me till I screamed for mercy, stirring up a wild tempest that he probably didn't bargain on. With earthquaking shudders we collapsed together, sweaty and slippery, our chests heaving, trembling all over. I felt completely undone as we lay together in silence, our hearts beating as one.

A shuffling noise on the rocks sent me scampering for my clothes.

Silas yanked on his faded, denim cutoffs. "You can hide over there," he said, pointing to some rocks large enough to shield me from view.

I slid into my flip-flops and darted behind the rocks to pull on my clothes. They were damp and sandy and gross and I was not *at all* thrilled in the least bit about putting them back on my damp and sandy and gross body. Still, I quickly dressed and then crouched out of view for a while, fidgeting, waiting for an "all clear" from Silas that never came.

Finally I called out, "Can I come out now?"

"Yes," a smug, female voice answered.

My blood ran cold when I recognized that voice. I emerged from my hiding place and strode over to where she stood, dangling Silas's boxer briefs on a long, slender piece of driftwood.

"Savannah, what the hell are you doing?"

"Here, slut. Here's your trophy."

I snatched Silas's undies from the stick. "Where's Silas?"

"What do you care? You got what you wanted from him."

"You're wrong, Savannah. I love the guy. I wasn't going to take his underwear. I never intended to *do* the stupid underwear thing. You don't see my name on that list on the refrigerator, do you?"

She blanched. Then her face crumpled. "Oh, gosh, Jill. What have I done?"

I pushed past her, pellets of warm rain bombarding me as I ran into the night crying, "Silas, come back! Silas!"

Rain streamed down my face and dripped from my hair and clothing as I dashed from one end of the dock to the other. I sprinted to his boat slip; his boat was up on the lift. No Silas in sight. Running toward Pelican Pink's, I slipped on a rain-slicked rock, went down on my knees, rose unsteadily with both of them torn and bleeding—palms, too—and kept right on running.

Think, Jill. Think. I stopped for a moment to compose myself. *Silas wouldn't be out in his boat because of the lightning, for crying out loud. No one's out on the lake. You're wasting precious time.*

I tore off again, this time for The Mimi. There, I paced in front of it in the driving rain, bellowing from the depths of my soul, "Silas, come back! Please come back! Savannah lied!"

Soaked through, I gave up and stood on the dock bawling. I was numb; it was over. I couldn't find Silas, I was leaving the day after next, and there wasn't a damn thing I could do to fix what Savannah destroyed.

Then it occurred to me that I needed to look beyond Silas. *It isn't about what I can't do, but what I can do*, I realized. And that was try to salvage the relationships I'd forged with my friends over the last ten months.

After all, I thought, *who am I to judge them? I haven't walked in their shoes. If they want to party their butts off and get wild, that's their decision. Yes, I've seen facets of each of their personalities that I didn't know about, but they're each who they are and I am who I am. We arrived here as friends and we need to leave that way, too.*

I boarded The Mimi and pushed open the door to the salon. A group of howling, hooting, grunting beachbums stood in a semicircle at the far end of the room. I squeezed my way through the teeming throng to see what all of the fuss was about.

When I finally did see, I was sick. Melora and Dylan were lying on the couch together, their limbs entwined, making out like nobody's business as the guys cheered them on.

My eyes narrowed as I pointed at the door. "Get *out!*" I ordered the voyeurs. When they all quieted down and just stood staring at me in surprise, I screamed, "*Get the hell out of here before I call the cops!*"

I wrenched Melora and Dylan apart as the scumbags made their reluctant exits. "Cut it out, you guys. What the *hell* were you thinking? Jeez!"

Dylan's face bloomed with embarrassment. Melora stared at the floor.

"You guys—seriously. It's *beyond* skanky to put on a live, lesbo sex show for the local hooter hunters. It's *repulsive.*"

Dylan looked shell-shocked. "I—I didn't mean—I mean, I'm sorry. Oh, gosh. How did this happen? You weren't supposed to see us!" Before I could stop her she darted through the galley and down the hall to her stateroom.

With a heavy sigh, I turned to Melora. She looked up at me sheepishly, her eyes glassy. "Wait here, okay?" I said. "I'll be right back."

Just when I thought matters couldn't get any worse, the door slammed open and in strode Amber's husband. His countenance was clearly further evidence of Savannah's handiwork.

"Where is she, Jill?" he asked in a deadly calm voice.

I can't save Amber, I realized with grim clarity. *It's too late. Nathaniel's going to find her, regardless.* "I don't know for sure, Nathaniel. I just got here myself. But her stateroom is the second door on the right," I said as I pointed to the hallway that led to it.

I dragged my hand down my forehead and rubbed my eyes as he stormed off in search of his desperate housewife, wondering, *When is this going to end?* I felt like throwing myself on my bed and crying my heart out over losing Silas. But I couldn't allow myself that luxury. There were things I had to do.

Walking resolutely down the hallway I knocked first on Mimi's door and then on Dylan's. "You guys, we need to talk."

Mimi came out first. I didn't say a word—just wrapped her in a big hug. Then I rapped on Dylan's door again.

"Come in," she said in a quavering voice.

I swung open her door to find her sitting on the edge of her bed looking miserable.

"Dylan, come out to the salon and let's talk, okay?"

She nodded and meekly followed Mimi and me down the hallway.

By some miracle, Melora hadn't passed out. She sat waiting on the sofa like I'd asked her to.

"First of all," I said, slipping my cell phone from my waistband, "we need to find Savannah."

I punched Savannah's number on my speed dial and waited for her to pick up. When she didn't, I left her a voicemail: "Savannah, please come back to the houseboat and talk to us. We care about you very much. We'll all be waiting for you in the salon."

I flipped my phone shut and turned to my four friends—the four friends I hadn't realized I held so dear till circumstances threatened that I might lose them all. "I need to apologize to all of you," I began. "I never intended to follow through with the one-night stand thing, but I let all of you think that I was game. That was wrong and I'm sorry. I'm ashamed to admit it, but I was afraid you wouldn't like me anymore if I didn't go along with the plan. I realize now that I should've trusted you more."

"Oh, Jill, we'd never think less of you because of something superficial like that," Dylan said. "None of us should've got caught up in the one-nighter thing, anyway. I hate to admit it, but Savannah was right about me; I don't think for myself. I wasn't crazy about the underwear idea, either, but I wanted to be like Mimi so I went along with it."

"The only way *I* could stomach doing it was to get wasted first," Melora said ruefully, looking down at her hands clasped tightly in her lap. "Savannah was right about me, too; I have a drinking problem. I've decided to get help for it as soon as we get home."

"*I'm* the one who should be apologizing and coming clean; after all, the whole thing was my dumbass idea," Mimi said. "Anyway, I guess it's high time I took responsibility for my actions. I have to admit that Savannah's words really stung me, too—mostly because they're true. I'm just a spoiled, little, rich bitch living off Daddy's money, bored with life and waiting for the next cheap thrill." She paused, hanging her head. When she looked back up at us, she had tears in her eyes. "You guys, I feel so *awful* about those cruel things I said to Troy and his friends about Savannah. How could I *do* that? Savannah's right; I am a two-faced bitch. But I'm not coldhearted. I'm really not. And I can be a better friend—to all of you. But especially to Savannah."

"Speaking of Savannah," I said, "we've got to find her. Make things right with her." I hit redial on my cell and tried calling her again. There was no answer. "Oh, gosh—I hope nothing's happened to her. I wonder where she is."

"I'm right here," she said, standing behind us in the doorway. The door was still open from Nathaniel's charge down the hallway.

She walked in . . . with Silas close behind. Hope trilled in my chest when I saw him—especially when our eyes met and I saw his love for me shining in his. He dropped Savannah's luggage just inside the door, and that's when I turned and saw Amber walking through the galley toward us.

"It's time to forgive and forget and move on," I said, reaching out to my friends.

Silas stood discreetly off to the side as Savannah apologized to us and we apologized to her. The six of us hugged and cried and sniffled and laughed.

Nathaniel appeared carrying Amber's bags, a stunned expression on his face. "I'll wait for you outside," he told her.

"Oh, God, Amber—can you ever forgive me for calling Nathaniel?" Savannah asked, fresh tears beginning to stain her reddened cheeks.

Amber managed a weak smile through her tears. "I know this sounds weird, Savannah, but I'm actually glad you did it. Our dirty laundry needed to be aired. I'm not proud of what I did and I'm not making excuses for my behavior, but Nathaniel and I have talked, and we're both willing to try to make this work in spite of everything. So I'm going home with my husband."

We all hugged Amber and Nathaniel and wished them well and then they left.

"Hey, does anyone know what happened to all the underwear?" Mimi asked suddenly.

We all looked up at where the undies had been hanging. The hooks were empty.

Savannah stepped over to her luggage and removed the items in question. "I'm afraid I took these over to Pelican Pink's and left them in a box at the door with a not-very-nice note that you guys don't even want to see. But then I felt bad so I went back and got them."

The four underwear thieves eyed each other and grinned. "Let's get rid of them," Mimi declared.

Snatching them up, she opened a window and tossed the bundle into the lake. We all went to the windows and watched as one by one, the water claimed them and they sank out of sight.

"Good riddance to bad rubbish," Dylan declared.

"One more thing, Savannah," Mimi said. "I just want you to know that I think you're a beautiful person, inside and out. *I'm* the ugly one, not you. I'm just so very sorry that we all had to suffer such pain in order for me to figure that out."

Mimi and Savannah embraced and clung together for several long moments. When they broke apart, Savannah said, "Let's all make a pact: No more negative dialogue for the remainder of this vacation. It's all good from here on out!"

We cheered and whooped and then as the merriment died, Silas and I just stood there staring at each other, love-drunk fools making goo-goo eyes. After a few minutes the girls diplomatically 'disappeared' under the pretense of returning Savannah's luggage to her stateroom.

When Silas folded me in his arms and kissed me desperately, my world *completely* righted itself.

We were married this past June and needless to say—
I had five bridesmaids. THE END